AND THE ANCESTORS SING

RADHA LIN CHADDAH

Text copyright © 2026 by Radla Lin Chaddah

All rights reserved. For information regarding reproduction in total or in part, contact Rising Action Publishing Co. at http://www.risingactionpublishingco.com

Cover Illustration © Nat Mack
Distributed by Simon & Schuster

ISBN: 978-1-998672-20-2
Ebook: 978-1-998672-21-9

FIC014090   FICTION / Historical / 20th Century / Post-World War II
FIC045030   FICTION / Family Life / Multigenerational
FIC144000   FICTION / Places / Asia

#AndTheAncestorsSing

Follow Rising Action on our socials!

Twitter: @RAPubCollective
Instagram: @risingactionpublishingco
Tiktok: @risingactionpublishingco

Contents

Part One: Da Long Village, China, 1978   1

1. Hooks   3

2. Blood Oranges   10

3. The Farmer Master   19

4. Long Worms   31

5. Eggs, Newspapers, and Slippers   39

Part Two: Shanghai, China, 1984   55

6. Halls of Heavenly Kings and Virtuous Works   57

7. Smoke Curls and Paper Meat   64

8. Pork Buns and Pink Shirts   79

Part Three: Da Long Village & Shanghai, China, 1986   91

9. Wheels   93

10. Brides and Bounty   101

11. Night Journeys   119

12. Wives   130

13. Husbands   150

14. Earth MaMa   162

15. Good Fortune   169

16. Trucks and Trains   182

Part Four: New Da Long & Shanghai, China, 1996   215

17. Swans and Scrolls   217

18. Cranes and Custard   234

19. Legacy Bearers   254

20. Homecoming   271

21. Daughters and Sons   289

22. One Day: Day One   306

Part Five: New Da Long & Shanghai, China, 2000   327

23. Seeds and Stitches   328

24. Sixes   354

25. Stars and Snakes   374

26. Old Home   389

Acknowledgments   417

About the Author   419

For Avery, Yani and Ayo.

AND THE ANCESTORS SING

Part One

Da Long Village
China, 1978

Chapter One

Hooks

It is a place of staggering beauty, this spot tucked away in the middle of nowhere at the heart of the Middle Kingdom. The land is rich with the darkest of soil and, at the right time of year, the hills are thickly carpeted with greenery so bold that the land seems to cry with life. However, for the men and women who dot this landscape with their hard-fought lives, knowledge of the land's capriciousness in delivering good fortune renders the image less vibrant.

In between the fields, outlined by irrigation canals furrowed by hand, wooden shacks protrude from the land. They lean this way and that, lacking any sense of fortitude; not one stands straight. When heavy rains flood the fields, the people of this land dare not complain that their leaky roofs leave them drenched to the bone. They humbly accept that these meekest of shelters, while unable to keep them dry, allow them to stay put, sparing the mud beneath them from softening to silt that might carry them away. The walls bear hooks that serve to pin all that these families own—collections of pots and hoes, plastic bags filled with roughly folded clothes and worn slippers, quilted coats, and sacks of rice—to their place on the land. Without these rains, life would be lost.

The tiny rice seedlings, each one transplanted by hand to its spot in a row of these carefully tilled fields, would be lost.

The children of the land are not told stories of mythical monsters. Rather, they are regaled with the horrors of a famine that once stripped this land bare. Their nightmares are filled with the howl of empty bellies, and their daydreams soaked with abundant rains that fall as rice grains into an eternally filled bowl.

Squinting to avoid the glare of a brilliant harvest sun, if one focused on the dark dots scattered on the fields, one would come upon Fang Lei, bent over at the waist and knee deep in water cold enough to leave her feet numb. She is surrounded by others similarly disposed; human hooks stuck in the soft earth.

"Hurry up! Cut faster!" Fang Bo spat as he talked to his young wife. "Get your stems tied up quickly. I want to catch up with the others." Bo stared after Pang and Shu as they waddled their way through the field, their full bodies wading steadily through the muddied water. Pang, nicknamed since boyhood with the common word for fat, was hampered neither by his corpulence nor by the considerable weight of the bundled rice stalks that he carried on one shoulder. Shu, Pang's younger brother, was smaller but no less robust than Pang, and waded stride for stride with him.

Bo's stomach churned at the thought of food. He was hungry and dreaded the long walk from the field to the Farmer Master's house. A thin strip of a man, Bo could only manage half the haul of either Pang or Shu. He would have to face the embarrassment of having his day's meager work weighed on the farmer master's scale, then stretch his hand out to receive half the wage collected by each of the brothers.

This was no fault of his own. As a boy, Bo had not had a belly filled up on the ill-gotten rewards of a mother who curried favor with the Party leaders, whoring herself for extra rations of sugar and white pork fat. Bo had swallowed hard on the saliva that pooled in his mouth when, on his daily walk to school with the pudgy pair, the glistening ring of animal oil smeared around their mouths and the smell of the pork fat on their breaths teased at his stomach. The thought of it now still soured him.

"You are so slow. You will do nothing but cost us our dinner. I don't want to wait around." He kept his eyes on the brothers, on their backs stained with sweat, watching them move further from him. Bo didn't look at Lei when he spoke. "I will not wait for you."

Lei did not take her eyes off Bo, though he did not know this. She was careful to keep her head bowed to her work, studying his face from under the brim of her hat. His words did not turn her this way or that, and neither did her heart jump nor strain at his harshness, simply for the fact that she did not yet know him. She searched his face for clues. Its smallness and tightness reminded her of a clenched fist. His dark eyes were so black, absorbing almost all the light even on this brightest of days. She hoped there was a softness hidden behind them that she could not see. She had looked for this same softness on the night of their wedding, but the moon had been shuttered out of his hut so completely that not a ray of light had fallen across his face. She had become a woman in complete darkness with a man who was invisible to her.

Lei reached her left hand deep into the chilly water. She focused on clutching a fistful of stems tightly and did not let her mind indulge in thoughts of what else might lie beneath the surface. In her right hand, she wielded a small sickle with a short wooden handle and a blade blunted from a full day's labor. She worked the blade against the stems, hacking repeatedly and using her full bodyweight to compensate for its dullness. The tension on the grasped rice stalks slackened as they were successfully hewn. Never loosening her grip, Lei deftly pulled the newly released bundle of stems out from beneath the water while hooking the sickle by its blade through a leather loop that hung from the rope belt around her waist. She had several pre-cut lengths of this same caliber of rope in her pocket, three of which she now used to tie up her bundle, starting with the stiff, green root ends and working her way up towards the golden crowns. Lei's face and body were moist with sweat even as her hands stiffened from their time in the icy water. She ran her hands softly over the rice crowns, grateful for the weight of their studded golden tassels. Each of these studs represented the plant's seeds. Seeds that, after many more days of nurturing, would release soft, tender grains of rice.

"What are you doing?" Bo barked.

"I am finished now," Lei answered softly.

Bo started off across the field, carrying his load with some difficulty, not looking back at her even once. She supposed he didn't need to as she was following right behind him, carrying a load equal in size to his own. She was close enough to hear his heavy breathing and the grunts he let out every few steps as he readjusted his slipping load upwards and back onto the scrawny ridge of his shoulder. The knobs of his spine protruded through the woven cloth of his shirt, and she wondered what they would feel like if she ran her fingers over them. She hadn't touched them once in their time together and wondered whether he might like it if she did.

The road to the farmer master's home had been no more than a widened dirt path in years prior. Now, it was paved. As the field workers emerged from the rice paddies onto the road, they used their bare feet to rummage through a mound of dusty canvas slippers. Though identical in style and cheapness, the shoes were easily sorted. The men's were solid in color, while the women's, fabricated from patterned canvas, were marginally embellished. Lei slipped her muddied feet into a well-worn pair of purple-striped slippers. She placed her bundle on the ground and quickly ran her hands over her bare calves and shins, feeling for leeches. She collected her bundle, balanced its weight securely on her shoulder and followed her husband as he trudged in front of her, walking only on the dirt edges at the side of the road.

Just as Bo said, he had not waited for her and was now chatting loudly with several other men from the village. Lei could have caught up with him but did not. From behind her came the giggles of young women. She hoped that, if she slowed down enough, the women would draw level with her and absorb her into their conversation. She missed the sound of her own laughter.

Twenty-three days ago, she had been unmarried. She had still been Little Sister, who curled up nightly at the end of her mother's bed and rubbed her mother's feet before sleeping. Now her mother would sleep alone, a two-day walk from here. Lei thought of her mother's feet, their cold, bony smoothness no longer warmed by her hands; she felt the weight of her load and readjusted it on her shoulder. She hoped that each foot would be warmed by the other and that, with enough mutual rubbing, they would produce heat.

"Fang Lei, why are you not up next to your husband? Is Fang Bo already making you an unhappy wife?" Two village girls had indeed caught up to Lei and snickered as they teased her.

Lei recognized them as the unmarried sisters. That's how Bo had introduced them on the day she and he had married. The teenage sisters had come over to Bo's hut carrying plastic mugs and expecting a share of the wedding day libations. They had worn the same field clothes they wore now. Patches of dried mud had dotted their faces and arms, and black semicircles of dirt lay encrusted under their fingernails. At the time, Lei had wondered whether they were unmarried because they were unwashed, or was it the other way around? As she looked at them now, she concluded that they had never washed properly. They were not made uncomfortable by being dirty, just like the sow that her father had kept throughout her childhood. They were creatures happy being muddied.

The unmarried sisters had each received a meager inch of warm wedding beer right at the threshold of Bo's shack. It had disappeared in an instant, downed in two noiseless swallows, and then so had they. Neither put forth her mug for a second serving, and Bo did not offer such. They hadn't spoken to Lei, who had been offered only boiled water for sipping.

Now they spoke to her. "Maybe his small chicken is too skinny for a big girl like you," one said. The sisters laughed in unison, kicking up dirt as they dragged their feet. Their legs were spare. If each girl were to have her legs bundled like rice stems, the width of the bundle would match the girth of her square hips, as neither sister carried an extra finger's worth of flesh. Their torsos ran seamlessly from their hips, with no indentation to mark exactly where their rope belts should cinch. Their faces were long and loose, as if the bones were arranged so as not to close their jaws properly.

They were not pretty.

None of this bothered Lei. She smiled weakly, unsure if their comment was meant to embarrass her. She was careful not to show her teeth, which were big, white, straight, and lay like two perfectly strung strands of oversized pearls in her mouth. The marriage broker had described them as Lei's most beautiful features and saw them as a selling point to compensate for her broad stature and lack of fair skin.

One night, not so long ago, Lei's mother, during her nightly foot massage, had warned her daughter not to show her teeth. "Don't open your mouth too wide. Others will be jealous of your smallest of fortunes." She told Lei that she was sorry that her only daughter had not gotten her small, delicate feet and fine features, but rather had the strong body of her father. Lei's fingers had traced the long bones of her mother's feet, following each down to the tip of a toe. Each toe was long with a soft pad at its end. As she did this, she wiggled her own toes and, without seeing them, lamented their short thickness. Lei's feet were solid and laid flat against the earth, touching it at all points. Her mother had told her that they needed to be that way to hold up her wide, fleshy hips, her too-full chest, and her broad shoulders.

For the first time since coming out of the fields, Lei felt the weight of the bundled stems on her shoulders and was ashamed that they did not feel heavier.

The unmarried sisters' laughter poured out over yellow, crooked teeth. They did not try to hide them. Lei pressed her lips firmly together as the girls walked right by her. She looked down the road, focusing first on the sisters' backs, and then searching beyond them to whatever lay ahead.

Chapter Two

Blood Oranges

The great balls of the sky had switched places by the time the young couple arrived home. Lei admired the full roundness of the crimson moon as it rose slowly, climbing ever higher into the night. Bo seemed not to notice the moon. He walked in its light and played with the coins in his pocket. He turned them over and over in his hand, clinking them against one another, as if enjoying their weight. Lei's pockets held nothing of interest, only leftover cuts of rope saved for the next workday.

As the moon reached its zenith, Lei was reminded of the precious blood orange her father had once brought home to share with his children. It was so beautiful that Lei had pleaded with him not to cut it open. It seemed somehow cruel. Her brothers had laughed at her, scoffing that she was scared, for everyone knew how the flesh of the fruit had gotten its color.

According to legend, there had once been a witch who, wanting to destroy her unfaithful lover, turned her bitterness into a toxin that coursed through her body and polluted her blood. Over months, she used leeches, plucked from the waters of the rice fields, to bleed herself. After allowing the slugs to engorge themselves on her poisonous blood, she slit each one lengthwise and drained it of its last meal. The old hag then took to the sky and sprinkled the orange groves with her toxic blood, gleefully harvesting the poisonous fruits that were borne. Upon eating these poisoned blood oranges, her lover met his death in a fit of vigorous convulsions.

Lei's three brothers had pretended to convulse around her as they teased her for foolish fears. Her father had commanded the boys to be still as he fastidiously cut the single orange into thin wedges. The juice of the fruit had been so fragrant that the children immediately stilled themselves and collectively inhaled deeply. Lei's father had then carefully selected the largest wedge to give to his only daughter.

"Call me when you have prepared the washing water." Bo's voice trailed behind him as he entered the hut, tossing a bucket out the door and onto the ground by Lei's feet. He closed the door tightly, leaving Lei by herself.

She collected the wooden bucket, made her way down to the village well, and pumped until the bucket was heavy. She kept her eyes on the moon the entire time and imagined that her parents and brothers might be doing the same. Upon returning to the shack, Lei carefully transferred the water into an iron pot. She warmed the water on an outdoor stove whose small fire she kept alive by sparingly adding dried twigs and straw to the flames, using only what was necessary to coax the water to a touchable warmth.

When the water was ready, Lei knocked softly on the door. Bo emerged with a small, rough rag, which he hastily dipped into the water. He scrubbed clean first his face and then his hands. He dipped the rag again into the bucket, carelessly losing some of the warm water to splashes as he scoured his thin neck and his even thinner arms and legs.

Lastly, he slipped the rag down the front of his pants and then further down into the cleft of his backside. The only sound that filled the space between the husband and wife was that of cloth rubbing on flesh. When Bo finished, he tossed the rag into the bucket and nodded at his wife.

"Clean up quickly and come inside so we can eat."

Lei reached for the rag. The water had already turned cold.

When Lei entered the hut moments later, all its remaining residents were already seated around the small, makeshift table placed at the center of the single-room abode. Lei squeezed in next to her husband, their legs touching. The corners of her pressed-close mouth turned upwards when Bo did not pull away from her. The nutty smell of cooked rice and the robust odor of garlic-seasoned vegetables relaxed the muscles of her body, making her grateful to have reached the end of the day. The unmistakably musky and pungent scent of a boiled egg made her mouth water. It sat shelled, but whole, in a small bowl with a dash of black fermented sauce staining its gleaming whiteness. It was the first one she had seen since coming to this new home.

"Aiyah! Finally, we start. Do not tell me if the food is cold. If it is so, it is because your wife takes too long to clean herself." Fang MaMa's slight, though spoken to her son, bit into Lei. Intense heat rose up into her face. Both Bo and his sister, MeiLin, who sat across from Lei, kept their heads low. Though they seemed not to move, Lei saw the muscles of MeiLin's lower face tense, suppressing a smile.

The older woman, on her feet, curved her body over the table, apportioning the food into the four identical bowls placed in front of each diner. Her hands, though bony and gnarled, authoritatively worked a single sharp-edged, metal spatula in such a way as to make clear that hers was the only hand permitted to wield it. First, the rice was scooped and plopped down into each bowl. Not a single brown grain was spared; Fang MaMa scraped the spatula's flat surface against the edge of each bowl, dislodging any grains that might have been stuck to it. The greens were similarly dispensed.

Each serving fated for Bo's bowl was bigger and heavier than the rest; Fang MaMa dug deeper into the pots of food to portion out her son's fill. Lei waited patiently for the egg to be sectioned. Her own father had always received the biggest share of every family meal she had ever witnessed, and as Bo was the only male in her new home, she knew this was his unspoken right. Fang MaMa sliced the egg in half. Lei marveled at its perfection. The two halves sat perfectly even with one another, and their soft, golden centers were silky. Without a moment's hesitation, Fang MaMa lifted both halves and placed them atop the small mountain of food peeking out from Bo's bowl. She then sat and bowed her head to her son.

"MaMa, we can all eat." Bo's voice came out in a soft mumble that barely moved the air in front of his lips and similarly did not move his mother.

"I don't want it." Fang MaMa looked at the egg with an almost genuine disgust. "Anyway, don't be stupid. You need all the energy. If you fail, we all fail. We owe everything on this table to your hard work." She did not look at Lei.

The pull of coins within his thin cotton pockets tugged at Bo, as did the sudden knowledge that more than half of their weight was the result of Lei's labor. Using his chopsticks, he sectioned one of the egg halves in half again. He then deftly denuded one of the egg quarters of its golden yellow yolk crescent and placed it to the side of his bowl. He picked up the now languid sliver of egg white and placed it in Lei's bowl. Lei thanked him without thinking, forcing her eyes not to look at the small piece of yolk that he had left in his bowl.

"Stupid boy!" Fang MaMa snorted, casting an unmasked look of anger at Lei.

On the day that Lei had learned that she was to be married to a man she did not know, aside from having glanced at him once at the Hundred Village market, her mother had talked for the first time ever of love. They were squatted outside their home, working through a pile of garlic chives, stripping the rotten strands from the still edible aromatic shoots.

"Lei, you are my only daughter, and I hope you have learned from me how it is to be a woman who honors her ancestors. A true woman is never soured by hardship or sweetened by fancy because she knows how to recognize love."

Wide-eyed, Lei had waited for her mother to say more, searching her face for guidance. The words made her uncomfortable, for they were unlike any she had heard before. Theirs was a language of practicalities, of mending things torn, of cooking things grown, of washing things dirtied. This new language of love and hardship and things of fancy caused her belly to clench. How could she have lived long enough to be leaving home, to be married, and yet not know of these things that now seemed sacred? Her mother gathered the greens and had handed them to Lei for washing.

Now, as she sat at her husband's table, she wondered if this shiny sliver of white that glistened in her bowl was that thing that she, as a woman, was supposed to recognize? She pressed her thigh a little harder against Bo's.

Bo focused his gaze on the face of his sister, who sat across from him; if he noticed Lei's gesture, he did not make it known. As if she could feel Bo looking at her, MeiLin raised her eyes, and the two siblings were momentarily transfixed. Her head was perfectly egg-like; her hair was pulled back revealing the roundness of her skull and the soft slopes that formed a perfect point at her chin. Her skin matched in color and smoothness the pieces of albumin that sat in Bo and Lei's bowls. When the brother admired the face of his sister, which he did often as it brought him a pleasure that verged on wrong, he saw with pride a beautiful version of his own. The face now pulled at his heart in much the same way that the coins in his pocket had pulled at his conscience just moments earlier. Without hesitation or fuss, he took the whole unblemished half egg that remained in his bowl and placed it, yolk and all, into hers.

Fang MaMa said nothing.

Bo did not consider how his actions would affect his young bride. He could not know that, just moments earlier, there had been a space in Lei's stomach that hungered to be filled. Now it was full. As Bo had transferred the half egg to MeiLin, the lightness and warmth that had puffed up Lei's chest had transformed into a hard, heavy stone that fell deep into the pit of her belly. MeiLin gave her brother an ingratiating smile. Lei looked at the two women across from her, one old and one young, each with faces identical to her husband's and, for the first time since becoming a wife, she wanted to sob.

"Pang and Shu are ready to be married." Fang MaMa shared the news with food still in her mouth. A few grains of rice flew forward from between her lips and landed on the table. "Their whore of a mother is telling everyone she has enough money saved to buy them worthy brides." She pressed at the grains on the table with the pad of her index finger, lifting them to her mouth.

A burp rose from Bo's stomach, and he tasted acid at the back of his mouth. "She will need to spend greatly to get those oily pigs wives. They are brutes. What type of woman would give herself to those types of men?"

"Don't be foolish. They may not have your shrewdness, but they are good workers. Their mother will manage their earnings well. Any woman will lie beneath a man's weight if some of it is made up by coins." Fang MaMa looked at Lei and sucked on her teeth. "The money will not be needed to entice their wives; it will go towards how pretty they will be." She spoke in conclusions. She did not invite discussion. Lei kept her head down, picking at the food in her bowl. She did not touch the egg white.

Fang MaMa continued, "They will have fine-boned, delicate wives. They have the money for such."

Bo saw his mother look sideways at MeiLin, who had not uttered one word during the entire meal. She worked her chopsticks elegantly between her long fingers, eating methodically. Each mouthful of food was carefully composed. First, she placed a small mound of rice in the side of her mouth and held it there without chewing. Next, she added a pinch of garlicky greens and a morsel of egg to the rice in her mouth, and only then did she chew, as if slowly savoring the combining flavors. Her thin cheeks ballooned out slightly, reminding Bo of the small field mice he used to capture when he was a boy. He liked to feed them little clumps of rice saved just for this purpose and would watch the movement of their pouched cheeks as they ate.

"They are uncouth and rough. Only the most mercenary of families would allow their daughters to marry into such corruption and filth." Bo huffed the words out, filled with air. Fang MaMa, lifting her bowl to her lips and using her chopsticks to shovel the remains of her meal into her mouth, said nothing.

That evening in their bed, curtained off in a corner of the hut by an old, dirty sheet, Bo climbed on top of Lei and made his way inside of her. Pressed next to each other, entwined into a ball that rocked noisily back and forth, neither husband nor wife was in the present. Bo was thinking of the harvesting season that lay ahead of him, and Lei could think only of her past.

Bo calculated how much money would be earned from this season's labor. Bitterly, he then figured out how much would remain after paying taxes back to the Farmer Master, for the same Farmer Master who paid him his laborer's wage also held the post of village tax collector. If all went well, there would be enough to start building a new home, one in which MeiLin would stay until she was ready to be married. Of course, this would require Fang MaMa to be satisfied with the new home. It would need to be built from brick rather than wood, and have a small indoor kitchen, as well as a covered outhouse; these were luxuries that Bo saw as necessary to his future.

A man's wealth was measured by the beauty of his wife, the amenities of his house, and the manliness of his sons. His wife's bride price had been counted in cartons of cigarettes and a clutch of eggs; that was all that Fang MaMa told Bo they could afford. Lei had been sold as physically strong and ready to work, with a healthy set of teeth, much in the same way that a cow would be advertised to the Farmer Master during breeding season. For Bo, Lei was not part of his wealth but rather a means to it. He pumped rougher and harder into her, causing her to let out a small cry.

Bo rolled off Lei and turned his back to her. The sound of her own voice had startled Lei and pulled her mind back from thoughts of her family and of her childhood. She longed for the shouting voices of her brothers running in and out of the house and for the smell of their sweat after a day of working alongside their father in the fields. She saw her mother sitting in the sun, outside their home, scrubbing clothes in a washbasin, her hands glistening as they wrung dirt in brown squirts from the well-worn cloth. She felt the heat of her father's lap, where she had sat as a girl and listened to stories about the land and thought again of the blood orange that he had shared so carefully with each of his children. Her father had shared everything with each of them, from stories, to fruit, to his own anger. He had beaten his wife and each of the children, but never unevenly or with such harshness as to leave a mark, and only when beer had reddened his face. This sharing had let them know that they were each part of a whole, the whole that was their family.

Bo had not struck Lei once since she had become his wife, and yet her body ached as she thought of the egg white stripped of its yolk. She did not know what to make of this man who lay so close to her and moved inside of her and yet seemed not to see her. Was this love? She did not know. Fang MaMa's snoring grew louder from the other side of the hut, rumbling through the darkness. Bo was Lei's husband, and she now belonged to him, to Fang MaMa and to MeiLin. She reached out in the darkness and ran her fingers over Bo's knobby spine. He did not move.

Chapter Three

The Farmer Master

T he second floor of Farmer Master Wang's home was the highest human-made point in Da Long Village, a fact that was known far and wide and most intimately by the Farmer Master himself. Standing in front of his second-floor window, with the wet heat of the day rising around him, the Farmer Master relished his distance from the ground. His breathing, deep and slow, was momentarily paced by his sense of satisfaction.

The land was rich with rice-to-be, though not his by sweat or toil; the grain was effectively his by way of control. The right to own one's spot of earth had washed away decades ago on the wave of revolution, when the Farmer Master's father had still been a young man. And while the letter of the law had made all Chinese equal, it could not erase the inherent inequalities of cunning. Cunning, the Farmer Master had inherited in spades from the older Wang. From this inequality, all riches had flowed, including the title of master, control of the land and, most important, control of the people hooked into it. The Farmer Master enjoyed pressing down on the people—of course, all in the name of The Party and beloved country—and squeezing toil from their muscles.

One of the brown dots working in the fields straightened up and called out to him, "Farmer Master, the workers will soon be ready for the day's weigh-in."

Wang nodded, enjoying the sound of this honorific as it reached his ears. His family name had long been subsumed into this ultimate title, and there were only two people who called him by anything different. AnRan, his wife, called him "husband"; she had done so from the first day they met, as it was on that same day they had wed. Their son, Jiang, called him "BaBa" if there was ever reason for the boy to address his father directly, though such occasions were rare. The son usually took the posture of silent listener and nothing more; Wang rarely invited the boy into conversation.

"Have everything ready for me," Wang called out over the field and waited as all the dots turned their heads upwards and acknowledged his instructions.

The lower edge of the second-floor window, which ran two meters wide by one meter in height, was exactly four meters from the ground. It was the only window on the home's second floor visible from the fields, and the workers referred to it as the Eagle's Eye. They were so aware of the Farmer Master's almost perpetual presence at the window's center that, when they made any type of mistake, they shuddered for fear of him seeing. If a few rice stems came loose from a large bundle that one of them was struggling to secure, the worker would immediately look up to the window, fearing their error had been noted. Experience of the physical world and of human limits should have let them know that a person's eyes, more than a field's length away, could not possibly see the details of the work at the level of their hands hovering so close above the earth. Yet, they lived convinced of the opposite. It was Wang's practice to scrutinize each worker's harvest for damaged, seedless rice stems and to scold his laborers for poorly tied bundles that implied stems lost along the way. The Farmer Master alone determined each worker's earnings at the end of each day, and it was his practice to dock any worker for such waste.

Presently, Wang moved away from the window and took a seat behind his enormous desk. His back was now to the window and, as demanded by Feng Shui, his face looked directly upon the room's entryway. Polished to a high sheen, the desk was crafted from high-quality wood with a black lacquer finish and embellished with inlaid mother-of-pearl in the form of figures, flowers, and birds. The desk had never seen a moment of neglect, and its exact age was hard to discern. It had been, to the older Wang, like a faithful servant with its hidden drawers and secret compartments securing all manner of riches and contraband. The Farmer Master enjoyed the firm smoothness of its surface and lovingly ran his fingers over its top.

In his father's day, when such items were seen as anti-revolutionary and bourgeois, the desk had been trussed in a tarp and hidden in a corner of the house, disguised as junk, behind an accumulation of worthless items, including a collection of brooms and buckets and a pile of empty rice sacks. Rather than destroy it, as would have been commanded by the rhetoric mill in Beijing, the older Wang had known that the day would come when ideology would curve back around, and when the cause of country would demand that prosperity be back on display. The Farmer Master was glad that he lived now, for indeed it was such a time.

Despite Wang's own youth having neither been wrapped in polished silks nor having had him sipping heady beverages from fluted glasses, he had still inherited his father's sense of entitlement. It took a crasser form than that of his father, who had taken care to wrap his ambition in the then-mandated language of communal patriotism. The older Wang had a gifted tongue and spoke the patriotic language with such eloquence, despite his ambivalence, that he was appointed Da Long Village Cadre. Vested with the authority to collect both the village taxes and the state-mandated quota of precious grain, the older Wang found ways to compensate himself for his patriotism.

Now, new leaders in the capital brought with them the winds of change, and the Four Modernizations of Agriculture, Industry, Science, and Defense slowly blew into the heartland. The Party ideology shifted. With hints of capitalism wafting into the country and the right to profit from one's labor becoming politically fashionable, the previous ideal of economic collectivization lost its luster. The young Farmer Master, having learned from his father, publicly donned the cloak of Party loyalist and was appointed to the newly created role of township leader. He was charged with collecting the Party's share of the township's prosperity and overseeing land leases. Such responsibilities, handled in just the right way, held the promise of substantial self-enrichment. The Farmer Master took his father's ill-gotten gains and stitched together a sizeable swathe of leased land plots. Finding laborers was easy. He took advantage of the villagers, most of whom did not have coins enough to seed lots or cultivate harvests of their own. Every inch of land seen from the Eagle's Eye was effectively under Wang's control, and every belly working the land was filled at his discretion.

Seated, the Farmer Master could see out and over the balcony railing framing the two-story square atrium that hollowed out the center of his home. Each side of the square balcony gave rise to a square room of identical size. If sky-borne and looking down on the house, one would note that the four rooms lined up with the cardinal points on a compass.

The Eagle's Eye was to the south, and directly to the north, across the atrium, was the bedroom shared by Wang and AnRan. The rooms had been set up this way from the time that the house had been built by the senior Wang. The ancestors believed that from the south came money and physical strength, both needed for any farmer to prosper. Charm and passion flowed from the north, hopefully into the primary bedroom, allowing for children to be conceived. The room to the east, believed to be blessed with love and trust, belonged to Jiang, and the room to the west lay empty and untouched. With its westerly direction, representing endurance, the room was held in reserve by command of the Farmer Master, for his future, first-born grandson.

No activity within the walls of the house went unrecognized by the Farmer Master. Every sound and smell was cataloged by his ears and nose.

Wang sank into his chair and relaxed his lower back, closing his eyes and waiting. Pots clanged against the iron grate atop the stove. He drew a deep breath into his nose and held it there. The aroma of smoked pork sent a deep rumble across his belly. He stayed like this for a while, breathing deeply with his eyes closed and his belly dancing, temporarily lost from the fields. Slowly, a rhythmic, swishing sound crept into his head, growing louder, and the deep meatiness he had been enjoying gave way to a musty smell. Before he could be fully annoyed and push a curse across his lips, the swishing was drowned out by a persistent splashing and gurgling. Water crashing against the tile floor of the washroom across the atrium alerted him to his wife's nakedness, a state quickly confirmed by the whispering smell of rose, from her wash oils, that clung to the air.

Cooking. Sweeping. Bathing. All activity was known to him.

His wife's nakedness brought Wang forward in his chair and straightened his back. He reminded himself that the fact of her state of undress was little more than a signal that the close of the workday was drawing near. This was a matter of his will. To be distracted by thoughts of his wife's slender, flexible body and buried, delicate musk was shameful. It was not the time of day for fleshy pleasures; the thought repulsed him for its fundamental weakness. The clinking of coins inside the metal box that he had unknowingly started pushing back and forth across his desk, between his soft hands, focused him. He controlled his breathing and was relieved. The sound was heavy and deep, much like this year's rains. Wang closed his eyes tight and tried to close his nose to AnRan's flowery fragrance.

The splashing transformed in the darkness of Wang's mind into an image of torrential rain; water pouring in sheets from the sky, filling every crevice on the earth's surface. First, the rain collected into irregular pools, and then it formed a solid, deep lake across the fields, a plane of coolness that cut through a blanket of warm air. This same rain, necessary for coaxing grain from the ground, put money into his box, but also turned the ground soft and clingy and made even the strongest of feet clumsy. Hauling the harvest to town along a road that swallowed all that strode or rolled upon it was costly. A smile, not a full one, turned the right corner of Wang's mouth. He again sank into his chair, unclenched his buttocks, and allowed himself to enjoy the fact that even the rain could be conquered by his will, wealth, and smarts.

The road from the Farmer Master's house to the market was to be paved this year, after the harvest and in time for next year's. Though much would be gained by easing the passage of his crops from the fields to his scale and then onto the market, more would be gained from the fee that would be paid by every other farmer whose grain laden wheelbarrows and carts were pushed or pulled along the blackened hardness of "Wang's Way." The dirt track there now was simply known as "that road." "That road is too dark to find your way at night," or "Search that road for fallen grain." Wang intended for the nondescript nature of the path to end once his money and mind had been brought to bear upon it. His name would blow across the lips of Da Long's residents for generations to come.

Reclining in his chair, Wang was suspended outside of himself, outside of this time and place, hovering somewhere in the future. He liked to do this, to disconnect from the present and travel to a time when his status and wealth were greater and more widely recognized.

Piercing the afternoon and instantaneously stirring Wang to considerable irritation, the bleating utterances of a goat rose from just outside and below the window. Jiang was nearby. Everywhere the goat went, Wang's young son was sure to be close at hand, sharing his lunch with the animal and pulling softly on its beard.

"Pointless. Useless creature." To which of the two creatures, nestled in the cool crook between wall and dirt earth, Wang was referring was not entirely clear, even to himself. He went to the window, convincing himself of a need to clear his throat and conjuring in his mouth a sizeable wad of phlegm, and spat forcefully outside. The wetness landed just in front of the two friends.

"BaBa?"

"Son. What are you doing?"

"Small Snow and I are just resting. It's too bright and hot out here, and we are both thirsty."

"Have the housekeeper bring you some water. Why do you just sit there? Water will not spring from the tap into your mouth by magic. And as for the goat, he can find his own water. Get going and clean up for dinner."

"Yes, Baba."

Jiang pulled himself up and brushed the dirt from the seat of his pants, running his tongue over his chapped lips. He cocked his head to one side, counting in whispers the whole time, and looked straight at the goat as if waiting for the creature to blink. The goat watched him steadily and waited for Jiang to stroke its head. Jiang called out "thirty-four" and then obliged the creature before disappearing into the house.

Wang pretended not to see any of this. Looking straight out over the fields, he focused on the line of men and women, shoulders sagging from their rice loads, making their way to his granary.

The men and women knew better than to grow impatient waiting for the Farmer Master to come and dole out their earnings. He would come when he was ready, and they would simply wait for him. They held their loads, never placing the bundles on the ground for fear of crushing the yellow tassels and having part of their labor cast aside, labeled as "damaged." Their shirts scratchy and stiff with dried sweat, the men distracted themselves with mindless chatter, passing time sharing dirty jokes. The women jockeyed to join the conversation by offering up gossip.

"A third girl has left HeLu Village to go and sell herself in the city. HeLu's crop yield is so low this year that the parents had no choice but to push her out the door," scoffed one of the women, shifting her weight from one foot to the other. "What times are these? Imagine. Young folk leaving their *laojia*, their hometowns and those of their ancestors, to work in the city. Bah! There'll be no one left to look after either those who are long in years or the little ones."

"Was she pretty?" asked one of the older men, wiggling his eyebrows up and down in mock interest.

"If you like sloping eyes. They say she's going to work in a factory, but what skills do you think she has?" The woman clucked her tongue. "She'll be working on her back before she ever sees the inside of a factory."

A particularly dirty-looking fellow snorted, "Well, if she's not pretty, then her yield there will be low too."

The men's laughter contorted their faces.

"She's likely one of those who is best working after dark. They have a lot of that type over in HeLu." The women joined in the laughter, letting their bellies undulate back and forth, supposing that this somehow was a compliment to the women of Da Long village.

Their rumbling laughter lost its momentum, fizzling to nothing as the workers turned towards the call of the snowy white goat. With mouths tightly closed and eyes wide open, they sought out a sighting of the Farmer Master's son. Jiang and his companion trotted into the granary courtyard. The workers bowed their heads and mumbled in unison, "Good evening, Young Wang." They looked at Jiang and waited. The boy stared back and seemed startled to see the workers. He immediately began counting out loud, his voice quivering, "Seventy-three." He looked to the goat as if waiting for instructions on what to do next. Seeming upset that his four-legged companion was voiceless, the boy looked back at the workers and spewed forth numbers even more vigorously.

"Strange." An anonymous whisper came from deep within the gathering of workers. Without any physical movement of the legs within it, the huddle moved slightly closer towards Jiang through a collective lean, as if to scrutinize him more carefully.

The boy's numbers flowed forth like notes in a strange ballad, and he began to vibrate. Small Snow began bleating uncontrollably, matching the fervor of Jiang's numbers, and he beat his front hooves violently against the ground. Jiang's hands reached out in front of him, and his fingers pinched the air, their pads thumping against each other.

The whole scene was spectacular. The workers stood absolutely still and silent, transfixed by the duo.

The boy's nostrils flared as his eyes danced in his head, his voice piercing the thick air. "Fire. Fire. I can smell it."

The workers pulled back and waited. They did not run or flee. They did not fearfully search for flames. They held tightly onto their bundles and let the scene unfold.

Only one head swiveled back and forth on its sturdy neck, casting one set of eyes in hurried glances all about, keeping pace with a heart that raced with the fear of being burned. Da Long's newest bride looked to the drying shed to see if its precious rice sheaths, dried of all water and perfect for kindling, had caught fire. Instinctively, Lei knew better than to drop her bundle and had steadied her fleshy feet even as her knees had begun to wobble; however, she did not know that there was nothing to fear, that nothing needed her attention more than what was right in front of her.

An agonizing screech ripped through the air and brought Lei's attention fully in line with that of all her motionless, soundless co-workers. She half expected to see the white goat with its throat slit, and for the smell of warm blood to curl up her nostrils, but, instead, the sharp acidic smell of urine cut through the air. The boy's slender, stiffened body thrashed violently against the ground while his head and neck arched back, seemingly tethered to the earth. All the muscles in the boy's neck and jaw and lips were pulled violently taut across their spans and his teeth, protruding and perfectly straight, shone with pure whiteness.

Avoiding even the faintest hint of culpability for the boy and his plight, the workers watched, pushing back ever so slightly as rivulets of pale, yellow urine inched towards their feet. The goat continued to bleat loudly and to stomp frantically against the ground, launching insignificant dirt puffs into the air.

Lei lowered her bundle carefully to the ground and, with the softest, "I'm sorry, please move aside," she began to wiggle forward through the mass of bodies toward the convulsing child. Frothy, white saliva ran down Jiang's face from the corners of his mouth to the hinge of his jaw.

Lei's movement into the sweaty stillness of the villagers must have created an unexpected dilemma in each one of them—which strange creature to focus on? Master Wang's only child? A soft-life child who knew nothing of their hunger or aches, who was so apart from them as to flail like a fish out of their common water? Or should they scrutinize Bo's full-bodied, paddle-footed bride?

Lei reached her trembling hand out in front of her. She wanted to place it on the child, to steady his thrashing, to rub her hands soothingly along the sides of his slender body. The goat, sensing her purpose, quieted ever so slightly. His bleating and hoof beating slowed to stutters. He, too, watched Lei expectantly.

Lei was moments from touching Jiang. She hesitated for a fraction of a second for fear of hurting him. Determined, she pushed her hand slowly toward the writhing boy.

Suddenly, she was on the ground, clasping her neck and watching one of her purple slippers sail overhead. All the air in her body was trapped, unable to pass through her throat. Bo's hand had grasped tightly at the back of his wife's collar, cinching it tightly around her neck, and had pulled her down and backwards onto the dirt.

"You stupid woman." Bo's words thumped down on Lei's head. As she struggled to suck air into her lungs, her body came back to life and moved ever so slowly.

Jiang's body went still.

Chapter Four

Long Worms

Water bubbled softly and steadily in the corner, where the old woman was squatting on the floor, rocking steadily on her bent-under legs. Her frail figure didn't turn to look at her husband, Old Doctor, but she listened intently to his chanting. His sounds came from deep within him as a low rumble sporadically punctuated by whispered words. These few words, barely decipherable and almost swallowed before becoming whole, served as instructions from the doctor to his elderly wife.

"Dark root." Old Doctor took a deep breath, put his chin to his chest, and paced in place. "Lotus powder. Yes. Lotus powder."

As Old Doctor's whispers floated over to her, his wife moved to the shelf crowded with jars of different sizes and shapes that were filled with all manner of things: pieces of tree bark, leaves both fresh and dried, berries, pickled animal parts, unctuous liquids, and other things not discernible through the layers of dust. Her little, claw-like hands authoritatively pulled down one jar at a time, picking from the lot of them with an implied certainty. Other whispers moved her in the direction of the large wooden trunk that sat beside her. She lifted the trunk lid open with one hand while rummaging through its contents with the other. Reading with her hands, she didn't bother to look inside, simply pulling forth little, folded paper parcels which she carefully opened to reveal dusty substances of various colors. Out of these jars and paper parcels were picked, poured, and pinched bits and pieces of this and that which, in turn, were placed in the small stone bowl on the floor between the old woman's feet. Small amounts of boiling water were ladled into the bowl, and the old woman smashed the ingredients earnestly using a pestle, putting the weight of her body into the endeavor, rocking back and forth.

A pungent odor began to permeate the room, somehow finding its place in a space already cramped with mustiness.

AnRan sat with her arms folded in front of her abdomen, nervously pinching each of her forearms. She pinched hard, willing her blood to move and her qi to flow. Old Doctor's soothing, soft voice made her lids heavy. Her eyes closed and mind open, the young woman wished to go back to the time, to four years earlier, when her uterus was swollen with the unborn Jiang. She wished not to be here right now with the out-in-the-world, pale Jiang laid out on the doctor's examining table. Her son was outside of her but looked like he should be back inside, safe and swimming in her body, letting her absorb all his movements, big and small. Each action he had made inside of her had been so strong and certain; she had never questioned their nature or purpose. She had not dreamt that his energy would be unbalanced, that he would have too many movements without meaning or function. He had been born too quickly, falling out of her before he was ready, before her qi had flowed fully into him and balanced him.

Now he was beyond her reach, beyond the power of her body to prepare him for this world. Now he depended on long worm, bark scrapings, and plant roots to bring him into balance, and on the knowledge of this old couple, who had never carried him, to pull him through this world.

Outside, a baby was wailing loudly. A woman's voice hushed the child, "Shush now. Stop your crying. We are here to make you better." The sound of her steps, back and forth in front of the Old Doctor's door, signaled that another mother was waiting for her time with the old healer.

AnRan squeezed her eyes shut. The smell of the tonic rising from between the old woman's feet caused bile to rise in her mouth and compelled her to pinch even harder at her arms.

Seated next to AnRan, the Farmer Master watched as his wife twisted the flesh of her arms over and over, turning it red and hot. He could see into the future when the redness would give way to pale, purple bruises. These small signs of penance, kneaded deep into her skin, would be visible only to him. He would stare at them as she lay next to him in their bed, her arms bare and not covered by the silk sleeves of a robe. He did not reach out now to stop her.

———————

One hour away by foot, the high sun of midday shone without a single cloud to intervene between its heat and the earth. Lei's back, bruised and sore, was sticky with sweat. A basket of wet and only partially clean laundry sat at her feet, a knot of Bo's and Fang MaMa's clothing. Lei had spent the better part of the morning washing and hanging a week's worth of wears. Bo's work pants and his oversized shirt, once dark blue, were almost grey. The fabric, which had never been made to withstand real labor, was soiled with ground-in dirt. Fang MaMa's two cotton shifts, made of fabric similar in color but looser in weave, were lighter in weight. The woman's frail frame couldn't really support anything much heavier.

As Lei had rubbed and kneaded the shifts in the washing water, the distinct smoky smell of the inside of their home had risen into the air. Lei now began to hang the laundry on the dry line already sagging under the weight of MeiLin's clothes. MeiLin's items had been washed first, separate from the rest of the laundry, with fresh water and honey locust soap balls; her garments were to be gently rubbed clean and pressed free of water, not twisted with force. Then they were hung immediately, spread out along the line without bunching, so to avoid wrinkling. Only after MeiLin's clothes were washed and hung were Bo's and Fang MaMa's clothes washed with the residual water and soap residue. This process had been outlined to Lei via a one-way communication from Fang MaMa to her. No instructions had been provided regarding the washing of Lei's own clothing. Wearing only her nightgown, Lei now submerged her own work garments into the remaining water which appeared dirtier than the clothing itself. She let her arms sink down into the water and enjoyed the creeping coolness of the waterline as it traveled up her forearms into the crooks of her elbows.

The heat had pushed all other living creatures into the shade. The air stood still and not a sound came to Lei's ear except for Bo's low, sleepy grunts. He was slouched against the solitary tree that sat at the end of the muddy path connecting the house to the fields. The tree itself looked quite deprived of attention and its leaves drooped with thirst; it cast only sparse shade and Bo's legs extended out in front of him into the light. Lei watched Bo's belly rise and fall and thought he looked rather content in that moment.

Her hand rubbed the part of her lower back that had landed hard against the ground when she last saw the Farmer Master's boy. She did not know what was wrong with the child, but knew she was not afraid of whatever it was that possessed him. She figured Bo had been scared, and that was why he had not wanted her to touch Jiang. The villagers had also stood by motionless and staring as the child had writhed and twisted. They, too, had been scared.

A puttering sound encroached on her thoughts. Lei looked to Bo, but he remained unchanged. His belly moved up and down in a rhythm that bore no relationship to the puttering which grew louder, coming from somewhere beyond her view.

A small, motorized scooter appeared at the head of the path and started coming towards her, past Bo and the tree. Lei squinted the sun out of her eyes and made out a large figure atop the scooter—Pang, the fatter of the two brothers who worked the rice fields. He looked too big for the scooter.

"Hello. Good afternoon." Pang struggled off the scooter, almost toppling the whole thing over as he brought one of his large legs behind him, over and across the seat.

"Good afternoon." Lei wiped her hands on her nightgown and carefully gave the man a polite, close-lipped smile.

"Who's here? Have you eaten? Are you full?" He spoke with a big open mouth and full voice, using this customary inquiry about food to show that his unexpected visit was a friendly and casual one, not necessarily one with a purpose. "Is MeiLin here?"

"What is this?" Bo had joined them. Awoken by the passing scooter and recognizing Pang's roundness, he had hastened up to the house and threw a limp wave of his hand towards the scooter. "Whose is it?"

Fang MaMa and MeiLin came out of the house to join them. MeiLin hung back, framed like a picture just inside the threshold of the door, out of the sun. Fang MaMa moved straight to the scooter, touching the handlebars and pinching the tires as if she possessed special knowledge about these types of machines.

"How much?" She looked at MeiLin as she asked this question to make sure her daughter was listening for the answer. Then, turning to Pang, "Probably you paid too much. Too expensive."

Bo pressed his lips hard and refrained from looking at anyone, angry that his mother had not felt the need to establish that the scooter actually belonged to Pang.

"Aiyah! You are probably right. I am not a skilled negotiator like you, Fang MaMa. It cost me the better part of a year's wage." Pang grinned off the old lady's chiding, his hearing cast beyond her prattle to the soft breathing sounds of the youngest Fang.

"Too expensive. Foolishly expensive." Bo snorted and then cleared his throat loudly, drawing phlegm to his mouth and spitting it out at a spot not too far from the front tire.

Lei cast her eyes to the ground, not wanting Bo to see her face reddened on his behalf. She looked at the spit on the ground and used her bare foot to brush dirt over the glistening wet spot. She smiled politely at Pang, acting as if this came naturally to her. A simple duty that any wife would do for a husband who had such a habit.

Pang did not notice Bo or Lei. His round face, always the color of brick, made him look perpetually breathless, but his breath was steady, as was his gaze. He looked at MeiLin and was overwhelmed. He wanted to pick her up and fly away with her, and so he tried to do so, "I wanted to offer my good neighbors a ride. I thought someone might like to ride up

Wang Road. The bike moves so quickly as to create a cooling wind." He paused, feigning to be offering the experience to everyone present and then, a little too quickly, "MeiLin?"

MeiLin moved ever so slightly forward, allowing one pale, bare foot to cross the threshold of the door, out from the darkness and into the brightness of the midday, and cocked her head to one side. She took in the whole scene: Pang, sweating and staring, the scooter, new but already covered in fine earthy dust, MaMa and Bo calculating and Lei with lips pressed and wearing her nightgown in the middle of the day.

"Don't be crazy, Pang. MeiLin cannot be out in this sun; her skin will become dark like dirt." Bo mounted the scooter. "Come. Take me down by Wang's Way. It is too damn hot out here."

Lei rubbed her bare arms as she watched the scooter stutter away from the house, with Pang and Bo awkwardly balanced on top of it.

———

Old Doctor whispered into the air, "The boy is hot with fright. He carries too much energy in him. This combination makes him quake." He continued without noting where his words fell, knowing that AnRan and Little Wang—he silently noted that "Little Wang" was no longer so little and that he should try to remember to call him by his official title of Farmer Master—would be listening to his every word. "The quaking will break him over time. It must be quelled through cooling liquids and general calm. Feed the boy the tonic daily in the morning, cool his feet, and don't let excitement creep into his day or night. Let him pass time sitting in the fresh air. No more numbers or school studies for now."

AnRan instinctively massaged Jiang's shins, pressing them gently, letting her palms feel her son's soft skin. Training her ears on Old Doctor's voice, she absorbed every one of his instructions, committing the sour-smelling tonic ingredients to memory, all the while rubbing the healer's words into her son's legs.

The Farmer Master wiped his hand down the front of his face and momentarily pinched his nostrils. His shoulders sagged, ever-so-slightly, with Old Doctor's last words. He did not question the old healer, who had been a close and trusted friend of his father's. Wang pulled his back rigid and fixed his eyes on Jiang.

The boy, his boy, was already too strange.

Chapter Five

Eggs, Newspapers, and Slippers

"They will be together. I know it."

"Aiyah! He's too fat for her. He will break her in half. "

"He's a man, fat or not, and he is ready to find a wife."

The whispers and giggles broke Lei's concentration and gave her an excuse to pause. She took a deep breath and pulled herself straight, stiffly unfurling inch by inch. Fully extended, she now let out a full and heavy breath, dropping one arm loosely to her side and letting the other, knife firmly clutched in its hand, rest in the deep crook that had developed between her hip bone and her belly. Her head was hot and wet strips of hair clung to the edges of her face. She watched the clouds moving curiously above her with an energy much greater than her own, lending a greyness to the sky.

Lei turned her face in the direction of the gossiping voices and was not surprised to spot the sisters. Across the fields, scattered several meters apart, were small clusters of field workers. Each worker was hooked onto the earth, crouched low, head down and covered, hands lost beneath the water. They were remarkably similar. All of them gathering and cutting rice stems; all of them identical in their desire for the midday mealtime to be at hand and for their bellies to be full.

Lei could now name every single hook on the horizon. Uniform as they looked, she recognized the uniqueness of each one. The gossiping sisters, with their angular, scrawny bodies stuck up and out from the earth like sparsely leaved tree saplings, the older one taller than her companion. They were Hong and Min, though Lei seldom heard their given names used in Da Long. Rather, the women comprised a pair of relativities: the older one and the younger one, the taller one and the shorter one, the ugly one and the uglier one, the one with more teeth and the one with fewer teeth.

Further afield, Pang and Shu looked like two balls of slightly differing sizes bobbing up and down on a sea of rice. Up and down. Up and down. The brothers worked in harmony to tame the stalks, Pang gathering a large armful of stalks and Shu working to harness them and cut them free from the ground. "Up." Shu's voice triggered Pang to heave the bundle out of the water and place it on an ever-growing pile. Their shirts and pants, tight and darkened with water and sweat, clung to their forms, outlining their muscled shoulders and legs and the thickness of their torsos.

Not far over from the brothers, Lei smiled at the fuller form of the butcher's wife. Like little schoolboys who were too scared to dive into the pond and who simply fell forward straight-legged, Chang TaiTai had knees that refused to bend. "These knees are useless and cannot carry so much, so it's a good thing I don't produce that much." She shared this thought daily during Lei's first harvesting season in Da Long. During lunch breaks, the hooks would straighten and move in unison towards the side of the road to rest while they ate. All the men and women sat with their legs folded either beneath or to the side of them, except for Chang TaiTai. She pushed her legs out right in front of her and vigorously massaged her knees with hands that smelled of meat on account of her being the butcher's wife and, as if needing to explain afresh, she would remind anyone who would listen of the useless nature of her "disobedient" joints.

"Why are you standing? What's happening? What are you looking at?" Bo pulled his hands out of the water. His wiry spine curved back on itself as he rose up quickly, and the counteracting weight of his head seemed to keep him from toppling backwards. Lei tried not to laugh. Raising her hand to cover her mouth, she pretended to belch. The pantomime elicited, "It's not yet time to eat," from Bo.

"I know. My body just felt cramped. I can't feel my feet."

"They've gotten so big." Bo cast his eyes downward, as if he could see Lei's feet through the muddy water. "You've gotten so big." These last words were said softly, even affectionately. Lei looked over at Bo, who as usual was not looking at her, but that didn't matter, for she did not see a scowl on his face. The corners of his mouth were cast ever so slightly upward. One of his hands was working the depths of a pant pocket. He pulled out something small and thrust it in her direction. "Eat this. It needs it."

Lei reached out to him with an open hand and received a small, hard, green sour apple. It was knobby and bruised on one side. She smiled at Bo, but again, he was not looking at her and did not notice the whiteness of her teeth. He was already crouched down with hands submerged, grasping for stems.

Lei nibbled slowly. Tangy sweetness pricked her tongue. She watched Chang TaiTai and thought her lucky despite her not being able to bend her knees. Never was she called a fool or laughed at for offering such wind-tossed logic about her meager earnings. The villagers, who were not necessarily cruel, never passed up the chance to point out fault or weakness in one another. Brutal honesty was a civic duty in Da Long village. Mistakes did not pass silently. But no one snickered at the butcher's wife, who always smelled of raw meat, or cast a word of derision in her direction for fear of retaliation when buying their meager portions from her husband.

Lei had no such protection. "Stupid egg" and "Simpleton" had rung in her ears for days after she had picked herself up off the Farmer Master's floor, bringing waves of shameful heat over her entire body. Bo, Fang MaMa, and all the field workers had reminded her, through an almost ritualized name-calling, that she was too obtuse to see the obvious, that she lacked the skills to assess what was right in front of her. The strange son of the Farmer Master was to be left alone, set apart, and certainly was not to be touched.

Lei spat two small, shiny black apple seeds into her hand and tossed them into the water. She then ran her hand over her belly and pulled its new inhabitant closer to her. She was glad the two of them were tied together with a fleshy rope and that the child could not float away under the water and in between the stalks. She understood that this fleshy rope would soon be severed and the creature at the other end would be set out into the world, untethered from her, but as certain as Lei was of this soon-to-be-parting, she was also certain that nothing would ever allow her to set this sweet creature apart from her. They were already one. She cooed comfort into its unborn ears when it kicked and moved about, rubbing its back and rump through her veiny belly skin which was pulled tight across its form. The child danced with each mouthful of tangy apple that Lei ate and kicked violently if she ate hot peppers in the evening, sending fire up the back of her throat. The child woke her up in the night to remind her that she was now fully responsible for its life, this message coming to her repeatedly as she made her way through the stillness and darkness that lay between the hut and the outhouse. Lei sang and spoke softly as she worked; stories of her family and her ancestral village came easily, and she diligently shared them with her firstborn-to-be.

"Get more bundles tied before the call to eat." Bo looked at her now squarely in the face, keeping his gaze from the rest of her. He had calculated the cost of Lei standing there staring out on the field rather than bundling rice stalks. He looked at her only from the shoulders up. He segmented her into different parts with different purposes.

Lei squatted and ran her fingers through the water. This was her husband's way. He gave her his affections in small pieces directed at small parts of her. Frustration and urging directed her strong shoulders to work and put coins in his pocket, where green apples and half smiles were reserved for her swollen abdomen, needed to carry his child. Bo's eyes didn't see Lei in her wholeness. He couldn't. If he could, he might not have brought her to the field to work. She might be home with MeiLin. Beautiful MeiLin, Bo's rural treasure, who sat in the shade of the shack, passing her days chopping garlic shoots, watching water boil, and briefly sweeping the smallness of the hut before resting back in her bed during the particularly hot hours of the day. Beautiful MeiLin, who had capable arms and hands and knees that worked, none of which factored into Bo's calculations of wages yet to be claimed. For all of MeiLin's parts melted together into a single, exquisite, fragile whole.

Lei wondered when Bo would look at her the way he looked at MeiLin.

When the midday lunch call finally made its way to Lei and Bo, on that day just three weeks prior to the birth of the couple's first child, a heavy rain erupted, drowning out the workers' enthusiasm for food. The men and women rushed to grab their bundles, secure their tools, and slosh their way to the road. The rain signaled that the workday had ended. The villagers scrambled to find their slippers, a task made harder by mud that was now obscuring some of the slippers' identifying colors and patterns, and trudged towards the Farmer Master's home for the day's weighing. Lei moved slowly, her swollen feet only allowing her to push halfway into her slippers. Bo struggled to pick up his own bundles as well as Lei's, anxiously aware that the Farmer Master would disqualify any bundles from the day's weighing that were too rain-damaged.

Pang approached the pair, "Come, let me help you with those. I can carry several more." His face glistened in the rain. He reached over to catch a bundle that was about to topple off Bo's shoulder.

"Well, help me then." Bo, teeth clenched and looking only at Pang's massive hands, said with reluctance.

"Shu, help Fang TaiTai to the Farmer Master's house. She could use a steady shoulder to guide her." Pang's words, "TaiTai," hung in the air for a moment as if looking for a place to rest. Neither Bo nor Lei had contemplated the idea that their union had resulted in the creation of an age-old pair: the "LaoGong," or Old Man and his "TaiTai," or Honored Wife. Lei wiped her hands down the front of her smock, pulling the wet and worn fabric neatly over her and her belly. She tucked straggling hairs behind her ears. Shu gathered her bundles from the soft ground at Lei's feet, and though she murmured a soft thank you at Shu, it was Pang who had her attention.

Lei watched as Pang twisted down to scoop up the rice bundles at Bo's feet under one arm while keeping his own bundles balanced on his other shoulder. With each twist, the fabric of his shirt cinched around his waist and outlined the breadth of his back. She followed the lines of his torso and of his bulging calves, both of which glistened in the rain. From deep within her, she felt a pressure and squeezed her thighs tightly together and tried to stop imagining that such a man could lift her on his back. Lowering her face, she focused on getting her slippers over her toes.

Hong and Min, soaking and silent, ran their hands vigorously up and down their sticky legs and quickly pulled their slippers onto their feet. Their light figures tried to take off after the men who had already started towards the weighing station, but, like butterflies with drenched wings, they could only pick up so much speed. The rain had slowed them down, yet they were still moving faster than Lei who stood still as she drew preparatory breaths. The warm rainwater brought little relief from the sweaty, heavy air, and heat rose out through the nape of Lei's shirt, her body a furnace.

Lei did not feel the need to rush. She moved slowly, her feet merely pushing her ill-fitting slippers through the mud. She thought of Pang and kept seeing his back through the wetness of his shirt. MeiLin had rested her pale white face against that back. How many times and for how long Lei did not know, but that it had happened was a certainty known to her and to Bo.

Pang had kept bringing himself by the house on his bike, each time looking at Bo but smiling through him to MeiLin. He never came empty-handed, not after that first time he'd ridden up on the new machine and, having had nothing with which to distract Fang MaMa, had been open to her chiding. After that, there were extra eggs he wanted to share, newspapers from the Hundred Village market that were filled with interesting stories that he would never be able to retell sufficiently, and slippers that he had bought in the wrong size for his own mother but that he hoped would be just the right size for Fang MaMa.

For Fang MaMa, the purr of Pang's cycle became much like the call to lunch, anticipated and greeted with excitement. Pang's gifts were always given to Fang MaMa, but everyone knew they were really for MeiLin. Each one an unspoken acknowledgement of MeiLin's beauty and an invitation to her to step out across the threshold of the shack. Presented nonchalantly, Pang would offer these items to the old woman as if the thought to come over and share had just sprung to his mind with no forethought. Like blossoms in a breeze that just happened to get caught in one's hair, Pang's gifts were presented as just lucky and inconsequential: "We couldn't possibly eat so many eggs, it's not good for the body, but I didn't want them to waste ..." "I was just about to throw the papers away ..." "I thought to take the slippers back to the market, but it's such a bother ..." His words made it such that the offerings couldn't be challenged by Bo as inappropriate or "too much."

In the same way that Pang's eggs, newspapers, and slippers slid their way into the shack via Fang MaMa, so did thoughts of Pang himself come to reside in MeiLin's head. In the time before Fang MaMa savored Pang's treats, if the idea of Pang as more than a neighbor had tried to sprout in MeiLin's thoughts, it would have fallen on non-nurturing soil. Even though several years had passed since her first moon of womanhood, MeiLin had neither a body nor a mind stirred to seek the attention of this man. Having spent her teenage years in much the same way she had spent her childhood, sitting on the bed she shared with her mother, waiting for the days to pass and for her father, when he was alive, and now, Bo, to come home, MeiLin was coddled and content. She had been this way ever since her memorable entry into the world. Whenever Fang MaMa told the story of MeiLin's birth, she would close her eyes and uncharacteristically lower her voice to a whisper. "Aiyah. When MeiLin came, I thought she was dead. She came out so quickly and quietly. Not like Bo. No, not like Bo. He fought his way out. Very noisy. Screaming, 'I'm here.' Not MeiLin. Like a white kitten, she tiptoed out softly and meowed, 'Look at me.' Your father almost fell to his knees when he saw her. She was just that pretty." And so it came to pass that MeiLin was born a rural rarity, a village child who was handled with extreme care and whose childhood didn't end with an early introduction to the ways of a crop knife.

When they were little, Bo and MeiLin were like two curious parts of a whole. They fit together, both slight and quiet, with eyes that spoke more words than any other part of them. While the other village children ran barefoot in the streets, fighting with mangy strays over scraps of food, the Fang children sat near Fang MaMa's feet. They passed their time together, with Bo working to amuse MeiLin. When they watched ants march across the dirt, Bo would place small obstacles in the little creatures' path just to make the spectacle more interesting for his sister. After the rain, when the ground was soggy, Bo drew pictures into the soft mud and waited for MeiLin to squeal with delight as she recognized familiar scenes—the family sitting at the table, the tree down the way, Bo and MeiLin holding hands. Bo worshipped MeiLin, and MeiLin was content to be worshipped.

"Where's MeiLin? Where's MeiLin?" These were always the first words Bo, or his father, would utter when they came home from their days away from the shack. Fang MaMa took pride in this. She had made something so valuable with the power to turn males into more than mere bellies with legs and arms. Other village women were greeted by their schoolboy sons and laboring husbands usually with nothing more than, "I want to eat."

Long, wet faces huddled around the scales. The rain made them shiver while bringing a light sheen to the cheekbones and eyes of the workers. The Farmer Master's face was hidden in the shadow of his hat brim. An unspoken order moved the oldest and weakest of the workers forward first. Chang Tai Tai's small bundle was lifted easily upon the scale and earned her a small, dirty, brass coin. She limped off towards Wang's Way and Lei, who stood at the back of the group, was thankful that the woman and her bad knees had a head start towards home. The heart of the group would easily catch up with the butcher's wife and keep her company as the sky grew darker.

Lei stood silently waiting for her turn. Bo had not seen her arrive as he had not been looking for her. She had not been looking for him, either. She stared at the ground and relaxed, as there was no rushing the weighing. As if the child inside of her had grabbed hold of her heart and head and was pulling her somewhere, Lei let her mind wander. She remembered how her father would carry her home from the market when it rained, running her into the house and placing her next to the open fire pit, her brothers dashing behind them the whole way. The boys would peel their wet clothes off and jump around naked, trying to keep warm, while their father would open a bottle of beer, sharing "warming up" sips with the boys. Lei would keep her underclothes on, letting only her outer clothes drop to the floor.

"You're crazy. Just simply crazy," Lei's mother would scold, half-laughing at the sight of her children hopping around the room.

Lei suddenly had the urge to hop. She wanted to jump and lift her two flat feet right off the ground. She pulled her feet out of their slippers and began to stretch the arches of her feet, pushing the balls of her big toes forward and down into the mud. She felt the sensation of pinpricks along her calves.

"Oh my God! There are hundreds of them!" Hong's shriek drew Lei's eyes upwards. The sisters were standing and pointing at Lei. Min's buck teeth and slack jaw were hidden behind her hands which she held up over her mouth, above which her eyes were horrifically huge and round.

Some of the women began to scream; others just looked at Lei's legs with disgust and spat on the ground.

Lei felt light-headed as she pivoted her right leg, bringing her right calf forward in front of her. The mound of her calf was mottled with black, dirt-like clumps clinging to her skin. Squeezing her eyes shut while trying to steady herself, Lei watched as the clumps wriggled in place, as if hooked into her skin. They were alive. Rank bitterness rose in her throat as she saw that her left calf matched the right one. She began to hop from leg to the other as she tried to scrape her skin free of the dancing clumps, using her alternating feet. Only a few of the leeches came free, falling to the ground with soft plops due to their being fully engorged with blood. The others, not yet full, held on fast.

Lei cried, "Bo! Bo! Help me!"

Before Bo could reach his wife, who had once again made a spectacle of herself, Jiang appeared at Lei's side. Coming out from the shadows of the house with his white, four-legged companion silently beside him, it was as if the boy had popped up out of nowhere. The goat cocked his head to one side and kept his eyes on the black clumps that were writhing on the ground. Reaching out with his hoof, he stomped squarely on the one closest to him, finding its approach menacing. Deep, red blood splotched the ground. Jiang put his hands on Lei's feet, pushed them onto the ground, and looked at her in the eyes for a long moment, as if commanding her to be still. Lei's panic eased, and the boy began to methodically dislodge the leeches one by one, working in rows up from her ankles to her the top of her calves.

The Farmer Master shook his head and looked away from his son. "Let's be done with this. Quickly, weigh up and be home with all of you." The workers immediately fell silent as Wang banged on the top of the scale sending the needle on its circular face flying.

———————

Lei fought to steady her head, which kept threatening to roll off her shoulders. She tried to pant away the waves of fire sweeping over her body. This roiling, fevered battle played out in stark contrast to the dark, strangely still, and cool emptiness of the shack.

Fang MaMa and MeiLin were outside, cleaning vegetables. Bo was gone to the fields. He had left her that morning after wordlessly looking at her wrapped legs. Soggy and swollen from hundreds of leech bites, the skin of her lower legs had fallen off in paper-thin peels. She was thankful for the cream-colored cotton bandages holding what remaining skin she had in place, though they were stained through with blood.

Her offer to help in the fields as best she could had been met by Fang MaMa's honest assessment: "Your legs are horrific. Blood oozing everywhere! No one will want to be near you. You will give everyone indigestion."

Barely raising her eyes from her breakfast, MeiLin added, more for Bo and Fang MaMa than for Lei, "Your blood has been weakened by the leeches. Your skin will not heal for days. You will not be able to work for at least a week." Like a broken piece of machinery awaiting repair, Lei was left to idle alone.

She lay in bed, drifting between onerous wakefulness and tortured sleep. Her thoughts, like steam rising from a boiling kettle, were real in one moment, lost in the next. She replayed her new family's words over and over in her head, trying to hear concern in their voices, to sense a touch of sympathy in their stares. She imagined the sweet taste of set-aside-just-for-her blood orange segments infusing the sour, soybean milk that had been left in the bowl at the side of the bed by Fang MaMa. She placed her head against the rough sack material that enclosed the mattress and imagined her head on her father's chest. She thought of MeiLin's pale skin pressed against Pang's back when she rode around on his motorcycle. She knew that Bo had imagined this as well, every day since the rides had begun.

MeiLin's head coming to rest against Pang had been spoken into reality, coming right out of Fang MaMa's mouth. "He offers to take you out because he respects me," Fang MaMa had stated, not inviting con- tradiction, on the night Pang had brought her the slippers she now wore ceaselessly on her feet. "He understands that I am an old woman who worries about her young daughter. He wants to do the right thing. He nobly offers to provide you that which I cannot: fresh air and stimulation for your senses. Sitting in the shack all day will spoil your skin and age you. Next time he comes, you take a ride with him and get some clean air."

And just like that, the evening rides had commenced, along with the whispering. Village voices speculated about what happened on those rides and what they meant for the future. As these musings crisscrossed the fields, eventually reaching Bo, Bo's ears turned the hottest shade of red Lei had ever seen.

Now, as she lay in the darkness, legs bleeding and pictures moving in her head, Lei was without bitterness. She understood that Bo loved MeiLin's beauty and could not let it go in the same way that Pang wanted to have it all for himself. She understood why MeiLin wanted to put her head on Pang's back and feel the soft solidness under her cheek. Lei longed for the same and felt tears fall on her cheek as she thought of her father.

Wrapped in loneliness, she fell asleep, waking hours later with new thoughts. She was not alone; she and MeiLin wanted the same things and shared the same feelings. As different as they were, as pretty as MeiLin was and as ugly as Lei was, they were alike in wanting to feel safe with someone.

Also, there was one other soul in Da Long with whom she shared an understanding. The strange little boy of the Farmer Master had touched her. He'd had the instinct to reach out to Lei, just as she had tried to reach out to him, because of what they could both see. He had recognized in her face what she had seen in his on that day when her husband had jerked her to the floor. What she had seen, looking past the crowd and closing her ears to the frantic bleating of the goat, ignoring the counting as it had grown louder and louder, focusing in on the boy's face and on his eyes before they had begun to roll up and beneath his forehead, was fear.

Lei stroked her belly and woke up the new life inside her. Clearing her throat, her voice rose softly in song, breaking the silence. She sang not to comfort herself, not because she was alone, not to bring herself back to the present, and not to brace her wandering mind. She sang because she was not alone and was determined to never be apart from this little soul who was growing inside her, a forever companion whose existence was borne of this new family and place.

Part Two

Shanghai
China, 1984

Chapter Six

Halls of Heavenly Kings and Virtuous Works

L uLu cupped each of her average-sized breasts with her hands and pushed them upward and over the pinching underwire of her lacy red bra. Thinking about what she would eat later that night, she bent over at the waist and ushered her breasts forward, making sure to keep her nipples covered. She then squatted on the small plastic stool and waited for business to start.

The road and sidewalks were jammed with bicycles, motorbikes, and bodies all moving relentlessly in every direction. Bells and horns sounded off, and people continued to scurry this way and that, not in response but with complete indifference, each body propelled by its own personal mission. Fried dough and oily meat scented the air, and Lulu's throat began to burn from the aerosolized flecks of hot peppercorns rising from the street hawker's wok just a few feet from her. She distracted herself with thoughts of dinner.

This period of waiting for the first customer of the night, though filled with the noises of the street, was experienced by LuLu in complete silence, as if the world was suspended before her and she was being given a moment to climb into the scene.

"Thank goodness it is Patient Man Night," YuZhen's voice broke through Lulu's silence. YuZhen was working her teeth around the husk of a betel nut and a small amount of saliva dripped from the corner of her mouth. She was an expert in stripping off the husk and getting to the small, softer green seed at the heart of the nut. Though YuZhen's mouth worked furiously, Lu was able to understand her as she continued, "I'm too sore for anything else."

"I know. I'm tired as well." LuLu watched as YuZhen's forever reddened teeth began to macerate the nut. "I just need to start and get to dinnertime."

"Don't be in such a rush. We will be busy soon enough. You know they will come. The Patient Men always have a few dollars left by mid-week. They don't waste it all on payday fighting with those drunk dogs that shove their way to everything." YuZhen offered LuLu a betel nut, as she had every night since the two of them had met, and LuLu, as was her custom, shook "no" with her head. YuZhen fixed her eyes and waited for the nut to take its effect. She closed her eyes without closing them, staring ahead without seeing anything. The skin on her neck was tight, and every vessel was visible; the thumping of her heart was present just beneath the angled part of her jawbone. LuLu watched carefully for the thumping to accelerate and for the vessels to become fuller. YuZhen's body straightened up and became rigid; she pulled her head towards the sky, stretching out her neck, and her eyes began to dance.

"This stuff is *so* good. I can't make it through the night without it. I don't know why you don't use it. I don't even mind the taste. I mean, I always use a little brown paste to make it sweeter and to bring it on faster." YuZhen's words were sharp and clear, rapidly flying from her mouth. "If you want some, you know I always keep a supply on hand."

"I don't want that stuff. I don't want to be that awake. I don't get paid extra for enthusiasm."

Ignoring LuLu, YuZhen stood up, wriggling her tight, sparkly skirt down the front of her thighs. She reached into the low-lying collar of her tank top and pulled up her large, melon-shaped breasts, leaving them almost hanging in the open. She moved into the stream of the moving crowd and called out to no one in particular, "Do you want to touch? Do you want to touch?"

The night was slow. Only two of LuLu's mid-week regulars, both migrant men from out west, had sought her services. In Lulu's experience, migrant men transacted their business faster than city men; as if niggled by the understanding that time was money, they kept their eyes on the clock.

Something in LuLu's belly kept distracting her. She tried to eat but only played with the rice in her bowl. YuZhen had been busy all night and was unlikely to join her anytime soon. Large breasts kept YuZhen in high demand despite her betel-stained teeth and hands. Anxiety grew in LuLu at having earned very little in tips and having brought so little into the house for Lao Fu. She stayed in the last room of the barbershop, the room that came off at the very end of a narrow hallway that ran through the rear of the building, and did not bring her food out onto the street to eat in the open air.

Two mattresses strewn with clothing, towels, cheap blankets, and several backpacks covered most of the floor. Tubes of lipstick and small, colorful makeup palettes spilled out of a makeup pouch that had been left open amidst the mess. The small plastic table that was pushed up into one corner of the room held a pot of white rice, some chipped rice bowls, chopsticks, and mismatched plastic cups. LuLu cleared some space on one of the mattresses, neatly folding a few blankets and towels into a pile, against which she lined up several backpacks after zipping up their pockets. Sitting down on the mattress edge, she flopped back to listen to her stomach, pressing her fingers into the flesh of her abdomen. She realized she was not hungry.

She grabbed her purple backpack, pulled out a small spiral notebook and a tiny, stuffed toy panda, and again flopped backwards onto the bed. LuLu methodically kissed each of the panda's paws and ears before tucking the black and white toy beneath her chin and snuggling it against her chest. She then carefully removed a pencil that had been secured within the spiral binding of the notebook. Turning the pages very slowly, taking in each one, LuLu tried to ease the roiling in her gut. Here was Zhang Li, swaddled and lying on the manger floor surrounded by hay, just as LuLu had drawn her the day before leaving her *laojia* for Shanghai. LiLi was just a month old in the drawing and looked a little sad, not that she could have known that her big sister was leaving and wouldn't be back for some time. LuLu's parents were drawn with a heavier, serious hand, the pencil lines being thicker and darker than those that had been used to depict LiLi. MaMa and BaBa stood pressed up against the crumbling stone wall of their home, anxiously peering out of the page. LuLu fought back tears as she rubbed her cheek into the panda's head.

Majestic stone buildings, crowded streets, throngs of bicycles and motor bikes, a river so wide that Lulu knew the first time she saw it she could not swim from one side to the other, and other Shanghai scenes filled the next several pages. All of this had been new and delightful to

LuLu when she had first emerged from the dusty Shanghai train depot almost a year earlier. The adrenaline associated with being part of a new frontier had overcome the girl in her first weeks as a city-dweller. Everything fascinated her and was beyond description, the necessary words never having sprouted within her during her years on her parents' farm. Libraries, grand embankments, public gardens, cathedrals, university buildings, and grand hotels were places too fantastical to have existed in her imagination. And though she had not yet seen it, LuLu had heard that at the city's heart was a famous golden temple with secret halls of "Heavenly Kings" and "Virtuous Works."

In those early days, Lulu had coveted all these details, painstakingly transforming each one, with her hands, into a precious picture recorded in the notebook that she faithfully carried around deep within her backpack. For LuLu, these details were now the details of her life, one she was eager to give to this city in exchange for calling it *her* city. All this she had felt then, before she had realized that this city would never be hers. This city didn't want to keep her; it merely wanted to capitalize on the best of her. Like a cheap piece of cloth, LuLu and millions of other rural migrants were there to wipe the mouth of this city before being tossed aside.

"What the hell are you doing? Have you gone stupid?" Lao Fu stood in the room's doorway. LuLu did not move; she had not heard him make his way down the hallway. "Listen. Listen to the sounds coming from next door. Do you hear that?" Saliva dotted her legs as he spat his words. The groans and grunts coming from the room next door were almost physically transmitted to LuLu through a shared wall, which vibrated with each utterance. "That's the sound of money being made. Now get up and earn your bowl."

LuLu sat up, grabbing the panda from under her chin. She quickly kissed all four of its paws and its two ears before stuffing it back into her bag. She picked up a tube of lipstick from under the blankets and applied the shocking pink color to her lips. LuLu kept her eyes on Lao Fu as this transpired. She secured the notebook in her backpack and then stood up and moved her way past him. She did not say one word to him. He was the type of man who enjoyed slapping a woman and was easily excited by sharp words. At only sixteen, she already knew about men and how to tread around them, when to smile, when to talk, when to laugh softly, when to pout. She excelled in being the quiet type who followed her clients with her eyes, always looking at them, and never being wild or physically too enthusiastic. Such tactics worked for YuZhen but would have come off as overtly false if LuLu had tried to work her clients this way.

Later, in the earliest morning hours, when her worknight had ended, and she found herself curled up on one corner of the mattress she had tidied earlier, LuLu stared into the darkness and began to draw her family with her finger, keeping track of every stroke. The girl next to her shifted in her sleep and threw her leg heavily across LuLu's knees. LuLu turned on her side, freeing herself from the sticky weight.

"Stop moving! I'm trying to sleep," a voice whined from the other side of the mattress.

It was never quiet in the city, and noises from the road streamed through the barbershop front to the back rooms. Even when she was working, LuLu could hear the city. The clanking of bicycle bells and purring of motorbike throttles merged with her own groaning and the whimpering of her clients into a chorus that never let her forget where she was. Now, she drew LiLi in the darkness in front of her face. LuLu imagined LiLi with straight black tresses that, never quite staying put, framed her full-cheeked face. Her lips formed a delicate, pale purple rose bud that was perpetually protruding in a pout. Next to be sketched were LuLu's parents; they were smiling and lying next to each other in bed, MaMa's leg thrown over BaBa's. Nested like birds, wings overlapping, MaMa did this because the bed was small and to keep BaBa warm. Lulu drew their eyes wrinkled with laughter, her finger moving noiselessly as she saw them come to life. Their foreheads were without a trace of worry as they watched LiLi play and waited for their elder child to come home.

LuLu's family hadn't seen or talked to her in almost a year, but she sent money home every month. The courier took his share, but the envelope was always heavy, as if a little part of LuLu herself went home every month in it. She imagined that MaMa always put the envelope on the table and rubbed it with her hands, as if absorbing LuLu's essence. Then BaBa would open the treasured delivery, take out the smallest silver coin, and place it on the family altar. A collection of worn pictures of his and MaMa's parents stared out from behind withering sticks of incense, all propped atop a wooden box across which a threadbare kitchen cloth had been carefully placed. One of LuLu's drawings of BaBa's childhood home also sat on the small altar. Kneeling before the altar with LiLi temporarily stilled, the small family, made smaller by the absence of its elder daughter, would call to their ancestors. They beseeched the spirit world to watch over their LuLu as they each envisioned her at a city factory, hundreds of miles away, stitching lengths of denim together into "foreign person pants," working day after day and late into the night.

Chapter Seven

Smoke Curls and Paper Meat

T he small window was tightly closed. Not even the slightest trace of air whispered across Du's fingers. He pressed his hands against the glass. Initially, Du made contact only with the pillowed parts of his palm but, after waiting for a few seconds, he pressed his whole palm more fully against the surface, measuring the intensity of the sun. Turning his body and placing his left ear against the window, he listened for other elements but could hear only the solitary stillness of the sun's heat. He felt certain that this was a good day for sharing the wisdom of the ancestors.

Du rose from his stool and felt his way around the room to the bed. He lay back and waited patiently, as he had been taught to do since childhood. Blind from birth, Du had been left wrapped in newspaper in the doorway of one of Shanghai's oldest orphanages by parents who, he assumed, could not find their way to feeding a child who would not, one day, grow capable of feeding them. Despite this hard start, Du had never felt unlucky or abandoned. From his early years, Du experienced his blindness not as complete darkness, but rather as a blackness broken up by spectacular intermittent patterns of light that floated in front of him.

He knew the patterns were communicating important things to him, and he never felt alone. The monks who ran the orphanage expressed amazement that Du was such a happy child, maybe even the happiest in the orphanage despite remaining parentless. The monks poured their love into Du, teaching him the old ways, to venerate the ancestors, and to seek their messages in the lights that came to him.

Currently, Du let the light creep into the void. It came from the furthest edge, a diminishing blackness that crept from left to right. And then it stopped. He waited for the golden light flowers to burst wide open. It had been a while since they had last appeared, and he could hear his own fear growing loudly with each beat of his heart. He waited and tried to still the commotion. He strained deep within his bowels, pushing down into his rectum, slowing the pace of his heartbeats. He stayed like this for a while. And then, with a full inhalation, they came. Dancing into the void came flashes of light, golden points of enlightenment moving chaotically. He was not forsaken. The ancestors still deemed him a worthy messenger. He pressed the hem of his shirt between his thumbs and forefingers, pulling each stitch from one set of fingers to the other, an exercise that allowed his hands to be still and not quake. He was then able to settle into the all-important task of discerning the wisdom encoded in the lights.

Sunlight never made its way back to the windowless room at the back of the barbershop, only heat.

"Aiyah! Why does it have to be this hot? Business will be slow tonight," YuZhen said as she pulled on her best shirt. Her face was pink from being freshly scrubbed free of all makeup. She shimmied into her "for foreigners" jeans and finished buttoning her shirt. LuLu had long recognized it as being the only shirt that YuZhen owned that buttoned all the way up to her neck.

"Here, move over so I can help you." YuZhen sat down on the mattress next to LuLu and pushed LuLu's raised hands away from her head and into her lap. "Do you want one or two?"

"Two. And please part it in the middle." LuLu let YuZhen pull her hair this way and that as she braided LuLu's hair into two long, lustrous, and perfectly symmetrical braids that framed either side of her face.

YuZhen patted down the braids, admiring how perfectly flat they lay. "Why do you always want me to do it the same way? Always two braids. You know I am good with hair. I can make it look good in many other ways."

"I like it this way."

"It's not so interesting. Look, I have some ribbons or butterfly hair clips. I could put those on the ends." YuZhen proudly presented two shiny pieces of silky, green ribbon, each festooned with white polka dots. "Pretty. No?"

"Next time."

LuLu looked into YuZhen's small hand-held mirror and moved it around above her head, trying to catch a glimpse of her whole body. Her school uniform still fit her. The pale blue, short-sleeved shirt and navy-blue skirt that fell just below her knees, along with her neatly styled hair, made her school backpack look very appropriate.

Lulu picked up a pair of purple strappy stilettos and shoved them deep into her backpack, making sure to feel the fur of her panda bear before zipping the bag closed. She slipped on a pair of navy canvas lace-up shoes. "Let's go. I'm ready." LuLu didn't tell YuZhen that her mother had always braided her hair this way on school mornings. "Let's not waste our free time."

The girls pushed their way out into the thick Shanghai air that hovered above the street. The sun blinded them temporarily but, through squinted eyes, they both made out Lao Fu. He was seated low down, just inches above the sidewalk, his bottom hanging off a small plastic stool and his bent knees spread apart on either side of his body. Whisps of cigarette smoke rose and disappeared above his head. He paid little attention to the crowds of people moving right up to and around him like water around a stone. Savory odors found a way to drift through the thick air and curled under LuLu's nose.

"Lao Fu, is your stomach full? You look quite satisfied, despite the heat." YuZhen's voice had a playfulness to it, and she addressed the scrunched-up old man as if he were a friend and not her pimp. The loud churning of LuLu's stomach caused Lao Fu to raise his eyes up to their faces. His body and head did not move, and he did not say anything.

"Excuse me. I'm sorry for the horrible sound. I have not yet taken my morning meal," LuLu said, keeping her eyes to the ground; she did not look straight at him. It was not night, and business time was over. It was not necessary for her to keep her eyes on him.

"Morning meal? You girls don't keep track of time, do you? The morning meal? Your stomachs don't know if it's day or night," he chided them with a touch of laughter, matching YuZhen's tone. "The soymilk boy was here hours ago. His milk was sweet this morning, almost too sweet, and the fried longs were nice and crispy. The oil tasted clean. You missed it all. Those came and went—passed you right by."

The earlier politeness had worked its way out of LuLu's mouth with conscious effort. She purposely used it to hold her steady in a daytime that contrasted so drastically with her nighttime. She pushed down her dislike of the nighttime Lao Fu, the wicked pimp who plied the back hallway of the shop, beyond the filthy barber's chair. Out here, in the light of day, he was a crumbly old barber, her employer, and she was a grateful, young shampoo girl from somewhere way beyond the bounds of the city.

YuZhen pulled on LuLu's elbow, the pressure of her grip belying her lighthearted tone. She wanted to get away. "We need to hurry along. We are going over to the temple to see Master Du."

"Humph. Master Du, the so-called fortuneteller? That blind bastard knows how to separate a girl from her money. He takes it in exchange for superstitious nothings." Little rings of smoke flowed out of Lao Fu's mouth; he enjoyed contorting his lips and cheeks to control the wispy, grey shapes. "It wasn't so long ago that The Party made sure his type was executed." Lao Fu began to laugh. "What makes him a master anyway? As far as I can see, the man produces nothing and owns nothing. He feeds and lives off of others."

"But that's because he gives everything away. He doesn't care about money. And, you know he's not a fortuneteller. He doesn't engage in such nonsense. He's never read hands or faces!" YuZhen had turned her body to face Lao Fu square on with both hands on her hips. Her face began to redden. "The ancestors speak to him. They took his sight but gave him their words. Our ancestors are always around us. Some will speak directly to you, but others choose to communicate only through chosen ones. Du is a master because he can speak all the way back to three generations of ancestors, not just one! Master Du is a good man. He's probably the best man I know. He gives his gifts freely and doesn't care what you give him in exchange. I've seen people pay him with days-old oranges and bean milk. I've seen him give an empty-handed fellow words for free!" YuZhen abruptly stopped talking, and LuLu detected a slight quiver of her friend's upper lip as if she were about to cry. YuZhen lowered her voice, "No man has ever given me anything for free."

Lao Fu stretched his legs out, forcing YuZhen to take a step back, and leaned forward, peering down the street as if he were searching for someone. "Go off and be back in time. You waste your money; you waste your time. Don't waste mine. You understand?"

———————

The fulsome shadows of midafternoon beckoned both girls as they cut back across Zhongshan Park, moving slowly along the knobby, stone pathways that sliced through the greenery. Having spent much of their day at the temple, LuLu and YuZhen searched for a comfortable spot in which to pass the remainder of their free time. People were scattered about like pieces of blue, black, and grey paper strewn about the grass. Men slept with hats pulled down over their faces. Small children toddled along, chased down by grandmothers wielding sticky skewers of taffy-covered hawthorn apples. YuZhen carried her shoes in her left hand and walked barefoot. She held LuLu's hand in her right.

"You should try this. These paths were designed to massage the soles of your feet and improve blood flow. Our ancestors had health wisdom we can't even imagine. They understood how to move with the spirits."

"I don't want my feet to get so dirty." LuLu scrunched her nose at YuZhen.

"Aiyah! We have to wash before we work anyway." YuZhen raised her knees higher and with her next few exaggerated steps, she slid forward, dramatically pressing her feet into the stone path for emphasis and al- most pulling LuLu off her own feet. "Think back to what Master Du told us earlier today; your life's course arises from the balance between your ancestral destiny and your present-day wisdoms."

"What are you doing? Be careful, I almost dropped our dumpling soup." Lulu pulled her hand loose from YuZhen's grasp and quickly cradled the contents of a plastic bag that was hanging from her other hand. "Let's eat before I lose our food to your silliness."

LuLu looked for a shaded spot, free of sweaty bodies, and found one just off the path beneath a blossoming cherry tree. Soft pink petals carpeted the ground, and the color stirred a feeling of homesickness in LuLu that she did not understand. She placed the soup bag carefully on the ground and knelt to pick up a few of the blossoms and rub their silkiness between her fingers. She watched her fingers, and the softness of the flowers transformed her hands into those of her sister. The image of LiLi's small, delicate fingers rubbing the pink blossoms between them was abruptly interrupted by YuZhen.

"Aiyah! LuLu, what is wrong with you? We can't sit on these flowers. Our clothes will be stained. Get up and let's move over there." YuZhen was already ahead of LuLu and moving onto a grassy knoll, walking between bodies and claiming a tiny patch of green beneath a tree just between the legs and torsos of strangers.

"Sometimes your mind is like these dumplings, soft and under-stuffed." YuZhen worked a pork-stuffed soup dumpling between her stained teeth, trying to chew as much flavor out of what was predominantly a broth-logged noodle wrapper. She slurped hardily at the soup, swallowing loudly before continuing, "Master Du gave you such special words, words I've never heard him utter before, and here you are worried about your dirty feet."

Turning her head away from her friend, LuLu scanned across the grass, over the people, and through the trees until her eyes came to rest on the park's northwest gate. There actually was no gate, just an opening in the low stone wall that surrounded the park. She wanted to escape through that opening and, for a moment, saw it as providing a transition point away from the current conversation. But truly, the gate would only lead her back to the barbershop neighborhood, where there was no respite. She turned back to YuZhen, pretending to be ready for whatever lesson was about to be shared.

"Don't worry, we have time before we have to return." YuZhen sucked on her teeth, trying to free some part of a green stem from between them. "We won't be late. Lao Fu won't lose his temper because of us."

"Please. Don't say his name." LuLu lay back and pressed her body into the grass. Caring for a fraction of a moment about staining her clothes, she began to pull off the ground but then, thinking of the northwest gate and the barbershop beyond, she let herself fall.

"He's not bad. Better than many men in this city. So many terrible men …"

"How can you say that about Lao Fu?"

"Simple, he pays us what he owes us. As long as you do your work when you're supposed to, stay out of his way, and don't open your mouth too big and too much, he pays you."

"He's rude to us. In the night, he treats us like dogs. He has no respect for us, the ones who are working to put money in his hands."

"Respect? What are you saying? Respect is getting paid." YuZhen finished eating and tossed the remaining soup out onto the grass in front of them. Small soup splashes came within inches of two men who were sleeping on their sides just in front of LuLu and YuZhen. "Respect is getting paid," YuZhen repeated, her voice constricted with frustration. "Where's the respect in having to give stuff away for free, having stuff taken for nothing?"

LuLu stared straight up at the intricate pattern of green leaves against the blue sky. She stared at the multitude of shapes that formed between the edges of adjacent leaves, like small pieces of blue glass. She wanted to draw what she was seeing and thought of reaching for her notebook, but YuZhen's voice was not going to let go of her.

"You hear me?" YuZhen demanded. LuLu sat up and looked at her friend, who was staring at her, examining her face. "You think those factory girls have respect? You saw them, no? At Master Du's?"

"I don't want to talk about them. I don't want to talk about the temple. I should not have let you take me there."

"Humph." YuZhen glared at LuLu, "Sometimes you are a stupid girl. You don't know luck just like you don't know respect."

During LuLu and YuZhen's earlier visit, the temple's confined courtyard had been filled with all sorts of people, everyone clambering around the fortune wheel, trying to get a moment with Master Du. Bodies pushed forward in the heat, hands thrust colored paper cutouts towards the master, and raised voices demanded answers: "Should I marry?", "Is this the right time for me to give my son the money he wants?", "Will my back be strong again?"

LuLu had avoided the throng, making herself as tiny as possible in the corner of the courtyard. She clutched a small yellow paper bird in one hand, the fortune ticket YuZhen had bought for her, its delicate lacy wings crushed in her palm. Next to her, a woman with the same clouded-over eyes as Master Du was warming her hands over a smoking metal canister and calling out, "Give to those who came before. Give to those who look down on you from the beyond." A few courtyard visitors, waiting for Master Du's arrival, had stopped in front of the woman, handing her a few coins in exchange for paper cutouts shaped like fruit, meat, and bags of rice. The paper offerings came in every color imaginable, and some were so finely cut as to resemble lace filigree. Gently cradling the paper cutouts as if they were the real objects they represented, the blessing seekers pressed their eyes shut and moved their lips soundlessly in prayer before carefully placing the cutouts in the woman's canister to burn and release smoke. All the while, after dropping the coins deep inside a small pouch tied around her waist, the old woman would chant wishes of good fortune. LuLu was sad to see the beautiful creations char and wither in the coal fire.

A brief communal silence fell over the crowd at Master Du's arrival as the slow shuffle of his sandals on the stone floor seemed to temporarily soothe the crowd. This silence was broken by a voice emanating from somewhere deep within the crowd. It was YuZhen, though LuLu only figured this out when she heard her name. "LuLu! Come. Come! Come now!" YuZhen spoke to LuLu as if no other person was present, as if a thick chord of believers did not separate her from LuLu who was still small in the corner.

Compelled by YuZhen's commands, LuLu began to squeeze herself through the smallest of spaces between bodies until YuZhen could grab her hand and pull her forcibly forward. A sense of gratitude filled LuLu at being received by YuZhen and, almost as if the same relief was felt by everyone present, a wave of celebratory noise was unleashed, and the crowd began to call out to Master Du. Excited pushing resumed. LuLu strained to hear YuZhen's instructions.

"Take your yellow bird and press it into the Master's hand. You must make sure he has it and that you touch his skin. Ignore the fortune wheel. Don't throw your bird in there. Everyone else will be doing this and waiting to see where their paper lands, trying to call out their lucky numbers to the Master. You just give him your paper. He knows it all. He doesn't need the wheel." YuZhen thrust Lulu forward towards Master Du, and LuLu felt herself falling through the crowd but somehow not actually landing on the ground. Her legs began to move beneath her, as though she were swimming without touching the bottom of a lake. The clamor of people screaming and weeping surrounded her and, as if tangible, the noise pressed on her eardrums and the sound of her heart rose in her ears. Thrusting her chin up and into the air, she pulled deep breaths into her lungs and let herself be jostled about by the crowd, trying to call out to YuZhen but having no sound escape her lips.

The weight of the crowd, pressing on her from all sides, made LuLu call out, "YuZhen! YuZhen! They're going to kill me." Tears flowed down LuLu's face as she called out for her only other sister, "LiLi. LiLi! LiLi!"

And then it stopped. Like strands of hair flowing free from an unfastened ribbon, the crowd spread out. Confusion came over LuLu and, for a moment, she questioned if this was the sweet release of death or if she was now paralyzed.

The warmth of a hand on the top of her head and the softness of a voice brought Lulu back to her senses.

"Please. Stop."

The crowd, astonished to see the blind prophet easily reach forward and touch the head of the girl who had fallen at his feet, had pulled back. LuLu looked up and found herself searching the smoky, grey eyes of Master Du. She quickly thrust the yellow bird into his hand and scrambled to her feet, thanking him repeatedly, until he silenced her with the raising of his hand.

The moment the prophet felt LuLu's fortune ticket in his hand, a bright, yellow light flashed before his eyes and flowers exploded. He reached for the girl with his hand, and she gave him hers. He thoughtfully translated the images for LuLu: "Look beyond today's life, child. Look to a life that will explode outside of the boundaries of today's walls." Slipping his hand out of hers, Master Du then stepped back and the crowd, swarming around LuLu, resumed calling out lucky numbers and simply trying to touch the man.

Presently, as she sat in the park next to an angry YuZhen, LuLu was filled with sadness. She wanted that feeling of being loved by the older girl to return and for her sense of gratitude to be in the space between them. "Sorry. Thank you for taking me with you today. I know how much you respect Master Du. I am just not as faithful as you."

"His words are powerful and come from the ancestors. What he told you will come to be if you heed his advice."

"I don't know where I am supposed to look. I don't see an end to the current situation. My father and mother keep getting older. They need this money."

"Of course. But what do you want after this life?"

"After? I don't know. I'm not sure there is an after."

"That's your problem. You don't see how good things are and can be. You put today onto tomorrow. Tomorrow can be different, you know?"

"I just feel the same every day. Tired. I don't feel luck or respect is part of this life. This life here in the city with Lao Fu and the other girls. "

"You have something to sell, don't you? You see Little Eggs. Look at what she has to offer. Two shriveled-up, old breasts that she can barely give away. Look at what I have: two huge, fleshy, satisfying mounds. Look at you. Small but upright, your tits make you a living. You could have shriveled-up dumpling sacs. What would you do then?" YuZhen leaned back, laughing.

"So, this is being lucky?" LuLu snapped. "I didn't come to Shanghai to sell myself or my parts. I thought I was going to get a respectable job in the factory making beautiful clothing. A job my parents could be proud of. The job my parents think I do now. I wanted to learn how to make things and to maybe find a husband. I have come here and have become a whore and a liar. The factory girls who came from my same home province look at me with disgust. You saw how they snickered at us as we left the temple? Even Master Du's blessings do not change me from what I am. What we both are. There is no luck in that. No respect. No different tomorrow." LuLu's words came quickly, and her breathing hastened. Her chest moved rapidly, and a prickly sensation grew behind her eyes. Tears fell down her cheeks.

YuZhen lifted herself over right next to Lulu and pulled LuLu's head into her chest, squeezing her tightly as if to wring the last of her tears out of her body. Lulu's sobbing lessened, and she grew still, relaxing into YuZhen, who started to speak. "One day, I am going to be gone from this place and this life. I am going to take the money I've made and my man, and we're going to go back to my village. We will be married and will return home with money in our pockets and new clothes and new haircuts. On mornings, we'll sell scallion pancakes with hot sauce and egg, and my man will serve the freshest soy milk. In the late afternoon, we'll eat dinner with our child, a little girl, I hope. And after dinner, I'll braid her hair and use all those ribbons I've been collecting."

"Your man? You mean Rong? He's going to go back home with you?" LuLu pulled herself back from YuZhen and searched her face.

"Of course. Why not? I keep him looking good and in new shirts, don't I?"

"Yes. I just ... I didn't know you planned to marry him."

"Well, I do. He loves me. He knows everything, and he loves me. That's lucky. I give him comfort and care because I want to, and he gives me affection and attention because he wants to. That's love. Giving and getting freely. You didn't get that factory job because you didn't want to get on your knees and put that factory boss in your mouth. Sure, that's what you do every night now, but you get paid for it. If you had done it back then for that man, you knew it wouldn't be just that one time. You knew it would happen again and again but there wouldn't be extra money in your envelope."

LuLu turned away from YuZhen now, wanting to stop her from saying any more.

YuZhen reached over and gently placed her hand on LuLu's chin, pivoting her head so they were again face to face. "You think those factory girls have respect? You don't think they are liars and whores? You don't think they suck on that man for free whenever he demands it? We lie to our families but not to ourselves. We know what we do, and we get paid for it. Those girls, they're dishonest with themselves. They can't admit what they do to be where they are, and so they don't fight for what they are worth."

The sun inched downward as the sky began to dim. The park had emptied, leaving the girls alone except for a few stray elderly men and women who sat on benches looking absently about, waiting for the dinner hour to start and for a reason to move. Their faces made LuLu uncomfortable, as each was filled with uncertainty as to what to do or where to go, as if they didn't belong to anyone.

Chapter Eight

Pork Buns and Pink Shirts

L azy spools of soft, red dirt swirled up from the ground with each gust of wind and came to lay on everything. This included the bicycles, which resided several meters from the gatehouse, in two distinct populations, along the factory's courtyard wall. With dirt clinging to their every surface and bearing soft tires held in place by rusted rims and bent spokes, the workers' bicycles were haphazardly leaned up against each other, their wheels and handlebars tangled. Some lay on the ground. None was secured in place. They looked much like their owners: tired, worn, and forgotten.

Nearby, another grouping of a half dozen bicycles, similarly banged up and poorly maintained, distinguished themselves by being neatly set upright and by bearing heavy chains and padlocks. Additionally, each upright bicycle had a one-foot cubic metal box fastened down with chains and padlocks to its rear rack, hovering just above the rear fender. The boxes were covered with partially torn, printed labels and hand-scrawled warnings. Their heft made the rear racks sag and strain much in the same way as would have a too heavy rider. These bicycles belonged to the plasma sellers.

The gatehouse, a single-occupant, wooden structure, had windows on all four sides which, choked by red dust, barely provided a view onto the outside world. This suited the gate guard. He was determined to do as little work as was required to make it through his shift, one cigarette and idle thought at a time. He had just placed a cigarette between his lips, when he shifted on his stool. He scrunched down and looked through a dust-free streak that had been created when a random finger had run along the outside of the gatehouse windowpane. He eyed the upright bikes and, seeing all six of them still in place, straightened up and leaned back against the wall. He was satisfied that he had done what was needed to justify the extra pack of cigarettes bulging from his front shirt pocket.

The rotation of his head—reaching with his chin over to one shoulder, down to his chest and over to the other shoulder—generated a crunching sound from deep within the joints of his neck that reminded the guard of his age. He suddenly wanted to close his eyes and take a nap before the lunch hour. Pulling a final deep drag off his cigarette and filling the gatehouse with grey smoke, he opened the door and slowly made his way around the backside of the gatehouse to urinate against its outer wall.

After zipping up his pants and wiping his hands on the front of his thighs, the guard made his way back around to the front of the gatehouse, where he noticed a distinctly female form approaching. She stepped off the road and moved across the dirt. Pushing his hands deep into his pockets, he waited for her. Watching her but not recognizing her as one of the factory girls, he began to think about what he wanted.

Watching the guard come around from behind the gatehouse, her chest began to jump. LuLu tried to keep her stomach from rising into her throat. She pulled down on the sides of her school skirt, trying to somehow lengthen it to well below her knees. She grasped the shoulder straps of her backpack, rubbing the sweat of her palms into the fabric. Her bag felt heavy on her back and sweat was collecting where the two made contact. She knew the heaviness of the bag was not real. Her mind was playing tricks on her. A dozen packs of cigarettes and two small pouches of money were the only extra items she carried with her today. She hoped that everything she needed to make her plan work was in this bag.

"Good morning, sir," LuLu addressed the guard, standing as tall as she could and thrusting her chin forward while trying to look him straight in the face. She wore her hair down, hoping to somehow drape out the childishness in her face. "I have come to speak with the factory boss." The urge to reach into her bag and pull out several packs of cigarettes was so strong that her hands began to tremble. Yet doing so would make her look like a desperate outsider; LuLu squeezed the backpack straps.

"Really? The factory boss? You are who?" Shanghainese rolled off his tongue and formed balls of sound that bounced in her ears rather than actual words. "What are you called?"

The guard did not take his eyes off LuLu. He followed her eyebrows, waiting to see if they arched upwards slightly with comprehension or drew together in a moment of hesitation. Likewise, she kept her eyes on him, but it was useless. She felt her tongue become leaden in her mouth, and unable to stop herself, she dropped her gaze ever so slightly for the briefest of moments. It was enough for them both to know what they each would do next.

Unable to rapidly fire off her answers in the city's native tongue, LuLu's migrant status was obvious. Not waiting for the answers to his previous questions, all of which were now irrelevant, the guard had moved on. "So what part of the rooster's ass are you from? Hmm?" His crass language defined all the significant contours of the relationship between these two strangers.

"Thank you for your help. My name is Zhang Lu. I know the boss. He offered me a job, but I could not take it before. I am ready to work now." LuLu spoke politely using Putonghua, the "common speech" of the nation, as demanded by the great leaders in Beijing. She took care to suppress any accent that might be associated with her ancestral home, keeping her tongue off the roof of her mouth.

"The boss is busy." The guard slipped easily from Shanghainese to Putonghua, decidedly pleased at having confirmed LuLu was not from around here. "Come sit with me inside the gatehouse and wait. Later, we will see if he has time."

The weight of her backpack grew, and LuLu felt as if she were being pulled backwards onto the ground despite standing perfectly still. She swiveled her backpack off one shoulder and around to the front of her body, instinctively erecting a barrier between her and the gate guard, who continued to take in every one of her movements. She opened the top of her backpack and reached deep inside. Feeling the familiar softness of her panda bear, she reached deeper until her hand secured the two small pouches that she had painstakingly prepared earlier that morning. She pulled the smaller of the two pouches out of the backpack so slowly as to suggest that it should not be brought into the light of day. She offered it to the guard.

"Sir, please accept this humble gift. I know it is not much, but I am not well, and this is all I have to repay any kindness you may show me."

"Not well? What's wrong with you?"

LuLu bit hard on the side of her mouth, flinching from the pain, letting it bring an unpleasant color to her face. "I am not made as I should be. As a woman."

The guard stepped back, slightly repulsed, but not before grabbing the small pouch of coins.

"Would you like me to show you?" LuLu had correctly anticipated his disgust. She had been with enough men who complained about the way in which their wives' bodies became deformed by childbirth and how the transformation sickened them.

The guard was now safely back in the guard shack. "You just wait there. Behind. In back. I will let the supervisor know you want to see the big boss when he comes out to eat. Make sure you stay quiet back there." He watched LuLu slip behind the shack, relieved when she was out of his sight. He closed the gatehouse door, and, only after keeping his foot pressed firmly against it so that it could not be pushed open, he relaxed enough to fall asleep.

The sound of the lunch horn accompanied a surge of factory workers that moved like a wave crashing through the gate and onto the dirt shore. Smells of meat and yeast began to fill the air, wafting up from the black, iron cooktops of the various food hawker carts that had begun to roll up in the minutes before the horn's wail. Clusters of workers soon surrounded each cart, and barbecue pork buns were distributed quickly in ones and twos in exchange for a few coins. Lulu's stomach churned. She feared someone would notice her crouched down in the shadow of the gatehouse. Her stomach continued to move, making her queasy and forcing her hand over her mouth and nose. Unfortunately, that particular spot was subject to a mingling of smells: the sweetness of the hawkers' meat combined with the sour acidity of the guard's urine and, whenever the guard opened the window of the shack to call out to a passerby, the smoke from his cigarettes added a dusky note.

LuLu was not alone in crouching low, hiding in the shadows, and awaiting opportunity. Only after the workers had settled into their meals and relaxed to the sways of useless chatter, did the plasma sellers slink out and into the open. They slithered silently forth from behind the trees where they had been patiently studying the workers. They looked at the men. Any man with two buns was ignored. Any man with one bun or no bun caught their attention. Did he eye the meals of his companions, yearning for more to fill his belly? Did his skin hang from his bones? Was his face strained and thin? Did he struggle to laugh and keep up with the chatter, the whole time feeling challenged by the emptiness of his pockets? Such a man was their prey. LuLu recognized the plasma sellers by their smoothness of movement and their complete lack of interest in eating. She had heard so many stories of desperate migrants succumbing to their disease-carrying needles, that she recoiled when they appeared, shrinking down lower.

LuLu's heart and head thumped in unison, and she felt her belly turn and rise. The nauseating mixture of urine and pork and sweat grew in her nostrils. She was about to jump up and run back to the room at the back of the barbershop, the one place in this city where she was certain of what she was doing, when the familiar sound of girlish chatter caught her attention and pulled her to stay where she was.

"These are good today, yes or no?"

"Taste good. Not stale."

"Yes, they are tasty."

"The oil is fresh."

"I want to get another one."

"Aiyah! How fat do you want to be? You can't do that until after you have an old man."

"Yes, you can be an old fat wife with an old fat man. Until then, only one bun!"

"Who wants a fat old man? I want a handsome, young man to keep me happy."

"I would be happy to have a fat old man if it means he'll pay for me to have more than one bun!"

Their words flitted back and forth, light and soft, and their heads swiveled and tilted on their necks. They were like a small coterie of chirping birds. Four ordinary factory girls with young, soft faces, leaning against each other in a row, chewing on the white fluffiness of their pork buns and speaking in the dialect of LuLu's home province. Their giggles took LuLu back to the school yard and a different world that seemed so far away, though it had only been a year back. Each factory girl had her hair tied back with ribbons and wore the short-sleeved, pink factory shirt she had been issued on her first day on the job. Their bare arms, clean faces, and hair were dusted with blue denim speckles, soft squiggles of thread, and lint. Lulu watched them, sticking her head out from behind the shack, careful to remain unnoticed, and saw herself sitting with them. She was so like them. They were the daughters her parents prayed for each night. She was one of them. She looked down at her own blue uniform shirt and realized that it was almost identical to the pink ones that they wore.

LuLu studied the girls carefully. One of them was quite pretty with full lips and naturally pink cheeks. She reminded Lulu of a girl from home, the younger sister of one of her own classmates. She stared at the girl now and convinced herself that she was indeed the same one from her school days, the same girl who used to chase behind the older students, wanting to join in their games. Lulu was so sure that she decided it would be okay to stand up and say hello, to call the girl out and to be invited to join them. Her blue uniform would be familiar to the girl; she would call out, "Little Sister, it's been so long since we met up." She had money and could buy a pork bun, maybe an extra one to share. She remembered how to talk as they did, without a care.

"Hey, you. Country girl. Get up. Get up."

Smoky words dirtied the air and drew heads down to the spot behind the shack. Seeing LuLu stand up and move awkwardly towards the guard, responding to his beckoning, the ordinary factory girls twisted up their faces and quickly looked away from LuLu as if the sight of her was distasteful. The plasma sellers surveyed the scene and quickly assessed LuLu as not being worthwhile, each one turning back to focus on the poor factory man in front of him, the poor soul who had already been separated from the herd.

"Well? Go on in quickly. The boss is a busy man, and you're lucky I was here to get you inside."

The guard watched LuLu as she moved quickly through the gate, disappearing behind the factory wall. He thought of how deceitful a woman's form was. How appealing it could look on the outside, only to be rotten at its core in some unforgettable way. He spat on the ground and watched his saliva slowly soak into the dusty ground and was relieved that he had not touched the country girl. He looked about and saw the plasma sellers leading their latest victims towards the neatly arranged cluster of bikes. They worked quickly to needle the men with tubes attached to plastic bags and to collect their bounty, placing each plumped-up blood bag carefully into the metal coolers on the back of their bikes. The newspapers often hailed the plasma economy, fueled by the medicine companies that purified and resold blood products to needy patients, as tremendously lucrative. The guard momentarily wondered if he should consider a career change, but seeing the plasma sellers do their work made him queasy and quickly gave him his answer. LuLu's small pouch of coins sat on the dusty shelf inside the gatehouse. The guard picked up his easy loot and pushed it deep into his pocket, certain that the girl had wasted her money.

Mindlessly making her way down the barbershop hallway, LuLu caught the voices of the other girls, barely muffled behind closed doors, getting ready for the night.

"You're late." Lao Fu leaned against the closed door leading to the last room. His body, while thin and not tall, was muscled and rope-like and seemed to almost lay slack. "I've warned you, girl, don't waste my time."

"I know what you've said. I heard you," LuLu replied, hard and fast, the words escaping her mouth without any modulation. There was no time to lower her voice and soften her bite, to slide it into the required apology. Lao Fu's body sprang into action, going from slack to hard. Her words had surprised them both, and in that moment, the pimp's hand was faster than LuLu's brain. He struck LuLu across her face, knocking her off her feet and sending her straight into the cheap door behind her. Her body slid down the door front, crumpling into a ball and then tipping over onto its side on the floor. LuLu lay perfectly still. At first, loud shrieks answered the loud thump of LuLu hitting the door, and then, after the door was open and the girls could see what had happened, there was complete silence. Stepping over LuLu, not daring to look at Lao Fu, the girls proceeded to the front of the shop and onto the street.

Tasting salt in her mouth, LuLu wondered what it would be like to live on tears and to never move again. If she were to lie here on the ground of this tiny shop, in the midst of this big city, and were never to get up or speak another word, what would happen to her? How would the outcome be worse than if she were to get up, dust off her clothing, wash up, put on her make-up, and work her way out to the front? Lao Fu had likely moved on, as his temper flared and was satisfied in seconds.

"LuLu? LuLu, get up. What happened? Oh, dear ancestors, don't look on this girl like this. LuLu! Get up!" YuZhen was now in the hallway, having emerged from the last room in response to the commotion. She helped LuLu stand and moved her slowly into the last room and onto one of the mattresses. LuLu lay motionless, her eyes wide open, leaving her tears unwiped. "What has happened to you? Where were you? Have you gone crazy?" YuZhen grabbed one of LuLu's thighs and shook it. "Don't ignore me. Tell me what happened." LuLu, sensing the fear in YuZhen's voice, was overcome with a sense of pity for her friend. She sat up, refusing to touch her face even though it throbbed, and told YuZhen about the factory, the guard, and the factory girls who had reminded her of what she was.

"Why did you even go there? What did you expect? Did you even see the boss?"

"I did."

"And?"

"And nothing. Nothing came of it."

"What do you mean? What did he say?"

"He let me know what I am worth. What girls like us are worth."

"What's that?"

"Nothing. Less than nothing. That was his answer." LuLu snapped her words out, as if they could bite YuZhen.

"You silly girl. He's not the person to ask such a question. I told you; *you* need to know your value." YuZhen tried to wipe the tears from LuLu's face with a soft towel, but LuLu slapped her hand away.

"What are we worth? This body of mine, that body of yours? They are worthless. Unofficial. Not even worthy of being registered on the city books."

YuZhen swatted at LuLu's anger. "Who cares? It's better that no one official knows who we are. If they did, they would be coming around for their share." YuZhen rubbed her middle and index fingertips with her thumb making the "pay me" gesture. She winked at LuLu and laughed, trying to lighten the mood.

"You laugh?" LuLu stood up. "Well, he laughed, too. I offered him this body. I took my clothes off and offered myself to him. He laughed. Laughed and told me that he didn't want what others had picked over. He told me he could have a fresh girl every day. What world is this?" LuLu's voice was low, but her words shot forth like bullets.

YuZhen turned away from her, trying not to listen. "Please try to remember what Master Du said to you a few weeks back. You have to think beyond this time and place."

"Master Du? Master Du can't even see what's right in front of him. What beyond is he talking about? I reached for a beyond today. I went to the factory to get back my respect and to be the girl I was supposed to be. I was willing to pay for the chance to wear a pink shirt and to ride the train home for the Lunar New Year, back to my parents as their respectable daughter. That world is closed to me, YuZhen. There is no beyond. This is where we are. This stinking room is my beyond." LuLu was pointing her finger at YuZhen, making her listen. "Don't look away from me, YuZhen. We are the same. We are the same, and there is no more pretending, not for me."

Grabbing the neck of her own blue shirt with one hand, LuLu ripped open the front of it, tearing buttons loose and letting them fly onto the floor. She took the unfastened shirt off her body, and holding it in her two hands, she pulled its material taut and began to frantically tear it apart. First a sleeve was torn loose, which Lulu tossed onto the ground, then the other sleeve tore off the shirt along the shoulder seam. Next, LuLu grasped the remaining intact buttons, one by one, and yanked them off the useless garment, whipping them onto the floor.

YuZhen dove to the floor and began to gather the strips of fabric, trying to fit them together like puzzle pieces. LuLu grabbed the pieces from YuZhen's hands and continued to shred them into ever smaller pieces. Pale blue thread and fabric debris floated in the air, landing on both girls, sticking to LuLu's sweaty face and falling softly onto YuZhen's bare arms and legs.

LuLu breathed heavily, panting.

YuZhen began to weep.

Part Three

Da Long Village & Shanghai
China, 1986

Chapter Nine

Wheels

A plethora of rapeseeds slept beneath the earth's surface; each night their good fortune was prayed for by the families of Da Long. The grey skies of winter hovered low above the land, as they had for some months, carried from beneath by a cold, drying air that leeched everything and everyone of spirit. The brief steaminess and warmth of summer was long gone, and the terraced hills, having given up the last of their rice pearls, were now left parched like empty soup bowls waiting to be refilled.

The soil of the lower plains seemed to have aged, having turned from a luxurious, rich black to a sickly color that matched that of the sky. The cold had turned the soil unforgiving; it did not give over easily to shovels, and bedding the rapeseeds came slowly. Weeks had passed with little progress. The farmers had little to show for their labor other than chapped lips and hands that let loose small drops of blood. No one complained. There was no point.

The tilled rows of earth grew so slowly that the Farmer Master's joy at the fall's abundant rice harvest quickly withered, being replaced with a general sense of disgust with his workers and the whole industry of farming. Standing at the Eagle's Eye, Wang looked out over the now dormant rice terraces to the flatness beyond. The weight of stagnation crushed down on his head. Was this what he was supposed to be? Was this the tiresome way in which his fortune was to be made? His road was complete, on time and under budget as demanded, and had brought him some small compensation from The Party. Ultimately, however, it was no more than a minor artery in the rapidly expanding circulation of roads that connected the heart of the kingdom to the powerful east coast cities.

Wang imagined all the wheels turning around the nation, making progress towards richness, but none was here on the flat plain before him. He could recite The Party line: some people in some places would prosper first, thus allowing all people, eventually, to prosper faster. He wanted to be among "some people" turning the nation's wheels ever faster. Instead, he felt he was being crushed by all those rotating wheels. He was as useless as a rice sheath thrashed against the ground, bringing forth nothing but dust. Wang's breathing grew rapid, and his hands grasped at his chest as though he were trying to pull something heavy off it. He cried out for help, but no one heard him. He was sweaty and, in a panic, he fell to his knees, bringing his head into his hands. He started to count. One. Two. Three. He slowed his breaths. Four. Five. Six. He at least had control of the air moving in and out of his body.

Downstairs, AnRan leaned against the sill of the kitchen window, letting the pale light of the winter sun brighten her face. Her eyes closed; the cool light still managed to elicit a warm redness from the vessels in her pale lids. The soft grinding sound of stone turning on stone comforted her, and she was thankful for her devoted friend Hu Lin, whom she, and everyone else, simply called Ayi. Ayi worked a small mortar and pestle, crushing dried herbs for Jiang's morning tonic.

The two women did not need to speak with one another to exchange ideas. Their intimacy, which welded them inseparably together, had been born from a lifetime of interdependence. Hu Lin was only two years older than AnRan, and the two of them had been raised first as playmates from AnRan's birth, only to transition into TaiTai—the honorific for wife of the house—and Ayi—both a functional term for a housekeeper or nanny as well as a term of endearment akin to "Auntie." There really had not been a transition but rather an unspoken, natural evolution that both accepted without need for acknowledgement. In truth, they were simply friends.

Through the window, AnRan saw Jiang and Small Snow waiting outside, anticipating Teacher Zhou's arrival. Jiang moved in and out of the courtyard, crossing back and forth across the threshold of the main gate. Over and over, Jiang took one step out and then took one step back in, stopping momentarily while outside the gateway to look down the road for the teacher. It was the same scene every school day morning. Small Snow did not move.

Watching her son, AnRan smiled and was momentarily filled with hope, just as she had been every school day morning for these past few months. Jiang had grown tall, a good head above herself, but was yet to develop the full-bodied thickness of a man. He moved easily, without any stutter in his movements; no hint of his episodes made their way into his everyday motions. He was quiet, that was true, but was capable of expressing a reasonable amount of noise when appropriate. Like now, as he moved back and forth, she could almost hear his breathing grow louder and more rapid. Five years had passed since Jiang had attended the village school with the children of Da Long. For five years, AnRan and Ayi had watched carefully over Jiang, ensuring that he was not overcome by household noises or left alone in the sun for too long. He received his tonic every day without fail, and AnRan would sit with her son as he read, painted, played with Small Snow, or made calculations out loud that she could not follow. He would multiply, divide, and square numbers of any size and did so with ease. His formal education, by way of private tutelage with Teacher Zhou, had only just resumed with Old Doctor's approval as Jiang's energy had become more balanced and his fits less frequent. AnRan forced herself to smile again and was just about to part her lips to share her thoughts with Ayi, when her mouth closed tightly, and the beginnings of concern crept into her eyes. Her own feelings confused her; the strong sense of hope and joy quickly seemed to darken.

"How does he look? Happy, no?" Ayi's voice pulled at AnRan's attention and saved her from the encroaching anxiety. The maid had not raised her eyes to look at AnRan's face, she had asked her questions while looking down on the ginger root she was mashing in the mortar.

"Yes, I think so, but ..." AnRan kept her eyes on Jiang.

"He is full of stable energy. He knows Teacher Zhou will be here soon. He understands that his studies are about to commence, and he looks forward to the day." Ayi was practiced in voicing these daily assurances.

"Yes. I think you are right." AnRan allowed. "He is a sweet boy who so enjoys Teacher Zhou's company. He anticipates his arrival."

"Yes. Right. What more could you ask for?" Ayi did not wait for AnRan to answer. "Come. Let the boy be and taste this. Make sure it is not too bitter."

Both women knew that there was so much more that could be asked for, prayed for, and demanded to be, for they had hopelessly asked, prayed, and demanded for such things to happen. It was easier now to simply pretend that such things were happening, and that the future would likewise be the same way.

"Teacher Zhou's coming! Teacher Zhou's coming!" Jiang's voice, directed at Small Snow, grew louder and more urgent. "Teacher Zhou! Teacher Zhou! Teacher Zhou!"

Hearing his name being shouted out into the morning air did not compel the teacher, who seemed to be floating between the fields, to move any faster. Zhou circled his legs steadily, keeping both hands on the handlebars of his bicycle and took in the spectacle. He ran his tongue over his lips, and the fact that they were slightly dry filled him with a sense of relief. Another winter was fully upon him, and, with three more moons, the Lunar New Year and all its promise of change would arrive.

Despite having spent years laboring, all in the service of re-education in the then foreign fields of Da Long, Zhou was still not used to this ill-tempered heartland with its mercurial air and sky. Not so long ago, grateful to have survived the urban purges of the bourgeois intellectual class unlike so many of his humble teacher friends, he had dutifully tilled the land, planted seeds within its folds, and carried thousands of buckets of water to quench its thirst. His hands had blistered, his skin had charred, and his back had contorted with pain. Zhou had been forced to know these fields *too* well. But now, with the title of Teacher resurrected from the bloodbath of Cultural Revolution history, he could willfully ignore the cold, cracked fields on either side of Wang's Way.

The teacher kept his eyes straight ahead and took in the stout figure of Ayi at the gate as she put her arm around Jiang and coaxed him inside for his morning tonic. The boy, on the cusp of teenhood, was tall and looked from a distance to be fully grown. Thankfully, he had his father's height, although he was less fortunate to have inherited the litheness and delicateness of his mother. Jiang's face, with its fine and pointed features, and body, with its light-weight limbs, cast him as an awkward bird.

Zhou pressed firmly on the brakes of his bicycle and dismounted carefully. He ran his well-oiled hands, thankfully once again soft, down the front of his robes, smoothing them into place, and walked the bicycle into the courtyard. He looked towards the kitchen window as a greeting to the Great Wife of the house, lowering his eyes respectfully. He didn't linger a moment longer, the weight of her expectations being more than he was willing to bear.

Zhou was the Esteemed Teacher to the Farmer Master's household, commissioned to educate Jiang. Patriotism had been reconfigured and endeavors of the brain, not just labors of the body, were once again fortuitously recognized as crucial to the nation's prosperity. Young folk from across the country were to show their love of country by taking their education seriously, and for the most serious lovers of country, The Party promised that great opportunities would arise. Jiang, when calmed and focused appropriately, had a strong intellect amenable to lessons in math, science, history, language, and the fine arts. Though his studies had been delayed, Jiang showed great aptitude for most subjects.

What troubled Zhou was that the boy's family expected more, especially the Farmer Master. They wanted Jiang to be prepared for life beyond the Eagle's Eye, for him to emerge from his sheltered childhood, readied for manhood and engaged with the world. But Zhou was a teacher, not a sorcerer or a mystic healer capable of dismantling or transforming the course of biology. The boy was not merely naïve and unexposed; he seemed emotionally incomplete, disconnected, and, episodically, overcome. There had been early gains misinterpreted as progress. From the start, the boy had shown great affinity for his goat and seemed to anticipate its needs; however, he showed less interest in his own parents. He barely looked any person in the eye and rarely initiated conversation. He tolerated his mother's and Ayi's touch, but not in any sustained way: a hand on the forearm, a quick arm around the shoulder, a gentle hand on an elbow leading him to his bath or bringing him to a meal. Nothing more.

Early in his tutelage, the boy had seemingly come to admire Zhou. The mother had rejoiced, and the Farmer Master had nodded with approval and satisfaction. The morning "greeting" ritual was seen as evidence of intimate intentions, a reaching out to another person, the establishment of human connection. Secretly, Zhou's heart was not turned; he knew Jiang's ritualistic display of affection had commenced the day after Zhou had pulled a beautiful abacus from his satchel. Jiang had mastered the ancient calculator very quickly and took delight in solving math problems with his mind and fingers, unaided either by pen and paper or by the teacher. Initially, Zhou had marveled as he watched Jiang's fingers fly across the wooden frame; the boy never got a question wrong. Yet he was honest enough with himself to never mistake the boy's ritual for anything other than what he believed it to be—demonstrated impatience to have the abacus in his hands and not a heartfelt longing for the teacher.

A three-wheeled scooter cart filled with villagers passed by and a chorus of female voices clamored, "Teacher Zhou! Good morning! You look so handsome today!" Zhou did not turn his head but simply lifted his robes off the ground and proceeded into the house.

The Farmer Master lifted his cheek up off his desk to decipher the noises coming from outside. Finding them unimportant, he put his cheek back down on the top of his father's table. Wang took solace in its smooth, cold, perfect surface. He focused on the whooshing sound that swirled in the space between his ear and the wood, silently begging his father to speak to him. But he could only hear his own son's voice rise excitedly up through the atrium, calling out large numbers in response to the teacher's questions.

As Zhou asked question after question, the beads of an abacus clattered ferociously, and Jiang's numbers flew forth. Wang was aware that Jiang was smart. He answered the teacher's math questions before the teacher could calculate the solution on his own abacus. He could recite ancient poetry flawlessly with perfect tone and recall the most obscure detail about the nation's history with astonishing accuracy. All this Jiang did repeatedly when prompted, but without any sense of purpose or ambition, and never with any attempt to apply his knowledge to the real world. Answer after useless answer and question after pointless question rose up through the air, each one dropping into the one upturned ear of the Farmer Master. The teacher's voice irritated Wang most and made him want to scream, "Close your mouth!" It was this voice that reminded Wang that most useless of all things was a man unable to work with resources to yield a desired result.

Each called-out number reminded Wang of how far from normal Jiang was.

Chapter Ten

Brides and Bounty

F estooned with red and gold crepe paper streamers, colorful pyramids of exotic fruits and vegetables rose from the concrete slab, each one just tall enough to tower over the youngest children. Mounds of bright green jujubes, fuchsia-skinned, spiky dragon fruit, shiny orange mandarins, pale yellow pomelos, and ruby red cherry tomatoes were beautifully adorned and displayed. Like young brides, they appeared, brightening the drabbest of ceremonial halls. It was the time of year for mountains of white turnips, mustard greens, and bright yellow cabbages. Butchers happily put full hogs on display, hanging from their hind feet, their cavities halved, and their excavated organ meats bagged. Each bag of entrails was placed neatly beneath its carcass, right next to a downward-facing pig head, as if each slaughtered animal were being made to acknowledge its fate.

Human bodies pressed and pushed through the small market. The men and women took their time to look at each stall, to see what seasonal specialties, through trade and transport, had journeyed to the heartland. Each of the edible delights particular to this season was considered a good luck charm carrying with it the promise of prosperity. The smell of lucky mud carps mingled with all the other strange and wonderful odors that filled the Hundred Village Market. In the midst of the hustle and bustle, each marketgoer took the time to inhale deeply, to fill their nostrils with the unique perfume of the Lunar New Year.

Most weeks of the year, the market was a flat affair with long-faced, short-tempered merchants, their meagre wares spread out on newspapers thrown down on the ground. Exchanges ran short, and all conversations were punctuated in a manner consistent with the simple understanding that at their heart, all such communications were transactions. But in this festival season, the place had a topography to it, made partially of mounds of goods and partially of swells of excited people, each landmark a tangible display of abundance. Furthermore, on this day, five days before the cleansing light of the new year moon would break through the night sky, a rare element swirled amidst those present. Hope.

As if the heavens knew that the land would be doomed without it, hope surfaced just as the days grew discernibly longer and the sun considered stepping out from behind the clouds. Two moons earlier, the villagers, gnawed thin by the harsh winter and aching from their considerable battle with the land, had been consumed with fear of starvation. The aches that weighed down their arms, shoulders, necks, and backs, and the pain that rippled through the cracks in their hands and lips, had driven them to utter hopelessness. Memories of the frightfully cruel Great Famine of '59 swirled in the villagers' minds and drove them into an almost stupefied silence.

It was at this point, when husbands were not speaking to wives, mothers were not speaking to their children, and when the children knew better than to call out in the night, that the progress and industry of the East finally seeped into the fields of Da Long and its neighboring villages. On an otherwise unexceptional morning, a new class of worker arrived. Carried on flatbed trucks that rumbled along all the Wang's Ways that crisscrossed the great expanse between the heartland and the powers-that-be came a smooth and unfeeling three-wheeled machine with rear-mounted iron claws. This new worker was greeted with stiff hands and frozen mouths in a scene that played out time and time again from one field to another. Not admitting that they feared they might be thrown or carried away, most villagers stood still, encircling the tractor plow and not daring to mount it. Eventually, each community offered up one brave soul, who, embracing the new arrival, climbed aboard and took charge. After a few fits and starts, the metal beast began to stutter and to haphazardly churn up the land. The men and women ran in all directions, scared that the machine, uncaring and unyielding, might pull one of them under, by the arm or by the leg, and return them to the earth.

In time, the villagers came to earnestly respect the machine, especially when the work was over, the fields were sewn, their aches and pains began to wane, and a period of relative stillness settled on the land. The villagers stared out at the planted parcels with a deep appreciation for the precarious nature of rural life. None could divine what their efforts would bring forth. They silently issued persistent pleas skywards, calling on their ancestors for merciful intervention. This was the only way to "work" the soil as they waited. Eventually, the days began to lengthen, and the air began to thaw. Not a single villager saw this occurrence as an inevitable climactic cycle but rather prudently acknowledged this shift as a gift from their forebears, a heavenly granted opportunity for renewal. An opportunity that had been understood and appreciated for centuries.

It was in this spirit, on this late winter market day, that the villagers felt obliged to spend, sparingly, a portion of their earnings to be renewed.

Beyond the fresh meats and produce, the street dentist and the market barber had arrived early that morning knowing business would be brisk. Each had set down a plastic stool and a plastic basin of water for cleaning their respective tools in between customers; one had a battery-operated drill and pliers, and the other had a similarly powered shaver. Both men had salves and balms, and the barber had an additional bottle of fragrant oil. If you had just come upon the two men, it would have been easy to confuse one for the other on the basis of their professional accoutrements. The constant whirring of the barber's shaver, along with the frequent yelping of the dentist's customers, drew a large crowd of onlookers.

"NaiNai, look. Look at his mouth. He's bleeding. Why is he bleeding? What is the tooth doctor doing to him?" Jumping up and down, sending two silky plaited pigtails flying about, the pale-faced, little girl who had wiggled her way to the front of the crowd clutched onto two of her grandmother's fingers. She emphasized each of her questions with a forceful pull and jump. "What is he doing?"

"Aiyah! Hush, Yan. Do not move so much. If you make so much noise, the tooth doctor will think you want to be next." Fang MaMa started to laugh as she attempted to scold Yan into being still. She placed her hand on her granddaughter's shoulder and tried to press the motion out of her body.

"He will not think that. I am a little girl and still need all of my teeth." Yan's huge eyes focused on the old woman and, as she furrowed her brow, it was clear she was not taking any of her grandmother's words seriously.

Yan turned to search the long queue of men and women that curled like a tail from the dentist's stool. Face after face had the same wincing expression.

"BaBa. BaBa!" Yan spotted her father and called out to him; she wanted him to know she was there watching.

Bo looked across the clearing to the crowd and spotted Yan being held back by Fang MaMa; he acknowledged her determination to join him with a forced smile and motioned with a raised hand for her to stay put. His stomach turned several times as he heard another dislodged tooth rattle down into a small ceramic bowl that the dentist kept by his feet. Bo suppressed the instinct to run his tongue along his back, lower left ridge of teeth; he knew doing so would elicit a sharp pain that would supersede the dull, pulsating ache that had been there for months. The dentist meted out only three treatments: the twisting and pulling out of rotten teeth with his pliers, the drilling and packing of salvageable teeth, and the rigorous brushing of bleeding gums with a salve that burned more than it soothed. Though he could not know which of these fates awaited him, Bo knew it was guaranteed to generate considerable discomfort.

Straining to smile, Bo called out to Yan, "Go find your brother. Go on. You do not need to wait for me. Go see what's in the rest of the market." Pleadingly looking at his mother to move Yan along, Bo winced as he continued, "There is so much to see."

"Come, Yan. Let's go find your brother. He will be missing you, and we don't want him to start crying. "Right, not right?" Fang MaMa took Yan's whole hand in hers.

Yan wrestled her hand free. "Not right. I want to stay here and see what the tooth doctor does to BaBa."

"You are too strong-willed and do not listen so well. Are you this way in school? I hope not!" Fang MaMa's bent frame curved over the girl. "Come. Immediately." Yan reluctantly took Fang MaMa's hand and allowed herself to be pulled along, out through the crowd. She looked back behind her but could only see a swarm of legs.

When Bo finally sat on the dentist's stool, his stomach swam and he began to sweat. He gripped his knees with his hands, trying to dry off his palms. Craning his head back and opening his mouth wide, Bo felt faint.

"Two of them need to come out. They have rotted through to the root. They will not be easy to pull. Seven Kuai." The dentist's clinical assessment took less than a minute.

"Seven Kuai? That's too expensive." Squeezing his eyes shut, Bo willed his head to settle and gathered himself for an argument. However, when he saw the pliers in the dentist's hand and the look of disinterest in the man's face, something inside him withered. The dentist held out his hand and Bo placed seven heavy, one Kuai coins into his palm. The palm remained open and held out in front of Bo's face. Bo's hands fisted up inside his pockets. The dentist did not move but smiled, revealing his own crooked but complete set of teeth.

"They are not easy teeth to reach." It may have been in his imagination, but in that moment, Bo heard the voices of his children calling, "BaBa. BaBa." He looked around and could not see them. Perhaps they were further back in the crowd. The last customer had left with tears streaking her face. Bo spat on the ground, pulled one more coin from his pocket, and pushed it hard into the open hand, which immediately snapped shut.

The dentist bowed. "You are too kind. Your New Year generosity compels me to take extra care."

In between the fruit pyramids, Yan spotted her mother's distinctive sway and weaved her way through the crowd and straight into Lei's skirt, leaving Fang MaMa calling after her.

The force of Yan's weight against Lei's legs and their ability to absorb Yan's energy filled Lei with delight. Her toddler son, Long, was resting on one hip, and, undisturbed by his sister's arrival, he patiently pulled at the strands of Lei's hair that had fallen loose across her face.

"Are they both yours?" The fruit merchant pointed at both children. "The boy looks like yours, but not her." He was now looking straight at Yan. "She is very pretty, isn't she?"

Lei pulled the children more firmly into her. Long squirmed under the pressure, the fullness of his body collapsing over his mother's arm. Yan's thin frame seemed to collapse into the folds of her mother's clothing.

Yan looked straight at the merchant. "We have the same teeth. Look." She thrust her upper teeth outward and over her lower lip, revealing beautiful pearly white squares set perfectly, one after another.

Lei smiled, revealing the same set of teeth. "My daughter takes after her BaBa's side. She has my teeth, but she is fair like him. My boy follows my side; he looks like my brothers." Long grunted while pointing at the apples, wanting to put one in his mouth.

"Well, they both should taste my apples. They are sweet, crisp, and the best for the health." The merchant held a perfect apple in one hand and a knife in the other. He cut into the apple partially liberating a sliver which he offered to Yan.

"Thank you, sir. Go ahead, Yan. You can taste it." Lei pushed Yan forward, and the girl freed the apple sliver and popped it whole into her mouth. The vendor cut another sliver and offered it up to Lei who pulled it loose and gave it to Long. Fang MaMa, having come up behind Lei, thrust her hand forward towards the vendor who sliced a very thin sliver off into her hand.

"Too sour. Where are you keeping the sweet ones?" Fang MaMa asked as she swallowed and held her hand out for another piece. The vendor ignored her and looked at Lei. "The children love apples. At two Kuai per kilo, that is a wonderful celebratory price. What do you say?"

"Waste of money. They taste like crab apples." Fang MaMa snorted.

Long pointed to the apple in the vendor's hands and grunted for more. Lei took his outstretched hand and pressed it to her lips. "One kilo we could do, for the children."

"Easy to spend my son's money, isn't it? His teeth are no good. He couldn't even eat these apples."

Lei shifted Long to her other hip, moving him away from his NaiNai's words. She took a deep breath. "Maybe some bananas would be nice. When they are ripe, they can be quite soft. Bo can have those to celebrate the Lunar New Year." Lei spoke softly and slowly and began to rock back and forth; she sensed Long becoming frustrated at not having his desire for more apple satisfied.

"Bananas? What luck do they bring? How many hands touched them before they came here?" Fang MaMa looked away from the fruit vendor and scanned the market. "There are many other worthy merchants here. We will find better prices. Give me the boy. He looks uncomfortable from the sour taste." Pulling Long from Lei's arms, Fang MaMa transferred the boy into her arms and pressed him against her chest. She then pushed into the slow-moving crowd that filled all the space between the vendors, not looking back once at Lei. Lei watched Fang MaMa and Long until they disappeared. She felt unsettled by a sudden sense of lightness.

"MaMa, the apple tasted good. Can we have more?" Yan tugged at Lei's skirt.

Reaching down and pulling Yan up into her arms, Lei smiled at the fruit merchant. "Yes, one kilo please."

"And the bananas? I have some ripe ones, which are very sweet. Only four Kuai per kilo."

Lei put one hand in her right pocket and fingered several coins. She thought of Bo and the rotten teeth in his mouth, small and crumpled looking, making his breath foul over the past several weeks. His pain had been so intense, he had lost all interest in food. "Ah, sir, I cannot afford a whole kilo. That's too much money. Can I buy them by the piece?"

"Usually not." The vendor turned his back on Lei. "But it's the season of prosperity, and I want to be looked upon kindly; I can offer you these two right here." He handed her two bruised bananas with mottled skins that he retrieved from a box of discarded fruit. "They're not pretty, but they will taste just as good."

"They are for my husband. I am not sure he would eat these ones, not the way they look."

"Ah, for your husband. Well then, wouldn't he prefer the proper fruit for a woman to give her husband, one that empowers the loins? You understand?" Laughing and surely enjoying the redness that rose in Lei's face, the vendor pointed to a display of small, clear plastic bags that were filled with some type of dried fruit. "I only ever have these during festival time. Very special. Everyone wants a Lunar Baby."

"Can I try a piece, MaMa?" Yan had scrambled out of her mother's arms and was trying to touch the bright orange strips that glistened through their clear plastic packaging. She began to trace the strips with her fingers.

"Oh, no. This is a very powerful and passion-filled fruit. It's not for girls like you, little sister." Taking the bag out of Yan's hands and placing it into Lei's the vendor continued, "It's for a big girl, like your MaMa here." The man's eyes circled from Lei's full chest to her even fuller hips. "Mango was cherished by our departed Father Leader Mao with good reason."

Yan demanded his attention, for which Lei was immediately grateful. "I am not a little sister. I am an older sister. I am not scared. I can try a little bit."

Lei looked at Yan and was fascinated by her. Her face was delicate and fine, and yet her jaw presented a sharp edge that was accentuated in moments of determination, like a knife in a fight. Yan persisted, "MaMa, you're not scared, are you?"

Meeting her daughter's direct stare, Lei turned the small package in her hands and tried not to lie. "I don't feel scared, Yan. I'm just looking at it." She had never tasted mango, having known it was famous for inflaming one's insides. Thinking of how her mother would warn her that it simply was not a womanly fruit, Lei put the package down.

"MaMa, there's enough for us all to have a piece. You can cut it up and we can all share." Hearing Yan's voice, Lei could almost feel her daughter's words coming out of her own mouth, out of her own childhood body and into the home of her parents. She could feel her father and brothers around her. She remembered that sense of belonging fully in that place, of being connected so deeply to those around her. Lei reached out for Yan, who had picked up one of the packages and did not let it go even as she allowed herself to be hugged.

"I can let you have one package for just three Kuai. You won't find that type of deal anywhere." The merchant looked at the bag in the small child's hand and did not move to take it away. With only five days to go before the onset of revelry and the turning of the market into nothing more than an empty, poorly poured slab of concrete, the merchant's sense of salesmanship was sharp. "Certainly, your father will enjoy them, older sister. You are a good daughter."

"What is this? Lei, what are you doing?" Voice muffled and words garbled, the anger in Bo's question was still immediately recognizable. His customary greeting for her was rarely more than a string of questions and accusations. "Put that down, Yan. Your mother should never have allowed you to touch that." Yan handed the plastic bag to Lei. Both mother and daughter looked at Bo as if waiting for a cue on what to do next. Bo's mouth was stuffed with shredded pieces of cloth, and one side of his face was swollen and distorted. His head appeared even larger than usual, and Lei marveled that her husband was able to keep it balanced atop his neck.

"Sorry, BaBa." Yan looked downward and her voice was now softer than her mother's. Putting the mangoes down, Lei looked back and forth between the young child and her husband, holding her breath and wanting the moment to quickly vanish.

"Come here. Let your BaBa show you the appropriate foods for a pretty little girl to buy." Bo crouched down and pulled Yan to him. The two of them melted together, and, forgetting her, they left Lei to pay the merchant. When their business was finished, the merchant turned from

Lei to his next customer, but he made sure to eye Lei's hips as she moved away from his stall.

Hong and Min called out to Lei, but she did not hear them.

Hong shook her head, "Aiyah! There she goes, moving like the ocean."

The sisters' eyes had also focused on the slow sway of Lei's lower body. Lei's roundness titillated them. They had enjoyed watching her ever-increasing fullness develop during her two pregnancies; the fullness of her breasts gave way to the fullness of her belly, which in turn was met by the fullness of her thighs and bottom. She ripened each time like a succulent fruit, so different from either of the sisters who over the same years had changed only slightly, each now carrying a small but discernible roll of fat that belted their mid-sections.

With the sweet fragrance of coconut rising from their hands, Min and Hong worked the barber's perfumed hair oil into their tresses and scalps. They then took turns weaving chords of each other's hair into singular, long, tight, glistening braids that hung down their backs.

Hong rubbed her hands together and rubbed her palms on her face, trying to use the oil's residue to moisten her dry skin. "Enough. Enough." She smoothed her rough smock. "We don't need to spend much more. We both have shined ourselves. Let's find some oranges for the ancestor altar and get home. Nothing too expensive." Hong looked at Min, who was rubbing her hands on her lips. Hong continued, "We can buy new clothes after the rapeseed harvest. Things will be cheaper once the holiday has passed. The merchants will be desperate to sell off their festival goods."

Min said nothing and did not look at her. Hong raised her voice, "Agree?"

Min still did not look at Hong as she spoke, instead looking around distractedly. Searching the market, she finally answered, "Sister, why are you so small-pocketed? Maybe the dead will appreciate your stingy ways, but everyone else will shun us as fools for wearing cheap leftovers."

"And who are you? Who will look at you? You think clothes will suddenly make you sewn-up pretty?" Hong started to laugh, though her words carried a sting. "I know whose eyes you hope to catch."

"You know nothing!" Min briskly walked away in the direction of the fruit stalls.

Hong ran after her and slipped her bony arm around her sister's. Linked together and feeling no resistance from Min, she softened, "You know, it's not Teacher Zhou's eye you should be trying to catch but his snake. It's hiding somewhere in those fancy silk robes. He is the teacher, but he has much he could learn from a village girl. Maybe you can change his mind about leaving this place. It's not just city girls that have lessons to share."

Min pulled her arm free and began picking through a pile of tangerines. Her hands moved quickly. "Do not talk to me about that. I don't want to hear anything from you." She threw a slightly browned orange back into the pile.

"What? You don't think you could use the help? Don't act so high-nosed with me. We have the same teeth and dirt under our nails. You want to be with a man, you want to compete with the factory girls?" Hong joined her sister in sorting through the tangerines, tossing one after another back into the pile, not placing a single one into the plastic bowl the vendor had given her to use as a basket.

Min laughed. "What snake have you caught? You forget that from the time we crawled on the same floor, we have shared a bed. Snake catching?

If a snake came after you, you'd run in fear it would bite you." Min placed two perfect oranges into Hong's plastic bowl. "Here, these two are nice."

"Yes, these are very pretty. You know how to pick fruit but not men. The teacher has his nose so far up in the sky he can smell the ancestors' hot wind. He has his eye on a fancy factory girl and city life. He wants to join the rest of the young men who want out of this rural life. He will be gone soon."

"Maybe not."

"Oh? You think you know something I do not?" Hong sucked on her teeth. "What is it?"

"You big head. What? You think you know everything, that I just walk around waiting to hear the world through your words?"

"Aiyah. Get on with it. You are too bothersome to be of any use." Hong pretended to ignore her sister and looked down at her hands, scrutinizing each orange carefully.

Min moved closer. "He is not allowed to leave. The Farmer Master has said the dear teacher is to stay until Little Wang is fully schooled, maybe even until he is married." She pursed her lips with self-satisfaction.

"So what? That shouldn't be too long from now." Hong did not look up at her sister. "The Farmer Master has more than enough money to ensure that feeble boy finds a bride. He has money to reach the sky above. He could buy a girl bride for that damned goat if he wanted. You really think that's going to keep Teacher Zhou here? He will be off to make his fortune shortly."

"Fortune? Is fortune not coming here soon enough?" Min's voice rose with irritation. "The clawed machine will continue to churn the earth and bring abundant harvests. Village air is clean, and village water is pure. In the city, the filth fills your pores. The girls smell like the streets, and their insides are tied in knots. Who knows if they can safely carry children? Surely a learned man cares about that?"

Hong was now looking at her sister with disbelief. "Learned man? You are a stupid egg. Every man wants one of his pockets filled with coins and the other filled with the hand of a good woman who knows her way around. I'm certain that you have neither of those things."

Min did not look at her sister. "I am no snake charmer. I also haven't run off to the city and learned all types of tricks. I haven't whored around the village. Ugly or not, I am clean. I thought you could say the same. But you seem so determined to sing the virtues of whoring. Maybe I'm wrong? Have you been spending dark hours in the fields?"

"Who are you? What type of animal are you? You look at me!"

Min did not look up.

Hong threw an orange in Min's direction; it landed just in front of her on the pile.

Min looked up and now spat at her sister, "What is wrong in your head?"

Hong picked up another piece of fruit and threw it forcefully towards her sister's head. Min swatted at the small ball, sending it straight onto the ground, amidst a swarm of feet. Hong's mouth dropped open; she raised her eyes in time to see the regret in Min's.

Before either woman could move to retrieve the lost fruit or to make amends, a voice called out, "Hey! *Hey!* You two. You idiots. What the hell are you doing?" A skinny, pock-faced fruit seller shrieked at the two sisters, punctuating each word with a shaking fist. "I see how you touch my fruit. You will pay me for every piece you've touched. Do you hear me? Every piece."

Knowing that any spectacle was considered free entertainment, and that many sets of village eyes were now happy to strike them down with visual daggers, both women's faces burned red. Without a word between them, they reacted in unison. Both stretched themselves as tall as possible and fixed glares upon the vendor.

"You shut up! Shut up! These fruits are half rotten." Min's eyes were wide and seemed to protrude at the man.

"Who do you think you are? Don't you dare speak to my little sister that way. I'll box your ears till they bleed. I'll run you and your filthy fruit right out of here." Tossing the plastic bowl onto the pile of oranges, Hong grabbed Min and pushed her way past the gawkers. When safely out of the man's reach, Hong looked back, calling out, "Stupid fool! There's rat shit all over your fruit."

No one paid her any attention. No one except Min, who began to laugh.

On one of the dirt tracks that radiated away from the market, Bo struggled to turn the pedals of the family bike. Balanced carefully on its frame were Bo and Fang MaMa, who wore Long around her front and Yan across her back. Both kids were bundled into place by a long piece of tightly wound fabric. The collective was moving so slowly that Lei, following on foot, was able to keep a constant distance between herself and the rest of the household. Fang MaMa was enjoying the ride. She was surrounded by her wealth: a son who labored to feed her and two grandchildren who were close enough to keep her warm.

"This year, I will have the Lunar Festival dinner I deserve."

Bo did not answer her. He kept his eyes straight ahead, wanting to see only the road and not the near future.

"Both of my children are married and have enough coins to prepare the propitious foods a woman of my age should enjoy. You have a new brother. The two of you are quite similar. Right, not right?" Fang MaMa watched Bo's back as she spoke, focusing on the slow but steady up and down motion of her son's torso, waiting to see if these last words would change his rhythm. "You and Pang both work hard and think of family as number one. You both like the same things—"

"What things? What are you talking about?" Bo interrupted his mother. He couldn't turn to address her and risk losing control of the wheels beneath him, but he made sure his mother could hear him.

Before she had a chance to answer, Yan started to whine. "I want to walk with my MaMa. I want to hold her hand. BaBa! Stop! Please stop!"

Bo put his feet down and brought the family to rest. He turned and looked at Yan, implying that her words had made him stop, that he had ceded to her wishes. He had actually needed to stop to catch his breath and was grateful to hide his relief behind feigned exasperation with Yan. "You cannot walk with your mother; you are safe on NaiNai's back."

"Yes, child. Your legs are too skinny for the long walk, unlike your mother's. She has such thick legs," Fang MaMa cautioned Yan, just as Lei had caught up with them.

Yan reached her hand out towards Lei. "I want you to hold my hand." Lei took Yan's hand. Long was fast asleep.

"It's okay, Yan. I am right behind you. I will watch you the whole way home. Can we do that?" Lei pressed Yan's hand to her lips.

Bo spat on the ground, and his stomach began to turn at the sight of his blood in his spittle. He turned his back on the lot of them, and, without saying a word, pushed off hard on the bike. He did not hear anything that either Fang MaMa or Yan said from that moment on. Only his mother's last words, calling Pang his brother, thrummed in his head. Pang was neither his brother nor, more importantly, was he Fang MaMa's son. As this thought turned over incessantly in Bo's mind, punctuating the strain he felt with each turn of the pedals, he fought back the nascent pricks of anger he was feeling towards MeiLin. Breathing heavily and struggling to understand how his life had come to be tied to Pang's, Bo settled on the obvious answer. Trickery! Surely that was the only way MeiLin could have married that fat son of a whore!

Lei looked after the lot of them, pushed off and away from her. She smiled, thinking of Yan and Long both tucked safely against Fang MaMa, being loved so fully by the whole of the old woman's body. She wondered if Bo's mouth would cease to stink after his visit to the dentist. The ride home would certainly cause his back and neck to be sore. When the family bicycle was far gone and almost out of sight, Lei immediately missed Yan and Long and found herself walking faster. She laughed; was this the love of which her mother had spoken?

Dusk approached and a warm glow bathed the road home. A bag of apples hung from the crook of Lei's right arm and bounced softly against her hip. She reached deep into the left pocket of her skirt and felt the smoothness of a small plastic bag. She pressed the bag and its contents between her thumb and her index finger. A rush of pleasure ran through her. Lei let her fingers linger, pinching the golden mango strips which were tucked safely away in their secret spot, deep in darkness.

Chapter Eleven

Night Journeys

S hanghai's sidewalks were clear of the usual crowds, shops began to shutter, and the city's families turned to preparing for feasting and reunion gatherings. The next fifteen nights, marking the start of the new year, would be alive with endless exploding firecrackers and bottle rockets whizzing up from the streets, while the days would be relaxed and pass with little fuss. Like a napping cat, the city was coiled up and content, largely oblivious to the few pockets of activity that simmered.

Brightly decorated carnival booths rimmed Zhongshan Park's stone walkways. Vividly painted with cartoon-scapes and bold, red bulls, for it was the Year of the Ox, many of the booths were already emptied of their games and celebratory knick-knacks. Hints of merriment could be found in the rubbish that littered the ground: colorful pieces of punctured balloons, skewer sticks with charred points, Hawthorne apple cores, glitter sprinkles, and cigarette butts. A few children, dressed in silky, new, red outfits embroidered with gold thread, were being carried or pushed about by grandparents hoping to find a small, afternoon sweet treat with which to spoil them.

On one of the narrow dirt streets to the north of the park, a pack of stray dogs nosed through a garbage pile looking for food with no one to chase them along. The barbershop was open, and a few men stood just inside the door waiting to have their heads and faces shaved, their nose hairs and eyebrows trimmed, and their ears cleared of wax. It was the last day for such services to be rendered in time for the festival of renewal. The fruit and meat vendors who usually worked the same road were long gone, and the residential courtyard doors were closed.

The only other business open on the street was that of the neighborhood seamstress who, upon ushering LuLu out of her store with a kindly, "May you have good health! May everything go as you wish in the new year," locked her door and turned off the lights.

Standing in the street, Lulu stopped to listen. She looked around her for some time, taking in the quiet. A particular beauty came upon the city only when it was vacated of its people. LuLu looked across the street to the barbershop and imagined that just beyond the men on the sidewalk, inside the shop, YuZhen was preparing gift boxes and red envelopes. The swirling red, white, and blue of the illuminated barber pole hypnotically beckoned her.

LuLu's feet did not move, but her heart ached and set her mind to dreaming.

She made her way through a maze of narrow streets, past homes and stores to which she did not pay attention. She knew that the railyard was heaving with a mob of rural migrants, each one of them trying to return to their ancestral village. Several streets over from the train station, a chorus of desperate voices broke the serenity of the evening. These voices, pleading for tickets on the last trains bound out of the city on the eve of the Lunar New Year, were indistinctly fused together into a roar that rose and fell. This undulating wave of sound pressed and pulled LuLu's body.

Moving more quickly, LuLu made her way closer to the station. She was dressed for a homeward journey. She wore creamy, silk stockings and a beautifully tailored, blush colored qipao. Delicate, aqua-blue songbirds whistling on winding branches were embroidered along the length of her torso. Her black hair was smooth and bobbed, falling just below her chin, her face powdered, and her lips were dabbed with a touch of pink. She was the embodiment of a pretty spring peach, fresh and enticingly sweet; a vision of loveliness set against the greyness of the city.

"Liar! Liar! Liar!" thousands of voices rang out. LuLu could clearly make out their words. She was so close.

"You all go home." The singular voice originating in the ticket booth and emanating from a mounted blow horn was dispassionate and mechanical.

"Liar! Liar! Liar!" The words scraped out from hoarse throats, accented in a way that LuLu recognized. These were her people. These were the voices of the farming villages that lay so many hours westward.

With a snap, the ticket booth blinds were pulled down, and its insides went dark. "Sold out! Sold out! No tickets available. It is not possible. Go home."

"*Liar!*" The crowd moved aggressively in several directions. One faction pressed against the ticket booth, crushing up against its glass window. Another segment of the crowd surged towards the train tracks, threatening to storm the sole train that sat at the platform.

LuLu clutched a white strip of paper with one hand and her bag of gifts in the other. Bracing herself, she began to navigate the crowd. "Please move. Please move. I have one. I have one. I have a ticket." She waved her fist with the white paper strip up in the air. "I have to make it to the train." The words barely escaped from her mouth. She kept her head up, trying to suck in air from the sky and trying not to get pulled downward by the undertow of the human mass. She tried to fight against the pressure of the mob. Hands pulled at her clothes, at her limbs, at her hair. "Please, I have to move forward." She whispered the last words. She closed her eyes tightly, praying to be propelled to the platform.

LuLu opened her eyes. She was still standing in front of the darkened storefront of the seamstress, gazing out on a barren street. She looked across the way to the barber shop; it stared right back at her. The swirl of the barber pole—round and round and round—had kept its pace.

In her hand, LuLu held a piece of crumpled white paper, which poked out of the top of her tight fist. She opened her fist and looked carefully at the paper within. The numbers on the paper, obscured by fresh crease marks, had been neatly written out by the seamstress and served as a receipt for the clothes she had made at LuLu's request. LuLu had no business at the railyard; not today. She had not had any business there in three years.

"Hello! Hello! LuLu. LuLu!" YuZhen and Rong emerged from the barbershop. YuZhen's arms were filled with bright red and gold gift boxes, and Rong carried two plastic bags filled with oranges. "You look beautiful. The seamstress knows how to make a festival outfit!" YuZhen admired LuLu's qipao. "I hope she did as fine a job on the clothes for your family. My goodness. Looks expensive."

"Happy Lunar New Year to you and your family," LuLu addressed Rong, who stood next to YuZhen and was smiling and nodding his head in agreement.

"Very nice, LuLu. Your dress is very nice." Rong's words managed to escape around the cigarette that seemed to perpetually hang out of his mouth, balancing on his lower lip.

LuLu tried not to stare at Rong, but she could feel her eyes being drawn to the distinctive topography of his cheekbones which rose too sharply from the plane of his face. "What is all of this?" LuLu gestured to the boxes in YuZhen's arms.

"Rong is going home tonight on the last train. I have sent presents for his parents. It is only right." YuZhen smiled at Rong. He stood silently and let her talk. "You know, Rong is practically my husband, and his family is my family."

Rong pressed out a smile, still saying nothing.

The outline of several red envelopes caused the stitching on his shirt pocket to pucker and made LuLu wonder how much money had been stuffed into the paper pouches. The shirt itself, unstained and still a sharp white, was certainly new. LuLu wanted to ask YuZhen, "How much? How much for his new shirt? How much money are you sending to his family? A family that does not know you exist."

She turned to Rong instead. "I wish you fast travels. You are a fortunate man. To have a ticket at this time of the year takes no small fortune. The migrant people at the railyard were out of luck ..." LuLu paused. "I mean, I can imagine that tickets were sold out weeks ago. You must have waited a long time at the railyard? No?"

"Aiyah! Why so many questions?" YuZhen snapped. "We have to get going. There is not that much time before your train leaves."

"No issue. No issue." Rong slowly raised one arm, as if exerting considerable effort, and put it around YuZhen's waist. Though the bare skin of his arm had been exposed only for a moment as his shirt sleeve slid down, it was long enough for LuLu to see puncture wounds. Rong went on, "LuLu speaks correctly. I am a lucky man to have an almost-wife like you, my YuZhen, who was clever enough to secure a train ticket for me. I pray the Lunar New Year brings me good health so that I may work and be worthy of such a woman."

YuZhen glared at LuLu as she pushed Rong's arm away. "Nonsense. Master Du told me my ancestors wished to ease my burden, and then I found Rong. We are a good couple. We help each other. Little Sister," she continued, looking pointedly at LuLu, "I'm sure you have gifts to prepare for your family at home. I know I am right about this. They must be anticipating the generous abundance of your labor."

The two women looked at each other and knew that the conversation was over. It was time for YuZhen to walk her "husband" to the train and for LuLu to send auspicious gifts, filled with implicit understanding of LuLu's "good life" in the city, back to LiLi, MaMa, and BaBa. YuZhen lived her lies and LuLu lived hers. They were friends welded together by the truth of their complicity. Each quietly helped the other build one lie upon another.

The backrooms of the barbershop were empty. Across the country, men of all ranks were tethered down by their familial obligations, ties that were made heavier by the fact of their being celebrated. The other girls were out exploring the city, enjoying each other's company, walking around in twos and threes with arms linked and donning their new outfits, and trying to look like everybody else.

LuLu sank back onto the bed and forced herself to be still. She tried to clear her mind of YuZhen and Rong, their skinny bodies making their way through the city, holding each other up, pulling each other along. She tried to stop imagining all the heartland-bound train journeys setting out that night. She saw her village dressed up with hung lights and streamers, little children running in the muddy streets clenching sizzling sparkler sticks, her village neighbors gathered around fires and food, and LiLi lying on the bed they would have shared—all of these things floated across the screen of her closed lids. Sounds invaded her quiet. The popping of firecrackers seemed so close to her. She opened her eyes. The room was silent.

Plastic bags with knotted-closed handles, backpacks, a cheap trunk with a heavy padlock, several woven satchels—all stuffed with evidence of the lives lived in the meagre room—were crammed into an undersized, incapable closet. LuLu carefully dislodged a small suitcase from near the top of the closet. Made of stiff brown-red leather, the suitcase bore no marks of use scuffed into its sides or edges and had a shiny, gold combination lock. After inspecting the lock and looking for any scratches, LuLu opened the case. Her backpack, flattened and void, was rolled up and pushed neatly against one side of the case. The panda bear sat on the opposite side, staring out at LuLu, waiting to be picked up and held. She grabbed it to her chest.

Water moved in the distance, down the hallway, sending a gurgle and swooshing noise through the thin walls. The shuffling of Lao Fu's feet moved LuLu to kiss the panda's paws quickly and to place it back in the suitcase.

"I will have everything ready for you, soon," she called out, first running her fingers over a green-yellow bruise on her upper arm. She pulled a purple silk scarf, trimmed with a pale-yellow border fringe, from the suitcase. It was a gift from a long-time client, an older regular who felt better about himself for having bought her such a luxury. The scarf was wrapped around a white, cardboard box that was filled with pieces of jewelry that matched one another only in their relative worthlessness. LuLu tried to remember who had given her what but realized that, for the most part, she had long forgotten or perhaps had never really taken note of such details. She pulled out a thin, gold-colored chain with a blue enamel butterfly pendant which was too heavy for the cheap chain.

Several sketchbooks filled up the remainder of the case. Each one was dated with the year and month in which it had come to be part of her collection. She opened the newest, almost a year old, to a page that was deformed along its edge by a small color photograph clipped in place. In the picture, a young girl stood in a country yard wearing a pale blue, cotton dress along with an expression that made it clear she was nervous having the lens focused on her face. On either side of her head, just above ears, that lay flat, were two rosettes made of rolled plaits, a few stray strands of hair softening her look. She was not smiling but looked as if she might when the moment passed. LuLu had drawn a few faint lines on the blank page, the beginnings of a crude outline of the girl in the picture, but nothing more. She traced her fingers along the girl's cheeks, still full, the only part that still seemed familiar. The picture had been taken recently, arriving in the latest letter from LuLu's parents. This was LiLi, as she was now, having just turned three.

Having unclasped the necklace, LuLu removed the butterfly pendant. She untied the package from the seamstress and counted the items of clothing within: three new outer jackets, one each for LiLi, MaMa, and Baba, each one quilted with precise machine stitches. Three pairs of pants, in a heavy, black cotton, and three white collared, button-down shirts. Each family member would receive a complete outfit. There was also a black, shiny tie for BaBa. From the suitcase, Lulu pulled out a new box of colored pencils, a small unused sketchbook, and a small tin of dried Oolong tea leaves. LuLu took the freed butterfly and placed it between the pants and shirts and, from her purse, she pulled out a roll of Kuai notes that she placed in the same spot. She tore a piece of paper from her sketchbook and penned a note blessing each member of her beloved family with the most auspicious of all New Years.

The clients who occasionally slapped LuLu, or worse yet, thieved her money, did not make it into the letter. She did not mention how this "lost money" flared Lao Fu's temper which, in turn, resulted in painful bruises up and down her arms. She also left out her fear of becoming diseased and unemployable after being with clients who used needle drugs and frequented plasma sellers when they were desperate for money.

Rather, lie after lie filled the page, with true love floating in between.

She told them the year had been a good one for her, filled with a new promotion and long, busy hours at work. She wished she could be home with them this year, but the factory boss needed her. Next year, she promised, would be the year for her homecoming.

LuLu's pen hand moved too quickly, messily laying down one line after another. She dared not look back over the sentences taking their place on the page. She folded the note and placed it on top of the clothes and then tied the package back up tightly. LuLu placed the whole package into a heavy cardboard box, along with the sketchbook, the colored pencils and the tin of tea. She secured the box lid with a beautiful red and gold ribbon that she pulled from her purse, and then she sat and studied the box. It looked appropriate. Heavy with goodness, the ribbon added a light element of fancy. She wished it safe travels and saw it, as it soon would be, fastened down on the back of the courier's motorcycle, waiting to be received. She anticipated her family's excitement at its arrival and felt them kissing it with joy and appreciation. Turning away from the box, LuLu looked at the wall. She was jealous of the welcome her gift would receive: a real homecoming.

Lulu ran through each of her gifts, picturing the joy on the face of each family member as they lifted each item carefully from the box. She imagined the enamel pendant falling out from between the layers of clothing, maybe landing on the ground. LiLi would dive onto the floor, her eyes widening with delight at the color and shape of it. Her parents' eyes would scrutinize the pendant, trying not to show any signs of concern in front of LiLi. They would wait until that night to ponder the blue of the enamel surface, the insignificance of a butterfly, the whimsy of the item. They would wonder at its cheap extravagance. *They would know.*

Gasping for air, trembling, LuLu quickly untied the gift box, trying not to destroy the ribbon. The courier would be here very soon. How could she have been so stupid? She usually sold the gifts given to her by her clients promptly, almost as soon as she received them. How could she not have realized that such a gift would cheapen her sister, cast her in a role in which she should never be? She unwrapped the clothing package and pulled the pendant out from between the cloth layers, tossing it into the still-open suitcase. She removed the elastic band from around the roll of Kuai bills and added several more Kuai notes to its thickness. She unfolded her note and added a single line at the bottom: *Please use a little of the money for LiLi, for a wish made true by her ever-devoted, big sister.*

Once everything was put away and the gift box sat waiting for its ride, LuLu took a bowl from the corner table and filled it with soft, fragrant, white rice from the rice cooker. She poured a spoonful of sesame oil over the top of the steaming mound, adding another of soy sauce. She unwrapped a small, tin foil parcel that had been left on the table by YuZhen and, using a set of wooden chopsticks, pulled free several ruby red slivers of smoked sweet sausage which she laid carefully atop the rice. She wiped the spoon clean with a tissue and carried it, the bowl, and the set of chopsticks out into the hallway and through to the street.

"You hungry?" LuLu came up next to Lao Fu, who sat in his chair on the sidewalk alone.

"Of course. You kept me waiting, didn't you?" He was grumpy and at first didn't look up at her. There was no business to be had tonight. There was nothing worth fighting over.

"Sorry. I just heard you come from the bathroom." LuLu handed him the bowl and utensils. "Everything is ready."

Lao Fu now looking at LuLu asked, "Is your stomach full?" His eyes turned to the empty spot on the stoop next to his chair.

"Yes. I have eaten," LuLu lied and quickly sat down to wait for the courier.

After the box had been collected and was safely on its way home, LuLu knew to retrieve Lao Fu's bowl. The dusky glow of the day's end had given way to the darkness of the night. And so quiet was the night that Lao Fu, largely unchanged, had fallen asleep on the sidewalk. She picked up the used bowl and dirty utensils from the ground, placed her hand on the back of the old pimp's chair, and waited for the sky to start exploding.

Chapter Twelve

Wives

Flowers in a basket are fragrant
Listen to me sing a little
Sing for a little
Come to Nanniwan
South Muddy Bend is a nice place
Nice place
Nice place and beautiful scenery
Nice place and beautiful scenery
Crops everywhere
Cattle and sheep all around
  - Nanniwan (South Muddy Bend), folk song

Cast against the clearest of blue skies, a blazing yellow seam cut a sharp line across the horizon. So marked and vivid was this line that it was only natural for those looking at it to shield their eyes with raised hands. The prayed-for fullness of spring had arrived, setting a scene of seduction. Brilliant ribbons of yellow blossoms shimmered and rippled, highlighted by the sun and subject to the whims of the winds, along the contours of the earth. A singular woman's high-pitched voice, singing of far-off Nanniwan, originated from several metal, bonneted loudspeakers that were mounted atop sporadically placed wooden poles. A gaggle of long-necked performers, the metallic horns transforming the singular singer into a chorus of sirens, crooned above the rapeseed fields. Three decades earlier, when the metal singers had made their debut, their voices had been stiffer and menacing, commanding obedience to The Party; village cadres had used them to humiliatingly broadcast the names of workers deemed lazy or selfish. Today, the chorus sang sweetly. Listeners could set loose their imaginations and enjoy taking in deep whiffs, for the surrounding yellow blossoms clung to the earth and seeped her curves in a sweet honey musk.

Hundreds of miles away, the muddy river bend known as Nanniwan was being dredged. Men, thickened with clothes drenched in silt, swarmed the site, guiding the vacuum head of a dredging barge to chorale the liquid earth that was first sucked vigorously up into the air from deep beneath the water and then later cast off to run loose on the river's banks. These men could not imagine the future their labor was setting in motion, that this muddy bend was destined to be a major waterway between the east and west. They were merely grateful to be full and to have their country demand their sweat and not their blood. Times were peaceful now and the men's paychecks were steady. This was enough to secure their loyalty to whatever government was in power and to whichever leaders were driving change across the heartland; the metal singers needed not issue warnings or threats.

Lei knew neither the men nor the Nanniwan of the future or of present day; however, she cheerily sang along to the words of its namesake song. In her mind, Nanniwan was simply a "nice place" with "beautiful scenery" and "crops everywhere," much as she saw before her now.

"MaMa. MaMa." Yan tugged at Lei's smock, demanding her attention, stomping her feet in the shallow water at the pond's edge. Long swatted at Yan with his fleshy hands, trying to defend his mother from the intrusion and to keep her energies focused on him. Lei moved her thighs up and down to the music and kept singing the words, looking from child to child, coaxing them with her eyes to join in with her. Bouncing heavily on her lap, his chubby thighs and bottom pressing repeatedly against Lei's bare lap, Long resumed clapping his hands and mimicking his mother by silently opening and closing his mouth.

"MaMa, listen to me. Tell me a story. Tell me about the witch. The witch whose blood colors the special oranges. Tell me about the leeches." Lei reflexively pulled both of her legs up from the water, sending Long straight into her chest. She saw nothing on her legs and, laughing, pushed them back down into the water, creating a big splash that lapped up against Yan's slender body and Long's dangling legs. Both children squealed with delight. A clutch of brown ducks that had been puttering along the shore hastily waddled off with panicked quacks and Yan, distracted by their departure, followed them demanding they come back.

Lei took Long's feet into her hands and kissed his soles. "You are so sweet. You are so sweet, Baby Dumpling. I must keep you so." Long squirmed with ticklish pleasure, pushing his feet with all his might into his mother's hands. She reached into the pocket of her smock and pulled out a small, orange nub and popped it into the boy's mouth. Sucking vigorously on the sugary mango piece, Long looked eagerly at Lei for another. She obliged him and studied his face as it contorted to force-fully acquire every mote of sweetness. After the piece had been fully consumed, the baby continued to suck vigorously on his inner cheeks, almost fighting against himself in the quest for sugar. The determination in his face caused Lei's chest to rise and, for a moment, she felt herself capable of flight, of being beyond any force on the earth.

"They don't do as I say. They won't come back." Yan's face scrunched in a pout, and Lei felt her disappointment.

"Come. Come here and sit by us, and I will tell you a story."

Yan dragged her bare feet in mud. She looked at Long and at Lei, and Lei instinctively lifted Long out of her lap, placing him on the ground. "Here, come sit on me." She reached her hand out to her daughter. Knowing that her love for both of her children was whole and complete, Lei did not offer Yan one of the mango pieces that remained in her pocket. She would not feed her such sweetness and tell her not to tell Bo of it. Lei would not make a liar of Yan.

Yan crawled into Lei's lap and put her head against her mother's chest. "They went into the water just as I was going to grab the bigger one."

Lei took a deep breath and let out a heavy sigh empathizing with the frustration she heard in the girl's voice. "They are just like us, Yan. They want to be free. They too want to enjoy the sun and to put their feet in the water."

"I just wanted to hold them. I wanted to keep them near us."

"Sometimes we keep things closer to us by letting them go. If you had grabbed one of them, it might have fought to fly away from you. It would not have stayed close to us as they do in the water. Look, they are right there." Lei pointed to the ducks floating on the pond's surface.

Yan turned her head toward the pond briefly before returning her cheek to Lei's chest. Long grabbed onto his mother's thigh and pulled himself up, feet planted steadily in the soft earth. Fully satisfied in the moment, with the feeling of her children's warm flesh against her own and the cool water soaking her feet, Lei closed her eyes and held her face up to the sun before whispering, "I have an important story to tell you."

"Is it scary? I only like scary stories." Yan did not lift her head.

"It depends on which way you listen to the words." Lei smiled down at Long who seemed mesmerized by his mother's low sound. "You know the same sun and moon have shone in the sky since the beginning of time? Right, not right?"

"Right." Yan looked up into the sky.

"Good. Then consider this. Just as you have a grandmother, Fang NaiNai, I too had a NaiNai. Her name was Xu NaiNai, and she told me so many stories, just like I'm doing right now, right here. Well, Xu NaiNai once told me the story of her own great-grand-uncle."

"Her ShuShu? Her oldest ever ShuShu?"

"Yes. Huang ShuShu. Well, as you know, the same sun and moon that we feel on us every day were felt by Huang ShuShu. But his life was different in some ways from ours. He grew up in a city quite far from here, filled with old buildings and stone streets. He passed many years there in school, even when he was much older than you are now, learning how to heal through the powers of nature and massage."

"Just like the Old Doctor!"

"Yes. Just like Old Doctor, but many, many years ago. Huang ShuShu was dedicated to his studies and never missed an opportunity to learn from the wisdom of his elders."

"What is wisdom?"

"All that one has learned in life."

Yan scrunched up her face and as though trying to think of what that would look like. Everything one had learned.

Lei continued, "He listened to his teachers and read all that he could about the healers who came before him, and soon he, himself, became a master healer. Sick people traveled from all over to receive his advice and his treatments, and Master Huang traveled all over the great country helping those in need. If you had a rash, he had just the right ointment to soothe the skin. If someone had a cough that lingered for too long, Master Huang had a tonic that would quiet the chest. He knew which muscles to massage to calm the stomach and which energy points to pierce to soothe one's head. He was a wonderful healer made happy doing good work, but he was not quite content."

"Content? What do you mean?"

"Well, he was comfortable and enjoyed his work, but he wanted to do more."

"What more? He wanted to heal more people?"

"It was not that he wanted to heal more people, it was that he wanted to see more than he had seen. Master Huang wanted to go beyond the world that he could walk and see. He knew that there were lands far away that could only be seen by traveling across the great waters. He wanted to go to the Beautiful Country, to America. He wanted to see that place and meet its people."

"The Beautiful Country? That is so far away. No one I know has been there." Yan thought of the impossibility of such a dream and momentarily wondered if Huang ShuShu had not studied very hard in school, had not realized just how far away the Beautiful Country was.

"You are right, it is quite far away. But our people were strong, and, more importantly, some of them were fearless. Workers from the great Middle Kingdom sailed across the greatest of oceans to help build the tracks for the first great iron horses, the first trains that would travel high into the mountains and across far stretches of land. Now Master Huang was not a man accustomed to the hard labor of railroad building, but he, too, was fearless and knew that these brave men would need one of their own healers to travel with them and protect them from any illnesses they might encounter in the Beautiful Country."

"Do you think he was scared to go?"

"Yes. Certainly. But he burned with excitement to see something new."

"MaMa, would you go to the Beautiful Country if you could?" Yan's eyes were wide and focused on Lei's. She held her breath, waiting for Lei to answer, anxious to feel her mother's voice and to still a sense of unease that fluttered in her stomach.

"I would go, Yan."

The girl squirmed in her mother's lap and held her breath.

"But only if I could take you and Long with me."

Yan exhaled and closed her eyes. "MaMa, I would go with you, too. And I would bring BaBa with us."

"Where would you bring me? Where are we going?" Yan's head sprung off her mother's chest at the sound of Bo's voice.

"BaBa, you came. You came. Would you go to the Beautiful Country to build the railroads and see a new place and meet new people?" Yan smiled excitedly at her father, looking up at him and finding his face hard to find in the glare of the sun. She scrabbled out of Lei's lap and ran into Bo's stick-like legs, somehow finding comfort in pressing against them despite their thinness. Bo pulled the girl up into his arms and looked straight into her eyes, commanding her to listen to him.

"Why would we ever want to go to another country when our own country is so great? What need do we have for outsiders when we have each other right here? You are a Chinese girl from Da Long and that is where your energy should be focused. Be grateful, daughter, that you will never head to a foreign land to build for foreign people." Bo kicked up the dirt with his foot as he spoke, watching dust settle on his wife's motionless back.

Two swans appeared on the pond, gliding as a pair across the dark surface. They were known to the villagers and were considered husband and wife, bound together for life and bound to Da Long. They frequently rubbed necks and touched beaks, a ritual of mutual admiration.

Lei rose to her feet, picking up Long, and without looking at Bo, said, "Yan, come. Let's wash our feet."

Bo carried Yan to the water and began to rinse her feet.

"BaBa, do you know about MaMa's oldest ever ShuShu? Huang ShuShu who traveled across the oceans and took care of the Chinese workers who helped build The Beautiful Country? MaMa, tell BaBa the story."

"Yan. Stand still. Give me your legs so that I can clean them." Bo splashed the girl more vigorously as she lifted one leg out of the water at a time, grasping her father's pant leg to steady herself as he used his toes to squeeze himself in place on the pond-bed. Several of the ducks took note and rose off the surface. "I don't have time to talk about such big tales and nonsense about bone bearers. Do you? Stories of blood oranges, iron horses, bone polishers—this is what you fill your head with, huh?

Have you finished your schoolwork? How many characters did you copy today? Not enough. Am I wrong?"

Yan did not answer him.

He continued, "I am off to the Farmer Master's. I expect to find you all at home when I return." He looked at Lei the whole time he spoke. "I have important business to discuss." Bo stopped speaking and stood still, allowing time for his profound words to be felt by his audience. He waited for a moment longer, noting that the lower rim of his wife's skirt was darkened by the pond water. The solid curve of her back remained unchanged as she held Long seated atop one forearm in front of her, his legs dangling just above the water. She used her other arm to reach down and scoop with the large cup of her palm, pulling water steadily up and over Long's feet, gently breaking the surface with each scoop.

Bo lifted Yan back onto the shore, gesturing her towards her slippers as he left. She struggled her wet feet back into the plastic shoes, watching her father disappear into the tall grasses that surrounded the pond. She did not call after him, though something in her young heart made her feel as if she should. Looking at Lei, she knew that her curiosity was better directed at her mother, "MaMa, what is a bone bearer?"

Lei did not hear Yan.

She saw her husband's face without seeing him. She saw grooves running across his forehead, grooves pulling down at the corners of his mouth, deep and unchanging as he moved away from her and made his way across the fields to the Farmer Master's courtyard. She knew nothing of Bo's important business; he had never made her privy to his plans.

She did know that after collecting their wages, Bo would touch every one of the coins in his pocket. Over and over, each one would be turned.

He would then stop in the village center and buy a small bag of sesame paste balls, later sharing them amongst Yan, Long, and Fang MaMa. Never taking one himself, he would simply watch the children chew on the sticky treats and struggle to scrape the thick paste off the roof of their mouths with their tongues. And then, a rare smile would push up onto his face. Her mouth empty, Lei would always wait to see Bo's face in this moment.

Lei knew later, in the dark of the night, she would stare at the back of his head. Looking into the inky darkness of his hair, she would patiently wait to see something. In nights now long passed, she had waited to see something of Bo, something that would explain him to her, explain her life as she lay next to him. But now the night was filled with thoughts of a place so far away from their bed.

Faces in a migrant army seeking the cities to the east moved in and out of the darkness, taking with them Lei's inner eye. There were so many sights she did not recognize, so many smells she could not place. She struggled to hear faint sounds. She dared not close her eyes for fear of falling asleep before Pang's familiar face came to her, shining so brightly as to light up the room. With animated and excited eyes, Pang spoke to Lei of his dreams for the future, his words cascading over her. His distinctly masculine lips moved rapidly, speaking of a new economic landscape with a blazing horizon across which paraded the silhouettes of buses, trucks, trains, and motorcycles. Then it was just the two of them, Lei and Pang, traveling across the horizon, riding a train that suddenly rose up into the mountains of the Beautiful Country, where Greatest Huang ShuShu waited for them. He called to them, "Come to me children of the Middle Kingdom. Come and help me to fulfill my duty to your ancestral countrymen who dared to dream before you."

Carefully, the great healer placed the polished bones of a dead, Chinese railroad worker into Lei's and Pang's open arms. "Take this man home, from the mountains of America to the fields of Da Long. Join him with his ancestors." Together, the couple brought the dreamer home.

Pang would then look at Lei with tears of joy and love. He pulled Lei so close to him, allowing them to feel each other in celebration. Her body always filled with excitement at this moment, and Lei would press her lips firmly closed to avoid making any sound. "Pang. Pang. Pang!" she would silently cry out his name, careful not to knock Bo out of his sleep.

"MaMa, you didn't answer me!" Yan tugged at Lei's smock.

Standing at the water's edge, the weight of Long in her arms and Yan looking at her quizzically, Lei apologized, "Sorry. My head was in the clouds. What did you ask me?" She took Yan's hand in hers and began to head for home.

"What is a bone bearer? BaBa said he didn't have time for stories about bone bearers. His voice was angry when he said it. He didn't seem to think going to the Beautiful Country was such a good idea."

"Don't worry about that. Your dad was not angry, just distracted with the business of the day. And, to answer your question, the correct term is bone keeper, not bone bearer. You now understand that Master Huang was a fearless adventurer who had many responsibilities to the men of China with whom he traveled?"

"Yes."

"Well, you must understand that he was responsible to care for their bodies both in life and in death."

"In death?" Yan shivered.

Lei was not sure whether the girl was scared or responding to the wind that now blew cooly across the fields. She continued, "Yes, in death. No Middle Kingdom man leaves his ancestral homeland without the belief that he will one day come back, that he will be buried in his ancestral grave mounds. The old-time railroad workers were no different. They went to the Beautiful Country in search of adventure and good wages, but only after being guaranteed by contract safe passage home, either in life or in death. Dreams of a journey to the Beautiful Country were only possible for those brave men because of healers like Master Huang. Healers who would make sure that for those who died far from their *laojias*, and there were many, their bones would be polished, prayed over, and returned safely to their ancestral homes. He was a bone keeper. That was no small job. Without a bone keeper, those men's souls would never have been at rest."

The fragile roofline of the family home was visible just beyond the turn in the road, and Yan pulled away from Lei to run towards the familiar structure without asking a single question more of her mother. Patches of laundry whipped about, straining the line that ran from a ragged roof corner to the tree. The day remained bright and the sun shone, but its heat was outdone by the blowing of the wind. Strains of music could still be picked out, but Lei could no longer hear the words describing the beauty of Nanniwan. She pulled her smock-skirt tightly around her, breathed hot air onto Long's neck to keep him warm, and made her way to the house.

————————————

Moving across the crop plain and up the sides of the surrounding mountains, the same cold rush of air that lifted Lei's smock made its way to the Eagle's Eye, rattling the windows as if demanding entrance. The first floor of the house was cool, resting in the shadows cast by the wide-hanging eaves of the roof. The persistent call of the wind against the glass panes shook loose a sense of fear inside the mistress of the premises. Feeling suddenly chilled, her flesh pocked with goosebumps, AnRan bit her lower lip. She moved as quickly as she could, not daring to run.

"Ayi. Ayi," AnRan's voice punctuated her short mincing steps, "Ayi. Ayi?"

"Relax, dear TaiTai. I am here. In the kitchen. How can I help?"

AnRan entered the kitchen to find her only friend standing over the stove, warming oil in the thick iron wok. A small bowl of peppercorns sat nearby on the cement block table next to the wood-burning stove. "Yes. I see you are here." She exhaled hard with relief. "You are making pepper oil for Jiang's tonic?"

"Yes."

"Good." AnRan wiped hair strands off her face and secured them behind her right ear. She relaxed the muscles of her chest and tried to quiet the racing of her heart. "Well, the air has turned suddenly, and the wind has hastened. I don't want the house to be cold. It's not good for the boy, as you know. I feel the windows should be secured. Probably immediately, as a summer storm may be coming."

"Of course. I will do that now. You rest here. You look flushed. I will return shortly and make you some tea. May I?"

"Yes. Good. Good. Tea would be good." AnRan perched herself on the small wooden bench beneath the kitchen window and, pulling her knees up onto the bench to the side of her body, tucked her legs neatly.

The window looked out onto the world in a contained way. Gazing up, she could see only the square of sky outlined by edges of the roof eaves that framed the inner courtyard. In this moment, that square was clear of clouds and was a beautifully bright blue.

The Farmer Master was in the courtyard speaking with a worker whom she knew went by the name Bo. He had his hands balled up in his pockets. She heard nothing of what they said and focused on the language of their bodies. Bo had been paid, likely quite a bit; enough for two pockets and for two clutching fists. His body was stretched as if being fully lengthened and he'd puffed his small chest up. He was looking at the Farmer Master, straining to look him straight in the eyes, but he was too short for that. The Farmer Master stood close to Bo, facing him. She did not know if her husband noticed Bo's puffery, and though he was taller and heavier than his companion, the Farmer Master appeared deflated.

The snaking wind wound around the inner courtyard and persistently rattled the kitchen window. The men's pants pulled against their legs and their hair blew back from their faces; their outlines were ghoulishly distorted. AnRan gasped and turned quickly away from the window and faced the kitchen. As she closed her eyes, her hands moved to her face and her fingers began to smooth out her brow, massaging deeply into her forehead. She opened her eyes without stilling her fingers, and focused on the small, embroidered flowers scattered along the silky flares of her sleeves. She had created each of these herself, using fine filaments of silk thread to diligently replicate the flowers found in the fields near her childhood home. Detailed and distinct, each bloom was a reminder that she and Ayi had once been girls with few worries. Lost from sight in tall grasses, the girls had crafted garlands and wreaths for one another, weaving together flowers by their stems into long, colorful chains.

The Farmer Master's wife looked out of place in this room with its darkened corners and low ceiling. She was delicate and perfumed and had a weightlessness to her frame. Heavy furnishings and a thick musk of oil and food gave the kitchen a rough feeling. A headless chicken carcass had been left unattended upon a central butcher block, a heavy-handled cleaver protruding from between its breasts. Drying herbs and plant roots hung from hooks wedged into the ceiling beams. The wok on the stove had a surface that was black and permanently crusted with stubborn char. It was so hefty that AnRan would have had to use two hands to lift it off the frame, not that she had ever tried.

Of all the rooms in the house, this one was the mistress's favorite. Here, Ayi was always to be found and, more important, it was the only room in the entire house in which AnRan had never seen her husband. The smell of it put him off. Here, she could take full breaths and exhale loudly. Her body was hers to inflate and deflate at will. She did not have to trap air inside of her and, like a balloon, float silently about her husband's house. When the Farmer Master was out in the fields, she could feel his heaviness upon her. Even when hundreds of miles separated the two of them, when he was gone to the city on official business, she felt him in almost every inch of the home as if he were waiting to knock her down. Only in the kitchen did she stop floating to avoid him. Only there did she settle onto the earth, perching herself at the window, moving her head about, looking up at the square of sky. She counted clouds as they moved overhead and studied the shades of the firmament for signs of what was to come.

From this window, she spied on Jiang and his goat, watching her son's face very carefully to see how it changed from moment to moment, to see if it even changed at all. She smiled as she watched Jiang secure a tarp over a stockpile of wood, convincing herself that Jiang endeavored to please his father. From this same spot, she had watched the teacher move across the inner courtyard every morning. For how many more mornings would the teacher's bicycle be placed next to the gate, and would that man make progress with her son? She did not know, but she knew Teacher Zhou had eyes that betrayed his frustration. She knew the look well; it was the same one the Farmer Master had when he looked at Jiang. The Farmer Master was waiting for Jiang to be *his* son, the son he wanted and not the boy he was.

"Tai Tai. Sorry. Sorry." Ayi was wiping her hands down the front of her smock and had flicked off her cotton house slippers.

"What is it?"

"Your tea must wait. I must bring in the washing before the rain comes."

Outside, the sky had turned dark and several bed sheets were snapping against a wooden drying rack as if trying to liberate themselves. Ayi moved quickly to free them, pulling the sheets firmly into her arms. She called out for Jiang and Small Snow, and the two appeared from behind the tarped stack of wood. They followed the woman into the kitchen. Jiang sat down next to his mother without saying a word. Small Snow pushed his way behind the boy's legs and sat down on the floor beneath the window bench.

"Peony. Plum blossom. Chrysanthemum." Jiang started naming the flowers on his mother's sleeve. He often meticulously painted the flowers on butcher paper and left his artwork on the bench beneath the kitchen window for his mother to find. AnRan sat and focused on her son's voice; the flowers of her childhood were a part of her son's, and for this she was grateful. She sensed Small Snow shaking beneath her and reached one hand down under the bench to soothe him by stroking his back. She understood that the creature, like her, was waiting for the storm to start. Jiang continued to name flowers.

That night, the light of the moon shone down on Da Long in fits and starts, coming and going as clouds moved across the sky. The afternoon rains had been brief and had filled the world with noise. Now, Lei sat in relative quiet and, from the corner of the shack, watched Bo sleep. Her hands were busy folding clothes. Even in moments of darkness, she knew each garment that she lifted from the laundry basket by its stitching, size, and softness. Bo's breathing, the shudder of his spine, the movement of his legs, all released small sounds into the night.

Lei pulled Long's cotton shorts from the basket and immediately rubbed her face into the unseen fabric, its softness filling her with wonder yet again. She had never known anything so soft existed until Long was born. Entering the world under an auspicious moon in the Year of the Dragon, the housewives of Da Long forecast a lucky life of abundance for the boy. At his first moon celebration, the villagers rejoiced in the boy's round body and full cheeks and congratulated Fang MaMa on having such a fat grandson. The old woman, delighted by the obvious abundance of her grandson, came home from the Hundred Village Market with the softest pair of shorts she could find and had them wrapped in red crepe paper. The shorts, being too big even for such a chubby baby, were used as Long's blanket for much of the first year of his life, covering his legs as he slept. Finally, Long had grown into them, and he cooed each time they were pulled up over his ample bottom. As Lei placed the folded shorts onto the growing tower of folded clothing at her feet, she was filled with happiness knowing that her son had spent his young life wrapped in something so extraordinary. She thought this might be a prophetic sign and quickly asked to the ancestors to make it so.

Lei climbed into bed next to Bo and made herself still so as not to wake him. The heat coming off his body warmed her, even though she was careful not to touch him. She lay on her back and relaxed her shoulders. She lay there for a while and the only face that came to her was Bo's. She could see his narrow face and the thin line of lips.

She waited.

The room remained dark.

Her mind's eye began to roam, but it took her no further than to the table in the middle of the shack and to that evening's meal. Bo had arrived home for dinner with his teeth chattering from a fully wet head of hair and wet clothing, and yet he had entered the house without complaint. He had shared his food with Yan and Long, spooning equally from his bowl of bone broth into their open mouths. He had said very little during the meal, as was his way. When the meal ended, he had simply reached into his pocket and pulled out a larger-than-usual bag of sesame paste balls.

"Aiyah. You waste money on such things. Why so many?" With her hand already in the bag of treats, Fang MaMa had customarily chided her son.

Bo, keeping his eyes on his children, answered simply, "Today I have enough money to build our new house. My children will know a better life right here in Da Long, their *laojia*."

That was all Bo said. He did not say how much money he had or how he had secured it. He did not mention where this new house would be located, how big it would be, or how the kitchen was to be set up. Lei knew nothing of doors and windows, of bricks or stone. Lei had looked to Fang MaMa, expecting a torrent of tactless inquiries to fly from her mouth right into her son's face, but the old woman had simply nodded a silent approval. Lei realized the old woman already had all the answers Lei wanted. In all the years that Lei and Bo had worked the Farmer Master's fields next to one another, Lei had loyally stepped back at the weighing scale and allowed her wages to be placed in Bo's hands. Lei had neither counted her wages nor questioned Bo's handling of the money; Fang MaMa had clearly done both.

After the children and Fang MaMa each had their fill of Bo's sticky treats, and when they stopped asking Bo for more, there had still been one ball left in the bag. Without a word or a meeting of their eyes, Bo had pushed the bag across the table in Lei's direction. For a sliver of a second, Lei had wanted to push the bag back at Bo. In the next sliver of a second, she had popped the sweet ball into her mouth and accepted that even she had secrets.

Presently, Lei stretched out her legs and focused her efforts on the face she longed to see. When she saw Pang, a flutter rippled along her lower abdomen. She stared into the darkness and willed him to turn and look at her. Pang was looking elsewhere. He disappeared into a field of burial mounds and Lei started to chase him. A purring noise sounded in the distance, and a motorcycle began to weave aggressively around the mounds, picking up speed, and eventually coming to a screeching stop next to Pang. The rider pulled off her helmet. It was MeiLin. Pang reached out and lovingly placed his hand on MeiLin's lower back. Lei pinched her eyes closed and felt her neck tense. She studied MeiLin's pale, narrow, lovely face. She recognized what she saw in the softly pouted lips and the ever so slight upward turn of MeiLin's head: desire for her husband.

Lei's lower back tightened and the fluttering across her lower abdomen ceased. She turned on her side and faced the back of Bo's head. Just beyond the curtain, Yan and Long lay curled up next to Fang MaMa on a bamboo mat with bellies full of sweet sesame paste and dreams full of the new home Bo, *her* husband, was going to build for them. Lei thought of her mother and wondered what she would say about secrets between a husband and wife. Before falling asleep, Lei reached over to Bo and placed her hand on his back.

Chapter Thirteen

Husbands

On the day of his wedding, Bo noticed that his bride-to-be's fleshy feet sank easily into the mud ridges outlining the rice terraces. The deep-set impressions made by her heavy tread punctuated her position, trailing behind her just as she herself trailed behind her brother and mother. Bo kept his eyes focused on her feet, not wanting to seem overly eager for the girl's arrival.

"My little sister is still by nature." The girl's older brother smiled at Bo. The girl's mother pulled gently on her daughter's upper arm, bringing her up to the front of their tiny delegation. Bo continued to watch her feet. Her approaching footprints muddled those of her brother and mother. She stood still, and he felt obliged to look at her. The marriage time was here and the whole of it would pass quickly. Bo felt little as he looked up, assessing the girl in one sweep of his eyes as open-faced and not pretty.

The nuptials were sealed with an exchange of gifts. The fields were empty, save a few birds that served mindlessly as witnesses. Two cigarette cartons and a small basket containing a clutch of eggs were pressed by Bo into the hands of the brother and mother, respectively; they, in turn, pushed the girl, Lei, forward over an invisible line into the territory of "his family." A few wishes for a future of full bellies and ancestral favors were uttered, followed by a series of rapid "goodbyes." The whole ceremony was over. The brother and mother turned around and walked away, each step they took landing squarely in the footprint of the one they had left behind.

Bo had not really expected more of that moment several years back, the one in which he had become a husband. He was not put off by the brevity of the event or by Lei herself. Her place in his world would be determined primarily by function. Her eyes, set widely into a round face of perfectly smooth, bronzed skin, looked straight at him. She was neither scared nor defiant but was simply looking to him, silently asking him, "What next?" She was ready to be led and seemed to be of the mind to follow him. Her body was thick, and Bo supposed it capable of surviving childbirth. He was confident that this was all he could ever want of a wife.

Now, as Lei placed her hand on his back, Bo felt the heat of her pressing into him in the middle of the night, and he did not move. He was certain her gesture was not a request of any sort. Aside from this, he was certain of very little about her. He tried to let the soft purring sound of her snores soothe him. He closed his eyes, wanting to fall back asleep, but the heat of her hand and her arm, which now lay across him, did not let him. He tried to shake Lei's arm loose, but it was heavy and did not fall so easily. Irritated, Bo forcefully rolled himself free and sat up on the edge of the bed.

Outside, the air was still wet, and the ground remained damp. Bo moved away from the shack quickly and cut straight into the fields. The fragrance of the maturing rapeseed crop filled his nostrils and made him feel drunk and powerful. He stopped to enjoy the moment. He lay down in the field and let the rapeseed plants absorb his weight and, as he stared up at the stars, he felt completely alone. An absolute stillness pressed against his body and rang in his ears. Alone, the world before him was his, and he felt his heart race with excitement. Bo scrambled back to his feet and began to run. He was little more than a thousand feet from his starting point, but suddenly the darkness and stillness made the shack seem a million miles away. Bo kept moving, seeking the far side of the pond.

At the point where the footworn path that tracked through the fields abruptly ended at the water's edge, Bo stopped running and stood still. Even in the dark, he could make out the contours of the pond and all its landmarks. He had spent almost all the non-claimed time of his entire life, the moments that arose between the demands of Fang MaMa, his teachers when he was a child, and now the Farmer Master, somewhere along the inlet's edge, right where the narrow river birthed the pond. Unlike tonight, in most of those moments, he had not been alone. There was a grouping of rough grey rocks just to his right that, during the day, was often covered by the stretched-out bodies of villagers who had just bathed.

MeiLin and Bo had often looked at the bodies, making fun of the collection of saggy bottoms and breasts. Beyond the rocks, thick marsh grasses grew taller than a man and obscured the water's outline all the way around the far side of the pond. He had to be careful not to lose his footing while walking this way, as it was easy to misjudge the boundary and end up knee deep in water. MeiLin had almost drowned this way as a child, paying little attention to her steps as she chased after Bo who was questing after dragonflies. Fang MaMa had thrashed Bo's buttocks for endangering his sister; Bo did not cry, believing the punishment to be fully deserved.

Bo moved with ease, completely aware of where his feet were at all times, making his way around the water's perimeter until he was at the point that put him directly opposite where he had started. His back was to the hills that rose gently up from this side of the water's edge, their slope starting several yards back. The earth was wet and easy to mark. Bo walked with purpose, watching his footsteps draw into the willing surface. He shook his head and, kneeling down, ran his hand over the dirt until it met the hardness of a stone which he dug free. Crouched, stone in hand, Bo drew a large square perimeter into the mud, waddling along as he pushed and pulled the stone through the dirt. He moved to the center of the square and was pleased at its size. He began to outline spaces within the rectangle's boundary: a room for Fang MaMa and the children, a bedroom for himself and Lei, and a third room that was just as large as the others.

Sweat collected on Bo's brow. He squatted in the center of his future home and looked about. He calculated the cost of each wall and window, of the door, and of the cement that would be poured for the floor. He closed his eyes and took in the rustle of the marsh grass. As soon as the rapeseed harvest was completed, this earth would be broken. He would break the ground himself, working side by side with a small crew of hired villagers to mark his spot. He would have the best mud-dung bricks brought from BeiHe, the town sitting downstream on the river that ran just to the south of Da Long. The brickmaker there made beautiful, deep red rectangles, using an ox to combine mud and dung into a stable mixture. And when the house was finished, at its very center, Bo would place a round, heavy, wooden table that would be brought from the Hundred Village Market by horse and cart. Bo saw his daughter and son on either side of him, with Fang MaMa sitting across from him and Lei seated next to Yan. There was room at the table for one more person, his MeiLin, but not for two more.

Bitterness crawled up the back of Bo's mouth before he could catch it and brought with it feelings that, though months old, tasted fresh. "The table will be crowded." That is all Bo had managed to say to MeiLin on the night of the Lunar New Year, offering none of the customary felicitations of the season. MeiLin had said nothing to her brother as he and his family had entered her married home. The two of them had hardly spoken since her wedding day almost a year earlier.

"You close your mouth," Fang MaMa sniped that night, pushing Yan and Long ahead of her into the house. "I remind you, it is my right to have both of my children, whom I have carried into this earth, honor me."

"MaMa, there are too many of us now with Yan and Long to sit at a small table."

"Aiyah. Pang's table is large enough for all of us. You are an ungrateful creature. Neither of you children was guaranteed a long life; both of you thin and weak. MeiLin is pretty, but pretty doesn't toughen a hollow belly. I saw famine and kept you fed. I saw death up close, and you two survived. I married you both well enough." The old woman showed her teeth to Pang who held the door open in welcome. "You will honor me for such."

"Of course. MaMa, you take the seat of honor. Come, my brother, you sit next to your mother." Pang had put his hand on Bo's slender shoulder, making Bo feel somehow smaller, and he then scooped up Long, who had been tugging on his pants. "MeiLin, come, sit next to your brother."

Without any hesitation, the same hand that had weighed heavy on Bo's shoulder traveled to the small of MeiLin's waist with such tenderness and confident affection that Bo's face prickled with a deep flush. With the fullness of Long's body in one of his arms and MeiLin's back secured by his other arm, Pang smiled easily. The three of them, Long, Pang, and MeiLin looked like they belonged together, like they were a family. Lei took Long from Pang and bumped Bo's shoulder as she passed him to take her seat, placing Long in her lap. Bo rubbed his aching shoulder, completely unaware of why it hurt. He did not utter one more word or look in his sister's direction for the remainder of the night.

The vivid memory made Bo jump up, his cheeks hot with tears. He slapped his own face and cleared his throat, stepping forward to the water's edge and spitting into the pond. He turned and walked "into" his house and, using his feet, he stomped along the outline of the third bedroom so as to erase it. One less wall meant less brick and less money spent.

"Good," he called out into the darkness and started to laugh, tears still filling his eyes.

He began making his way back to the shack. Before disappearing into the fields, he turned one more time to look back across the pond at his land, wiping the back of his hand under his eyes. His heart drummed in his ears; a mixture of sadness and self-doubt planted him on the spot. He had a plan and needed to stay resolved; he hated his weakness and cursed his mother, recalling her Lunar New Year scolding. He was building a home for his family. He would show MeiLin that he could provide for her, that she didn't need to let Pang put his hands on her. If Bo built it,

MeiLin could come back to her real home. Maybe that third room would be needed.

Bo's land had not come to him easily.

The Farmer Master, who oversaw all leases in the township and thus controlled the land that surrounded the river and the pond, had for some time resisted Bo's red envelopes—a generous monetary gift that would serve as a thank you of sorts for allowing Bo to lease his desired land plot. Wang was looking for a thicker envelope, one that was filled with several more years of Bo's good harvest wages. For this reason, it came as a surprise to both Bo and Wang when a strange meeting of the minds between the men had brought the transaction to fruition earlier that day:

Rain was threatening to arrive, and the Farmer Master moved to tarp a pile of wood that had been delivered to the courtyard earlier in the day. Wang could see AnRan sitting at the kitchen window, uselessly looking up into the sky. He knew that she watched him as he moved about the courtyard, but he did not indulge her attention in any way. Her looks no longer moved his body. He had taken control of himself.

The Farmer Master pulled at a folded, heavy plastic tarp, waved it loose, and created enough lift beneath it to float it over a pile of wood. He saw a slight strip of a man enter the courtyard and bristled with irritation.

"You come for your wages?" he spoke gruffly at Bo.

"Farmer Master, sir, I am here for the extra wages I earned from the first rapeseed harvest."

"Hmm. Extra wages? You are sure?"

"Yes ... sir."

"I see. It is good that I remember these things." Wang saw Bo's anxious eyes follow his hand into his pocket and watch as it pulled out a sizeable coin pouch. Wang counted out Bo's bonus in two parts, handing him two handfuls of coins. He turned away from Bo to tend to the tarp, not bothering to ask for any help.

"Sir, sorry to bother you further. The land on the far side of the pond. May we talk, sir?"

"Talk." Wang looked at Bo and noted that his frail frame looked somehow heavier and that the worker was puffed up. The Farmer Master wanted to take a finger and poke Bo in the belly to deflate him.

Bo continued, "The land is nice but not perfect. The water comes to its edge in the heavy rains, and it will take extra preparation to ready it for a modest home."

"So, you are telling me that it is not so 'nice'?"

"No. No. I only mean that it will take some doing to make it perfect. Some extra effort which may be considered as we settle on how much I would offer for your assistance in securing its lease."

"I see. I did not know we were necessarily bound to settle on how much you might thank me."

"Of course. Of course. This is a matter of your prerogative and wisdom."

"I am not a fool for flattery."

"Of course not."

"I have told you how much my *guanxi*—my favor and mutually ben-
eficial cooperation—is worth, but you are a persistent bother, are you
not?"

"Yes. I am so very sorry. I was hoping that we could find some terms
that would benefit us both."

"Benefit me? What would you know about my benefit?"

Bo stuttered several apologies and was composing his next words
when Jiang and Small Snow entered the courtyard, the boy counting out
loud as was his way. Bo looked at Jiang and could not stop his body from
repelling away from the strange boy. He looked at the Farmer Master and
saw his face fall in a moment of uncertainty.

"Jiang. Be useful. Secure the tarp."

"Three thousand one hundred and thirty-six. Three thousand two
hundred and forty-nine. Three thousand three hundred and sixty-four."
The boy counted and moved to the backside of the wood pile and started
placing rocks on top of the tarp's edge.

"You have children, right, not right?"

"Of course. Yes, sir. I have a daughter and a fine son." Bo consciously
looked straight into Wang's eyes, not looking in the direction of the
woodpile.

"Your son, he is strong? Healthy?"

"Yes, sir. Long is a fine boy."

"And your girl, is she fair?"

"My girl, Yan, she is just six. She is delicate with pretty features and
small, tender feet."

"What are your plans for them? Will they be sent to work in the
cities?"

"My children? Sir?"

"That's what they all do, go off to the cities to make money?" Wang looked in the direction of the woodpile and heard Jiang's voice.

"Five thousand one hundred and eighty-four."

"Not my children. One day, I will choose a suitable husband for my daughter. A man who will not take her away from the land of her kin. And my son, he will work our land."

Wang looked at Bo and sized him up quickly; the man had almost nothing, but he had two things that interested the Farmer Master: his family and his ambition.

"I understand. I, too, will keep my boy close to me."

Bo looked at Wang as if, for a moment, they had shared a moment of mutual understanding, maybe even appreciation. Jiang's voice rose from behind the woodpile, calling out another apparently meaningless number. Bo involuntarily looked in the boy's direction but saw only the small white goat stuttering its heels against the ground. He quickly turned his eyes back to the Farmer Master. He hoped his actions did not betray his thoughts; where else could the Farmer Master's strange boy go? What roof would he have to lie beneath other than that of his father?

Wang followed Bo's eyes as they stole a look at the woodpile and then moved too quickly back to face Wang's eyes. What stared back at Wang were not the eyes of a man who presumed to be his equal, but worse yet, the eyes of a man who pitied him.

Now Wang's hands were clenched deep in his own pockets, pushing down his anger and straining as he commanded himself to reason. He made himself convert Bo and his dreams into usable parts. More hooks on his domain to be placed, as proved most useful.

Wang offered his hand to Bo. "I understand your way. It may well be of benefit to us both. I will accept your red envelope, as it is, as a starting token of your appreciation. I will also lend you the money to build your house. This money will be paid back to me two-fold, as a more complete expression of your gratitude. And there is one more thing."

Bo swallowed deeply, squeezing the coins in his hands and bracing himself steady against fear. "Yes. What is it?"

"You and your children will owe me loyalty. *Guanxi* will bind us. You will all remember this moment when I, the Farmer Master, did you a favor and you will pay me back in kind should the need arise." Bo wiped his right hand against his pant leg. He could not imagine what the Farmer Master had in mind; he could only focus on the man's outstretched hand, which he eagerly took in his.

The land was his.

———————————

The spring rains became less frequent, and before the air and earth began to parch, the patch of land on the far side of the pond was taken to by Bo and a small crew of hired masons. The masons arrived at the patch each morning, each dressed not so differently from the average field hand in loose linen pants, muddied loose-fitting shirts, and canvas slippers. Their only real distinction was that each of them bore a well-used shovel over one shoulder and carried in his pockets a trowel, a pack of cigarettes, and a lighter. Two of the younger masons were responsible for dragging along an old wheelbarrow with a wobbly front tire secured in place by a worn leather belt. The men dug foot deep, narrow trenches into the earth, marking out the perimeter of the house-to-be and then continued to whittle into the interior of the house, laying trenches for the internal walls. Into these trenches, foundation bricks would be laid to serve as the base for the outer and interior walls. Bo paid for the bricks in cash, and they would be delivered by the cartload every third day. When the walls were complete, a cement floor would be poured and spread evenly using long planks of wood that the men would swiftly swipe in semi-circles across the still formable liquid surface. Finally, a roof of vaulted wood beams and grey clay tiles would cover the modest single-story structure.

"Our new house will be ready very soon. Isn't that right?"

"Your father is very, very smart, Yan, and he has planned for it to be ready before the first frost. My bones will not suffer the cold this winter." Fang MaMa's mouth closed in a firm line, punctuating her sentences with a sense of certainty. She spoke loudly, ensuring that the resoluteness in her voice carried beyond Yan's ears, falling into the ears of the villagers who lounged about the rocks, peering across the pond at the masons who were sweating as they labored in the afternoon sun. Occasionally, Bo would pause from digging and look across the water at Yan and Fang MaMa and offer a nod of the head, the whole time his chest puffed up.

A collection of older men and women, too fearful of cracking a rib or bruising a tailbone to scramble up on the rocks, used small, wooden fruit boxes as makeshift stools. They sat for hours, looking upon the same building spectacle as the others, as they gummed candied ginger or dried sour plums. Yan kept her distance from them; her stomach turned at the way that their lips seemed to have disappeared, as if pulled into the blackness of their toothless mouths. Beyond the coterie of village spectators, the marsh grasses stood taller than Yan but had already begun to lose their vitality; several stems, given over to the rains, had folded back on themselves.

Chapter Fourteen

Earth MaMa

The ancestors, much like summer flies, swarmed around the great
Earth MaMa, whispering complaints into her ears. Earth MaMa
listened patiently at first and then swatted the ancestors away in irritation. That the hem of Earth MaMa's dress moved this way and that as she
rose from her sleep, and that she cried tears of frustration down the front
of herself as she thought of the fickle nature of her millions of children,
both past and present, was a vivid explanation of the natural world that
generations of heartland children carried deep in their imaginations.

In Shanghai, as Earth MaMa tossed about, city dwellers awoke
abruptly, pulled out of sleep by the roiling of their own stomachs, and
were propelled to vomit into the closest basin, bucket, or open toilet.
The girls in the back room of Lao Fu's barber shop had collectively
retched into whatever was on hand: an open suitcase, a
half-empty plastic take-out container left on the floor from the night
before, a high-heeled shoe that now oozed vomit through its open toe.
Thankfully, most of the girls were half-naked and few of their working
garments were soiled. LuLu and YuZhen, having been closest to the
bathroom, were the first to get cleaned up and worked together to mop
the back rooms whilst the others took turns rinsing their mouths and
washing their faces.

Many blocks over from the barbershop, heading westward, the tree-lined boulevards of the city's most prestigious center of higher education remained calm, and its people were not concerned. They were reassured by that cluster of academicians whose job it was to describe such events in exacting scientific detail that the origin of the crisis was far away and that only the very outer ripples of the disruption had touched the city. After pouring over maps and scouring the transmitted needle scribbles made from thousands of seismographs, each one carefully placed in areas close and remote, they could say, with a high degree of confidence, that the origin of the disturbance was two thousand one hundred-and ninety-six-kilometers due west, just on the outskirts of rural Da Long village.

Measurements of the event were plentiful; fault slippage, affected surface area, rock rigidity, wavelengths, amplitudes, and the speed of seismic wave propagation were all quickly calculated. The graphic details of the events at the epicenter and its surroundings, however, were scarce. In Beijing, central authorities tried to piece together a picture of the event from reports that were communicated by telephone.

From above, the land of Da Long was a roughly torn loaf of bread with its crust disrupted and its soft middle jagged and uneven. The river, previously long, skinny, and snake-like, had overflowed its banks at irregular intervals and a multitude of new lakes and ponds dotted the devastation. Macerated rapeseed plants, with root bundles pointing skyward, this way and that, were blended into the soil. The mounted metal singers who had towered over the fields had been felled, many of them losing their bonneted heads. The shiny arm and head of a mechanical harvester could be seen protruding from the earth's surface, its body buried deep in the mountains of mud and rock. Across the region's fertile plain, a disorderly patchwork of irregularly shaped land plots, their once-neat borders disrupted, lay razed and colored primarily by brown and grey wooden shack shards. This new surface was eerily pockmarked with occasional bursts of color: a red, woolen sweater, the cover of a magazine, a yellow-labelled tin of pork grease, an orange motorbike fender, the blue canvas body of a baby carriage, a decapitated, yellow timber roof frame. This was what was left of the homes that had once clung to the earth.

Da Long village center was an ill-formed and strange-smelling collection of wood, mud, brick, metal, and flesh. The torn and cursed bodies of humans, pigs, dogs, cats, chickens, cows, and fish, as well as their blood, could be smelled in the air. Few here had escaped what came without warning in the early hours of an otherwise unremarkable rural morning.

The Eagle's Eye inexplicably stood largely unchanged. The two-story, stone building had been shaken but not broken. Objects had taken flight—as Earth MaMa stood up and turned about, tossing her arms into the sky—and had shattered against the building's outer facade. A deep red splotch marred the building just beneath the Farmer Master's window, marking the spot where a small animal, perhaps a bird or small rodent, had met its end. Wang himself had heard the animal's body crunch into the outer wall but was unaware of exactly what had happened. The man had seen nothing from beneath his desk. Pinned to the spot by the invisible but very real force of self-preservation, Wang had been unable to get to his feet.

Similarly situated beneath the heavy kitchen table, AnRan, Ayi, Jiang, and Small Snow had crouched as low to the kitchen floor as was possible; the two women trembling uncontrollably in the darkness. Both the goat and the boy remained uncharacteristically silent and still. When the world had started to wobble and roar, they had all held onto each other. Jiang had allowed his mother to pull him close to her; he had not cried out as did the two women, each one begging in her own way for the disaster to pass.

Even when the world had stopped moving, when Earth MaMa had settled back in her bed, the inhabitants of the Eagle's Eye remained crouched beneath their tables, daring not to move for several hours.

In that same moment, just after the earth had stopped rolling, Yan and Long were buried in Lei's bosom, pressing hard into her body and daring not to look anywhere other than into the darkness of their mother's chest. Bo had already struggled to his feet. He waited for nothing and, though his legs trembled, tried to push past his brother-in-law.

Fang MaMa clutched at his sleeve and raised her voice in panic. "You are crazy. You cannot go outside. You damn fool."

"Please, Brother. Listen to your MaMa. There is nothing to be done right now. We must wait a little while. I will go with you, when it is safe." Pang, facing Bo, reached out with both of his hands and placed them on Bo's shoulders. Pang, with his back to the front door of his and MeiLin's home, was thankful that the door was still in its frame and that the walls had not come down and entombed them alive.

"Listen. I think I hear something," Bo said.

Pang closed his eyes.

"MaMa. MaMa. I hear someone crying." Yan herself started to cry, and Long joined her.

"Shut them up!" Bo snarled at Lei. He pushed Pang's hands from his shoulders. "Move out of my way."

165

"You have no manners or sense. Aiyah! You ungrateful wretch." Fang MaMa pulled hard on Bo's sleeve. "Pang saved you. He saved all of us. If he had not been out early making the Farmer Master's deliveries to the market," Fang MaMa said, visibly trembling as she spoke, "he would not have been there to collect us with his scooter cart the moment the rumbling started. The children and I would be dead now. We would have been swallowed by the earth. We could not all have run up this road. We could not even move. Think! Would you be here if you had to carry me and the children? Our shack must be gone, carried by the shifting ground into a deep hole. What is it that you think you are going to do out there? What power do you have to use?"

Bo jerked his shirt sleeve free of his mother's grasp and shoved past Pang. He did not look at MeiLin who was huddled on the floor next to Lei and the children.

Bo opened the door and stepped out into the relative stillness. A few dirt-covered souls staggered about outside, looking around, trying to make sense of what had happened. Bo began to jog. He was nimble on his feet and moved quickly down the dirt road as it wound around the belly of the mountain. The road remained largely as it had been. That the earth had shaken in this part of Da Long was evident from shattered clay pots that lay in front of people's homes, from bicycles that lay flat on the ground rather than propped up against trees, and from baskets of rice that had vomited their contents onto the ground.

Seeing scattered wooden shacks and a few brick homes still standing confused Bo. His heart raced with hope. He began to move even more quickly, eager to reach the point on the mountainside road from which he could look down on the lower plain. He knew that just around the next curve, the crop fields, the river, Wang's Way, and most importantly, his patch on the far side of the pond would all come into view. He reasoned that it was likely that fields would be disordered and that segments of the Farmer Master's road would require repair; as for his new home, maybe several rows of brick would be lost, but as long as the foundation and fortified outer walls of the house lay intact, he would easily build the internal walls again. The construction of the internal walls had started just a few weeks earlier, and the rudimentary structures had stood just above Bo's head when the workday had ended less than twelve hours before. Bo could still feel the bricks in his hands, each one laid carefully to follow the plumb lines the masons had rigged, ensuring that each successive layer of brick was level. It was slow work, but certainly no more than a week's labor would have to be repeated.

On coming around the curve of the hill, Bo froze and was felled. He collapsed to his knees and pulled at his hair with both hands. He shrieked up to the sky, his neck and belly muscles painfully contracting.

The valley that lay beneath him, the only land Bo had ever known, was now one that he had never seen before. The banks of the skinny, narrow river, that previously had hugged the base of the hills on Pang's side of the valley, had been pulled apart and were no longer level. The river's far bank had collapsed, as had the earth beneath it and beyond, and had shifted several feet downward. The river's waters, no longer contained, had roared down the newly created gradient and flooded the valley as well as an enormous swathe of the lower plain, smothering everything in their path.

Gone was the Farmer Master's road, except for a tiny black tail that curled up the hill on the other side of the valley. Gone was the patchwork of abutting crop fields with their neat rows of tilled soil and fledgling plants. Gone was the path that cut through the fields, running along the once-narrow river. Gone was the small pond at the end of that path, with its edge circumscribed by rocks and marsh grasses.

And gone was the leased lot with its nascent brick structure. Not a piece of Bo's dream remained visible.

All that lay beneath the water was lost.

Chapter Fifteen

Good Fortune

"Too expensive! Too expensive it is. Aiyah!" The older woman shook her head as she swept up the debris. Shards of glass, pools of oily liquid, clumps of leaves, soaked bark bits, and fragments of animal parts were strewn across the pressed mud floor. She gathered all the bits and pieces up with her brush, pulling all of it together into a small mound that grew in the center of the room. Permanently bent over, Old Doctor's wife could only manage to generate swift, short strokes with the broom, but she was efficient, nonetheless.

The door to the small, wooden home was pushed open, allowing in a blaze of sunshine. Two figures filled the doorframe, then stepped into the house. In the light, the true extent of the mess could be seen. The old woman, knowing that the visitors sought out her husband, kept sweeping while muttering to herself, "What a waste. What a waste."

"Old Doctor, look at my girl. Her skin is pimpled and creased." Fang MaMa pushed MeiLin forward and clutched the front of her smock. The lines around her mouth pulled harder than usual at her thin face.

"No one is well these days." Old Doctor motioned calmly to the table that stood in the middle of the room. "Leave the door open. We have no light."

MeiLin climbed on the table with Fang MaMa's help and lay down on her side. She drew her knees to her stomach and did not open her mouth.

"Her stomach does not lie still. It cannot since the soil shook. I feel she is wasting from fright." Fang MaMa tried to sound angry, to get the Old Doctor to sense her impatience.

"Take ease, MaMa. Take ease. I will see." Old Doctor put his hand on MeiLin's shoulder and pushed her firmly onto her back and tapped on her knees. MeiLin straightened out her legs and said nothing. The old man held his hands out, palm down, over MeiLin's body; starting at her feet, he hovered his hands just inches above her and slowly moved, trembling continuously, up over her shins and thighs, and then stopped for a moment over her lower abdomen. MeiLin winced without being touched. Old Doctor's hands continued their slow flight up over MeiLin's breasts and neck, stopping just above MeiLin's face. MeiLin closed her eyes. Her nose twitched. The old man's hands smelled sour and MeiLin had the sense of floating, but it was only her stomach that moved. Saliva collected in her mouth as he pulled down on her chin. He brought his face close to MeiLin's, examining her tongue and cocking his head to get a better look at the roof of her mouth. He then placed both of his hands on MeiLin's belly, one above the umbilicus and the other below, and, slowly, through the thin cotton layer of her tunic, massaged the flesh that lay between his hands, pressing ever deeper with each push of his hands.

Fang MaMa stayed at the foot of the table but did not dare to touch MeiLin, though she wanted to hold her daughter's feet. The doctor's wife, who had not looked at MeiLin or Fang MaMa, continued to work her broom and pushed Fang MaMa back from the table with the business end of her broom, sweeping the tiny space between Fang MaMa's feet and end of the table with added vim. Fang MaMa glared at the woman's bent body but kept quiet.

Old Doctor continued to warm his hands via the young woman's body, enjoying the heat under his palms. In his younger years, he would have lifted her shirt and pressed his flesh against hers, enjoying the current that would flow through his body and the excitement that would linger long after one as lovely as young MeiLin had generated it. But now his body was too frail to carry such energy, and he knew it not wise, or necessarily enjoyable, to have such pulsations caught up in a body incapable of discharging them appropriately. He closed his eyes.

"Conceived. Conceived. Conceived ..." Old Doctor whisper-chanted as his hands came together over MeiLin's belly, forming a diamond-shaped opening between his forefingers and thumbs. He closed his eyes as he measured the energy that swirled in MeiLin's body. "... right before the earth shook; six moons to come still."

"What is this you say? Good fortune! Good Fortune has come to us! Praise and honor to the ancestors! Praise to those who look after us. Thank you to the honorable ones! Thank You!" Fang MaMa grasped MeiLin's feet in her hands and squeezed them repeatedly with joy. "Little girl of mine, do you hear the old man? Do you?"

MeiLin stayed reclined on the table, her stomach still turning on itself. She dared only to turn her head to the side, facing away from the Old Doctor and not looking at her mother, seeking a moment of privacy. She tasted the salt of her own joy as tears ran across her face and into her ear. Her pale face turned pink as she thought of her husband, and she swallowed down the saliva pooling at the back of her throat.

Lying there, the young mother-to-be could not possibly know that the small ball of cells that grew inside of her, slowly transforming itself with each day that passed, would change everything. The world housed by the four walls of Pang's and MeiLin's home was to be turned upside down. The mere existence of the baby would generate shifts and rifts that, though not measurable by the inky needles of a fancy seismograph, would be of a greater magnitude than those brought by the Da Long earthquake that had rumbled but a few weeks after this child's very conception.

"Girl, you wait here. Let me run home and have that worthy husband of yours come and collect you. We cannot let you get too tired. Your energy has a claim on it now. Old Doctor, she can stay right here, on the table? Correct?" Fang MaMa was full of color, worry having evaporated right off the top of her head in an unseen vapor. She rushed to the open door, undaunted by the blinding light, and took off without waiting for anyone to speak. The air in Da Long was still grey with earthquake dust that had not yet settled back down to the ground. The winds swept it up and circulated it overhead, leaving no one be clear-eyed.

Since the quake, Pang and MeiLin's home was full of bodies. Bo, Lei, Yan, Long, and Fang MaMa all slept in the back bedroom on rolled-out bamboo mats and were kept warm in the night by a mishmash of blankets and Pang's old work clothes. Their own shack was now invisible, hidden beneath a body of water that showed no signs of receding. Not even a speck of roofline was visible; Lei wondered if anyone would ever believe that the low plain had once been dry and dotted with many small structures and humble lives. The old pond was gone, subsumed into the bed of the new lake. And, with it, all the neatly laid bricks that had been placed along its far side were also gone. The only sign of the little house that had almost been and that now was never to be, sat on Bo's face in the form of a permanent scowl. He slept in the corner of Pang and MeiLin's back bedroom and, though the room was crowded with his wife, mother, and children, such that the children's soft arms and legs were entwined with those of their mother and their NaiNai, Bo touched no one in the night, not even in his sleep.

As the extended family crowded around the table in the home's front room, Lei was careful to keep a thin sliver of space between herself and her husband. She knew he did not want to be touched, that he was barely there and didn't want to be brought into the present by something as meaningless as the pressure of his wife's thigh against his own. Bo had not been inside her since the great quake and, while the current sleeping arrangement alone would suffice as explanation, Lei knew that Bo truly had no interest. He had lost interest in almost everything; only Yan got an occasional direct look from her father, and every few days, Long would be carried off by Bo to accompany him on one of his walks to nowhere in the later evening hours.

The village center would take many months to be cleared of debris and refuse. The government had sent troops, little red-helmeted, ant-like armies, to help and offered compensation to all able-bodied men who could assist in the clean-up effort. There was no other work to be had. Life had come to a standstill; no crops to harvest, no fields to be tilled, and so few animals left to be milked, fed, and herded. School was closed and children were left to while away their time, usually trying to avoid fatigued and anxious parents. Most of the men took to the streets each day, using bare hands to pick up pieces of everything. The pay for such work, coming from central authorities, was minimal and would take time to arrive. Food rations were disbursed every third day to one member of each officially registered Da Long family: one kilo of white rice, half a kilo of white sugar, a small tin of pork fat, a plastic canister of soy milk powder, four two-liter bottles of water, a half a dozen eggs, a small sack of random root vegetables, and the occasional piece or two of fruit, usually oranges or bruised apples.

Comprised of two registered families, Pang's household now qualified for double rations and Fang MaMa, keeping a keen tally of the family's state of relative abundance, decided to celebrate. On the night of the day that Old Doctor had delivered news of MeiLin's fragile but fruitful condition, Fang MaMa took extra care to slather the mashed turnip cakes with a thick layer of pork fat, almost doubling their thickness. And, when the small bowls of creamy congee were ladled out, each one carefully apportioned by Fang MaMa, the children squealed with delight as they immediately noticed that there were a generous number of brown and white marbled pieces dotting each of their bowls, each one representing a tiny piece of salty, broth-soaked tea egg.

"Don't be so disruptive! It's as if you have never seen food before, like little animals with no manners." Fang MaMa playfully swatted Yan's back. "Come. Come. Eat now."

Fang MaMa ladled an additional portion of soup into MeiLin's bowl before pushing it in her direction. MeiLin immediately pushed her bowl in front of Pang, who was easily thrice her size. Pang broke out into laughter, drawing all eyes to his glowing face, and pushed the bowl back to his wife. "You eat."

"Smart husband. Listen to him. You eat," Fang MaMa chided MeiLin, who looked at the jelly-like egg pieces and felt her stomach expand uncomfortably and heat rise in the back of her throat.

Before the quake, Bo would have noticed every action and reaction that flowed among Fang MaMa, MeiLin, and Pang. He would have been quick to interpret what was transpiring and even quicker to insert himself in some way as to lay claim to his family's attention. But today he saw nothing and simply spooned gruel into his mouth. It was Lei who observed a difference and immediately sensed that change was coming.

"It is time." Fang MaMa was deftly peeling the skin off a bruised apple, her one knife as sharp as ever. "Prosperity should always be shared quickly with family." She kept her eyes on the knife, but her voice was thrown in Pang's direction.

"Yes, MaMa. So wise you are. Well, there is prosperity to share."

"Why is your face so hot? So red?" Yan looked at her uncle. "Like a tomato. Are you ill?"

"Oh no, Little Face. Not at all." Pang slipped his hand along the table, palm up, and under MeiLin's. Her white, pale hand looked so small and precious, surrounded by his fleshy pinkness. Pang continued, "We are going to have a child, just after the new year in the early spring. A little rabbit."

Fang MaMa clapped her hands, and the children joined in, Long clearly not knowing why.

"Will it be a girl, like me? Please, can we have a girl?" Yan exclaimed, wanting to claim her stake before anyone else could say anything.

"We, as of yet, do not know. But it can be." MeiLin spoke softly and tried to smile.

"I will pray for a girl. I will ask the ancestors every night to give me a little sister."

"Hush, Yan. We must just pray for health." Lei was gentle in her admonishment. "Congratulations, dear brother and sister." Lei forced a sweetness into her voice and kept the heat from rushing to her neck and face. She looked at Bo, who still had not spoken.

Yan climbed off her rectangular, wooden stool and ran around the table to MeiLin. She placed her hands on MeiLin's stomach and then put her ear on the same spot. "Hello. I am Yan, your older girl cousin. If you are a girl, I will love you and show you everything important in Da Long." MeiLin rubbed Yan's back and did not push the child away. "If you are a boy, I will try to like you and to still show you some things."

Pang roared with laughter and grabbed Yan and started to tickle her.

"Silly child. Really. Did she really say such a thing? It is time for these children to sleep. And you too, MeiLin." Fang MaMa tugged at Yan's shirt, letting Pang know to put the girl down. She turned her attention to her son. "And you, have you nothing to say? Your long face is all we see." Fang MaMa pulled the corners of her mouth downward and drooped her lids over her eyes, mocking Bo.

"Come. Let's go to bed." Lei lifted Long into her arms, pulling the boy free of the table. Long held on tightly to a piece of egg, trying to work it into his mouth while he was midair.

"Well? Speak now, boy." The blade of Fang MaMa's knife caught the light as she jabbed it in the air, thrusting it in Bo's direction. The old woman was standing now and leaning across the table, blade in front of her. A slithery piece of tea egg plopped onto the table as Long opened his fist and reached for the knife blade.

"Aiyah! What will the ancestors think of us fools?" Fang MaMa threw the blade flat down onto the table.

Lei pushed Yan into the back bedroom. The girl flopped down onto a small pile of blankets and clothing that barely lent softness to the thin, bambooed sleeping mats spread out on the floor. Lei ignored Yan's pouting mouth, quickly putting Long down beside her.

"Stay here with your brother. Understand?"

Yan looked at Lei, her lips still squeezed together.

Lei went back to the front room and stood next to Bo, who remained seated with his congee half eaten, and placed her hand on his shoulder.

Fang MaMa looked at Lei and snorted. "Your husband. My son. Aiyah!" She sat back down and started to pick a piece of rice from her teeth. "Go tend to your children. I will talk something sensible into his head."

Bo moved the spoon in his bowl between the islands of egg and then pushed each one down, deep below the surface of the congee. Lei watched as the small pieces of preciousness were submerged, one by one.

"MaMa, I will stay to hear my husband speak." Lei eyed the knife on the table and then looked at the squinting eyes of the older woman.

"Humph." Fang MaMa pulled the knife in front of her. "So, you have tongue tonight for the first time and your husband has none? The world is truly upside down."

Bo pushed his bowl towards his mother, as if offering up an exhibit. "What do you want me to say? We have lost everything. I am in debt this way and that way. Each way I look, I owe someone something." His voice came even and calm, even as he shot a glance at Pang before looking back at his mother. "Another mouth to feed? It is not mine, and so I can say, good luck to you." Bo did not look at MeiLin, as if not seeing her would allow her to remain unchanged. "I'm getting up."

"Wait, Brother, please do not be so disheartened on such a happy day. The ancestors will think us all ungrateful." Pang gestured to Bo's place on the bench.

"I can hear you without sitting."

"MaMa, are you coming to lie with us?!" Yan called from the back bedroom, not daring to come out into the front room.

"In a little time. Be patient, Yan."

"Brother, I know this has been a hard time for our family." Pang's voice was soft.

Again, Bo did not look at his sister. "My family. My house is lost. Yours still stands, and, evidently, it even grows."

"Come. We are one family, are we not?" Pang looked at Bo and wondered at how small he looked. He was really no bigger than MeiLin.

"One family?" Bo saw himself pulling Pang's lips away from his face, stretching them out and distorting them so that they could never close again. He saw the knife lying in front of his mother and wondered how quickly he could grab it. Could he get the blade deep into Pang's groin before it was too late, before someone grabbed him and made him stop? A sense of urgency came over him and his blood pulsed loudly. Tingling, his legs were ready to launch.

"I will go to them." MeiLin's soft voice cut through the noise in Bo's head. She gestured to the back bedroom.

"Are you okay?" Pang reached out to MeiLin as if to steady her as she rose from their shared bench.

"Don't worry so. I just want to lie down with the children. You talk."

Outwardly, MeiLin looked much as she always had. Her slip of a frame and the fairness and fineness of her face remained unchanged. She moved as she had since childhood, floating as if her feet barely touched the ground. However, in her eyes, which were the only part of her Bo wanted to see right now, she was completely unrecognizable to her brother. His "one family" was destroyed. MeiLin, his MeiLin, was seeded by this man. In a flash, Bo, for the first time since MeiLin and Pang had been married, understood all that must be true. He was already too late.

"Brother," Pang began, turning his attention back to Bo, "there is always opportunity in any disaster." He saw defeat in Bo's face, the face that reminded him so much of his wife that to see it now was certain to bring him a degree of heartache. "We are one family, and we can recover together. The government will not let us down. Our great leaders have told us that this is the time for the 'four modernizations.' It will happen here. Advancement in agriculture, in farming, is on The Party's list! Right, not right? We've all heard the message over the loudspeakers, those that still stand, and in ration hall. There will be rebuilding and investment. The new economy will be here."

"Smart. Smart. This one is so very smart. Are you listening?" Fang MaMa was back to plucking at the debris between her teeth and wishing for the more dexterous fingers of her youth.

"Our brother, Shu, is in Shanghai right now working with a transportation company, learning how to fix and refurbish moped carts and produce trucks. How will all that is made here in the heartland be sold to those on the eastern edge and outside of our country? It must travel its way along roads like those built by the Farmer Master and along many more. We will be part of that."

"*Our* brother, Shu?" Bo burped loudly as soon as the words were out of his mouth and grabbed his stomach.

"Yes. He is developing our family *guanxi* in Shanghai and even as far as Beijing. Everything is about relationships. He is good in that way." Pang tried not to wince as he looked at Bo's face, streaked with discomfort.

"It is so, how you say, about little brother," Lei floated soft appreciation into the air, hoping it would land on Pang. "And is he okay? In Shanghai? Does he like it? What has he seen?"

Pang looked straight at Lei, his eyes wide at hearing her voice. It was a small, edgeless sound, unexpected from a woman of her shape and seldom, if ever, heard. His face broke into a smile, and he parted his lips to answer, "Sister ..."

"Girl, stop with such stupid bothers. What is there to like or not like? See or not see. The issue is opportunity." Fang MaMa's words would ordinarily have cut Lei to size.

"I know, MaMa. I just ..."

"You know. What do you know? Let the man speak of his plan. Don't ever interrupt a man who speaks of his plan for prosperity. Without it, where would you be?"

Lei watched Fang MaMa's lips tremble with anger and realized that it felt as if the world was still shaking with the hostility of the great quake. Her hand rested on Bo's shoulder; he did not seem to notice. Pang, whose imagined, fulsome hands touched her and made her back arch in the middle of the night, though sitting just across the table from her, was truly out of her reach. And the gnarled tree of a woman at the table, the "MaMa" on her lips, had shaken a knife in the air and had feet that Lei would never touch.

The world was spinning.

Without a word, Lei went to the back room and found MeiLin lying on the ground with Yan's back curled up against her belly and Long, on his back, just next to MeiLin's head. All three were asleep. Lei maneuvered onto the mat and covered them with several blankets before lying down and facing them, leaving a little space between herself and the dormant trio. She listened to the chorus of their night sounds and recalled those of her youth. Her brothers' snores grew louder over the years as their bodies took on hair. Almost weekly, her mother's moans, uttered so evenly as if she were setting a pace for her father's more erratic groans, would be loud enough to keep her awake. She could make out all their faces even now, after so many years, just as easily as she could outline those of her own children.

She woke up chilled and found Fang MaMa in MeiLin's spot; a shrinkage of vertebrae that led the woman to have a curled-up shape, much like that left behind by her daughter. Lei imagined Pang had come and carried *his* sleeping sliver of moonlight back to their room and into the warmth of their bed. She moved her legs slowly and tried to reach into the room's corner with her toes to touch Bo's feet. She only met cold air.

Chapter Sixteen

Trucks and Trains

P ale pink and sharp white blossom petals, each one a velvet tear, sprinkled the factory courtyard. The cleansing light of spring shone down on the flower pieces and the place looked set for hope and renewal. Slinking around each other in a hideous dance, those with the needles ready to pinch and those with skinny, shaking arms extended, the leech men and their prey drained the place of such illusions.

The guardhouse was quiet, wreathed in smoke, and pungent with the smell of an unwashed body. The guard looked out, unfazed by the familiar scene. Except for the movement of his chest, lips, and nostrils as he worked the well-smoked butt of his last cigarette, he was inert. His eyes moved ever so slowly, following the dance. He neither bothered to laugh at the feeble, who closed their eyes and jiggled their bodies away from their own outstretched arms, nor did he flinch with the pinch of each needle into their skin. He had winced at the sight many years before, and he may even have held his breath along with the feeble as they were bled, but not anymore. He could not hear any of their chatter, and he was glad of this as he barely had the inclination to watch.

"When again? When can I go again? Today? Tonight?" The man's eyes darted about as he peppered the air with his questions and coughs. He tried to focus on a single blossom petal as it made its way from branch to ground, but he got distracted by another petal and then another. He didn't look at the plasma seller who was roughly placing a plaster on his oozing puncture site.

"What are you? A strong man?" The pimple-faced plasma seller laughed. "No. You are simple. You are a stupid one."

"Of course. You are right. You are too good to help me. When then? You tell me." The man's cheekbones seemed to scrape against the papery thin skin of his face, and, with his arm now free, he began to pick at the scabs that dotted his arm with the good veins. "You are right, I am stupid. You know. You tell me."

"The authorities say every two weeks, you know that. You can only sell your stinking blood every two weeks!"

"Aiyah! To the ancestors!"

The plasma seller, repulsed by the numerous scabs and partially healed needle sites that pocked the man's inner arms, ignored the man's plea and squeezed the last drops of blood from the collecting tubes into the blood bag. When he was finished, he looked about the courtyard, searching for anyone else to bleed. There was no one.

"Listen, if we do this again tomorrow, I am taking a great risk. You understand?"

"Yes. You are too good. Too good."

"Shut your lips and listen to me. I will collect from you again tomorrow, but I will only give you half the fee."

"Half? But why? A full bag is a full bag!"

"I put my ass on the line for you, and you ask why? No issue. Leave it." The plasma seller disconnected the used needle from the plastic tubes and wrapped it in tissue before placing it in his shirt pocket. He collected the dirty tubing and shoved it into his backpack and then placed the full blood bag into a metal cooler box that sat at his feet. He took a twenty Kuai note from his pocket and shoved it towards the man, who grabbed it.

"Thank you! Now, please listen. I am called Rong, and sometimes I speak too fast. You know I am not smart like you. I speak too fast without stopping to look in my head. I will take half. I will be here tomorrow. Okay? Half is good." Rong got the words out quickly between short breaths, before erupting into a coughing fit.

"We will see." The plasma seller moved towards his bike that stood unlocked and propped against the guardhouse.

"Tomorrow," Rong called after him, waiting to see the plasma seller turn around.

The plasma seller focused on the guardhouse and its open window. The guard's palm thrust out before he reached it. Spitting on the ground, the plasma seller pulled another twenty Kuai bill from his hand and slapped it into the open hand. The hand disappeared. No words were exchanged.

Rong made his way back to YuZhen, who was lying down and barely discerned his return to their home beneath the bridge. The chipped glass of herbal tea he had left beside her was untouched and only a small bite's worth of the onion pancake was gone. Rong picked up the remainder and stuffed it into his mouth.

"You're full? You didn't eat much." Rong's words came out garbled around the chewed pancake. He rubbed YuZhen's back with gentle circular motions, trying to pull her out of grogginess. "You need to drink more. You don't want to dry up. Sweeping hair out of YuZhen's face and tucking it behind her ear, Rong slouched onto the ground and leaned his back up against the mattress. He pulled the twenty Kuai note from his shirt pocket, along with a loose cigarette and a matchbook. The note he tucked under the tip of one shoe. Trying not to take his eyes off it, he fumbled the cigarette into his mouth and steadied his hands to light it.

"Rong? You back?" YuZhen pushed her arm in Rong's direction. "You get it ... the medicine ... did you ..."

"You are up? You are feeling better?"

"No. So tired. I can't be up." YuZhen rolled on her back and pushed her forearm across her brow. She was warm and wet with sweat. "The medicine. Do you have it? Did you get the money to get ..."

"Rest. You are tiring yourself out." Rong moved his foot squarely over the note on the ground. "I don't have any money, yet. I will find a solution."

"Please ... Pl ..." YuZhen drifted back to sleep.

A pulse of guilt hit Rong about hiding the money from YuZhen, his almost-wife, who could not lift her head up off the saliva-crusted mattress, but only for a moment. He immediately homed in on the sounds above him. Overhead, throngs of cyclists and pedestrians jostled across the bridge, and Rong saw each of their paths illuminated in multicolored threads of light. He tried to count each bright line but kept losing his place.

While Rong's strung-out brain strained to follow each bridge crosser, those above him took no notice whatsoever of the migrant shanty town that sprawled in the dank darkness several meters below their feet. Low-lying, single-story cubicles made of assorted cinder blocks and brick, covered with rusted, corrugated sheet metal, ran in several rows along the river. The mud floors of each home were a continuation of the embankment that ran down to the water's edge. The structures were no more than a collection of crude walls and roof fragments that divided the terrain and were devoid of power and plumbing.

"Hello? YuZhen. Are you here?"

Rong, startled, leapt to his feet, grabbed his money, and shoved his hands in his pockets. He recognized LuLu's voice and quickly unfurled his shirt sleeves, pulling them down over his arms.

"YuZhen?" Lifting a thick, muddied plastic tarp that served as the door to the home, LuLu called, "YuZhen? What has happened? Are you okay?"

Rong stumbled back, away from the mattress, as LuLu crouched next to YuZhen and began to shake her awake.

"What? What is it?" YuZhen tried to open her eyes.

"What have you given her?" LuLu jumped to her feet and turned to Rong, who believed he had made himself invisible by pressing his body into the wall.

"Nothing. I haven't given her anything. She has a cold, that's all. She needs her medicine."

"Where is it?"

"I have no money. I haven't ... she hasn't worked in some time. You know." Rong pressed harder into the wall and hoped, if he pressed hard enough, the wall would absorb him whole.

Weeks-old newspapers lay at YuZhen's feet on the end of the mattress. A few fancy men's dress shirts on cheap, wire hangers hung from nails jammed into the spaces between the cinder blocks of one wall, and several pairs of ladies' heels were lined up neatly on the floor below the shirts. A small, wooden dresser and two red plastic stools were the only other pieces of furniture, aside from the mattress, in the room. Along with Rong's shirts, a single sheet of sketchbook paper adorned the sparse walls. LuLu recognized it immediately as one of her sketches of YuZhen from years earlier. LuLu wanted to jump up and open the dresser drawers. She wanted to throw every single piece of fancy men's clothing that she knew had been bought, carefully folded and then put away in that dresser by YuZhen, in Rong's face. But what would the point be? Rong was the paid-for-husband of YuZhen's arrangement. YuZhen had sought Rong out and bought him; bought him with clothing, food, rent money, and a pocket-change allowance. In return, he was to be loyal to YuZhen, treat her like his TaiTai, be the respectable 'husband' who appeared in her letters home to her family, and never discuss how YuZhen's money was earned. The man was useless.

"You are a good friend, LuLu, to come see us. YuZhen, she is like your older sister. Isn't she?"

Eyeing Rong carefully, LuLu worked through the best use of him. She lifted YuZhen's head and tried to coax a few drops of tea into her mouth; the drops ran down YuZhen's face and off her chin.

LuLu stood up. "I have money."

Rong peeled himself from the wall, springing into a false state of readiness. "How glorious. I will go now and get her medicine."

"That is good of you, but I know you are worried for YuZhen. Take ease and stay with her. I will go now to the druggist. I need to buy medicine for my own BaBa."

"Does he have a cold as well?"

"No. He will be fine. His back is hurting from working too hard. I will be back soon."

"You are so good." Rong's shoulders slumped, and his voice came out as a whimper.

As LuLu lifted the tarp to leave, Rong climbed onto the mattress behind YuZhen. He curled his body to fit the contours of her back and threw one arm across her. He wiggled in place, trying to draw some of her warmth. "You are so right, LuLu; I have been so worried for her."

Not looking back at Rong, LuLu muttered, "Yes. I am sure. You and Lao Fu have been worried much in the same way."

LuLu made her way through the dirt alleyways that ran a grid between the rows of shanty homes. A spring rain had visited earlier, and she tried to avoid soiling her shoes in the soft mud. A cluster of women chatted around a barrel fire, and, on spotting LuLu, they saw opportunity. "Pretty girl. Pretty girl! You hungry? Your stomach full? Come. Come look."

The women wore dark grey and navy linen smocks. One sported green men's socks on her feet, while the rest were bare-legged; all of them wore plastic house slippers. Their faces were creased and unpowdered, allowing the natural bronze of their skin to shine. "Come, pretty girl. Looking is free. Come see our delicious gems. Round and like orange gold." A small, straw sack filled with unwashed sweet potatoes sat at their feet, and the smell of caramelized sugar hung in the air. LuLu wanted to be gone from this place, but she knew that she would need to return with YuZhen's medicine and wearily anticipated passing the women again.

LuLu knew better than to offend them. "Thank you, Aunties, but my stomach is full. In a little bit, I will be back with medicine for a friend who lives over on the second row."

The women's heads all turned to look over in the direction of the river, back behind LuLu, and then quickly turned back.

"Your friend? Is her stomach full?"

"No." LuLu felt the sting of tears coming to her eyes.

The women, feeling LuLu's sadness pressed in closer, "What makes her sick?"

"Does she pass water?"

"Is her stool fiery and loose?"

"Sweet potatoes are powerful for healing poor tempers."

"Aiyah, but, most important, they must be roasted not boiled." One of the women pointed into the barrel fire for emphasis.

"Listen to what she says, she is good with sickness."

Sensing their concern, LuLu managed a small smile. "Thank you, Aunties. You speak truth. I will ... I must go now and when I return ..."

"Healing cannot happen on a cold stomach." The women all nodded in agreement.

LuLu continued, "It is possible, what you say. When I come back, I will see if you have any left and bring one to her."

As she climbed the dirt embankment back up to the bridge road, LuLu looked down on the shanty town. Hundreds of migrants clotted together, under the bridge, clinging onto the earth with no foundation for their lives. The city dwellers did not care to see them; their tunnel vision brought into focus only those body parts that washed, cooked, cleaned, or pleasured them. The aunties around their barrel fire began laughing and teasing one another the moment she had left them. They had tried to sell her what they had, and she could not dislike them for that; their advice they had given freely. She knew they would not forget her and would ask after YuZhen when she returned. They would be easy to find, for the orange blaze of their fire marked their location as did the tufts of soot-filled air that arose right above them.

Blossom petals carpeted what was left of Wang's Way, and the children leaned over the cart's edge, hoping to see what would happen as its wheels kicked up the pieces. The ride up to the Farmer Master's marked a new time; the time after the great quake, when life was still not normal, but when Da Long's mothers had stopped clutching their children and keeping them strictly within the perimeter of their own gazes. Crushed spines of math books and readers, pieces of pencils, the metal legs of desks, and a slab of blackboard protruded from a mound of rubble in the village center. This marked the spot of the old schoolhouse. The surviving tail of Wang's Way led the way to what the government troops called the "just-for-now" schoolhouse.

"Sit still."

"Not possible, the ride is bumpy. Ahh! You're pulling too tight."

"I am not."

"It is too tight. I cannot braid this child's head if you pull on *my* head."

Three school-aged girls sat on the floor of the cart, each with her legs spread, one sitting just inside the legs of the girl behind her. Each one worked to braid the hair of the girl right in front of her, and the youngest, who sat at the front, simply kept still, trying not to move or pull her head while keeping her free hands in her tiny lap. Extending the hair-braiding chain were Hong and Min, who had started the activity, with Hong in the first position, her back up against the side of the cart.

"You are impossible." Hong pulled sharply on one chord of Min's hair. "Your braid will be deformed and crooked like your teeth."

"Big Sister, if it is such, of course, I will not even touch that nest on top of your head." Min held the braid of the girl in front of her in one of her hands as she tried to reach back and grab Hong's face with the other.

"You don't want to do that." Hong pulled her hands back and took Min's braid with her. "The teacher will think you a mess. He is sweet for sure, but his nose is still crooked. He wants a girl with oiled hair, not one strand out of place, that is swept off her brow and twisted respectably into an even tail. You still have your eyes set on him? Then close your lips and sit still."

Min pulled her arm back and quietly resumed braiding the hair of the girl in front of her.

Hong waited for her sister's tongue to wag and kicked her when no insult came back to her. "What? Words all lost in your big mouth?"

The adult villagers on the cart started to howl, except Lei, who covered her mouth and laughed softly into her hand. Chang TaiTai, rubbing her knees and showing all her teeth as she laughed, looked at the sisters and shook her head. "Listen to these two. The only pretty thing they have hangs right off their heads, and even that they cannot keep precious."

The cart pulled up in front of the Farmer Master's courtyard, and the children scrambled to the back of the cart, waiting eagerly for the tailgate to be unlocked.

"Slowly. Slowly. Please take care." Chang TaiTai's commands carried no force. The excitement to start the school day and the potential for all sorts of curiosities to reveal themselves was too much for the little ones.

They climbed over Chang TaiTai's extended legs, taking no notice that they were made of feeling flesh. Min and Hong hopped down over the side of the cart and went around to help the children down. Bony and childless though they both were, they were strong and enjoyed this part of the day. Min carried two children at a time and jogged them into the courtyard, taking notice of Teacher Zhou's bike just inside the courtyard entrance.

The Farmer Master's courtyard was festooned with paper birds, tigers, lions, dragons, and a few more assorted creatures not found in reality. Each one, inscribed with well wishes, had come from an elementary school in Shanghai; in the aftermath of the Da Long earthquake, the city children wanted to do their part to help their countryfolk. AnRan, seated at the kitchen window, watched as "Long Life," "Good Health," "Prosperity," and "Eternal Blessings" all dangled in the breeze, as if just waiting for the taking.

Jiang sat next to her. "Are they here again? All of them?"

"Yes, son. They are here again for their lessons."

"Will I have my lessons?"

AnRan tried not to hear Jiang's repeated question. She did not answer him; she watched the children run into the courtyard, some holding hands. Others eagerly found their spots in the circle of plastic stools, arranged that morning by Ayi, that now occupied the center of the courtyard, where the weighing scale had once prominently stood.

Teacher Zhou greeted the children. "Welcome. Welcome. Good morning! Soon we will start."

Yan pulled Lei's hand, impatient to claim a stool very close to Teacher Zhou. Once on her perch, she began to move in circles, letting her bottom rotate on the seat. She looked over to the kitchen window and froze. Jiang stared back at her, watching as she grabbed Lei's skirt.

"MaMa, why does that strange man never come outside? Why does he watch us from the window?"

"He is just a boy, Yan, not so much older than you."

"Strange! And much older."

Lei smiled as she raised her hand and waved at Jiang, a small kindness in return for his help so long ago and one she had given Jiang several times over the years. The boy never smiled back. One might have thought he did not know her, but Lei knew differently.

AnRan saw Lei and smiled back on behalf of her son and then, filled with sadness, she looked at the teacher's relaxed face. The stiffness he had carried into her house for so many years seemed to have eased.

Allowing the children to run their hands over the silkiness of his robe and greeting each one individually with their familiar names, the teacher was content. He was happy to be with these children, these life forces, each one eager to see him. Their little bodies and faces looked so healthy and robust. Each of them a little package of potential energy waiting to be opened and ignited with knowledge.

AnRan remembered when her own son had looked that way. Now he was not such a small child, in age and body. And his potential energy? It seemed to have dissipated long ago, given off in epileptic bursts so strong and violent, yet meaningless. The fits had mostly disappeared—Old Doctor's daily tonic having doused their flame.

"Will I have my lessons today?" Jiang persisted, his voice impatient, and now Small Snow stood up and stared at AnRan as if also waiting for an answer.

"Jiang, you can try today with the others. Your teacher is there. Look outside." Ayi spoke to Jiang from the other side of the kitchen table where she ground the herbs for the boy's tonic.

"I am not like them. I do not do the same lessons." Jiang looked at Ayi as if she should know better. He covered his ears with his hands. "They make too much noise."

"Yes. I understand. You could help Teacher Zhou, help teach the little children, like a big brother."

"I am not a big brother. I have no siblings. I am not a teacher. I am a student." Jiang's hands remained pressed against his ears.

AnRan sighed softly. "What you say is not wrong."

Once the children were settled, Hong, Min, Lei, and the village parents climbed back into the cart and waved frantically at their young ones who took no notice. Without the children, the cart grew somber. Several of the villagers placed small paper masks, brown with accumulated dust, over their nose and mouths. The cart rumbled back down Wang's Way and onto a makeshift gravel path that traveled along the new water's edge, past what used to be the low plain, and into the center of town. The smell of ruin still filled the air, and all wished they could smell something other than the burning of trash and the rotting of organic matter.

Chang TaiTai held her hands over her nose and breathed deeply; she no longer smelled of pork. The great quake had taken those smells, along with the husband who carved meat, away from her. Each villager was grateful for the Farmer Master's courtyard and the magic of escape it provided the children; the well wishes of faraway school kids dangled enticingly for them as much as they did for anyone.

The smell of fresh chives and the sounds of busy hands lured the Farmer Master's stomach into growling and marked the approaching midday hour. Wang put his pen down and ran his hand over the open pages of the ledger. He then ran his index finger up and down a column of green-ink entries on the far right, looking at each neatly inscribed amount carefully. He looked for movement: leaps up, tumbles down, small changes that over time would be of consequence. That the red ink pen sat untouched on the gleaming black surface of his father's desk, listless amongst the inlaid birds, made him feel most full.

Wang closed the leather-bound ledger and placed it into the desk drawer. He stood and stretched his arms over his head before walking over to the Eagle's Eye and looking out and downward over what had been the lower plain. After years of counting rows of crops and farmers hooked to the land, the Farmer Master accepted what he now saw without sentimentality. What had recently become a "lake" was dotted with waterfowl, and he took to counting how many winged creatures floated on *his* new body of water, before guessing at what bounty might come to live in its depths.

"I wake up with the sun up high." The teacher's voice interrupted Wang's calculations and threw him back to his own school days and his learning of the famous poem, "Early Spring." The children's voices came slowly and precisely, up through the atrium, as sing-song words parroted lovingly back to the teacher. The lesson continued, "Birds chirp everywhere in the sky." Wang focused back on the water, whispering the poem under his breath,

I wake up with the sun up high.
Birds chirp everywhere in the sky.
Last night a rainstorm passed by.
Flowers must have fallen down.

A storm of sorts had indeed passed on by and flowers had fallen, and he, the Farmer Master, son of Wang Li, had been there to pick them up. He shifted on his feet and pressed into the floor, enjoying his own weight. The pale gravel path that wound around the flooded plain would be blackened soon enough, maybe into the "New Wang Road." This was a project to be overseen and profited from by New Da Long's Township leader Wang. The powers-that-be in Beijing had agreed to such, rewarding Wang for his part in "Restoring the Patriotic Heartland." The courtyard school, Wang's humble offering to his beloved village comrades, had brought much-needed forward momentum to the recovery effort in Da Long, curbing the growing despair of the villagers. Children laughing, running about, coloring cartoons, inking their hands with calligraphy brushes, and reciting poetry pulled the villagers back onto the track of love and loyalty for country and its great and generous leaders. Demands for quantification of recovery and aid, the "how much" and "how quickly" questions, gave way to "thank you" and applause for "our blessed leaders." The coin box on Wang's desk grew heavy with the fees he collected for housing Da Long's "just-for-now" institution of learning.

"Farmer Master, excuse my being too bothersome." Ayi stood at the office door, hesitating.

"What is it? Is the food ready?"

"Very soon, yes. I have a letter for you. The courier just delivered it at the gate."

"From whom?"

"It has The Party seal."

Wang moved quickly to close the distance between himself and the letter, his heartbeat picking up speed. With the letter in his hand, he dismissed the woman and went back to the window. The Farmer Master wanted to let the full light of the midday sun illuminate the message and whatever potential for profit it contained. A contract to fill, a crew to command, a new venture to bring forth, maybe a trip out east to clarify his duties. All riches flowed from the powers on the coast to their loyal comrades in the heartland. And Wang, grinning to himself, knew how and when to be loyal.

MeiLin sat in the front yard of the house, in the full heat of the midday sun. Covered with nothing more than the light cotton, sleeveless shift she wore to sleep, the fullness of her breasts and belly, accentuated by darkened areolas and a protruding umbilicus, was on display. The tops of her shoulders and legs were pink, and Long, pointing to his aunt's sun-kissed skin, asked, "Pain? No pain?"

Fang MaMa stood in the doorway and took in the scene. "You have gone mad. Why are you out there, exposing yourself in such a way?"

"MaMa, the sun feels too good to not be here." MeiLin took Long's pointing hand into hers and kissed it. "Not painful. How are you so cute and delicious? Hmm? Can you pick me some flowers?" The boy looked to the clumps of weeds and crabgrass scattered about, his face hardening in determination to do as MeiLin requested. With the boy gone, MeiLin spread her legs apart and allowed her shift to rise up her thighs. She ran her hands over her body and squeezed both of her breasts, marveling at their firmness.

"You are truly mad. Like a feral bitch." Fang MaMa snarled. "Come inside! Your husband will not want to look at you or put another child in you if you cook your skin and act like a fool."

MeiLin laughed ever so gently at her mother. "There is no worry there. I tell you the truth."

"No manners!" Fang MaMa glared at MeiLin and then called to her grandson, "Long, come inside. Immediately!" Long, as if not wanting to disappoint either woman, dropped two dandelions in MeiLin's lap and ran into the house.

How could MeiLin explain how she felt to her mother? Her entire life she had been looked at by others, men and women alike. Her every movement watched and admired while she was largely invisible to herself. Now, ripe with life, she understood what it meant to want to look at her and to touch her body. She understood Pang's desire to cup her breasts and kiss her belly and other parts. Just a few hours earlier, before anyone else had awoken, Pang had kissed their baby, starting at the top of her dark mound and working his lips up and over the crest of her abdomen. The scratch of his shaved scalp and cheeks and the softness of his lips on her bare skin were exquisite.

Her husband's head had come to rest on her chest, and he had laced his hand in hers. The child growing inside of her, the one constantly heating the fluids of her water bag with the kick of its feet, was also kicking Pang. The child had ignited her husband's energy and filled him with fire. He talked in feverish whispers of all that he saw ahead of them, the three of them present in their bed on this morning and the many more who would come in the future. The nation was ripe with possibility. New connections were being forged every day; tracks and roads were being laid and paved. Trains and two-wheeled, four-wheeled, and even eight-wheeled motor vehicles were moving between points close and far. Men and women would be needed to drive, maintain, and repair these moving wonders, men and women like himself, his MeiLin, and this little one who was about to join them. MeiLin listened and did not protest. He had taught her how to ride a motorcycle, though she was not so steady as to ride it without him right behind her, his hands shadowing hers on the handlebars. Pang's words flowed like a river rushing to meet the ocean. MeiLin listened and whispered, "I follow you." That was all she needed to say.

"Girl! Come inside!" Fang MaMa begged from inside the house.

MeiLin pressed the pinkness on the top of her shins and watched her skin change colors, from pale white to yellow and back to pink. She turned her face to the sun and wanted to submit to its power. She did not need protecting or to be hoarded by MaMa and Bo; she laughed by herself, basking in the freedom of feeling so completely alive.

That night, the shimmering crescent in the black sky, shining with a brilliant, pure white light, cast its perfect reflection on the still surface of the flooded valley. Bo, sitting on the mountainside road that wound above and away from the water, appeared to be afloat between two heavenly bodies. His teeth chattered wildly and tried to find space inside his sunken face. His body, thinned, was like an over-whittled piece of wood. He stood stiffly, his long hair lashing his face. Staring at nothing, he did not try to warm himself or fight back against the wind.

Wrapped in a blanket and holding another one to her chest, Lei walked steadily down the mountainside road. She could neither see her feet nor her surroundings, but she knew her way. She also knew where Bo would be, though he had never told her where he went on all those nights that he disappeared. He simply reappeared each morning, sharing fewer and fewer words with the rest of them and leaving more and more soybean milk in his breakfast bowl. That Lei had to find him on this night and bring him back, back to the world of the living, did not change the cadence of her breaths. That it was dark and that the night wind bit at her face and neck did not make her change the pace of her stride. All change had happened at the level of Lei's heart, months prior, on the night that she learned of MeiLin's condition. There were no more night rides on the celestial train with Pang. His face did not come to her anymore. All that she had in the world was right there, in the small room at the back of her brother-in-law's home: Yan, Long, and Bo, if she could pull him back and anchor him in the now.

A decade ago, when Lei's mother had pushed her across the crop rows into the realm of her new husband and into the role of wife, Lei had felt unprepared for Bo. His face and body she had accepted. What choice did she have? They were as they were, with no power to change. But his manner and ways, she had tried to understand those, to find her way into his rhythm, to yield to and find space within them. That he loved

MeiLin more than he wanted his wife did not upset her. She understood the power and ease of loving something so simply beautiful.

She saw Bo's back and called out, "Are you hungry?"

Bo turned his head and looked at her and then turned back to look out on the nothingness before him.

"You did not eat tonight." Lei walked over to Bo, unfolding the blanket she had in her arms and pulled out a paper-wrapped sesame ball; she held it out to him, in front of his face, from behind him.

He pushed her hand away. "Why did you come here?"

"To find you." Lei wrapped the blanket over Bo's shoulders and sat down next to him.

"Go back. Go back to the children."

"They are asleep. They will be that way until morning."

Neither one of them looked at the other as they spoke, sending words into the emptiness.

"We cannot stay any longer, husband." Lei waited for Bo to say something, to see if any seed of a plan existed in his mind. She did not expect one. In his silence she continued, "If we want to build a home ..."

"We have nothing. I have no face to show." Bo cleared his throat, but his words still scraped out. "I sold our lives, the lives of our children, to Wang. We are beggars at the doorstep of my sister and her ..."

"I know," Lei cut him off, trying to help him preserve his pride. "There is no real work for us here. We need to find real work and, slowly, we will pay back the Farmer Master, the masons, and the brickmaker. We will start anew."

Bo groaned, put his head in his hands, and started shaking it "no."

Lei continued steadily, "We can go to the city, to Shanghai, to work better jobs. We are both strong." She did not look at his scrawny legs, covered in goosebumps. "We will come back and rebuild. The government will give every villager who lost their home a new lot of land. We will come back and start over. Brother Shu can help us find work and ..."

Bo stood up, sending the blanket from his shoulders to the ground. He turned and looked down onto the top of Lei's head, his eyes wide and wild. "You speak nonsense. Leave? Leave Da Long and go to the filth of the city? What about MaMa and MeiLin? What about Yan and Long? I won't ever leave Da Long. This is my *laojia*!" Bo gesticulated frantically into the dark void. "This is why you came to find me? To talk this craziness to me? To talk about sewing my future with Brother Shu? He is not my brother. He is a swine. To leave is to become no better than beasts!"

Lei did not move. "What do you think you are now?"

"Say it again! What do you say to me? Say it again, wife." Bo raised his open hand into the air and hovered over Lei, threatening to bring it down on her head.

"You are devouring yourself." Lei stood up and looked Bo straight in the eyes. They were the same height. "MeiLin's body grows larger each day with life, while yours withers and shrivels. Pang makes plans for the future, while you come here each night and live in the past. The children call you to be with them, and you push them out of your sight. I am going to find work. I will go alone if I must. You can stay and explain your decision to your mother, to your sister, and to your children. My behavior they will understand. Yours, they will not."

Bo looked at Lei, searching for something he recognized. He backed away from her. "My sister's body grows larger. How will she, who is but a sliver of your size, survive this? Did she not see how enormous you became? She risks herself for him ... Yes. I am shriveled." His stomach growled painfully, and his body suddenly felt heavy with fatigue. He stumbled backwards and fell, Lei moved towards him, her hand outstretched to help him up. Bo jumped up with an unnatural jerk and stumbled to the road's edge. He looked down over the side of the mountain and then back at Lei, who instantly froze with fear. Bo then turned back to the open space. He lifted one foot off the ground and willed himself to step forwards.

"Stop! Stop!" Lei's words leapt out of her mouth with such ferocity she feared they would push Bo over the edge. Forcing calm into her voice, she begged, "Please, Bo, think of the children! Yan. Long. You are their father."

Tears flooded his vision, and Bo began to sob; he crumpled onto the ground. Lei rushed to him and put her body on top of his, pinning him to the ground. They both trembled. Then, when she felt his body release its energy, Lei reached for the blanket and covered them both.

———————————

"Daughter, Shanghai is far, too far. Pay attention. Look out for opportunities. Care after your husband."

Lei traced each character of her mother's message with her finger, hoping to feel her maternal presence. Pang had brought her the letter from the village center two days earlier, just in time for the departure. Lei had looked at the letter repeatedly as she packed her and Bo's small duffel bag with their clothes and food for the two-day journey, as she sat down to draw a butterfly on the note that she had given to Yan right before climbing onto the long-journey bus, and now, as Bo fell into an uneasy sleep on the cross-country train, letting his head bob up and down on his neck.

The note Lei scribed for Yan had been a simple one, "I love you." Yan had read it, and then, not letting go of the note, she had turned away from Lei and put her face into MeiLin's body. None of the sweetness of the mango pieces Lei had secretly shared with Yan when telling her of Lei's and Bo's plan to go to Shanghai to find work remained. Yan's mouth was dry, as were her eyes. Lei pulled Yan to her and hugged her tiny body as tightly as she could. "Yan, I will sing to you every night." Yan had no more tears to cry and refused to understand her mother's departure. Long, secured in Pang's arms, reached for Lei, but did not cry when he could not have her. This temporarily helped Lei to wave goodbye and board the bus.

Bo mirrored Yan; his eyes were dry, his mouth set in a firm line, and he, too, did not understand the woman whom he followed.

The world whizzed by in a continuous blur, making Bo vomit into his mouth. Squeezed between the weight of Lei's body to his left and that of a larger, unknown man to his right, Bo had to exert effort to swallow the sour curd back down into his stomach. The train was packed with warm bodies, and he dared not move from his spot on the floor of the aisle to search for a latrine. Closing his eyes and trying to find solace in sleep, Bo began to swim knots; he swam in the new lake, moving away from Da Long and the family he left behind, only to swim ashore in Shanghai and have his lungs filled with smoke. He dove back down deep into the lake, away from the past and the future, trying to seek refuge in the infinite darkness, only to come back up to the surface and have his breath squeezed out of his body from either side.

Lei gently braced Bo's bobbing head onto her shoulder and stayed still until she heard him snore. She tried to imagine just how fast she was moving and wished she could see what the train looked like from outside as it sped past fields and small towns and disappeared into the mountains, only to reappear seconds later.

She had had a singular moment of trepidation earlier, just before boarding the train. After traveling for the better part of the day by bus from Da Long to the provincial capital, Lei had initially been relieved to have her feet back on the ground and for the bus ride to be over. She felt steady moving under her own power. She had never seen so many people and quickly feared that she would lose sight of Bo, who made no effort to lead the way and lagged several paces behind her. Pang had told Lei how to navigate the transit depot: "Look for the massive blackboard with the train schedule and, at the right time, let the crowd move you along, under the board and onto the train track." Seeing the train up close for the first time and watching people disappear into its belly, Lei's heart raced. She was seized with the urge to turn around.

How could she have left Yan and Long behind? She needed to go and get them. She stopped and tried to swim against the tide of migrants clamoring to board the train. Turning her head back and forth, looking for Bo, Lei saw hundreds of hardened faces filled with dread, desperation, and fatigue; all of them old enough to have these feelings written in lines running across their foreheads, around their eyes, and down from the corners of their mouths. Not a single, soft child's face was to be found. The nation's urban centers had no patience for migrant children. City schools and hospitals were reserved for children born into families holding a city *hukou*, which conferred upon them city citizenship. Shanghai would not open its purse for outsiders.

Bo grabbed Lei's shirt. Having caught up to her, he began to scold his wife for moving too fast; he only went silent once they were aboard and fighting for spots on the aisle floor, as all the seats had already been taken.

Presently, the train cabin cooled as darkness fell. Hundreds of migrants, collectively rocking to and fro, huddled together. Glad for the warmth, and unsure of what the city frontier would bring, they forced away their worries and gave over to sleep. Lei struggled to stay awake, wanting to watch the stars shoot across the sky. Eventually, her lids grew heavy, and her chin came to rest on her chest.

This was when Huang ShuShu appeared to welcome her on her journey. "I've been waiting for you, Lei."

"Thank you, wisest and greatest uncle. May I ask a question?"

"Certainly."

"Dearest ShuShu, what advice do you have for me?"

"Ah, dear child, Shanghai is so very close. Pay attention. Look out for opportunities. And care after your husband."

Lao Fu swept the trampled, browned blossoms from in front of the barbershop door into the street gutter. He pulled his stool onto the sidewalk from inside his shop, set it down on the swept-clean spot, and settled in for the evening. His eyes followed the men who walked by, sizing each one up and hoping to make customers of all of them.

The sounds of heels clattering on the sidewalk let him know that one of his girls was hurrying in to start her shift. Seeing YuZhen, her gaunt frame scantily dressed and her mouth stained a garish red from messily applied lipstick, Lao Fu was caught off guard by a momentary sense of sadness.

"I'm sorry I am late, my dear boss." YuZhen's brown teeth filled in her wide smile.

"Why?"

"Fortune was waiting for me. Master Du had special words for me tonight." YuZhen held out her hand, revealing a lacy, pink paper rabbit cutout.

Lao Fu pushed her hand away.

YuZhen chattered on, "He told me that the ancestors see us for who we are for all time, not just for this moment when we are on the earth. What we do here does not have to doom us forever. We are much more than what we see; more than what we do. All of us are."

"And you paid the blind fool good money for that shit?"

"Lao Fu! Have you no respect?" YuZhen's leg shook while she stood balanced on her heels, hands on her hips.

Sneering, the old man pointed to the barbershop door. "I respect him as a businessman. He has it good. Now, go inside and get ready. I have no time to talk rubbish with you. We are on this earth and then we are not. If you want to stay on this earth for another day, then you better pay to stay." He waved YuZhen inside, not wanting to look at her too closely.

"That man will be cursed. He has no sense of anything." YuZhen entered the back room and found LuLu getting dressed.

"Lao Fu? He is already cursed. Why do you bother with him?" When LuLu looked at her, YuZhen could tell her friend was trying to examine her arms without staring. YuZhen had covered them with makeup and had powdered over her bruises. "I'm glad to see you, YuZhen. Are you truly better?"

YuZhen, following LuLu's eyes, started to gush, "Well, look at you." She came up close to LuLu and ran her fingers along LuLu's silky, purple scarf, gently combing her fingers through its yellow fringe. "You are meeting your special someone tonight? Right, not right?"

"I am meeting someone, that is right. That's our job." LuLu did not press YuZhen to answer the question about her health.

"Is he still 'work,' a part of your job?"

"Of course. I'm meeting him at the train depot."

"You will not come back here with him?"

"He never wants to come here." LuLu looked around the room. "That's no surprise."

"Is he good to you?" YuZhen continued to playfully run her fingers through the scarf's yellow fringe.

"He is a customer. What do you mean?"

"He is more than that. He's been faithful to you for all these years."

"Faithful? You mean he has been faithful to me as his whore of choice." LuLu pulled down sharply on the ends of her scarf, freeing it from YuZhen's fingers.

YuZhen winced. "Why do you do that? Always take something beautiful and make it ugly with words." YuZhen pulled the scarf forcefully off from LuLu's neck and sat down on the bed, repeatedly running her hands over the fabric.

"I'm sorry, Big Sister. I just don't think of him as anything more than a customer."

"You are special to him. Look at all the things he has given you over the years. He cares for you, accepts you, like Rong cares for me."

LuLu smirked. "He is with me because he can talk freely and it will not change our arrangement. He can tell me anything, lies or truth. He does not care for me. He enjoys how he feels when he is with me. A lie only burdens you if the one you are fooling gives it any weight. I give no weight to his words. That is what makes me attractive to him."

"Aiyah! You are too serious. You think too much. Just enjoy that you have a man who keeps coming back to you, for whatever reasons." YuZhen came up behind LuLu and placed the scarf around her neck. "You look beautiful."

———————

LuLu sat on the train depot steps, twirling the scarf in her hands. She always wore it when she met him, her "special someone." She laughed to herself for even letting YuZhen's words become part of the description of one of *her* customers. Not far from her, pacing back and forth at the top of the steps, a man in bell-bottomed pants, large-lensed sunglasses, and a too-small-for-his-head red cap kept checking his watch. LuLu watched him and wished he would stand still. The train from the heartland was just under two hours past due, and the man's movements would do nothing to change this. As if reading her mind, the man came to a stop, lowered his sunglasses, and smiled appreciatively at LuLu's stockinged legs.

"How much longer do you think?" He threw the question out to LuLu.

"I'm not sure." She tugged on the two scarf ends, evening out the way they fell on her breasts, covering them. The man turned away. LuLu let out a breath and forced her shoulders to relax.

Twenty minutes on, the depot began to vibrate, and a low rumbling sound grew slowly louder. LuLu moved quickly into the arrivals hall.

On board the train, the last hours of the ride had every passenger praying for the journey to be over and for the swaying of the carriages to stop. Visions of the earth collapsing, riverbeds being torn apart, and water flooding Da Long had Bo grinding his teeth and sweating uncontrollably. Lei tried to soothe him, reminding him repeatedly that they were safe and on the train to Shanghai. When the train finally stopped, its passengers tumbled out of its long belly, desperately trying to find their legs.

Lei, who was carrying a small duffle bag on one arm and dragging a green-tinged Bo with the other, searched the platform station. Pang had told her that Brother Shu would be waiting for them in Shanghai; it would be easy to spot him by his red cap. It had been some time since Lei had worked alongside Shu in the fields, and now with Bo being of little help, she worried that she would not find him. She focused on finding a spot of red in a sea of people.

"You have arrived! Welcome! Welcome to Shanghai. Sister! Brother! Let's find you some rest." A red-capped man came pushing forward through the crowd, reaching his arms forward to grab Lei and Bo. He raised his oversized sunglasses to let them see more of his face. Lei, recognizing Shu, let loose a heavy sigh and broke into a toothy smile.

LuLu waited patiently and saw, in her periphery, the red-capped pacer disappear through the crowd with a mismatched pair of villagers: a larger, golden-skinned woman with a perfect smile and a pale, sickly looking man with a fear-etched face. She turned her attention back to the train and waited for the first-class passengers to disembark. She smoothed out her dress and pulled a powder compact from her purse, quickly dabbing her nose and cheeks with the pinky white dust and checking her teeth for stray lipstick. YuZhen's words popped into her head, and LuLu wondered, am I fool enough to think he cares for me?

Farmer Master Wang climbed off the train and into his other world. Shanghai, with its bright lights, construction cranes around every corner, and burgeoning commercial Bund, moved at a frenetic pace and exuded a sense of non-stop striving. This place seemed to call to him by name. This was the city that had birthed his ancestors and from which his father had fled, striving to survive the new order. Shanghai was his true *laojia*. Now, Wang returned whenever he could to reclaim the life that could have been his. The Party letter in his pocket was his calling card in this world of opportunity, but business would wait until tomorrow.

He looked around the platform, feeling completely in control, and saw her standing there waiting for him. She was fresh and young, but far from innocent. She wore her knowledge of men with quiet confidence, not hidden beneath flowing silks and masked by perfume.

"You know, you don't need to wear this scarf every time I come to see you." Wang pulled at LuLu's scarf as he moved in close to her. "You don't need to impress me."

She pulled back, putting her hand on his arm and stopping him from pulling the scarf completely free. "It is you who needs to impress me. This is the only scarf you have ever bought me. If you don't want me to wear it next time, buy me another."

Wang laughed, grabbing LuLu into an embrace. "Of course!"

Later that night, LuLu leaned, naked, out over the balcony of Wang's hotel room. Reclined on a lounge chair, the Farmer Master, wearing a hotel towel and LuLu's purple scarf, was completely relaxed. He enjoyed smoking his cigarette and watching her body. He enjoyed that his body worked when he was with her.

"What do you see?" He studied the muscles in her back and legs.

"I can see the Huang Pu River from here. I could follow it back to the Yangtze and then even further back to my *laojia*."

"You miss your old home?"

"I miss my sister. She was just a baby when I left."

"You like babies?"

"No. I don't. But I love my sister. She is my baby. She is the only child in my life." LuLu came and sat next to Wang. She took his cigarette and inhaled deeply. "You? Do you like babies? Did you enjoy your son as a baby? Will you have more?"

"More babies? No. That cannot happen. I have opportunities that come packaged in playing The Party Patriot. No, I only have one child—will only have one child. And Jiang as a baby? What was that like? I can't really remember that time. In some ways, he still seems like a young child to me now."

"What do you mean?"

"He's just shy. You understand?"

"With women? Is that your meaning?"

"Yes. That is what I mean." Wang did not look at LuLu directly when he spoke. He did not tell her that Jiang's only attachment was to a four-legged creature and that he spent his days hiding from other people, aside from his mother and Hu Ayi.

"Relax. He will find his way—with the right woman. All men do." LuLu turned Wang's face so that she was looking straight into his eyes. She stroked his cheek. "I speak correctly, don't I?"

"Yes. You are not mistaken." Wang pulled LuLu so that she was lying on top of him. "Your sister is lucky to have you."

"I just want to give my little one, my little sister, a complete education. She will have all the opportunities I did not have. Everything else will come later, much later. She will understand that my choices created choices for her, that I did this for her."

Wang stroked LuLu's hair. "We really are so very similar, you know? You and I, we think the same way—we do what we do for our families."

Wang and LuLu fell asleep on the balcony, two strangers entwined in each other's half-truths, keeping each other warm under the Shanghai night sky.

Part Four

New Da Long & Shanghai
China, 1996

Chapter Seventeen

Swans and Scrolls

F loating rainbow fragments, baubles of red, orange, yellow, green, blue, and violet, bumped across the surface of New Lake. The sun had climbed three-quarters of the way to her zenith, and the earth had already warmed enough to send dogs hunting for shade as shore vendors fanned themselves with their caps. Several families milled around the wooden dock and down the skinny slip that extended fifty meters over the water, perpendicular to the eastern shore.

The encroaching lunch hour seemed recognized without the need for a clock. The fiberglass swans on the lake, as if imprinted on a particularly speedy yellow one of their kind, began to paddle for land. The vendors added coals to their grills and began to boil pots of water in preparation for the cooking of purple rice. Freshly sliced brown, nubby mushrooms were thrown into the water. A little while later, as bodies began to emerge from the swan bellies up onto the bobbing dock, the vendors opened their coolers and pulled out basins of water filled with vigorously splashing, silver-scaled fish. Banners with intricately painted, stylized piscine bodies reminded everyone that these creatures were auspicious symbols and encouraged the eating of the famous New Lake carp for one's health. Luck and longevity characters adorned all manner of souvenirs, including T-shirts with cheap iron-on artistic renderings of the New Lake. Judging by the desperate sucking sounds made by their pink-tinged gills as they writhed in the crowded waters of their plastic ponds, the carp were clearly out of both luck and longevity.

Clusters of travelers sat along the lakeshore, eating just-cooked food from paper plates with throwaway, splintered, wooden chopsticks. Fish bones collected in little piles. The vendors knew these were the last of the spring holiday visitors and were happy to have the few stragglers to feed and add to their take. The annual tomb-sweeping festival had brought a good number of tour buses down the Lake Ring Road. Some of the riders, those from these parts, called the road by its local name, New Wang Road, and knew it as an extension of an older and narrower version. But for others, the road and lake held no past and were attractive primarily for their newness: evidence of the new economy having beautified what a natural disaster had once blighted. These latter riders, coming from the cities, were impressed by what The Party had accomplished in the rural hinterlands and enjoyed their visit to the lake as a prequel to New Da Long, the model rural village paternalistically rebuilt and romantically reimagined.

The New Lake covered a large swath of the place once known as Da Long village. That submerged and lost beneath the water's surface were the dreams, homes, fields, and lives of hundreds of villagers was hardly noted by any of today's visitors. There was a small plaque, somewhere along the lakeshore, drilled into a boulder; far from the dock and pier, the plaque's engraved blessing for all that had been lost was seldom read. This was a country that The Party knew how to move along.

Sending her long legs straight out on either side and letting the wheels of her bicycle pick up speed, aided only by gravity, seventeen-year-old Yan tried to hold her breath down the winding length of the mountain road. Her clothing fluttered, and she lifted herself out of her seat, wanting to feel her ever-increasing speed along the full length of her body. On the last turn of the road, New Lake came into view, and she could not stop the air from rushing out of her lungs. Yan pumped the handlebar breaks vigorously, fighting the pull of the grade, determined to stop.

Straddling the now still bike with both feet on the ground, Yan opened and closed her eyes, trying to capture the image with full detail in her mind. Her eyes slowly surveyed the scene; she consciously planted all the colors, movements, and emotions associated with the scene deep into her memory. Yan would not have forgotten this place even if she were thousands of miles away from it. She checked that her books were still secure on the back of her bicycle and then hurriedly pushed off, whizzing down the last section of the mountainside road before carefully merging with Lake Ring Road.

She was late.

Yan propped her bicycle against the wall, next to the one that had definitely arrived on time.

She gathered her books and made her way through the courtyard where she saw Ayi struggling with a heavy basket of freshly washed laundry. "Ayi. Ayi, I can help you?"

"You are kind. But no need. You are late." Ayi wiggled her fingers in a running motion, urging Yan to move faster.

"Come, we will make fast work of it together."

"The teacher and Jiang wait for you. What were you doing?"

"They will be happier to see me being made to wait. I took a moment to study the valley, from up on the mountain."

"Study the valley?" Ayi shook her head. "Yan, you have so much to prepare before you sit for the *gaokao*. The High Test is your priority."

Yan placed her books and pencil case down on a wooden bench under the eaves of the courtyard and joined Ayi in hanging several large sheets onto the line. Though wrung out, the sheets were still heavy with water, and Yan's long arms were soon wet. Being much taller than Ayi, Yan easily hoisted the sheets up and over the line and quickly pegged them securely in place.

"Yan, please do not let me make you tired before your lessons. You are too skinny and need to eat more." Ayi clucked at Yan and gently shooed her away from the basket with the remaining wet sheets.

"You speak the truth. I am too skinny and too tall, and my face is too thin, Ayi, but somehow, I manage." Yan laughed and collected her books. She took the pencil case and tapped it against the top of her head. "My only chance is to grow my brain."

"Silly child. You know there is not even the smallest piece of truth in what you say."

The door to the kitchen opened and AnRan stood in its frame. Her hair was fully down, hanging loose on either side of her face, letting Yan know that the Farmer Master had not yet returned. She wore a pale purple silk robe that reflected the morning light. "Yan, come quickly. Jiang is impatient for you both to start."

"Yes, Wang TaiTai. I am sorry for making you wait."

"No matter. Why is your head not covered? You shouldn't be out in that bright sun. You have lovely skin and do not want to become like a raisin."

Sheets of butcher paper the color of peaches hung from the windows of the first-floor study; each piece was covered in calligraphy of different styles. Dark, square block characters in the modern style stood solidly between curl-filled "running style" characters and more demure, semi-cursive, "walking style" ones. Every character was rendered in black ink, and the uneven hands of their creators were evident in the patchy brushstrokes highlighted by the sunlight.

Teacher Zhou and Jiang sat at the long, wooden table. Neither looked up when Yan entered.

"You are late." The teacher, keeping his back perfectly straight, held a loaded ink brush firmly in the fingers of his right hand.

"You are six minutes late. Teacher Zhou is never late. He arrives every school morning between 8:55 and 8:56 a.m.." Jiang, back stiff and inkless paint brush in hand, was seated next to the teacher and proceeded to mimic the man, who presently sent his brush dancing across a sheet of paper which, being weighed down by two large stones, lay perfectly flat on the table.

"Thank you, Jiang." Yan slipped off her slippers and set her books down on the floor by the door before slipping onto the bench on the far side of Jiang. She focused on Teacher Zhou's movements. His wrist always remained at the same height from the paper, his brush hung perfectly vertical, its nib never touching the paper with too much of an angle, and his painting arm remained relaxed allowing for even strokes on the page.

"Yan, why are you late?" Teacher Zhou's brush did not stop moving.

"I stopped to study the valley midway along the mountainside road." Yan began to prepare her calligraphy supplies.

"Studying or dawdling, which one was it?"

Yan's neck grew tense and warm. "I was observing that the flora and fauna around New Lake, ringing the lower valley, is more diverse than that of the upper valley. The Great Shake, in destroying much of the lower valley, seeded a whole new ecosystem. I was trying to think of why this would be."

"And?" Inky letters flowing from his brush, the teacher did not take his eyes off the paper in front of him.

"I think several factors are likely involved: differential rates of soil erosion and re-composition of the minerals in the growth beds would have resulted after the Great Quake denuded much of the lower valley and churned the earth so violently. Different plants would have found the new growth beds hospitable, and, in turn, they would have become new, or more importantly, different sources of food and shelter for a new complement of animal species than had previously inhabited the area."

"Interesting." The teacher pressed his lips together, and Yan knew he wanted to smile but would not let himself do so. He continued, "Are you ready to start writing the required classical poetry verses? The *gaokao* requires you to recall and write each verse perfectly from memory. Remember the ancient wisdom: to miss by an inch is to fail by a mile. Be more diligent. Arrive on time to your future." Teacher Zhou nodded in the direction of Yan's calligraphy brushes.

Yan's neck relaxed. She reached for a brush and began to write when she let out a shriek, "Oooh! What is that?" The toes of her right foot felt wet and warm, and Yan pulled her legs up and back over the bench, jumping up.

"Bleeh. Bleeh."

Small Snow stuck his head out from under the table and rested it up on the bench next to Jiang, depositing a small pool of drool where Yan had just been seated. Jiang and the teacher stood, understanding the goat's demand, and silently pulled the bench away from the table. With all four of its knees swollen from arthritis and having lost sight in one eye following an infection several years earlier, the animal moved slowly and unsteadily and would not be hurried.

"Come. Come with me." Ayi appeared at the study door and coaxed Small Snow towards her with a baby bottle full of sweetened milk. She eyed Yan with one eyebrow raised before disappearing in the direction of the kitchen.

"Sit, please." Teacher Zhou, already seated once again, resumed the calligraphy lesson.

A slow burn crept along Yan's shoulder blades and down the top of her back. The light in the study took on different hues as the afternoon progressed, and, stretching out her arms, Yan turned them slowly and studied how the color of her skin had changed. Jiang remained poised. He held his brush as instructed, with firm fingers and a light palm. His cursive characters flowered beautifully, without effort. His eyes held still without blinking for long intervals and his face was relaxed. Yan watched him for a while and was grateful that she understood that he could be this way; in the space between agitation and confusion was his peace. Recognizing this had brought her to this point in her life: to her lessons with the teacher, to her companionship with Jiang, to her closeness with Ayi and Wang TaiTai. While one could imagine that these connections had come together to prepare Yan to sit for the *gaokao* in just two months' time, it would be harder to appreciate Small Snow's role in putting this constellation of humans in place.

———————————

Back in the early years after the Great Shake, when the Farmer Master's courtyard school had its brief tenure, Jiang had terrified the village children. He was the shadowy figure always looking out through the kitchen window, never blinking, never joining the lessons, just watching and covering his ears with his hands. The children simply called him The Strange One and, after hearing stories of his violent fits from their parents, they convinced themselves of how wicked he was. Yan feared The Strange One would hurt them all if he wasn't locked up in the house. She outright dismissed her mother's assessment, rendered shortly before Lei had left for Shanghai, that Jiang was just a boy in the same way that she was just a girl.

One afternoon, Teacher Zhou had asked Yan to go to the kitchen and ask Ayi for a large head of white cabbage. Stepping towards the kitchen door, Yan had felt fear rise in her and threaten to come out in a forceful, "No." Even at that young age, she knew it would be a "No" borne of weakness and she disliked this idea. She went to the kitchen door and knocked loudly, readying herself to run should The Strange One be waiting for her.

"Come," Ayi's gentle voice had reassured her. The kitchen, filled with the aromas of spice and sweetness and with the sound of water bubbling, immediately filled Yan with a sense of familiarity. Maybe all country kitchens embraced those they loved via the senses.

"What do you need, Yan?"

"Sorry to interrupt you. Teacher Zhou asked for white cabbage. He wants to show us how one object can be made to share its vital energy with another."

"Is he right?" Ayi teased gently.

"I think so."

"I will have to go to the root cellar and see what there is."

Bamboo steamers, bundles of long onions, a small parcel wrapped in peach-colored butcher's paper, and a column of silky white, paper-thin dumpling wrapper discs brought water into Yan's mouth. Shortly, Ayi would sit down and methodically wrap several hundred perfect pockets of seasoned pork which, in turn, would then be set afloat in a broth flavored with ginger root and dark-skinned mushrooms. Yan pinched one of the long onion stems, listening for the soft crunch to verify freshness; Fang MaMa had taught her this lesson many times. She moved over to the column of wrappers and, driven by her stomach, tried to estimate how many there were. "Ten wrappers to the centimeter times twenty centimeters of column height equals two hundred wrappers which allows for two hundred dumplings, which means ...'"

"Six point six seven dumplings per student or six point eight six if the little girl with the scar above her right eyebrow refuses to eat again." The Strange One's voice, punctuated by the thumping of Small Snow's hoof against the kitchen floor, sent Yan's heart galloping and her body into flight. Tumbling backwards against the kitchen table, grabbing at the air, Yan landed on its surface, crushing several bamboo steamers and sweeping the tender dumpling wrappers onto the floor. Jiang moved towards the mess and Small Snow began trotting around the kitchen, bleating wildly at the chaos. Yan trembled, and a wet warmth trickled down her leg.

Carrying an enormous head of white cabbage in one arm, Ayi returned to the kitchen and grabbed the wayward goat by the scruff of its neck. "What happened? Jiang? Yan?" Right behind her, hair knotted neatly at her nape and with creases of worry across her brow, stood AnRan.

"Sorry! Sorry! I ... I ..." Yan tried to stand up, but her legs shook, and her face was red hot. She could neither bring her eyes to meet Ayi's nor could she move.

Jiang stared at Yan's face for a moment, then he took a dishrag from the table and began wiping the source of Yan's embarrassment off the floor. Ayi, moving towards Jiang, motioned for him to hand her the towel so that she could take over the clean-up, but she was stopped by AnRan who stood mesmerized by her son's behavior: Jiang had looked at Yan and had apparently felt sympathy for her.

In the moment in which Jiang had stared at Yan's face, he had instantly noted exactly how many centimeters apart her eyes were, how long her nose was, and how her mouth was perfectly symmetrical. This was something he did reflexively; he measured and quantified the world around him, all the time looking for meaningful patterns.

Jiang's love for Small Snow was manifest, in part, by his very specific knowledge of the creature. He knew that the goat was exactly fifty-eight centimeters tall at the shoulder, ninety-two centimeters long, that he weighed twenty-nine kilograms, and ate four kilograms of mixed grains, grass and vegetable scraps daily. Jiang's closeness to his mother was such that he knew that on sixty-eight percent of days, AnRan wore her hand-stitched flower robe. Curiosity about his father's work had led the boy to know how many rows of seedlings were planted in the beds of the upper rice terraces. He had even calculated that, if the rows were to be planted on a diagonal, the crop yield for the same plots would be increased by six percent.

Jiang had never shared any of this information with anyone, for no one had ever asked.

What started out as a love for numerical squares and cubes and for raising numbers to the power of four, five, six and so on, in time gave way to harder and more interesting calculations. Looking at any length, be it of a rope or road, Jiang's mind would get to work: how many pieces of fine rope would be needed to create a net big enough, and strong enough, to catch a barrel's worth of New Lake carp? Or, how many paved strips of road, and in what configuration, would suffice to create a highway network extensive enough to ferry all the heartland's crops to the port of Shanghai?

This situation, here on the kitchen floor, did not require such complex calculations. Jiang recognized a very simple, familiar pattern in what he saw. Yan's expression was just like that of Small Snow whenever BaBa was near: scared. And, just as Jiang wanted to protect Small Snow, he now knew he wanted to help Yan by cleaning up her mess.

Yan, sitting in her urine on the Farmer Master's kitchen floor and witnessing Jiang come to her aid, was flooded initially with gratitude for Jiang's kindness and then with shame. She had wrongfully judged and feared Jiang, joining with the other children in calling him The Strange One. That would never happen again. Lei had been almost right. Jiang was not *just* a boy; he was so much more.

———————

"Yan? Yan!" Teacher Zhou's voice clapped against Yan's ears. Calligraphy scrolls lay strewn on the table before her. "Daydreaming will not train you for the *gaokao*." Teacher Zhou had put down his brush. "Today's lesson carries the virtues of the ancestors. Calligraphy is a spiritual gift. To master its form is to master one's own nature through the practice of control and focus. Bringing your head and heart together as one will allow the flowing forth of answers. Being so easily distracted never serves one well."

Jiang nodded as the teacher spoke, as if he were listening very carefully to every word that the teacher said, and continued creating. Yan pulled a fresh piece of butcher's paper onto the table. She secured it with two polished stones, straightened her back, picked up her brush, and started again.

That evening, pushing her bike up the mountainside road, Yan was frustrated with herself; she worked to control her breathing and maintain her pace and to not give over to the aching in her arms and legs. She did not look back over her shoulder to see the New Lake disappear, but rather she focused her eyes straight ahead of her and was thus startled by the sound of the horn.

"Little Face! Little Face! Come. Climb on." Pang and his ten-year-old twin sons, Wei and Tao, approached on a blue, motorized flatbed trike.

"Little Face! Little Face! Little Face!" The boys began to chant Yan's nickname, excited to see their cousin. Yan pulled her books and a calligraphy scroll loose from the back of her bicycle and was glad to allow her uncle to lift it onto the flatbed. She squeezed in next to the boys, happy to smell their sweat, and began to tell them about the rainbow of swans she had seen earlier that day.

———————

Three weeks before Yan was to sit for the most important test of her life, Long was roused by the noise of small voices in the night. They beckoned to the boy to come quietly and to take great care to listen to what they had to share. Long climbed out of his bed and searched for the voices. He looked about the room.

"Down here! We are down here." Long's eyes darted to the floor and began to scan the darkness. He stumbled in the dark to find his school bag and grabbed a flashlight pen from its outer zippered pocket.

"Don't you see us? We are right here. Hurry!"

Meticulously pointing the beam of light to the ground and directing it back and forth, Long found the source of the voices: three black mice, standing on their hind legs atop a peach-colored dais. They had whiskers that twitched in unison and front paws that gesticulated for Long to come closer. Long lay down flat on his belly and put his face level with the talking rodents. He strained to hear what they said and finally tuned into their frequency, understanding their message: he, Long, was not safe in this place and needed to take heed of the predators lurking in the corner.

Long flipped violently on his back and saw two growling goblins. Despite being large in frame and strongly built, and not one who would appear to be easily scared, Long shrank back with a cry. He turned back to the mice for help. He yelped as their bodies disintegrated into black ribbons that fell to the ground in tangles that he could not decipher.

"Help me! Please, help me!" Long screamed.

"Long. Long. We are here. We are here." The goblins approached, calling his name. Long begged them to leave him alone as tears streamed down his face. More and more voices filled his head; the sounds were so horrible, Long pulled at his ears. All the voices knew who he was. Why did he not know who they were? And then, suddenly, the sweetest notes of a song rose out of the cacophony. The melody of a familiar song grew louder and closer until Long knew it to be the voice of his mother singing that all was safe.

It was Yan, not Lei, who was singing to Long. Her words gently evoked a bend in a river, a place their mother had sung into their minds as young children. She strained to keep her voice even, to modulate the panic in her throat, and kept moving closer to Long until she could take him into her arms and bring him back to reality. At first, Long spoke with a rapid and ferociously fearful tenor, almost without pause for breath. He told Yan of the mice disintegrating into coils of black ribbon, pointing to the floor, and then of the two goblins that had filled the corner of the room.

"They were real. They were real!" Long insisted, his words a plea for Yan to believe him.

She tried to soothe him. "It was all a bad dream." She fought to keep uncertainty, the questioning of her brother's mind, out of her voice.

As Long settled back into the quiet reality of the small bedroom in the small house on the side of the mountain, the one he had shared for as long as he could remember with his twin cousins, he grew still and curled himself into a tight ball. "I'm sorry, Yan. I don't know ... I don't understand what is happening to me. I can't make it stop." His words, soft and spoken directly into his chest, were almost impossible for Yan to bear.

MeiLin and Pang, who had rushed to the shared bedroom of Long and the twins, wiped the tears from Wei and Tao's faces, reassuring them that Long meant them no harm.

"We kept telling him we are not goblins. He didn't hear us. It was just like the last time. Why does this keep happening?" The young boys looked to their parents to clear their confusion.

Pang repeated, "It was all a bad dream." He raised his voice over theirs, trying to sound convinced of what he said.

Yan, Pang, and MeiLin silently shared the same thoughts. The voices and visions of Long's dreams were coming more frequently and with increased fervor; they no longer stayed within the confines of dreams, if that was even what they had truly ever been. Now the voices and visions intruded into Long's life with equal frequency during both the days and nights. They had the power to pull Long out of the real world.

Wei and Tao had begun to whine about their boy-cousin being less fun and more bothersome: Long had wandered off in the middle of a game of hide and seek, never coming to find them after many minutes of their being carefully hidden up in the branches of a tree; he had suddenly accused the boys of hiding the wash sponges used on the yard vehicles and had stormed off with the full bucket of wash water; and he now often wanted to eat lunch alone, carrying on conversations with himself.

The room was still, and Yan carefully moved her legs from beneath Long's head; he had fallen asleep, comforted by her song and skin.

MeiLin and Pang had returned to their room once the twins had settled, trusting Yan to keep order. She spent her days learning the taxonomy of organisms, the formulations of higher math, and the measure of ancient poems. She endeavored to order the world around her with the implicit understanding that there was an *order* to be discovered. Long's was a world in which the normal patterns and rhythms of life were fraying—one in which logic was unraveling. Searching Long's sleeping face, Yan wondered, how does one order the disordered?

Above Long's bed, photos of Bo and Lei were taped to the wall in a long line; the couple appeared to be keeping vigil over their sleeping son. The pictures showed how their parents had changed, maybe aged, over many years; a sure transformation that Yan had studied fastidiously in an effort to make Bo and Lei seem familiar to her.

"What would you do," Yan whispered to the squinting version of Bo and Lei standing in front of a very tall building on a sunny day, "to fix Long?" Tears pricked Yan's eyes. She could not possibly know what they would or could do. Other than recognizing them as the ones called "BaBa" and "MaMa," she did not know the people in the pictures, and they did not know her or Long. Lei's letters, along with the photos, came but a few times each year, with short notes and a few Kuai for Yan and Long. Usually, Lei would pen a short description about some aspect of city life that she observed on her way to work: a new building, taller than any she had ever seen, that looked like it was made of green glass or the swarms of bicyclists clogging up the roads. Also included, without fail, would be a line or two about Bo: how he was sleeping, how he was eating, or how his teeth were improving. For Yan, each letter was like a flower that was missing all but a few of its petals.

Looking to the floor where Long had pointed, insisting that she would find the tangles of black, mouse ribbon and the peach-colored dais that had raised the talking rodents off the ground, Yan found only a scroll of peach-colored butcher paper. She had gifted it to her dear brother and recognized her uneven brushwork. Long's chaotic, breaking mind had brought her inked words to life, turning them into imaginary creatures. The calligraphy characters for "Luck" and "Longevity," gracefully rendered in full-bodied loops that exemplified the ancient "running style," lay flat on the floor.

Chapter Eighteen

Cranes and Custard

A flock of tall-necked, metal cranes was gathered on the east bank of the Huang Pu River. Deep in the mud, they worked tirelessly, creating prime real estate out of refuse and topsoil. All around them, high rises filled the Shanghai sky. Growing out of the earth like sun-drenched weeds, the next one growing taller than its neighbor, each high-rise buzzed with human life. At their feet, throngs of mopeds and bicycles swarmed en masse like steely gnats guided by lights. Further along, where the river opened its mouth to the sea, shipping containers clogged the port and trucks waited anxiously to be fed. This urban machinery ran full throttle day and night, guzzling human fuel, consuming human hours by the millions.

For the officious ones charged with governing such a place, division and categorization served as first-order principles. From urban planning to the safeguarding of moral virtues, all civic responsibilities were more easily handled when the people could be divided into the haves and have-nots, the polished and the unpolished, the urban elite and the rural underclass or, as The Party officially proclaimed, the registered, *hukou*-holding city dwellers and the unregistered migrants. In this way, the distribution of all resources and goodwill was rendered simple: the haves kept getting to have, and the have-nots did not. The city's unique nightscape scheme, planned with precision and acute attention to detail by the finest lighting architects, followed this simple math.

Progress made its way to the shanty under the bridge in the form of a new, solo streetlamp. Lighting up only long after the sun was gone, its harsh, glaring white light shone down, forming a singular, circumscribed cone of interrogation, beyond which migrant life remained unlit. Not far from this spotlight, in the direction of the river's ritzy upscale promenade, the Bund was bedazzled with countless strands of neon lights that served no purpose other than to be admired as signs of prosperity.

A cool, evening wind came off the river and rushed down the front of Lei's shirt, prompting her to pull her coat lapels tightly together. With river boats gliding behind her, she closed her eyes and turned her face, letting the deep yellows, reds, and fuchsias of the Bund's night lights fall on her face.

"Hurry! It's too cold for this." Bo stood by Lei's side, spiky strands of hair flying straight up from the top of his head and, with so little on his body to insulate him, he vibrated in the cold. "I have to get up early."

"This is for the children." Lei stomped her feet in place, trying to keep warm.

"No need." Bo sucked his teeth. "Wasting money." Despite his words, he stepped in closer to her and ran his fingers through the front of his hair.

Lei linked her arm through Bo's, trying to share some of her heat. He kept his hands shoved deep into his pockets. "This will be the last one. Show them that you are happy about that."

"Ready now? You two? The flash is exchange charge." The greasy-

haired photographer held up his camera and pointed to the bulb.
"You don't want to risk it being too dark. You choose."

Bo clenched his fists, muttering, "Bastard," under his breath.

"Flash. We want the light so our faces can be seen. Five Kuai?" Lei
knew to establish the price before the man clicked his button.

"Oh no. Ten Kuai with the flash. Light is expensive."

"You are expensive." Bo began to pull away from Lei, but she held him
firm.

"Seven Kuai, or we find someone else to take the photo. You choose."

"Fine, lady. You haggle like a real outsider."

"So do you."

Mist rose from the corner cot, and Lei could just make out Bo's form
under a mound of blankets as she returned late one evening to their
one-room dwelling. He was asleep, despite the cold. Waving her hand in
the air, she felt for the string, pulling it gently to turn on the yellow bulb
above the shaky folding table.

From the other corner of the room, a soft groan answered the light.

"Shh. It is Sister Lei." Shu's voice eased his wife back to sleep. "Lei, eat
quickly now and turn off the light."

"Sorry. I will be fast." Lei sat at the table and saw that Bo had left her
his half-eaten bowl of noodle soup, covered, on the table. Lei removed
the plate covering her own bowl of soup and, though she was tired, and
the others all slept, she decided to indulge herself by warming it. Having
carefully separated the clear soup from the noodles into a small pot, Lei
ignited the single propane burner. A spectacular, blue flame flowered
and quickly brought the broth to a boil. Lei poured the broth back into

her bowl over the cold noodles. She used her chopsticks to wade out the few green stems Bo had left in his own bowl, adding them to her own. Chopsticks in one hand and a soup spoon in the other, sipping and chewing as quietly as she could, Lei composed each mouthful carefully combining the broth, noodles, and a wrinkle of green leaf.

When she was finished, Lei put on her coat and slid her feet back into the boots she had left by the door. Carrying the soup bowls and the pot in a plastic basin, she walked in the dark towards the garishly lit clearing near the end of the shanty row. She joined the line of women standing beneath the only lamp in the entire shanty, waiting for the water pump.

"Lei, your belly is full after a long day?" a woman near the front of the queue called out to her.

"Almost, but it is better than that, it is warm. And yours?"

"No gas to heat anything. Only cold scallion pancakes and pickles tonight. Makes for quick dishes."

Lei looked up at the lamp, squinting into the glare, and in her mind, she tried to take it apart and put it back together. Had hands like hers made such a thing? She followed the thick, black lamppost down to the ground; it stood firm. Would it have gone down in the Great Shake as had its cousins, the skinny posts that held up the bonneted singers in the fields of Da Long? Maybe there were similar lamp posts now in New Da Long. The nation was booming, just as the great leaders had promised, and prosperity demanded that factories, highways, and other modernities be planted in the land of fields, alongside the regular crops. The women of the shantytown would excitedly share news of a shoe factory or a furniture plant that had been built in their hometowns; "Just like a little Shanghai," they'd brag. In Lei's heart, Da Long stood unchanged, just like it had been before she left, with Yan and Long still wanting to hear her voice.

The women were well-lit and silent. One by one, they took their turn at the pump, bringing icy cold water to the surface. They rinsed their dishes and then their hands and mouths. Each one calling out to no one in particular, "Meet tomorrow," making a shared promise before trudging back to her make-shift home.

"Meet tomorrow." Lei rolled the words repeatedly in her mouth, walking slowly back to the folding table with its yellow light. She opened her backpack and removed her cleaner's uniform, hanging it with care over the back of her chair. In nearly ten years, she had only owned one uniform and had never been docked for poor appearance. The office building she cleaned housed the city's largest bank and the headquarters of Shanghai's third-largest textile exporter. She was proud to clean such a place and prepare it each night for the work of the next day; it was her little contribution to her country.

She reached deeper into the bag and pulled out her purse and a paper bag; she fingered through her purse, past her bus pass, past a one Kuai note and two ten Kuai notes, until she found the small, square photograph encased in a protective cellophane wrapper. The photographer had been too impatient to zoom in, and the couple looked tiny compared to the river and the buildings on its banks that sprawled out behind them. She studied the two people staring out at her and wondered how much they had changed over the years. Bo's face, even bathed in neon lights, looked more deeply creased and his body more stooped, but his eyes were the same. He stared out at the world, hard and demanding. Lei was stronger than before; grueling work had shaved her leaner, but she remained nonetheless solid. She too looked straight out of the picture, smiling and holding Bo tightly. She and Bo were standing so close to each other, that Bo's hair, whipped by the wind, was obscuring part of Lei's face.

From the paper bag, she pulled out an envelope and a clean sheet of paper. Wanting to turn the light off quickly, Lei penned just a few lines to Yan and Long, "The city has installed a new light at the end of our lane. It is very bright and makes washing up in the night more convenient. BaBa and I will be home soon after so long and will share so many more stories then. BaBa sleeps well in preparation for the journey home. Until it is time for us to meet again." She folded the message around the photograph, added the two ten Kuai notes from her purse, and sealed it in the envelope which she addressed. She kissed it before setting it on the table, pulling off the light, and joining Bo beneath the blankets.

Bo's feet were warm against Lei's, and she was thankful he did not pull them away.

In the silence, she could hear her voice loud and clear in her head, singing out to Yan and Long.

Rising early, before the sun, Bo climbed over Lei and pulled on his work overalls, cursing their dampness. His boots, muddy and well-worn, chafed his bare feet, but he could not be bothered with finding socks in the dark. As he opened the door to leave, he felt his way along the wall to the folding table and ran his hands over its surface, knowing Lei would have left the envelope there for him.

The streetlamp was already out, but Bo could have found his way out of the shanty with his eyes closed. Several dogs barked as he approached the bus depot gate, and Bo reached his hand out to let them sniff his identity. He found the others gathered in the workers' lounge, a tiled room with few furnishings and posters featuring coyly smiling, semi-nude women taped to the walls. Cigarette smoke filled the room; Bo inhaled, pleased to be smoking for free.

"Fang Bo, come. Eat now." One of the men pushed a bag of oily pastry sticks towards Bo.

"Thank you, but I am not hungry." Bo sucked in another deep breath.

"What? Are you a girl watching her figure?"

"No, It's my—"

"Aiyah. Fang Bo, you need to prepare to go home. You need to get fat and look prosperous. Eat, now."

Bo accepted the fried dough stick and began to chew on it slowly. Already cold, the dough stick was hard, and its oil clung to Bo's mouth.

"How long have you been here, Old Fang? We hear you have a pretty daughter waiting for you at home."

"Too long. It is true, I have a fine daughter." Bo paused. He rarely spoke, but on this morning, he felt his tongue loosen and felt the need to add, "I also have a son who is stronger and taller than any other in our village." Even as Bo spoke of Long's growth, he remembered both of his children as little ones splashing in the waters of a pond that no longer existed.

"Is that true?" The men feigned surprise as they teased Bo's rare show of pride. "You didn't bring them here with you? Such fine children might have become corrupted without their father's hand."

"Not mine. My daughter is waiting for me to come home and arrange her marriage, and my son will work the government land that we were granted. They understand the importance of the ancestors, of their *lao-jia*."

"Humph! These days, those young people all want to come to the city, to give up the old home and even old ways. More opportunity."

"They will stay in Da Long!" Bo offered too quickly. "They don't need to come to this place. I kept them away." Bo wiped his oily fingers into his hair and became anxious for his stomach. He immediately regretted saying anything.

Bo wrapped the remainder of the dough stick in a paper napkin for later and was about to shove it into his front, chest pocket when he remembered Lei's letter was there. He pulled it out and stared at the first line of the address: "New Da Long."

"New! Humph!" Bo muttered to himself as he stuffed the envelope back in his pocket.

What would he find in *New* Da Long? What changes possibly warranted the addition to its name? A new town square, a new school, and a few roads had been slapped together after he left. That didn't make the place new. New buildings were going up all around him, but Shanghai didn't change to *New* Shanghai. He had heard rumors that the roads had allowed riches—refrigerators, black and white televisions—to trickle into the heartland along with some vices, including drugs and a few plasma sellers looking to leech off desperate farmers, but he didn't believe it. No one ever gave specific names about the drugs and such. Da Long was still his *laojia*, where food was grown that fed the nation and where his children were waiting for him.

Bo made his way into the yard.

The other men had started soaping the buses and Bo grabbed a hose. He braced for the back-spray from the nozzle, and, when cued by the others, he began to rinse down the first vehicle. Soaked through to the skin, the men hopped in place to keep warm. As pools of suds collected around their feet, they grabbed towels and started drying the buses. At the right time, two of the men came and picked Bo up, as he was the smallest of them, and threw him up on the hood of the first bus. From there, Bo scampered up the windshield and onto the bus roof which he began to work with two toweled hands.

For the better part of a decade, Bo's body had been tossed onto one bus after another, on every morning of every week, year after year. He had moved thousands of miles from home, lived with strangers—not just Shu and his wife in one room, but legions of migrants from all over the place crammed into the shantytown, sleeping and pissing on top of one another—and worked a degrading job divorced from the land, all to get back to Da Long. He had paid off, bit by painful bit, his debt to the Farmer Master. Somewhere in *New* Da Long, near the base of the mountainside road, there was a bare, small lot of government land with not a single brick laid upon it. That was what the mighty, modern government had deemed his due restitution after The Great Shake. He had given himself to this city in exchange for being put back to square one. Bo shook his head. All around him the *new* China supposedly grew, evidently even spreading all the way to *New* Da Long. But, for Bo, there was nothing new.

Even the envelopes Lei used twice or thrice a year to send a photo home, as if pictures could substitute for the real thing, were unchanged. At the post office after work, Bo counted his money carefully, checking his arithmetic twice before filling out the remittance form. He then placed a stamp on Lei's letter and considered it for some time. He asked the postal clerk for a pen and scratched out "New" from the face of the envelope.

Walking quickly away from the post office, through the narrow back alleys of the hutongs, Bo saw a collection of painted street ladies in front of a barbershop. He crossed the alley, not wanting to catch the "love" diseases that spread through their sort; he did not notice their wedding revelry.

Bo did not see that in the center of the short-skirted, high-heeled grouping was a sad-looking couple dressed in traditional, matrimonial, red silk robes emblazoned with matching golden phoenixes.

Ash tumbled down the front of the groom's clothing, falling from the half-smoked cigarette perched between his visibly dry lips. He tried to push the girls back, not wanting any of them to touch him; he already had lip imprints in two different shades of pink on his right temple. The bride's full mouth was painted a startling shade of red, and her face powdered a stark white, almost as if to cast the whole scene as a comedic ruse of some sort. She took the groom by the arm and helped him into the barbershop, telling the others to leave them alone.

"Come. Maybe you need to rest." The bride spoke softly, but without a hint of tenderness, as she guided the groom to the first room off the rear corridor, the one next to the bathroom. The bride had seen the room only once before, but she was still surprised at how different it was from the back rooms further down the hall. Those spaces were dingy and bare, outfitted only for their primary function of selling sex. This was a room for living. A high-backed sofa with tufted upholstery and soft, hand-embroidered cushions filled the far corner and was surrounded by books, newspapers, and popular magazines. Dark wooden end tables flanked both ends of the sofa and held up a pair of painted ceramic-based lamps with oversized teal, silk shades. Before stepping into the room, the bride slipped off her shoes and used one free foot to help the groom kick off his sneakers. She relished her first steps across the threshold, letting the soles of her feet sink into the thick rug. Taking in the scene, the bride was momentarily filled with a sense of accomplishment. Not a single wall was bare, from an immense curio cabinet filled with hundreds of glass and porcelain figurines to the poetry-filled scrolls that graced the far corner, hanging just above the sofa. Here was her new world, filled with endless items to examine and reimagine with pencil and paper. Even the deep windowsill was occupied by a half dozen flowerpots, each one home to a different variety of exquisite orchid.

"Girl, let's bed now." The groom pulled at the front of his ceremonial jacket, standing next to the large, four-poster, wooden canopied bed. With its delicate carvings and gracefully thin spires, the bed was a work of art that harkened to the days of the Ming, but, for the bride, seeing her groom waiting for her, it reminded her of the cages at the city zoo.

"Remember. We have an understanding. I am your wife, not 'girl.'"

"Yes. You are the clever one. We have a deal, and I will not forget any of it." The old man patted the top of the bed.

"Of course you will not." The bride looked at her purse sitting over on the sofa table and visualized the neatly folded, stamped, yellow piece of paper that it held. As if reading her thoughts, Lao Fu patted the bed more forcefully, "LuLu, you have your Shanghai *hukou*, your city citizenship, and I have my wife, my TaiTai."

"Yes … TaiTai." LuLu swallowed the words and began to fiddle with the buttons of her qi pao. "Let's go over the rules one more time. To be clear." She did not look at the old barber-pimp.

"Is it not too late for that?"

"I just want it all to be clear. I am your legal wife, and you will recognize that. I do not work for you anymore, not in the way of the past. I will cook and clean as I have always done, but I will also help you run the business. The girls will work hard for me, and I will ensure that we are not cheated of what we are due from any of them."

"And?"

"I will service your needs."

"As I demand."

"Yes. But only with my hands."

"Those will suffice for my needs. They are well practiced." Lao Fu climbed into the bed. "Okay, LuLu TaiTai, let us celebrate our wedding night. Let me see all of you."

LuLu wiped her hands with a napkin and climbed out of the bed. Lao Fu lay on his back, shriveled and naked from the waist down and already sleeping. Covering all of him but his head with a sheet, LuLu pretended he was not there and went to recline on the sofa. She lifted her legs straight up in the air and opened and closed them repeatedly, intermittently forming a deep "V" shaped aperture through which she focused her sight. The figurines in the curio cabinet caught her eye.

The menagerie of animals and human figures seemed trapped behind glass, pleading to be freed; LuLu obliged them, bringing a handful of creatures back to the sofa table. She sank down onto the carpet, enjoying the feel of it under her naked backside, and arranged the figures on the table in a perfect circle. She pulled a cigarette from her purse and lit it. Holding her new Shanghai *hukou* up to the lamp light, she saw her new name officially typed in blue ink: Fu Lu.

Studying her new surroundings, LuLu could see that the room, though pretty, was stale. Dust motes sprinkled the air like the remnants of a firecracker. The wallpaper seams were visibly lifting, and yellow water stains seeped from the ceiling down the top part of the walls. The pillows smelled of cigarette smoke, and the sofa table magazines were over twenty years old. The room had been decorated by the first Fu TaiTai. LuLu immediately felt sorry for the woman whom she had never met, surmising that her predecessor could not have possibly known how this place, filled with items chosen with love and longing, would be used in future days. LuLu's work life had begun in this room, the only other time she had ever been here, as it had for all the girls, with an "audition" for her once-pimp-now-husband.

LuLu walked over to a free-standing, full-length mirror. A woman's robe hung over one corner and there were several pairs of heels clustered around the mirror's base. None of the items belonged to LuLu, but she didn't feel any shame in having them remain. She looked at her body and ran her hands over her breasts and thighs and thought of how many men had touched her without knowing anything about her. Now that was going to be different. The old pimp was on a leash. She would let him bark and then stroke him to calmness, but he would never bite her again. And Wang, her forever client by choice—he was the only one she planned to keep for now. When she had told him of her deal with Lao Fu, of her marriage, he had laughed out loud with admiration, "Ah, LuLu, you are a clever, clever girl." They understood and satisfied one another. For LuLu, that was enough.

On the morning after her wedding, the new Fu TaiTai woke while it was still dark. She stretched out her new body, mindful not to touch the one beside her. She poured a glass of sweet soy milk and plated two egg custard tarts that had gone uneaten during the previous day's short-lived wedding celebration. She placed these items on a round, lacquer tray that she left on the sofa table for Lao Fu, moving so softly as to not awaken his sleeping form. Two additional tarts she wrapped individually in bright red wedding napkins and placed carefully into her purse. LuLu dressed neatly in a tailored, European-styled, office dress and modest, cream leather pumps, pulled her hair into a tight bun, and smoothed clear jelly over her lips. Making her way down the alley as the sun was beginning to rise, she was greeted warmly by the seamstress who sat on her front stoop sipping cautiously from a steaming tea jar, "Good morning, Fu TaiTai."

"Good morning." LuLu reached into her purse and gave the old woman one of the tarts. "Still fresh enough. Please enjoy it."

"Too rich for me. But I will keep it. I know to take small bites."

Even at this early hour, the Shanghai Number Three Hospital was overwhelmed by would-be patients waiting to register. LuLu barely made her way through the front door, pushing her way into a crowd. A mosaic of bodies—some standing, some lying down, some curled over, others leaning on others—decorated the floor. Flies buzzed around, drawn to the smell of sickness and discarded food. The drab yellow light combined with the smell of warmed urine forced LuLu to cover her mouth with her hand.

A heavy-lidded man approached Lulu. "Lady, my ticket is for the number eight spot in the queue. You will have your needs tended to for certain. Only forty Kuai."

"I don't need your help," LuLu spoke through her fingers.

"Too many people here. The line started forming at midnight and it already counts all the way to three hundred and seventy-four. You have come too late to get an entry ticket for today." The man ran his eyes over LuLu and appeared impressed by her stockings. "The ticket girls don't care how you look. It only goes by the numbers. Number eight, it's a lucky number, you know? Forty Kuai is nothing when you are sick." The ticket scalper moved in closer to LuLu, and she could smell spirit on his breath. "I can help you, lady."

The man was desperate to sell her the only thing he had, the space occupied by his physical being, something that did not even belong to him. "I appreciate your offer, but I have a Shanghai *hukou*. I will be called in first."

As if put out, the man's mouth fell open. "What in heaven! You could have said. Aiyah!" He looked LuLu over one more time and then, resigned to her being a waste of his energies, he moved towards the door to look for a fresh customer.

By the time LuLu made it to the bridge road, the dinner hour had long passed. She held the folds of her dress skirt tightly to her body as she came down the embankment.

"Pretty LuLu, why so serious today? Look at the proper-lady dress."

"She is a married woman now, a TaiTai with an Old Man. Isn't that right?"

"Still, why so? Too old for you. Na!"

"Which one, the dress or the husband?" The shanty women howled with laughter. One of them deftly reached into the barrel fire and pulled out a steaming sweet potato, tossing it quickly to another woman who caught it between the two halves of a piece of foil.

"One or two today, LuLu?"

"Just one. I have just come from the hospital and have no appetite." LuLu warmed her hands on the foil wrapped potato. "I was finally able to get the right medicine, the real stuff, with my *hukou*."

"Ahh! That place is full of crooks, better known as doctors. I would never go there. You must pay the staff under the table even with a *hukou*, and everyone still dies." All the other women immediately fell silent and looked down at the ground. "How much extra did they make you pay? How thick was your red envelope?"

"Too thick." LuLu pushed the potato into her purse and paid the woman quickly. "But it worked. The doctor gave me the pills."

"You paid too much for them, no doubt."

"Yes, what you say is not wrong. But I have them."

The tarp and tie cords across YuZhen's doorway had been replaced with a proper door and lock a year ago, back when she was still working and just after she had become scared in a general way that was not easy to pinpoint. Despite this, LuLu was able to push the door open and enter the home without difficulty. A singular, overhead bulb had been left on and a collection of partially eaten sweet potatoes sat on the dresser and on the red plastic stool that had been placed next to the mattress. LuLu grabbed a plastic bag that she found partially filled with garbage—fragments of foil, a still full carton of milk tea, and a fermented soy pudding container—and began to collect the uneaten food from around the room.

YuZhen lay stone still on the mattress, unaware of her visitor, and as LuLu moved closer to her, she could smell the rot rising off the mattress and struggled not to vomit. LuLu sat down on the red stool, took the egg custard tart from her purse, and placed it in her lap. She then crushed one of the just-acquired pills in her palm and sprinkled the powder over the top of the tart, thinking it could easily pass for baker's sugar.

"YuZhen? YuZhen? I have a treat for you. It's your favorite." YuZhen did not move. LuLu put her hand on her friend's shoulder and immediately withdrew it. The feeling of barely covered bone sent a chill down her spine. YuZhen startled awake and began to cough, and, though the cough rocked the totality of YuZhen's frail body back and forth, LuLu was relieved.

"Water. May I have some water?"

"Of course," LuLu grabbed a plastic bottle of water from the dresser and helped YuZhen take a few sips. "I got your medicine. I've put it right here on this lovely tart."

"I couldn't eat all of that."

"You must. You used to eat these three at a time."

"That was before." Lifting a shaky finger to her mouth, YuZhen slowly opened it as wide as she could, grimacing at the pain coming from its cracked corners. The soft, pink skin of YuZhen's mouth was pocked with dozens of lesions, some crusted over and others raw-red with ulceration. LuLu tried not to gasp. YuZhen continued, "They are all over my body. Just like with Rong ... before he was gone from this earth. I think it *is* the Love Disease, the one in the blood. Rong said it wasn't. He didn't want to admit it. Do you remember, LuLu?"

"Shh. Here, please try to take a small bite." LuLu broke off a tiny piece of the medicated tart and tried to push it past YuZhen's lips and in between the rows of darkened teeth. YuZhen slowly moved her jaw, trying to work her mouth, but cried out in pain. Globs of yellow custard and shards of crust fell down her chin.

"I'm sorry, LuLu." Speaking caused YuZhen's tender mouth to explode with pain and she winced with each word.

"Shhh. It's okay. You don't speak, just rest. Let me tell you something funny. You know I'm a married woman now? I married the old bastard, Lao Fu."

YuZhen's eyes slowly popped open with surprise.

"You always told me he wasn't that bad and that he always pays. What more could I want? Right?" LuLu stroked YuZhen's hair. "You were right."

"No. Ddd ..." YuZhen's face scrunched up. "Dddu."

"Oh, yes. Master Du. Master Du told me to think outside of 'today's walls.' I don't know. Somehow, I feel like I'm even deeper inside those walls right now."

YuZhen half-laughed, nodding her head slowly and closing her eyes. She began to shiver as she drifted into sleep.

LuLu found YuZhen's wash basin and walked down to the pump, taking her place in the line of women waiting for water. In the light of the streetlamp, she could see each of the women's faces and bodies. Different in shape and size, some pretty, some homely, young, old, bent over, straight-backed, each one was waiting for her share of what the city offered her. All these migrant bodies were given in their totality in exchange for some small ration.

LuLu squeezed her eyes closed in anger.

Millions of migrant body parts, swept by waves of water onto the eastern coast of the nation, floated before her. Disparate body parts came together to form whole, deformed bodies. Tears started to burn under her lids, and LuLu tried to will the images away, but she could not stop seeing legions of migrants lining up to give everything they had, but receiving so little in return. Bodies paid for providing sex by the quarter hour and feel-good pills bobbed up and down. Needles floated about, piercing veins and extracting red gold.

And then came an intruder, small and unseen, that worked its way into those plasma tubes and slid through those needles into the veins of the migrants. This intruder worked its way triumphant, for just like the city, it had dominion over the migrant body. The invader made itself at home in these desperate bodies and used the machinery it found to multiply and feed itself. LuLu felt herself shaking as she saw Rong covered in sores, stricken with the Love Disease that authorities refused to acknowledge. City folk derided the condition as the disease of the drug users, or of the love-for-sale girls, or of the filthy migrants who pimped their own plasma. All those bodies dismantled, vital organ by vital organ, their energy forces and immunity cells being stolen by the thief. And, like the unlit, low-rent shanty districts, these bodies were not worthy of saving, restoring, or rebuilding.

In the white light of the streetlamp, LuLu's face glistened with streams of tears. She made no attempt to wipe her face, and the others made no attempt to look away.

Upon returning to the shanty home of her only friend, LuLu sponged YuZhen clean, combed and braided her hair, and dabbed clear jelly on the corners of her mouth. She shed her own clothing and put her dress on YuZhen, bringing beaded sweat to her own upper lip. Then LuLu lay down on the mattress next to YuZhen and wrapped her arms and legs around her, trying to give the ever-colder woman all of her warmth.

Chapter Nineteen

Legacy Bearers

"Wah! Why that fat, huh?"

"Who? You speak of who?"

"You."

"And you? Why so thick? Your stomach is really that big now? Your old man is keeping you happy!" Hong emphasized her words by poking her index finger into the softness around Min's abdomen.

Min, laughing, grabbed Hong's finger, and pushed it away, "He just feeds me all of those fine fruits that he sells. The best around, as you must know."

"Bah!" Hong flapped the air. "The second best, right after my Mister's. Look. Come closer and look at these monkey heads. Just this morning they came, all the way from Hainan. They are so sweet!"

"Monkey heads?" Min eyed the custard apples her sister proudly displayed. "How did he get those?"

"*Guanxi!*"

"Connections? What connections? Which horse's ass is your old man patting?"

"I don't know. I don't care. I just enjoy." Hong spread open the handles of her white, plastic market tote and pushed it up towards Min's face. "Smell these. Too sweet."

Min reached one hand into the bag and licked her lips as she pulled out a head-shaped custard apple. She ran her fingers over its pebbled surface, suddenly losing her finger into a deep opening. "Aiyah! What is this?" Min sucked the creamy white flesh off her finger and spat a shiny black seed onto the ground, "Why is it so bruised up?" She used her finger to scoop more sweetness out of the fruit's center.

"The pretty ones sell. The ugly ones get left behind." Hong broke a piece of the monkey head free and sucked it clean of flesh.

"More people are coming." Min pointed her chin towards the square.

"There is only one person you are interested in seeing." Hong looked at her sister and puckered her lips.

It was Min who now swatted at the air and rolled her eyes. "Not me. No need. I have a man."

"You would make room for another if it were him."

Hong and Min both looked over towards the market side of the square. A low platform, swaddled in shiny red bunting, had been erected overnight and currently Teacher Zhou, the Farmer Master, and the Provincial President occupied the only three chairs at its center.

"Not now. He's strange. Never married." Min's voice dropped to a murmur as she turned her eyes away from the teacher.

"Never married. What a wonder." Hong shook her head.

Min tried to pull the last custard apple from Hong's bag. "Probably sick. You know, prefers other little rabbits like himself."

"Enough." Hong pulled the bag closed. "You are already fat enough. Hurry. Let's find our spots."

The heat of the sixth month was heavy, and Teacher Zhou resisted the urge to peel his thighs up off the seat; he occasionally rearranged the length of his robe. He took several quick sips of water from a plastic bottle that he then slipped behind his chair, as if not wanting to admit he was thirsty. The Farmer Master and the Provincial President smiled while gesticulating towards the square, which grew louder with the din of the gathering crowd.

New Da Long's central square measured a lucky eighty-eight meters by eighty-eight meters and was comprised of thousands of pieces of tiny, grey, cement rectangles. Each one had been meticulously placed in accordance with the design provided by the "Rebuilding and Reimagining" subcommittee of the Great Quake Relief committee, whose members reported to the provincial authorities who in turn answered to the Capital.

The completion of the square had taken Wang Construction's team of thirty men several months to complete and had required more than just the Capital's funds.

Working to level the earth in preparation for the laying of the cement tiles, the workmen of Da Long had come across scattered objects that refused to simply be crushed flat. Random pieces of brick and glass were expeditiously removed in the quest for a blemish-free surface. However, work came to a complete standstill on the morning that one of Wang's workers discovered a tiny set of teeth. The burials for the children lost had long passed, but the grieving had not. That these teeth had been found alone, separated from their earthly body and unidentifiable by loved ones, brought anger and pain back to all of the men. They refused to continue their work. None was able to set foot in the square, let alone clear it bare.

For many weeks, villagers gathered daily to cry at the dirt lot and the wheels of progress halted. Village officials initially participated in the show of grief, even genuinely so, but over time, they began to desperately hope for the time of re-mourning to pass. "Rebuilding and Reimagining" needed, per the provincial authorities, to stay on schedule. Tiny altars of mounded fruit, plastic gold coins, paper money, and incense sticks appeared around the perimeter of the would-be plaza. The Farmer Master, in his capacity as the construction company owner, was called upon by his fellow village officials to get his men back to work and avoid provincial-level reprisals. Wang watched his workers stand still and silent. Not held to the earth by their shovels and rakes, they appeared unmoored and ghost-like.

The Farmer Master's anger had been slow to rise and did not burn in a way that would have been consistent with his belief that all men needed to constantly prove their utility. For, in recent times, he had found himself consumed, almost plagued, by an unrelenting fear.

As he had walked the freshly paved roads of the New Da Long, he was aware of how his stature and monies had multiplied. His ability to harness men's labor behind his own purposes had allowed him to profit from all manner of government-funded reconstruction contracts. The new school, the new two-room health center, the first travel lodge and restaurant in the region, and the New Market were all structures put up by men whose livelihoods he controlled. While the buildings were spare in detail, constructed from the same red brick, single-storied and only memorable for the functions they served, Wang himself grew in reputation and detail. In the talk of the villagers, Wang's contribution to the New Da Long was acknowledged with flourish and a sense of admiration. And while this was all quite pleasing, Wang was acutely aware that not a single structure bore his name. His son remained practically mute in the presence of strangers and was still without a woman and, more importantly, without Wang's grandson. Who would be there to speak of Wang's cunning in the future, to remind people of who had "rebuilt and reimagined" the village beneath the quake?

Legacy fulfillment consumed the Farmer Master's every moment as did the need for the next Little Wang, who would someday become the New Farmer Master with shoulders broad enough to carry the weight of his grandfather's legacy. Watching his men cry, on the edge of the stalled New Da Long square, Wang understood that the men wept for those who would have remembered their names in time to come. The men were haunted by the loss of their legacy bearers.

Knowing all of this, Wang had gathered the men around him and unfolded a handkerchief just pulled from the pocket of his shirt, the one that lay over his heart. He revealed several tiny teeth, polished to resemble shiny pearls. "These are not to be discarded or buried, but to be remembered." He looked around him, looking into the eyes of the men. "I pledge to each of you that these will be placed at the heart of a memorial sculpture that I will gift to the people of the village." The men stared vacantly at Wang, listening with the politeness afforded any Party member. Wang continued, "It will stand here at the center of New Da Long and have the family name of every lost child chiseled into its base. We must build this square to be worthy of our legacy. Tell me, am I right?"

Before that moment, before hearing these words, the men, many of whom had worked for the Farmer Master since the beginning of their working days, would have been surprised if he could recall them by name. Now his voice was filled with passion, and his words spoke to their intimate pain. Spontaneous tears and cries of agreement sprang forth. The Farmer Master patted the upper arms of the men on either side of him, starting a chain reaction of arm clapping that connected all of them through touch and spurred them on like a team of horses tethered by a single harness. The rallying cry— *Jia You! Jia You! Jia You!* - "Add oil! Add oil! Add oil!" —rang out, spurring the men to pick up their tools and resume working. The square was completed in record time, and Wang's "finesse" with the workers was noted by the relevant authorities, even those seated as far off as the capital.

———

Currently, Wang continued to admire the square as the Provincial President walked to the small, wooden podium at the front of the stage. Wary of losing power during his speech, he was mindful not to trip on the microphone wire that, running just in front of the chairs, connected to an extension cord that continued off the back of the stage and disappeared into the entrance of the New Market. Several vendors had already complained to him about losing their perishable goods to the mercurial refrigeration system which suffered power outages several times a week.

Barely cresting the podium, the Provincial President stealthily stepped up on a plastic stool that had been rendered invisible to the crowd.

"Everyone, welcome to this very important day. We will recognize the achievement of our Old Family, thanking our ancestral benefactors for the great honor bestowed on our humble, yet mightily patriotic province." The Provincial President paused; the audience members took the cue and clapped loudly. "It is only right that we accept the honor brought to us by our own children in this place that honors those children not here with us today." Reaching his arm out to draw the crowd's attention to the other side of the square, the Provincial President gestured to an engraved monolith which, standing taller than the average man and wider than three shoulder to shoulder, could not have been missed by anyone new to these parts. Even from across the square, the engraved character for "WANG" was visible, beneath which several hundred characters fell in silent rows. Turning his body slightly around, the Provincial President clapped his hands in the Farmer Master's direction, effectively directing the crowd to acknowledge the memorial's benefactor.

The Farmer Master looked out on the crowd, his gaze sweeping past AnRan and Ayi, who were clapping obediently, to the far right and close to the stage. There, Jiang stood swaying from side to side with his hands covering both ears; he shook his head in disapproval and his eyes darted about. Yan, looking straight ahead, simply placed her hand on Jiang's shoulder, eliciting no clear, visible response. As the clapping began to cease, Jiang's swaying slowed, though he continued to cover his ears. When the crowd had once again fallen silent, Yan pulled her hand off Jiang's shoulder, and he came to a standstill and dropped his hands to his sides.

Bo, seeing the interaction between his only daughter and the Farmer Master's strange son, strained his fisted hands against the liners of his pant pockets and refused to clap. Lei, who stood next to him in the first row of spectators, clapped her hands softly together, as if in a trance. A peach tree blossom corsage made of fabric, with dangling congratulatory gold ribbons, hung awkwardly from her jacket lapel. Yan's hands, trembling with excitement when pinning it in place just minutes before the ceremony commenced, had not pinched the corsage's tiny pin through enough fabric to secure it steadily in place. Lei had let hers be and had helped Yan successfully pin similar corsages on AnRan and Fang MaMa.

"To award two Love of Country Scholarships right here in New Da Long is my deepest privilege. Knowing that these fine scholars can choose to pursue their studies at the nation's greatest universities is a testament not only to the success and wisdom of the 'Rebuilding and Reimagining' campaign, but also to the generous benevolence of our dear fathers in Beijing." Once again, the Provincial President took an extended pause and waited for the crowd to fill it in with exuberance and adulation. "Of course, let me mind my manners and show unending gratitude to the venerable Teacher Zhou, whose guidance helped bring these young ones to this pinnacle of achievement."

Teacher Zhou stood and bowed his head deferentially to the Provincial President and then to the crowd.

"To Wang Jiang and Fang Yan, who achieved the most success on the *gaokao,* more than all the students in the entire province, I present gold medals."

Even as the crowd erupted in applause, the whooping cheers of Pang, Wei, and Tao could be heard clearly, "Yan! Yan! Yan! Jiang! Jiang! Jiang!"

Fang MaMa's gnarled hands clicked against each other, following the beat of her son-in-law's and grandsons' cheers.

MeiLin and Long stood just beyond the edge of the crowd, far in the back. Long had asked his aunt to stay on the "outside" of those gathered as it was too hot to be closely surrounded by so many bodies. He was too ashamed to tell her that, in truth, he feared what voices he might hear amid so many strangers; he was determined to not humiliate his family, especially not Yan, on this day of celebration. MeiLin offered her hand to Long as the cheers grew louder. Long was happy to take it, to feel it, and to be tethered to the real world.

Yan started to ascend the wooden steps at the side of the stage, but Jiang did not move. He covered his ears again and began to tremble. Yan held out her hand to him, but he did not take it.

The Farmer Master looked over impatiently as Jiang stalled at the bottom of the steps; the Provincial President frowned, and then, seeming to remember the crowd, tried to smile in Jiang's direction.

In a flash, Wang and Bo were struck with the same question. How did blood mixing work? How had each man's seed combined with his wife's egg to create these next-generation legacy bearers? Bo and Lei were, respectively, neither handsome nor beautiful, neither well-spoken nor nimble of feet, and yet here was exquisite Yan, brimming with beauty, a writer of poetry, and endowed with grace and poise. Awkwardly standing next to her was Jiang, who, though several years older than Yan, looked like a frightened child. He was, to all who had pondered on the issue, the confusing and unlikely product of the cunning and firm-bodied Farmer Master and his elegant and eloquent wife.

Wang looked at AnRan and immediately saw her hands betray her; weakly held out to her son, they trembled with anxiety and uncertainty. If he had scrutinized her long ago, before they were tied together by agreement, certainly he would have sniffed out her defects, would have chosen a different egg, and would have had a different legacy bearer.

"Three hundred and eighty-six. No. No. Three hundred and seventy-four ... No! ... Three hundred and eighty-one!" Grasping his head, Jiang was now on the stage calling out his estimates of the crowd size as his brain processed the sound waves painfully vibrating against his eardrums.

This being the first day on which the Provincial President had met the younger Wang, he found himself horrified by the sight of the man-child writhing on the stage, spewing forth random numbers.

It was only Yan who understood the basis of Jiang's calculations, and she tried desperately to tamp the crowd down into silence. As Jiang's voice was grotesquely amplified through the microphone over the multitude of gasping and laughing faces, The Provincial President looked desperately towards the older Wang. The Farmer Master, hot sweat trickling down his back, picked up his foot and crushed the joint between the microphone wire and the extension cord, effectively silencing his son and bringing the ceremony to an end.

———————

Bo stared out at the New Lake without seeing it, his back turned to his family who were gathered noisily around a wooden picnic table.

"Strange ... so strange! No manners! Spoiling the most auspicious day like that." Fang MaMa shook her head. "It should not be ... not be allowed. I ..." The translucent eye of a perfectly steamed New Lake carp stared at the old woman. "Fresh! Look at that, son. Noth ... nothing like that in Shanghai." Bo winced at his mother's slurred and halting speech. He tried to remember what she had sounded like before he had left, but the sounds of her smacking lips made that impossible. His hand tingled. Without looking at her, without touching her, he could sense the cold, sunken skin of the now-collapsed side of her face. Bo had not been here when Fang MaMa had suffered the stroke that rendered her thus, just as he had not been here when his daughter decided to sit for the *gaokao*. Important moments that were simply lost.

"Let's ..." Fang MaMa searched for her next word, "... eat." A sliver of saliva escaped down the drooping corner of her mouth.

"Of course, MaMa, while it is hot!" Pang spoke to Bo's back. "Come, brother. Come and sit. We are celebrating with this fine fish."

Bo took a deep drag off his cigarette and flicked the butt into New Lake; he watched as it bobbed passively on the water's surface. He sat down at the table, saying nothing and looking at no one.

"The head for the head." Pang used his chopsticks to sever the fish head free and began to place it on Fang MaMa's paper plate.

"No! For ...for Bo." Fang MaMa pulled her plate back towards her.

Pang redirected the fish head to Bo's plate and gave him a wide smile. Lei circled the gathering, scooping servings of purple rice onto each plate, inhaling the nutty steam released with each scoop.

"Auntie, more."

"Also, for me." Wei and Tao asked their Auntie Lei for extra servings of rice; she happily obliged them, enjoying their exuberance and anticipation of good food. The boys were relaxed with her, accepting Lei as if she had never been anywhere but right there in their lives, as if they had once crawled into her lap and asked her to tell them stories before falling asleep. Yan, who had tried to serve the rice in place of Lei, politely thanked her mother who placed a generous purple portion on Yan's plate.

"Thank you, MaMa." The last word came out of Long's mouth and hung in the air for a moment too long, as if Long was uncertain of its meaning and unsure of how to land the word. He looked at Fang MaMa and immediately stared down at his plate. A New Lake food vendor emerged from one of the lakeside stalls and placed one plate of shelled, hard-boiled eggs and another of garlic-strewn, stir-fried pumpkin shoots on the center of the table.

"Is one fish enough? Maybe we need another?" Pang looked around.

"Enough, husband. It's enough." MeiLin gave her husband a quick smile and looked him in the eyes.

"Yes. You are better at this than I am, MeiLin. I am so thankful for us all to be here. For our whole family to be home." Pang smiled at Lei and then at Bo, who was staring back at the fish on his plate. Clearly impatient to start eating, the twins picked at the rice on their plates. Pang continued, "The ancestors have guided us well. Our table is full and all roads, those here in New Da Long and those further away, have humbly led us to prosper. On this day, none are as rich as dear Bo and Lei. Of course, all of us, especially Fang MaMa, are honored to have such a fine scholar in our home."

MeiLin pulled at her husband's shirt and looked from his eyes to the top of Bo's downturned head.

"Brother Bo, please it is your place to speak. Forgive me."

Bo looked deeply into the unblinking fisheye in front of him. What was there for him to say? For the past decade, he had been apart from his children, working to return to them, to come back to the land of his ancestors. Now he was sure it was Yan who would leave him. His own daughter had taken the *gaokao* to what end other than to be apart from him. Bo shook his head and laughed awkwardly. Just minutes earlier, this fish had been alive, thriving in the lake that had consumed Bo's dream.

Bo looked up at Pang. "You have said the best that can be said. Let's eat now."

Wei and Tao dove their chopsticks, in unison, into the fleshy fish belly.

After the meal, the twins and Long took to weaving on the bank of the lake in a high-energy game of tag. Pang and MeiLin helped Fang MaMa along as they took a walk down to the dock; Yan and Lei were ahead of them, though Yan stopped occasionally to look back and to let the others shorten the distance between the two parties.

Once at the dock, Yan relaxed and was glad to be surrounded by so many other people. She and Lei walked about slowly, diffusing into the Brownian motion of the other visitors.

"Have you ever been out in a swan?" Lei pointed to the paddle boats.

"A long time ago, when I was little." As she answered, Yan realized that Lei had only really known her when she was little. "I mean, after you and BaBa left for Shanghai."

"Yes. That would have to be true. It looks so lovely, to be out there in the middle of the water. You must be able to see things in all directions."

"Almost."

"I'd like to see that. Shall we go?"

"Out there? Now?" Yan looked out on the water; she felt her heart thud against her chest and noticed her mouth was dry.

"Yes."

Fang MaMa, Pang, and MeiLin came behind the mother and daughter, having overheard Lei's invitation to Yan.

Fang MaMa was breathing heavily. "I need to sit down and," she began, taking a deep breath, "rest a little."

"I can sit with you, Fang MaMa," Yan offered immediately. Lei kept staring out to the middle of the New Lake.

"No. Pang and MeiLin are with me. You go out with your other MaMa."

On the water, Lei peddled hard, propelling the purple swan quickly through the water. Yan, astonished at her mother's strength, tried to help but quickly realized that both sets of pedals shared a common axle and were being worked primarily by Lei's consistent effort.

Once at the center of the lake, Lei stopped and looked all around her. She then closed her eyes and felt the unfiltered sun on her face. The two sat for some time; Yan silent and Lei singing softly.

"Are you upset, like BaBa, about the test?" Yan fingered the gold medal that hung from her neck. Lei's eyes remained closed, and she seemed so very far away.

"Yan, do you remember when you were little we used to go to the pond, and you would chase the ducks?"

"I think so."

"Hmm. I loved watching you try to catch the ducks. You were so tenacious."

"But I never caught them."

"I know. It was your determination that warmed me." Lei felt her chest rise, and she wanted to hold Yan in her lap and place her head on her chest. "I felt that way again today at the ceremony."

"When I received the medal?"

"No. I mean, yes, certainly. But before, when you put your hand on the boy. I mean, he is now a man. On Jiang's shoulder."

"He just needs to be steadied every once in a while."

"Yes, I understand. I heard that was how he was able to finally sit for the exam after all these years. You were allowed to sit next to him in the exam room."

"I was only there for him to see something familiar. He gets scared. We all do." Yan looked at her mother and bit her lip.

"I sense you are not scared of the world. You never were."

"I remember when you told me about Huang ShuShu, the bone bearer. I was a little scared then."

"The bone keeper." Lei gently corrected. "Yes, you ran off when you heard that part of his story, but you were still curious to know all about him."

"Tell me again. What exactly did he do?"

"I imagine he provided healing to our people who built the railroads in America, the Beautiful Country. He tried to help them find peace when their hearts broke from loneliness and they missed those they loved back in the Old Home."

"But what about the bones?"

"Well, you know he was a Celestial?"

"A Celestial?"

"The Americans called Huang ShuShu and those of the Middle Kingdom, 'people of the stars.' They believed they were somewhat mystical.

That their bones carried their souls and were to be cherished and safe-guarded."

"By bone keepers?"

"Yes. I have seen Great Uncle in my dreams. He is awake late at night. He sits near a fire polishing a curiously long set of femurs, bringing them to a high shine; these are the bones of a dead countryman. ShuShu is preparing them to carry the man's soul first to an earthbound burial mound in the man's home village and then onto the spiritual realm of his ancestors. A true Celestial."

They sat in silence for some time, and the paddle boat was almost at a standstill. The temperature dropped, setting the hairs on Yan's neck up-right and filling her with an uneasy impatience. She shook her mother's hand, sure Lei had fallen asleep. "MaMa? I must tell you something." Tears began to well up in Yan's eyes and redness moved into her face; she was angry with herself. "MaMa, I need you to listen to me."

"I am listening." Lei immediately opened her eyes and looked directly at Yan without any hesitation.

Yan realized that she had not been asleep. "I ... I want to leave."

"Yes. I know. I understand."

Yan did not hear her mother's words and rushed on, "I want to go and study outside. Maybe become a doctor like Huang ShuShu. I should have told you about the *gaokao*, but I didn't know if I would do well enough. I need to go, but ..."

"Yan, do you know Huang ShuShu never came back to the Middle Kingdom? I think he knew it would be too hard for him and his family. Too much change in his absence on all sides. People make new connec-tions and relationships that have their own energy. Energy that is hard to escape."

"My score is high enough, MaMa. I can try to be like him, Huang ShuShu. But ... I ..." Tears ran down Yan's cheeks, and she hurried to wipe them away. "I know BaBa ... And Long ...Long fears what's happening to him. He needs answers, but none of us has them. When you were gone, I didn't know what to do and even now ..."

"Shh. No need to explain to me, I understand. Yan, BaBa and I have come home. That is our duty, not yours. We will find the answers for Long." Lei took Yan's hands into hers and gently rubbed them. "Talk with your father. Let him hear your plan. I cannot say what he will decide, but you have my blessing."

Yan did not know exactly what her mother understood, but her heart twisted with both relief and joy. She put her head on Lei's chest and allowed her tears to flow.

Chapter Twenty

Homecoming

J agged and snow-capped, even on the longest sun-filled day of the year, the Dragon Back Mountains bit crisply up at the heavens. Alpine air, swirling down from amidst the peaks, managed to modulate the extreme summer heat sweeping through the country's southwest to a level considered bearable. Nonetheless, every window on the non-air-conditioned, long-journey bus was open, and every passenger fanned their face.

The driver wiped a handkerchief across his forehead, focusing his waning energy on staying awake. Several minutes earlier, almost losing himself in the undertow of a wave of wooziness, the driver had swerved the bus dangerously into the opposite lane, narrowly missing a local tribal woman walking along the roadside with a basket of chickens. Calling out thanks to the ancestors, for the road had been clear, the passengers were anxious for their journey to end, and they nervously eyed the driver. The woman with her chickens continued walking without a sign of concern; the silver tassels hanging off her enormous black turban headdress swayed to the rhythm of her hips.

Rifling through the pages of one of her early sketchbooks, LuLu found the wizened face of a tribal woman, her headdress heavily sloping down over the top half of her left eye, with a basket of chickens, their feathers drawn with fine pencil strokes, on her back. She smiled peacefully out of the page. LuLu whipped her head around, searching for the woman on the side of the road, but she was no longer visible.

For LuLu, this bus ride was the last leg of her physical journey home. In the terms of a clock, her journey had started in Shanghai seventy-two hours earlier when she had embarked on a forty-three-hour train ride to Kunming. It had continued with the first long-journey bus ride of nine hours and, if all went well, it would end during the third or fourth hour of this one. To measure the journey in this way had not crossed LuLu's mind. She was counting down neither the hours nor the minutes nor the kilometers that were left until she reached the end. LuLu had made this journey countless times over the years, traveling this trail with every letter, curled Kuai note, and gift box that she had sent home. Every step towards home came as a picture; some scenes she had repeatedly recorded in her sketchbook, while others had just replayed on the screen of her mind. All details she knew like she knew her own body; they were lived in every day. Now, as the scenes came fast and real, one after another, LuLu was moving continually to and from the past to the present and into the future. She had been, and would be, coming home for her entire life.

Scrutinizing every passing frame, LuLu convinced herself that nothing had changed. The mountains had not moved, the clouds had not drifted up and away, but still hung low in the sky, and the land remained a patchwork of hard-worked fields. The tribal women in the square still dressed in celebration with multicolored folds in their thickly pleated skirts, and the embroidered patterns of their traditional vests almost sang out loudly above the silence of the mundane. There had been a few foreigners in the square, milling about and trying to capture the place with their cameras, but they were alien and largely ignored. LuLu took the liberty of leaving them out of her current sketch.

However, everything had indeed changed.

That LuLu, in body, was coming home for the first time in over a decade made change a fact. In the early years of her migration, LuLu had perpetuated her absence from her *laojia*—or as YuZhen would have insisted, the place where her ancestors were waiting for her—through a series of excuses revolving about the demands of her factory job. The ever-increasing weight and worth of her packages home served to validate her strategy of always staying in Shanghai and working every holiday. At some point, her parents became the ones to offer up the excuses for nonreturn: the journey is long and not safe; BaBa will go out for work and will not be here to see you; you must use your free time to rest as you work so hard. In the last few years, there were no more excuses, just absences. This changed when the telegraph from LuLu's mother had arrived at the barbershop, addressed to Fu TaiTai. Having been paid for by the word, it was brief: "Daughter come. BaBa dying."

LuLu knew there was a chance that her father had already left this world, that her mother's telegram had been sent in the moments before he had taken his last breaths. Still, she was unprepared to see the white banner of death over her home's entryway in Alley Number Seven. She was delighting in the feel of the cobblestones pressing up through the soles of her shoes and stretching her arches when she came around the curve and saw the banner barely moving, sagging limp in the center. It presented the perfect metaphor for what it symbolized. She quickly turned around and went back around the curve, glad to find the narrow space between the rows of buildings empty and leaned back against the crumbling wall of an abandoned house. LuLu breathed hard and waited for her tears to come; she planned to let them pass, but they never arrived. They had flowed when she lost YuZhen, but now her cheeks were shamefully dry. She waited for some time before retrieving a white, mourning smock from her backpack, which she put on over her shirt and belted at the waist. She pulled her hair neatly into a ponytail and wiped the powder and lipstick off her face and lips with a paper napkin.

At the door of her parents' home, LuLu recognized her mother's low voice engaging in conversation with a man. She also heard a soft, whimpering cry which confused her; it sounded human, but LuLu's idea of her LiLi, now a young teen, did not fit with the childlike sound.

Inside the old alleyway home, darkness lay in folds; multiple shades of black temporarily blinded LuLu. As her eyes adjusted to the darkness, she saw there were currently no animals on the first floor. Scattered straw covered the ground and hay bales were stacked against the back wall all the way up to the ceiling. The distinct mustiness of animal perspiration filled her nostrils.

She began up the back stairs, cautiously, as she recalled almost having lost her footing many a time on several loose boards. The treads were firm underfoot, and LuLu realized that they had been rebuilt since the last time they bore her weight but still remained just as steep and narrow. She followed the human sounds.

"MaMa? Little sister?"

The voices stilled, though the whimpering persisted.

"You have come? Daughter, you have come?" Zhang MaMa's deep voice pulled LuLu up the stairs.

"Yes, MaMa. I am home."

Zhang MaMa stood wearing a floor-length, white pinafore with a white T-shirt and muddied sneakers. Her hair was gathered into a single, impressively long braid that hung down to the small of her back. She staggered towards LuLu, looking as if she were about to collapse onto her, and then she caught herself and stopped within inches of her daughter. She embraced LuLu lightly, as if she were an apparition prone to fading. Zhang MaMa's arms did not quite close around LuLu's body. LuLu tried to hold onto her mother, to pull her deeper into their embrace, but the woman pulled back and wiped the skirt of her pinafore with her hands.

"BaBa has left this world." Her voice was controlled.

"Yes. I know, MaMa I am ..."

"This is my older daughter, Fu TaiTai." Zhang MaMa turned towards a simple-looking, young man with a soft face who was attired in a respectable black suit; LuLu correctly surmised that he was an undertaker. "She has just come from Shanghai. Her husband is from there."

"May the ancestors bless your father, Fu TaiTai." The man's voice conveyed a practiced sincerity.

"We are making the funeral arrangements. I could not wait. I ..." Zhang MaMa explained.

"LuLu! Oh, LuLu!" From the darkest corner, a flash of white emerged and rushed towards LuLu with such force that LuLu almost fell backwards. LiLi began to sob as she hugged her older sister. "LuLu, you have come. You have come to me. Oh, LuLu, you have come."

Hearing her given name uttered by her own blood broke something deep inside LuLu. Her name, mouthed by the tender lips of her sister, was like a siren call pulling LuLu back in time, up onto a welcoming shore, back to before she had ever heard it whispered by so many unknown mouths. LuLu cried, for she heard her father's voice calling her home again. She grabbed wildly at LiLi and buried her head into the girl's thick sheets of hair. LuLu convulsed and, despite squeezing her eyes tightly closed, tears sprang quickly onto LiLi's neck. The younger girl was immediately distressed by the wetness moving towards her collar and squirmed to be free. "I can't breathe," LiLi whimpered. "Stop. I can't breathe." She fell to the floor.

LuLu fell on her knees beside the child, "Sorry. Sorry. My most beautiful LiLi, I am overcome with happiness in seeing you. Please forgive me."

LiLi pouted her lips at her sister, her full cheeks puffing with upset. "I am happy, too. But I am too sad about BaBa."

"Yes, of course. I am as well." As she spoke, LuLu studied LiLi's face and manner, finding it hard to believe that the girl was nearing thirteen.

Not unaccustomed to such displays, the young undertaker turned away to save the sisters any embarrassment. He tried to bring the room back to order and addressed LuLu's mother, "Zhang TaiTai, as I was saying, the funeral arrangements need to be finalized to ensure proper passage for the deceased."

"Yes. I understand. What you so kindly recommended is how we will proceed." Zhang MaMa beckoned her girls off the floor.

"You will want to choose an appropriate urn."

"Urn? BaBa is to be buried. You agree with me, right?" LuLu was on her feet and looking at Zhang MaMa. "Where will the burial mound be? I would like to see the place and help prepare the spirit money and spirit gifts." She now looked past her mother and challenged the undertaker.

"Of course. You are a fine daughter, Fu TaiTai. However, there will be no mound. Just cremation. We follow the funeral reforms of The Party. The great leaders have set new traditions into place."

"New traditions?" LuLu looked at the undertaker. "What about those who wish for the old traditions? The ones that have ensured centuries of safe passage to the ancestors?"

"Well, I understand your desire, but the authorities do not look easily on illegal burial mounds."

"And legal ones, how are those looked upon by the authorities?"

"They are legal that are not looked upon too closely. Especially those not looked upon by the Ministry of Land Resources."

"How much?"

"Fu TaiTai, please." Zhang MaMa tried to stare LuLu into silence. "This is too much."

LuLu looked at her mother and wanted to ask her, *Why have you not called me by name? Why do you not call me like you did when I was still completely yours? What is too much?* But she kept these questions to herself. "My husband has sent me with a small offering of comfort," LuLu lied.

The undertaker's face turned red. "Three thousand Kuai."

LiLi gasped from the floor, where she still sat. "Three thousand Kuai! Three thousand?"

Zhang MaMa turned her face away in shame. "Impossible."

"Mister Fu will pay for this to be." LuLu stepped forward and pulled a thick money roll from her bag. "Please use this as a deposit. Mister Fu has sent enough to pay the remainder after a proper ceremony has been performed. Make it possible."

On the most auspicious day of the current moon cycle, as divined by the village elders, LuLu's father was buried several miles outside of the village center in the middle of a peach tree orchard. A local priest conjured the ancestors and beseeched them to open their hearts to the newest crossover soul transitioning from earth to heaven. Paper money, of denominations both large and small, burned in a send-off bonfire that raged for several days. Additionally, elaborate cardboard replicas of food, jewelry, a television, a European car, and even a small house were all added to the fire as a means of endowing after-world BaBa with enough resources to live well amongst his fellow spirits. Fireworks and food were provided for all members of the village on each of the seven nights. Children ran up and down the narrow alleyways, long past the point where the sun went down and the moon rose, with their mouths filled with candy and their bellies filled with roasted meat. Extra funds were paid to the undertaker to ensure that an abundant supply of spirit money, foods, and desirable worldly possessions, made only from the finest gold-foiled joss paper, would be burned and offered up to the ancestors every month for the next year at the base of the burial mound. Additional monies were paid for professional mourners to wail so loudly that the ancestors would be sure to hear them. All of this was made possible by Mister Fu, the venerated husband of the first daughter of the beloved deceased.

During this week of funerary display, LuLu fell in love. The sweet intimacy of sisterhood filled her up. On the morning of the burial, LuLu and LiLi bathed together behind their home in the alley. The sisters stood naked together, sharing a large steel basin of boiled water, and stared at each other's bodies. LiLi's had full breasts and dark, thick patches of hair sprouting from beneath her arms and atop the mound at the base of her abdomen. This confirmation that LiLi was no longer a child, but an adolescent, came almost as a disappointing surprise to LuLu who had been lulled by the girl's innocent manner into irrationally believing something different.

In the mornings before LiLi went to school, LuLu helped her milk the goats, feed the chickens, collect any eggs they had been kind enough to lay, and muck out the first-floor manger. In the afternoons, after milking the goats a second time, the sisters would take a few minutes to lie back in the wild grass. LuLu would bring out her sketch pad, and LiLi would call out a Shanghai scene for her sister to draw, recalling places LuLu had described in her letters home: worshippers praying at the Golden Temple, children playing in Zhongshan Park, the Bund's Lunar New Year sky filled with fireworks, Mister Fu next to the glass animals in LuLu's fancy apartment. The last scene LuLu sketched strategically, enlarging the glass animals and leaving no room on the page for Lao Fu.

At night, LiLi insisted on sleeping with LuLu, curling up in her arms and begging her to fill her head with visions of Shanghai. "Tell me about the flowers, are there just too many to count? And what about the temple where you live? Does it have a koi pond with fish of many colors? How do the city ladies dress? Are they too fancy?"

LuLu laughed, not wanting to disappoint the girl. "Yes. Yes, to all your questions."

"And what of the food? Oh, LuLu, are there the most delicious sweets in every store, around every corner?"

"There are a lot of fancy stores with fancy sweets."

"Mister Fu, your Mister Fu, does he write you poetry and bring you chocolates from Europe?"

"What do you know about Europe?"

"I know that the palest of all people come from those parts; my teacher says some of them are even paler than the Beijing Opera King."

"It is true. I have seen some of them in the city. Like ghosts they are."

"And you and Mister Fu, do you have a fancy apartment in a building that touches the clouds?"

"Not quite." LuLu stroked LiLi's hair, wishing she could say something nice about the old man.

"I know the clouds are not as low as the clouds here, so maybe it would be too hard for the building to touch the clouds."

"Yes. I live in a lovely room with a fine collection of glass animals."

"Really. I want to see them. When can I see them?"

"One day you will."

"Why not now?"

"Now. Really?

"Please, LuLu can I go back with you to the city?"

"What would you do?"

"What do you mean? What a silly question. I am a student. I will go to school and come home every day and have dinner with you and Mister Fu. You two would be like my Shanghai MaMa and my Shanghai BaBa."

"And what about MaMa?"

"She would be so proud to have two city girls! Don't you agree?"

"Would you really want to come and live with me?"

"Yes. LuLu, please take me."

"Shh. Go to sleep."

"Okay. Stay with me."

"I am right here." LiLi wiggled her pudginess right up against LuLu, seeking her out and not finding peace enough to sleep until enough of her skin's surface lay against her sister's.

Every evening, the sisters' conversation would end with a shared construction project: their life together in the city. Despite knowing all the vagaries inherent in a vision built by an innocent girl and knowing just how many fallacies lay beneath its foundation, LuLu allowed herself to indulge in the possibility that the vision might somehow become true. She began to weave elements of her real life into the dream, trying to reinforce or rebuild its weak spots. As the "daughter" of a city *hukou* holder, and with several red envelopes to pave her way, LiLi would escape relegation to migrant status, and would be entitled to attend school in the city. If Lao Fu claimed LiLi as his daughter through marriage, he could ensure that she had access to all the rights and opportunities of a city child. LiLi was naïve, innocent, and maybe even silly, but she was not a poor student and kept up with her studies. Eventually, LuLu believed LiLi could find a respectable job, a worthy husband, and have a life filled with the pretty dresses and fancy foods about which she dreamt.

Hadn't LuLu worked to create such an opportunity? Business at the barbershop was going well, for as the city prospered, so did Lao Fu's girls. Surely there might be enough money to rent a small place, away from the barbershop, big enough for just the two of them. LuLu convinced herself that she could keep Lao Fu happy in residence at the barbershop; maybe she could offer him more than just her hands.

"Each night you speak with your little sister about the city." Zhang MaMa and LuLu were sweeping the first floor of the alleyway house. The goats had been put out to pasture on the small square of grass on the backside of the house. The chickens ran away from Zhang MaMa's broom and left LuLu alone to scoop up the collected animal droppings, mud, and straw bits for the composting pile. "You will be returning to your husband in the city very soon. It is best to leave her head empty of wrong ideas."

LuLu felt her heart race and tried to compose her words carefully, "MaMa, it is not just an idea. LiLi can come back with me to the city. I am a married city wife. I can provide her with bigger opportunities."

"She will not go."

"No, she will. I mean, she wants to go."

"You do not understand what I say. I cannot let her go."

LuLu tried to look her mother in the face, but the woman turned her back and vigorously swept an already cleared part of the floor. "MaMa, I know you will miss her, but she has a chance to be fully educated and to—"

"I don't want it. I don't want you to speak." Zhang MaMa kept sweeping but without effect. The bristles curled under and back on themselves, for the woman leaned on the broom handle with her full weight, as if to steady herself. LuLu moved closer to help her. Zhang MaMa raised her hand and stopped LuLu from touching her. "I don't want it. I can love the both of you, but I cannot be ashamed of both of you."

"What are you saying? I don't understand."

"I know what you are."

"What I am?" LuLu flushed deeply and her voice shook. "I am a married woman. I work in a factory. My husband is a barber. I don't know what you mean."

"Please, daughter, stop talking."

"I am a wife." LuLu glared at her mother, willing the woman to look at her. "My husband owns his business. I ..." LuLu stopped speaking.

282

Her mother still had not said her name even once since she had come home. Wrapping her arms around herself, trying to hold herself steady, LuLu asked, "MaMa why can't you say my name? Why can't you call me as you did before?"

Zhang MaMa looked at the ground, holding the brush still, and shook her head. "Because you are not as you were before. I don't want to lose that girl. I don't want to replace that girl with the woman you are now."

A chicken walked across the space between the two women, pecking aimlessly at the ground, moving without purpose. On seeing the bird's head wobbling back and forth on its neck, LuLu ran to the corner of the room and threw up in the hay. She felt her spine melt and her legs give out from under her. She sat on the ground for a long time and did not move.

"How long have you known?"

Zhang MaMa walked over to LuLu and sat down next to her. She did not let her body touch LuLu's, "For years. For many years."

"And BaBa, too?"

"Yes."

For over a decade, LuLu had feared this moment but had never prepared for it. Shanghai had honed her skills as a perpetual liar for love but had given her very little practice in facing the truth. The coolness of the barn floor felt good against her skin, as it grounded her, and as LuLu leaned back against the manger, she began to order her thoughts. How could MaMa and BaBa have known all these years and said nothing to her? How did they let her do what she did and accept everything she sent home without ever begging her to stop? She was a fool. All these years, she had protected her family from the reality that strangers used their daughter's body to meet their needs. They had not needed LuLu's protection. Blood pulsed loudly in her ears, and a quiet rage began to rise within her.

"I want LiLi. I want to take her to Shanghai. You must agree I have earned the right." LuLu spoke with a distinct coolness to the woman next to her.

"Impossible. What are you thinking? What can you possibly provide her?"

"What can I provide her? Huh!" LuLu stood up and looked down on Zhang MaMa. Her voice raised slightly and her jaw stiff. "Can you really ask me that? I have provided her, and you, with everything you have. I have loved her, and you, in the best way I could. I have earned the right to have her with me; I want to love her completely and give her everything I did not have, every opportunity."

Zhang MaMa stood up slowly and faced LuLu. Her face creased to show her full age and grief, and her body seemed unable to hold up even the weight of her clothing. "LiLi is simple. She has known very little hardship because of you. Her opportunity lies in being married to a man who can afford to keep her soft. You cannot have her, LuLu. She will be married and matched to a good family. You can continue to love her, necessarily from a distance, as you have these many years."

"There is more out there. She can do and see more. There are *other* opportunities in the city."

"No!" Now, Zhang MaMa bit the air. "She is simple, but she is pure. She will be married that way. That is what your father wanted for her, and that is what will pass."

The Shanghai summer sun had begun its rise much earlier in the day and, by mid-morning, the window glass was hot to the touch. Usually, Master Du enjoyed such warmth but, on this afternoon, he feared there was something unforgiving in the energy captured in the pane. He began to prepare for the afternoon devotions and decided to stay in the sunlight, beside the window, and to wrestle with the uneasiness he sensed. He stood patiently, facing the window. He waited for the red, the only color he could see currently, to dim and yield to a message. His stomach bubbled, reacting to the hot peppers that had pungently flavored his last meal, and slowly he could feel gas moving through his intestines. His hands trembling, the Master worked the stitches of his shirt hem. He meditated on the entire front side of his shirt, from hip to hip, several times over, moving the stitches from in between one set of fingers to another. The flower bursts did not come.

The blind man spent an hour this way, waiting on the ancestors to show him what elements of luck and fortune were still there for those who would come to him for a wise word. But there was nothing. He bowed his head and moved from his window-side chair, down to the floor. On his knees, he eased his forehead to the ground and repeatedly beseeched, "For your mercies, I pray humbly." He understood the absence of the flowers. Luck and fortune were not to be had, only misfortune was left to play out.

The temple's afternoon worshippers were not plentiful, and LuLu found her way to Master Du without much pushing. She paid for three ornate fortune tickets, each one a piece of paper lace. Two of them she took to the old woman in the corner of the temple, tossing them into her fire after placing two coins squarely in the woman's palm. These two were for YuZhen and BaBa; LuLu's donation set the woman to fero-ciously chanting for their comfort and prosperity in the afterworld. The third ticket, blue and shaped like a butterfly, LuLu kept for presenting to Master Du. She waited patiently for the small crowd around the prophet to disperse and then approached him silently.

The Master might have sensed her energy, for he shivered despite the heat. He held out an open hand and LuLu placed the butterfly in it. She then opened her purse and pulled out the stuffed panda that she always kept with her. She kissed its paws gently and placed it on top of the fortune ticket into the Master's still outstretched hand. Only after the panda was in this spot did Master Du pull his hand back and cup over its contents with his other hand. The prophet looked to be perfectly still, and LuLu could not know that inside his body a battle of energies raged as he cried with so many questions. She waited, wondering if the man had fallen asleep.

"All things work by the will and wisdom of the ancestors to serve justice and restore harmony. Follow their guidance. We are only made whole when we see the whole." Master Du smoothed the dirtied fur of the panda, running his fingers along its worn and partially torn seams, before handing it back to LuLu.

Zhongshan Park was still light and the air still warm, even though the sun was en route to retiring. LuLu sat on a bench and took no notice of anyone else. She felt small and alone. She had sent smoke curls into the sky for YuZhen and BaBa; it is what they would have both wanted. She had also gone to the temple to find peace for herself. What was the "whole" she could not see? She turned the prophet's words over in her head. Maybe Lao Fu was right. Master Du was a master con.

"Stupid! Stupid! Stubborn! Stupid." Invisible YuZhen spoke to LuLu. LuLu looked about her, expecting to see her old friend just behind her, hands on her hips, brown-toothed grin on her face. "Be thankful for the Master's words; they are the answer."

"What is the answer? What was the 'whole' that I cannot see? Where is the wisdom of the ancestors in the life of a daughter who went unsaved by her own parents?" The sound of rushing blood intensified in LuLu's ears and her body stiffened.

"What would you have had them do?"

"They could have saved me!" LuLu turned her head, as if looking away from YuZhen. "What? Tell you they knew what you were doing at the back of Lao Fu's shop? Demand you come home to be the center of all village gossip for the rest of your days? To have no man wed you? To have LiLi be ruined as well?"

"What are you saying?" LuLu scrunched her eyes and held the panda in her hands, tears of anger escaping her closed lids.

"Did their denial not allow you to have a whole life? You have a husband and a Shanghai *hukou*; you've secured the right to be in this city. And, now, you are free of further pretense and obligation. LiLi loves you; even admires you. Don't be nearsighted!" YuZhen's voice grew soft. LuLu could almost feel her friend wiping the tears from her face. "Look beyond what is right in front of you."

LuLu conjured LiLi's presence, her softness, and felt the girl's skin up against her legs, her arms, her belly, her chest, her entire being. An aching for the girl tightened across LuLu's chest; it was a pain that felt so strong and powerful, so beautiful, and so much bigger than anything else LuLu had known. She let out a long, slow breath.

"YuZhen, was this BaBa and MaMa's way of saving me? What if I never see LiLi again?"

"You have opened her future; she will marry well and be secure. Is that not everything? You can love her without the weight of shame pulling you both down. See the whole."

Chapter Twenty-One

Daughters and Sons

Yan's departure from New Da Long defined two clearly distinct time periods in the lives of almost everyone who knew her. Strangely, the longer of the two, the "when Yan was still here" period, was almost completely eclipsed by the "once Yan was gone" period. Everyone who knew Yan remarked on her absence, repeatedly, and felt it profoundly. In the windows of the shops that lined New Da Long Square, newspaper clippings praising Yan's *gaokao* performance, the best score in the entire province, and her accompanying pictures remained taped on display long after they had yellowed. The students of the New Da Long school slavishly followed what they believed to be Yan's example: they sat perched at the feet of their new headmaster, Teacher Zhou, waiting to be fed crumbs of knowledge and dreamed of one day being legendary and "gone" just as Yan was now.

The growing wealth of MeiLin's and Pang's mountainside household was measured in wheeled machines. Dozens of bicycles, mopeds, electric trike carts, and one four-wheeled, rusted-out pick-up truck stood in neat rows, like tin soldiers, across the home's front yard. When Yan was still here, she had chased the twins in between the rows, throwing water-soaked sponges at their heads and making the chore of washing down the vehicles more fun. Now that Yan was gone, Long helped Wei and Tao clean the mud and dirt off the various sets of handlebars and wheels, while listening to the boys' stories about the pretty girls in the village. Pang and MeiLin missed Yan as surely as they would have missed one of their own children, for they, along with Fang MaMa, had practically raised her. However, the sheer enormity of her adventure and the almost tangible sense of striving that it embodied resonated so deeply with Pang that he effectively lauded her somewhere-elseness.

"Yan is probably meeting so many new people every day," or "Imagine all the different foods cousin Yan is tasting in the city," and "Books, books, and more books. Yan will never not have something to learn," were all common musings delivered by Pang over any given meal.

Fang MaMa, teeth loose in her mouth, used her gnarled hands to jab chopsticks in the air as a means of punctuating her responses: "Let's hope ... hope she doesn't get mixed up with ... fast ... fast and loose city people," or "Diarrhea will keep her from studying," and "May the ancestors keep ... keep ... keep her from going blind from reading too much in the dark." All were offered as dire warnings, but the old woman's body was puffed up with pride, affirming her son-in-law's exclamations.

For Bo, this chatter had no purpose as, after his daughter had left him, he fell back into his customary posture of perpetual silence, sparing his energy for teenage Long and their time together working the flatbread cart in the New Market. Long was strong and a fine worker, able to carry the weight of three men. Most important, he was here, not gone away to the city. The time for talk of Yan and her plans had been short, wrenching, and now long past. In the weeks that followed the medal presentation, father and daughter had conversations in which their individual ideas were like two streams flowing down different sides of the mountain. That a passionate love for family and Da Long, their *laojia*, was a shared point of origin only made their divergent plans ever more frustrating to one another.

***

Their last battle of consequence had taken place on the side of the road with Bo and Yan looking out over New Lake.

"Why would you leave this place, the place of your ancestors, when there is no need? Hasn't Da Long given you everything?" Bo, still refusing to use New to describe the Da Long that had been his since birth, asked as he searched the surface of the lake as if looking for answers. Yan was seated beside him, right up against him.

"I have been here my whole existence. It is all I know. I want to see more and must leave to get that."

"Bah! What is it you are going to see?" Bo did not look at Yan. "I have been where you want to go. The cities are filthy places. They offer nothing worthwhile for people like us. City people know money and how to fill themselves with it. They have no respect for Earth MaMa; she is a stranger to them." He nodded at the lake, humbly accepting its existence yet again.

"I am not scared." Yan closed her eyes, feeling for her mother's words and keeping anger out of her voice.

"Fear is not the problem in that place." Bo coughed hard, setting his chest rumbling. "Innocence makes you its victim."

"BaBa, are you okay?"

"You don't need to ask me that. Are *you* okay?"

"I want to see what is out there and to learn things I cannot learn here."

"It is the things that you will see and learn that trouble me."

Though their words pulled them further and further from one another, neither father nor daughter dared to physically separate from the other.

"I could forbid you from going."

Yan sat silently, working to hold her tongue.

"The Farmer Master came to the New Market today."

"To your cart?" Yan tried not to sound surprised, and her voice remained calm.

"Yes." Bo chafed at her manner and felt his jaw tighten.

"He was hungry?"

"He had a proposal for me ... or maybe I should say he had a proposal for you." Bo felt Yan squirm and continued, "I worked these ten years to pay him everything I ever borrowed from him, along with interest. There was a point a few years back when he offered to take my government restitution lot as payment for the remainder of my balance. But, if I had given him that, what would I have left to start over with? I stayed in that city longer to pay ..." Bo started coughing and curled over, struggling to bring phlegm up into his throat. Yan tried to clap his back, but Bo pushed her hand away. "... to pay him what I owe him. Now I can start again. I have the lot. I will save again to build again. You understand?"

"Understand."

"When the Farmer Master came to see me in the New Market, I was not scared. I felt we were clear. I did not have to hide my face. But then he reminded me that we are bound by *guanxi*; I owed him more than money. He had given me opportunity when I had very little, and in return, I had pledged him loyalty. I promised to never forget his giving me a chance. You understand?" Bo did not wait for Yan to answer. He could feel her thigh begin to tremble next to his. "The Farmer Master proposed clearing *all* my debt, truly setting me free. He had me looking at him in such a way as to curse him and his ancestors, for he offered me a red envelope, stuffed with just enough money for me to start building again, as a gesture of his 'goodwill.' He said it would be your bride price for marrying his boy. He told me how the two of you became friends while I was gone."

Bo searched Yan's face. Was she calculating how much she was worth to him? Did she realize that her leaving would cost him several more years of his life and the postponement of his dream? The family dream? He could stop her with a single word. She sat still, as if indifferent to what he had just shared. But, as Bo looked at her face, shaped like his, he knew where to search for clues. He listened to her breath; it had hastened. He looked at her lower lip; it trembled. He sensed her body; it had moved ever so slightly, leaving a slice of space between the two of them. A wave of nausea came across Bo; in her deep silence, he could hear inside of her and knew she was crying. Bo's heart dropped suddenly from his chest, and he was desperately ashamed.

Bo stood up. "We must return home. We will go now."

In the orange glow of the summer's dusk, father and daughter walked home, side by side, each one lost in their own thoughts. Millions of conversations filled the air as myriad insects began to sing their raspy love songs. Yan tuned into their noise and thought of Jiang. The sounds of humans scared him, but the call of crickets, thousands at a time, soothed him. She did not need to wonder what he was doing on this evening; she could see him in the study, with a window open, enjoying the intensity of the encroaching night.

From the day Jiang had helped her off the kitchen floor so many years ago, Yan and the Farmer Master's son had engaged in a deep and lasting conversation, albeit a largely silent one. They spoke with the exchanges of looks, small gestures, and, on Yan's part, reassuring touches of her hand. Words did exist between them but were not necessary and served only as occasional punctuation in a language of mutual understanding. The two studied side by side, learning from Teacher Zhou and each other for many years. They shared books, raced each other for answers to math problems, painted the same poems and compared results, and had shared meals on more days than not since that morning in the kitchen. And while Yan's intense intellect had certainly delighted the teacher, it was her heart that had made her his pupil. Not knowing exactly what it was that Jiang had seen in Yan as she sat on the Farmer Master's floor had not mattered to AnRan. It had been enough for the mother to decide that her boy needed what every other child in the courtyard school had: a friend.

How everything had been arranged had never been discussed with Yan. Fang MaMa had simply told her, "Yan, from today you will study with Young Wang and Teacher Zhou. Of course, you are to make yourself worthy of the opportunity."

Now, as the crunching of Yan's steps grew louder and louder, she realized that the sound was augmented by Bo's identical tread. The two were in lockstep. Their bodies moved at the same pace, their feet hitting the ground simultaneously and their arms swinging in unison. She was taller by almost a full head than him, for with prosperity had come nourishment, and she was more golden in color but, when Yan looked at Bo, she saw herself. In all the pictures sent to her over the years, it was his face that convinced her she had parents out there. Her mother, who always stared back at her, Yan respected. Her father, his familiar face not quite easy, Yan missed the way one longs for a lost part of themselves.

The song of the crickets swelled, and Yan remembered Teacher Zhou's words on the matter, "Their sounds are not solely calls to breed, but are sometimes cries over disputed territory and assertions of dominance." What had her father said to the Farmer Master? She loved Jiang fiercely and could imagine the future stretching out before her sitting in the study, painting with her dear friend. Jiang likely could be happy just like that for the rest of his days. But that did not make a marriage. Did it? What did she know? She wanted to cry out and mark her own territory, even if its borders were defined only by the space on which she stood. She wanted to assert her control over her own self.

The noises of the night irritated Bo. He wanted to look at Yan without distraction and draw himself onto every one of her features. He kept hearing her silent crying mixed with the vibrating cacophony from the trees above. Bo did not tell Yan that in the instant the Farmer Master had shared his cunning calculation with him, he, Bo, had started breathing hard, that his lower lip had trembled, and that he had taken a step back.

After all those years away from Da Long, years sacrificed in repayment to the man, Bo realized that he had something that the Farmer Master wanted. More important, Bo realized he had the power to deny it to him. All the years of toiling in the city had earned him this moment, the moment in which he could say, "No." Bo would want Yan to believe that his refusal of Wang's proposal came solely from his deep love for her, but he knew that a small part of his decision was fueled by his own quest to feel whole.

Pang and MeiLin's yard came into sight. One row of bicycles had started to collapse, the first poorly balanced bike having started a tipping cascade.

"I will set them straight and come right in," Yan said.

"Leave it. Let the twins take care of it."

"No matter. I will do it."

"No. They will need to learn." Bo held Yan gently back, blocking her from entering the yard. "You will not marry that boy. But now you will have to leave. Everyone will have to learn how to do things without you."

"But ... BaBa! I don't understand."

"The is no need for more talk. I do not want you to go, but I do not forbid it."

———————

From the moment it was decided that Yan would leave New Da Long, Lei and MeiLin began to fret. Neither indulged in worry for Yan and how she would navigate the new terrain of the city, but rather their concern focused on Long and how the boy would fare in the "once Yan was gone" period.

Living in that time now, they realized that their concerns were not misplaced. Talking mice plagued the boy more frequently; they danced and coaxed Long with their words at all hours of the day and night. When Yan had still been with them, she seemed to be able to whisper the creatures away, but now the hallucinations seemed emboldened and persistent. Long was taken to stealing away and disappearing for hours at a time, only to reappear with no explanation for his absence.

"Sister, our boy needs to be seen by Old Doctor. You agree with me, no?" MeiLin handed Lei a small, pearl colored onion.

Lei heard the word "our" and smiled, sharing her teeth with MeiLin. "I do not know. Maybe this is the way of boys at his age?" Lei worked a thick, threaded needle through the body of the onion.

"I do not know. Your brothers? Was this their way?" MeiLin's voice carried not the slightest hint of accusation. She passed another onion from the basket to Lei.

Lei pressed her mouth closed and shook her head, "No." She worked the next onion onto the thread and then held up the long chain of onions. "Enough?"

"Yes. Enough," MeiLin agreed.

Lei pulled her needle free and handed it to MeiLin, who began to thread it anew. Lei stood, reached up on the tips of her toes, and hung the onion chain from a nail on the outside of the house. "The heat will dry these very quickly."

Lei stared down at MeiLin sorting through the remaining onions, pulling out any that were already soft. She caught herself musing over how MeiLin's beauty had grown, never shriveling like a bloom on a branch.

MeiLin looked up at Lei. "Come now, let us finish this together." She patted the ground next to her. Lei sat down and drew strength from yet another of MeiLin's chosen words, "together."

"Bo says I should not create trouble. He says he will keep Long with him, working the cart in the New Market. He says it is okay for him not to be in school. That school does not have use for every child."

"In the market?" MeiLin steadied her voice to conceal her panic.

"He says the boy just needs a place for his mind to be free." Even as the words came from Lei's mouth, they were flat.

"Yes. The New Market is filled with people and sights." MeiLin handed Lei another onion.

"Including Old Doctor, who is at the New Clinic now." Lei took the cream-colored bulb and pierced its many skins with her needle. "Maybe Long can see him there."

"Yes. What you say is not wrong." MeiLin prayed silently for Long.

Yan's absence spread like ripples over the surface of the New Lake, into the heart of another mother also deep in thought over the future well-being of her son. AnRan became convinced that the house had turned cold and drafty, as if Yan's warm, youthful energy had seeped out through its cracks. Teacher Zhou was also gone, and scarcely a visitor came to the house, leaving three middle-aged adults and one too-old son within its walls. Gone were the laughter and the chatter that had once echoed throughout the house, up through the atrium, seemingly loud enough to fill the sky.

Jiang became even quieter as he missed his friend. He would occasionally share drawings of the fields and rice terraces with reconfigured crop layouts with AnRan, but she never shared them with the Farmer Master, who was now perpetually short-tempered. The few times Jiang sought out Teacher Zhou at the New School, he made short work of helping the teacher grade math exams. Most days passed with Jiang reading and painting, alone in the study for the many sunlit hours.

Ayi made meals that were barely eaten, and the old butcher paper scrolls peeled off the study windows. AnRan tried to sit in the study, her embroidery in hand, to spare Jiang the heaviness of complete solitude. After days of primarily silence from her son, it was AnRan who felt a weight crushing down on the top of her skull. She took to remaining in her bed chamber for several weeks and bathing multiple times a day.

Ayi tried to cajole Jiang into interacting with her, suggesting it was time for a new goat to join the household given that Small Snow had left this world at around the same time that Yan had gone to Shanghai.

When he showed no interest, she wondered if she had lacked sensitivity and started naming a litany of other possible companions. "Consider a dog, a cat, a bird, a rabbit, a field mouse, a—"

"Rabbits," was all Jiang said.

Ayi saw to it that one of the field hands built a large, raised hutch on one side of the courtyard and arranged for two red-eyed, white, neutered, male rabbits, not appropriate for stewing, to take up residence in the new abode. Jiang took to bringing the animals into the study, and soon rabbit droppings could be found in small clusters all about the first floor of the house.

Yan's absence did not stay confined to the first floor; it wafted up to the second floor and fogged up the windows of the Eagle's Eye, bringing about a new version of the Farmer Master.

Wang frequently and involuntarily replayed the New Market scene, the one in which that nothing of a man, Fang Bo, had outmaneuvered him. Years back, when Bo had negotiated with Wang to borrow money and secure a lease for his desired land lot, Wang had seen Bo as no more than a debtor. Later, when AnRan had approached Wang and begged him to allow Yan into their home as a companion for Jiang, the Farmer Master pretended that he needed persuading. In truth, he was delighted at having Yan hooked by obligation, just like her father. That Yan grew to be beautiful seemed, to the Farmer Master, a reward for his cunning. Yan would make the perfect wife for Jiang. He did not pay any attention to her brilliance, nor did he recognize the danger of the fame and recognition it would bring to New Da Long. If he had, the Farmer Master might have recognized a worm on a hook wriggling free. He would have made sure to press Yan firmly back into the darkness of the soil, allowing her to be plucked out only when he chose to do so and to be put to whatever purpose he found useful. That he had ultimately been the one to provide both father and daughter the means to humiliate him and escape his bidding, caused Wang to pound his fists against his father's black lacquered desk. He vowed that he would never be distracted from his mission again.

It was in this way that the wave of tumult caused by Yan's departure flowed from New Da Long to Shanghai. On a particularly stifling late summer afternoon, LuLu, ignorant of any change, found herself in bed with the "new" Wang, the Wang of the "Yan is gone" period. A small ceiling fan whipped the air about the room, but the heat remained intolerable. Wang and LuLu lay on the bed, panting. It was too hot for sleep, and they were both left awake and thinking. That Wang, a usually considerate and tender lover, had been unusually rough and determined to satisfy his own needs did not bother LuLu, but rather made her question the one man she did not mind having in her life.

"What is happening? Are you okay?"

"No issues. I have things to straighten out." Wang reached for a cigarette and looked up at the ceiling as if searching for answers.

LuLu sat up and pulled on her robe, tying its sash tightly around her waist. She took a sip of warm beer from Wang's can and plopped herself down on her back, next to him. "What is up there? Anything useful?"

"Nothing. Nothing at all. How's the old man?"

"Alive."

"Giving you any trouble?"

"Nothing I can't handle. Sometimes it takes a custard tart, other times a pinch, but I can usually get him fixed up."

"Really?" Wang turned on his side to face LuLu, propping his head up with one hand and keeping the cigarette steady in the other. "I didn't think of you this way."

LuLu turned to face Wang and felt the need to reassure him. "At times his mind turns foolish, and like a child he needs to be reminded of things. I have too many worries to coddle him; I never pinch too hard."

They studied each other for some time as night approached, their eyes adjusting to the incremental darkening of the room. Each was burdened with the troubles of living lives that were seemingly filled with dreams coming undone, and both wondered whether a small measure of relief could come from sharing their woes.

Given that Wang had never been fully truthful with LuLu about his strange boy, he immediately dismissed the idea. He couldn't truly lament Jiang's wifelessness without admitting to LuLu the primary reason for his status. Not to uselessly talk about himself, he asked her, "What worries do you have?"

"Aiyah! Family worries. Isn't it always about family?"

"I don't know," he lied. "If not your old man, then who?"

"It is my little sister; she is soon to be betrothed."

"Happy occasion, no?"

"No. Not at all. She is only a child, not quite fourteen, but my mother is desperate to secure her future. I will likely never see her again. Do you understand? She will eventually be married into her husband's family, and my mother will keep me from seeing her. She will not want to jeopardize my sister's respectability."

"Where is this husband to be?"

"There is none, yet. But my mother has just asked me to send the marriage broker's fee. Enough so that it will not take long to find her an appropriate suitor. One from a good family, preferably with means."

"And you know this broker? You trust them to make a good choice for your sister?"

"Humph! Good choice? It all depends on how much I pay, doesn't it?"

"And your mother, she is looking for a bride price to sustain her in her older days? I mean she has no son to take care of her." Wang tried to slow the conversation down; the wheels in his head were beginning to pick up speed. "It is only right that your mother be kept comfortable."

"I suspect she hopes for a little something."

"Your sister, is she like you?"

LuLu sat straight up in the bed and glared at Wang. "What are you saying?"

"No. No. I did not mean it in that way." Wang pulled LuLu softly back down next to him; he could not afford to have her closed off. "I mean, she is beautiful and smart like you?"

"More so." Though this was not quite true, LuLu was not entirely lying.

Wang looked at LuLu and thought of stopping himself, for in some way he cared for her. He had never thought of her as vulnerable, but then here she was, half-naked and lying next to a man who paid her for comfort. He bit down and reminded himself not to be distracted by her face, her eyes, her mouth, her breasts. LuLu yawned, stretching her body straight out and then back into a slight curl. In that moment, she looked like a young girl and not a seasoned woman.

"What if your sister were to marry a boy of your choosing, one with whom you could deal directly?"

"I cannot! My mother would not want this. And, she is right. I must be happy that my sister will be married into a good family and trust that my mother will ensure a good match. This is what I worked to accomplish." LuLu closed her eyes, wanting to hide their moistness. In her own darkness, she saw YuZhen nodding in approval.

Beyond the motel room's window, the din, comprised of hundreds of clanging bicycle bells, combined with the cries of street hawkers plying their savory dinner delights, and the scuffle of moving pedestrians, rose and fell. The ordinariness of the noises felt like a heavy weight, pinning LuLu and Wang down both to their bed and to their discontent. Wang struggled to push it off and persisted, "What if she, your mother, did not know? What if there were a way for your sister to be married and for you to stay in her life?"

"What are you suggesting?" LuLu sat up and looked directly at Wang.

"If your sister ..." Wang searched LuLu's face.

"LiLi,"

"Ah, LiLi. What if LiLi were to marry my son, Jiang, and I could then ensure that you would see your sister again, maybe on the occasional visit to Shanghai?"

LuLu's eyebrows furrowed in confusion. "But why? Why would you want this?"

"My son is a gentle soul. He needs a young and gentle girl."

"She is still in school. She must finish her education."

"Of course! LiLi can join my household in the new year, after the school term has ended. I will find her a teacher to complete her studies as she gets to know my son. I am sure my housekeeper can help her with her schoolwork." Wang hid his irritation; he had no intention of bringing Teacher Zhou back to the house.

"I don't know." LuLu chewed on her lower lip. "My mother sees LiLi's future so clearly …"

"Your mother will never know," Wang interrupted. "I will use her marriage broker and pay your mother a good bride price, not so much as to raise suspicion, but enough for her to bless the marriage. I will provide for your mother's care. Do not worry about her. Now, don't be angry but I must ask, is your sister pure?"

"One hundred out of one hundred parts."

"She must stay this way." Wang envisioned an untouched LuLu and was eager to hook her for Jiang.

"No issue. She is …" LuLu paused for a moment, "… young, even young for her age."

"Ah! This is good."

"And your son will want this?" LuLu tried to imagine a smaller, younger version of the man who lay next to her.

"Of course, if I tell him she is my choice."

"And your son will not keep LiLi from me? And you will never tell her about us?"

"You have my promise."

LuLu's heart raced with a mix of fear and excitement. YuZhen, MaMa, and LiLi swam circles in her head, waiting for her to make *her* choice. She felt her hands on the handlebars of fate for the first time and was giddy. She reached out to Wang and ran her palm down the side of his face, almost as if to steady herself.

Wang took LuLu's hand, not wanting the heat rising in his body to betray or distract him, and kissed it gently, repeating, "You have my promise."

Chapter Twenty-Two

One Day: Day One

This day started the same way it always did, in darkness and filled with Bo's protests. Lit only by the moon, just outside the door of the mountainside house, Long and Bo shoveled coal into a barrel-based grill that was welded onto the metal floor of a street hawker's cart. Lei, just inside the door, neatly arranged the contents of her backpack. When the shoveling was finished, Bo paused to catch his breath and Lei, standing in the doorway with her backpack in one hand, offered Bo a last sip of tea from the cup she held in the other.

Long did not pause; he went from shoveling to taking the backpack from his mother and hoisting its straps over his shoulders, to balancing two sacks of flour on the rounded, concave surface of the cart's grill. With a deep exhalation, he began to slowly push the precariously loaded cart out of the yard and onto the downward slope just beyond. Long's muscles reversed course; his arms pulled on the cart with considerable strength and his leg muscles fought gravity, trying to keep his pace steady. Every inch of Long's body was trained to keep the cart from flying down the road and from taking everything, including Long, careening over its precipitous edge. Every morning Bo would call out objections to Long's "reckless" actions and "dangerous techniques," all the while trotting next to him. This morning was no different. Lei remained silent, following closely behind her son and her husband, ready to rescue anything or anyone that might fall.

The family trio arrived at the junction of the steep, dirt road and the flat, smoothly paved Lake Ring Road. They moved silently into a new configuration. The inky night was just beginning to take on a pale greyness as Long took up the flour sacks, one under each of his arms, and Bo and Lei took to man-handling the now much lighter cart. A few minutes along the road, they passed several low-lying, rectangular, brick structures. Largely similar, each one had three openings: a front doorway flanked by two identical, square windows. These were the newly built villager homes, each one sitting on a government restitution plot, housing a family who had lost what the government considered "everything," and likely more.

As new as the homes were, nothing modern ran to or from them, no electrical current through wires and no water in pipes. The crow of a rooster warbled from behind one of the restitution homes and a spot of coal-generated orange glowed through one of its windows. A woman carrying a bucket of foul-smelling waste emerged from the front door.

The woman nodded and said, "Morning," to Bo and his family who were gathered in front of the plot next to hers and kept going in the direction of the lake, careful not to let the sloshing contents of her bucket soil her.

"Morning." Bo wrinkled his nose and watched her pass. Turning back to the lot in front of him, Bo scanned for any changes that might have transpired overnight, but the space looked as it had the evening before, which was largely the same as it had looked the very first time he saw it upon his return from Shanghai. Certainly, left to the will of nature, the lot's vegetation had grown thicker and more tangled but in essence, it remained a rectangle of grasses and green scrub. Bo stood for a while calculating and recalculating how much labor would be needed to clear the land, how much brick would be needed for a modest home, how many stuffed bread cakes he would need to sell, and, finally, how many months it would take to do this.

Lei watched Long, who had turned away from the lot and seemed to be listening to something.

Lei called to Bo, "Let's go."

Bo turned to look at Long, and, seeing the boy straining to hear nothing, he agreed, "We need to get moving."

Fluorescent bulbs flickered awake as the New Market doors were unlocked. Bo, Lei, and Long entered, along with dozens of other vendors. Bo pushed the flatbread cart, his arms straight and straining, and Lei pulled it by a front handle. The cart clattered along, getting stuck every several meters as its front right caster wheel set to swiveling uselessly in its casing. Lei lifted the heavy cart several centimeters and used her foot to reset the uncooperative wheel into a forward position before setting the cart back down. Long followed his parents, his arms and back occupied by the two heavy sacks of flour and the backpack containing Lei's wooden rolling pin, a thick wooden cutting board, a large metal bowl, a plastic container of pork lard, a bottle of peanut oil, several plastic bags filled with assorted spices, and a heavy, handled cleaver. Long stepped as easily now as he had done for much of the last two hours since first leaving his uncle's home.

The music started with a few percussive elements: Lei's knife thumping against the wooden chopping board as she sliced fresh scallions, the clapping of the metal bowl against the cart's counter surface as Bo vigorously kneaded a large ball of hot water dough, the tapping of the metal spoon against the plastic container as Long mixed the lard with a handful of ground pork and several pinches of assorted spices. Long looked at his mother and father to see if they could hear the music, but they seemed to take no notice.

The rows of stalls began to fill up with loud-voiced vendors arranging their edible wares and tossing about clipped vulgarities that crashed against the ear like the clanging of cymbals. Lei began to roll out the dough into skinny rectangles and smeared each one with a thumbload of meaty, spiced lard paste. She then rolled up the rectangles, turned the pinwheels on their ends, and thumbed them down into round discs. Each disc was treated to a rapid flattening with her rolling pin, producing a low thumping sound, and then plopped into the hissing puddle of oil at the center of the grill pan.

All these sounds leaned into a syncopated rhythm, but it was the shrill singing voices high above the beat that stirred Long into complete stillness. He listened hard, trying to hear what they were telling him, but the back beat grew louder, and he could not make out their words. Looking around him, Long spotted a cluster of mice singing in the shadows with their mouths wide and open.

"Sing louder!" Long called out.

Bo looked at his son, standing rigid and silent. He tapped Long on shoulder. "Make more paste now, for your mother."

"Why don't they sing louder?" Long looked at Bo, wanting an answer.

"Who? What singing?" Bo looked around. He saw nothing other than the New Market ready for the start of the business day.

Long looked at his father and immediately regretted asking him the question. The voices warned him, "Trust no one!"

———————

Whispers moved through the university library, hopping from one wooden table to the next and circulating around the stacks of medical textbooks and in between the students' tea thermoses that dotted the study tables. These hushed words came to rest in the ears of the students and then jumped to their tongues. Soon they were carried off once again on a fresh wave of rumor to land on new ears. The "fever without a name" was making gossips of everyone at the medical center.

"How many with symptoms?"

"Can the numbers be true?"

"In the country's heartland? Thousands of them?"

"I thought it was a migrant disease."

"*No!* It's a whore's disease."

"You're both wrong. It's a drug user's disease, spread by their and the plasma sellers' needles."

"Hah! Aren't those all the same?"

Yan kept her head down. Letting her hair hide her face, she pretended to hear nothing from behind the curtain-like strands. Deep, dark half-moons cradled each of her eyes, and her stomach grumbled for it was almost midday and she had not eaten. That she was a migrant from deep within the rural heartland was known to her student companions but was somehow always forgotten. Mesmerized by Yan's quick answers to almost every question posed by their medical mentors, as well as by her fine figure and face, the other students, mainly hailing from Shanghai's finest families, were quick to claim her as "one of us." They overlooked her worn clothing, her borrowed-from-the-library rather than new textbooks, and the way in which she carefully counted her change in the canteen when buying her meals. She had been their classmate for two years, but they did not really know her. Yan often wondered if her origins were truly forgotten or simply forgiven.

Hearing every single word uttered in speculation about the "migrant" disease made Yan feel even emptier; her stomach was awash in acid. She dug deep in her book bag for her purse. It was mostly empty save a few single Kuai notes, some coins, her student identification card, and one photograph. The Polaroid's colors were fading, and the picture was warped, but still clear were Bo and Lei standing on the Bund, their hair tossed about by the wind.

"What's that?" A hand from behind Yan reached down and pulled the picture from between her fingers.

Yan didn't turn around, instantly recognizing the voice. "My parents."

"You look like your father."

"I know." Yan's heart thumped harder and sweat collected in her armpits.

"I'd like to meet them someday, when they come to Shanghai."

"Maybe."

"Maybe? You think they wouldn't like me?"

"Like. Not like. What is the point?" Yan collected her books and study notes, stood up and looked over her shoulder at ZhiChao. "I have many friends here, don't I? Why would you be special?" Yan's voice was flat as her stomach roiled. The study tables around her were filled with clusters of students sharing school notes with one another, explaining genetic trees or organic chemistry structures, and pouring tea for one another as encouragement. Yan sat by herself, by choice, preferring to study alone. She could not go home on weekends to catch up with her family and draw comfort from home-cooked meals. She did not have the money to span the distance between her and New Da Long and was unlikely to see her family for several more years.

ZhiChao offered to help Yan with her book bag. She waved his hand away. "No need."

"Did you eat? Is your belly full?" ZhiChao gently pulled Yan's bag out of her hands. "You want to eat?"

"I am hungry," Yan conceded and let him carry her bag, even though it made her feel naked. She wanted to grab the bag and steady herself, using it as an anchor in a sea of biochemistry and cellular biology, a sea that she confidently navigated with fastidiously written notes and mnemonic devices. Without the bag, with ZhiChao carrying it as if it had no weight, she felt unmoored and somehow vulnerable to losing herself to something else, to an undertow that she could not name.

The basement canteen, just below the lobby of the university hospital, smelled of trapped people and food. The crew of women serving the food, sponging down the long dining tables, clearing the plastic trays of half-eaten plates and bowls of food, and washing the dirty dishes was comprised solely of migrant workers. They wore uniforms of khaki-colored polyester pants and collared shirts, donned pink hairnets, pink sleeve protectors that cinched at their wrists and elbows, and latex gloves. Evidently, no contact was to be made between their bodies and the food being sold.

Yan sipped her soup directly from the bowl, not letting the noodles past her lips. Her eyes followed the workers, and she wondered whether their outfits were designed to keep them clean or to protect the food from being dirtied by them.

"Still don't like the noodles?" ZhiChao pointed to the waterlogged clump in Yan's bowl.

"I still like rice better. I'm not used to them."

"Give it time."

"I don't need time. I'm not trying to be a noodle eater." Yan looked at ZhiChao, her lips pressed firmly together and shoved her bowl away from her.

ZhiChao remained relaxed and finished shoveling the last of his noodles over the lip of his bowl and into his mouth. He put the bowl down on the table and then leaned back in his chair. "Throwing a fit? Why?"

Yan liked the way ZhiChao's lips moved when he said, "Why?" Irritation at herself rose for even noticing this.

"Yan?" ZhiChao asked.

"Hmm?"

"Your mood is sour. Why? Are you not sleeping?"

"It's nothing." Yan handed her and ZhiChao's bowls to one of the serving women, who thanked her profusely for the unexpected gesture.

Watching Yan carefully, ZhiChao leaned back in and slightly forward, over the table, closer to Yan. "Really?" His voice was soft and gentle, inviting her confidence.

Yan looked at the boy who sat across from her and took him in; his handsome face with perfect teeth, the polished cotton dress shirt, his long fingers with soft skin and evenly trimmed, dirt-free nails, and his wrist with the fancy, leather-strapped watch. He was a creature unknown to her, a city boy. Was he one of them, one of her "friends," or was he something real?

Now Yan leaned forward over the table and lowered her voice, "The fever without a name, the Love Disease, everyone is talking about it, but they know nothing of how it works." Yan studied ZhiChao. He did not pull back.

"And?"

"They talk about the sick people with such contempt."

"Listen. The disease is contagious and attacks the immune system irreversibly. That is known. People are scared, Yan. It's natural."

"Natural? Is it natural for a doctor to fear sick people? They fear the migrants from the heartland, the ones they call peasants when they are alone. They are talking about places like my *laojia*. My family is from the heartland. Are they scared of me?"

"I'm not." ZhiChao tried to touch the tip of his index finger to Yan's.

Pulling her hand into her lap, Yan looked at him. "They think everything in the city is better, including themselves."

"Don't be so angry." ZhiChao stood up. "You came here for something better, didn't you?" He handed Yan her backpack and looked at his watch. "It's almost one. We have class." He did not wait for her to answer his question.

"Not *better*," Yan said to herself. "I came to see something new, something different."

The Farmer Master stared at the large clock that hung just above the entrance to the New Market and watched its black, plastic hands move incrementally. The south-originating, long-journey bus was late and Wang, growing ever more impatient, took to walking the perimeter of New Da Long's central square. He did not stop in front of the commemorative monolith for the children lost in the Great Shake, though he would have liked to spend a few moments right there. If he had, he would have undoubtedly noted, not for the first time, how the rock had been skillfully broken and penetrated by an artisan's chisel to inscribe his family name.

It was late afternoon, and, though the business day would be ending soon, the front doors of the New Market remained pulled back and pinned wide open by rubber stoppers. The entrance way was curtained with clear plastic strips that gave way to the autumn breeze. As the strips flapped back and forth, Bo was able to see into the square and grew tense when he saw the Farmer Master. The market had cleared considerably and there were few customers left to cajole.

"We should pack up," Bo said, facing the doorway.

Lei stood several feet behind him, facing the other way. The round, woven bamboo basket in her arms still had a half dozen flatbread discs left to be sold.

"The bus has not arrived yet. The riders will be hungry, no?"

"It's late, the bus. We can save them for the boys." Bo opened the lower chamber of the vending cart, pulled the ashtray out, and emptied it into a plastic bag. "Where is Long?"

"He went to the toilet."

"He's been there a long time. Loose stomach?"

"I don't know." Lei began to help Bo prepare for the journey home. She carefully wrapped the uneaten flatbreads in a small towel and set them aside. She began to layer the heavier items into the bottom of her bag, starting with the chopping board and the bottle of peanut oil. She then took the metal bowl and placed the container of lard within it.

"Where is the cleaver?" Lei looked about, as it was her habit to lay it inside the bowl, wedged next to the lard container.

Bo, hardly paying attention, muttered, "I don't know."

At the far end of the New Market, the men's toilet room was empty except for Long who had been standing in the middle of the room for almost twenty minutes. The tiled floor was interrupted on one side by three in-ground, porcelain, squat toilets, and a single sink jutted from the opposite wall. Absent any privacy dividers, the room was an open cube with nowhere to hide, and yet Long looked in vain for his watchers. He could not see them, but he could hear them counseling him.

"Be careful."

"It is waiting for you."

"It is looking for you."

"Be careful. It only wishes you harm."

Long's eyes darted around the room, and he dared not leave. He crouched to the ground, not wanting to be seen and began to shiver.

Outside the market, the long-journey bus pulled alongside the square and heaved to a stop. Min and Hong, seated in the square and surrounded by several cartons and trays of unsold fruit, waited for their husbands to pull around, behind the bus, with their carts. The sisters watched Wang move quickly towards the door of the bus.

"So, the day is here." Hong nudged Min with her elbow and nodded her head in Wang's direction.

"She comes today? Wah! Look at Wang." Min grinned and did not take her eyes off the bus door. "He is ready for her."

Hong scrunched up her mouth and sucked on her front teeth. "Yes, but it is The Strange One who needs to be ready for her."

"Sister, Jiang will not know how to play with his new toy." Min started to giggle.

"Sister, he doesn't even know how to play with his old toy!" Hong joined in her sister's laughter. "But he will have time. I hear from Ayi that the girl is quite young, and she must be allowed to finish her studies before they will officially marry. It is part of the marriage contract."

Wang watched as one passenger after another descended from the bus. He showed very little interest in any of them, clearly focused only on identifying the child bride.

Long heard his name being called from outside the market's toilet room. He shifted his weight back and forth from one leg to the other and began to bounce on the balls of his feet. The call of his name grew louder, and he let his watchers know, "I am going."

"Look out. Watch it. The dragon is coming for you!" the watchers shrieked after him as Long headed for the door.

"Where were you?" Bo yelled out from several meters away. All the stalls were being packed up, and the tired vendors paid no attention to either father or son.

Long did not answer but walked steadily towards Bo.

"Faster. Faster. We must go." Bo turned and started heading back to the flatbread cart, muttering, "That bastard Farmer Master is in the square, and I don't want to see him." Bo turned to make sure his son was behind him. "Come Long, your mother is packing up. She cannot find ..."

Long ignored his father. The voices in his head grew louder. "Be careful. Look for the winged dragon." He followed Bo back to the cart and saw Lei, who, in this moment, he eyed suspiciously. He recognized the cart and looked about, searching for the dragon.

"Son, are you okay?" Lei approached Long, and he looked at her with confusion, failing to understand what she was saying. "Do you have a fever?" Lei tried to put her hand to Long's forehead.

Long briskly sidestepped his mother. "I am looking for something."

Out on the square, LiLi descended the steps of the long-journey bus.

"Oh, to heaven!" Hong nudged Min's head with a rise and drop of her shoulder, waking her, and pointed in LiLi's direction. "Look at the child bride!"

In the manner of a chain reaction, everyone who was in the square at that moment found themselves following their neighbor's lead and looking in the direction of the child bride spectacle. The newcomer was short and chubby, with full cheeks that glowed pink against a heavily powdered face. Her glossy black hair was curled into a lacquered tower strewn with sparkly, artificial flowers and with dangling strands of faux pearls. Her thin lips, almost lost in the fullness of her face, were notable due to their being painted a deep pink color. Once down in the square, LiLi's clothing could be more fully appreciated by her impromptu audience. Her full-length baby pink, silk dress had a voluminous, gathered skirt, and her matching waistcoat, which strained at the buttons, was trimmed in white fur.

"Aiyah! But she is just a little girl!"

"She is adorable."

"So fat!"

"So pink and fluffy, like a prosperity cupcake."

"Too cute to be eaten!"

The appraisals of the crowd spread quickly, making their way from one side of the square to the other and into the New Market. Soon, even the tired vendors couldn't help but gather at the plastic strip curtain to look at LiLi. Vulgar jokes about how to best eat a cupcake started to circulate, and loud laughter reverberated off the market's corrugated tin roof.

Bo and Lei were too busy searching for the missing cleaver to note LiLi's arrival.

Long began to creep towards the crowd at the curtain, whose laughs he heard as shrieks.

As LiLi had initially emerged from the bus, Wang had been forced to catch his breath.

After looking her over very carefully and feeling quite pleased, Wang greeted LiLi, "Welcome to New Da Long, Little Daughter."

"Thank you, Mister Wang, sir." LiLi smiled at the Farmer Master and bowed her head.

"We will go home and meet my son, your husband, Jiang."

"Of course!" LiLi smiled again. "But we must carefully carry my dear MaMa's wedding gift."

Wang followed LiLi's pudgy hand as she gestured to the bus driver, who now emerged from the vehicle, dangling a scarf-covered bird cage.

"It's a songbird. She loves to sing and eat sweets, as do I." LiLi ran towards the driver and lifted the scarf, gleefully revealing a rust feathered, yellow-beaked bird, with distinctive white rings circling both of its eyes.

Wang grabbed the handle, jerking the cage free from the driver and eliciting a loud fluttering noise. This was the only manifestation of his irritation at having to accommodate yet another childish pet infatuation. Exerting considerable self-control, he kept his voice even and soft as he lifted the bird cage up to his eye level. Feigning interest in the bird's existence, he managed to say with honesty, "Well, your husband will be pleased."

"She has to be walked every day, in her cage of course, and if she is in a good mood, she flaps her wings and dances." Emphasizing her words, LiLi exuberantly raised her own arms straight out to her sides. The sun stretched her winged shadow eastward across the square.

At that very moment, Long, standing tallest in the crowd of onlookers just inside the New Market doorway, looked out on the square and saw a dragon. It was flapping its long, pink wings. "I see it!" he cried out in terror.

"Kill it! Kill it before it kills you!" the voices' commands sprang from between Long's ears.

Long reached his hand under the back of his shirt into the waistband of his pants and raised Lei's cleaver high above his head. "I must kill it!"

He began to thrash at what appeared to him to be tall grass surround- ing him. Trying to make his way through the exit, Long could not move. He thrashed the knife more violently.

Screams ripped through the air: "Oh God!" "What are you doing?" "Stop! Stop!"

Long grunted as he struggled to cut through the grass that had now morphed into thick, heavy vines with ghoulish mouths. The vines were reaching up and curling around his arms, legs and body. "Get off me! Get off!" Losing his footing, Long slipped into one of the many red rivers that had suddenly sprung up from the ground, flowing in every direction.

Bo and Lei ran towards the sound of screams and cries, hearing Long's pleas above the din. Bo dove on Long, grabbing at his arm and trying to wrest free the cleaver before it struck anyone else. Lei dropped to the ground and frantically used her skirt to try to staunch the blood pouring from the cuts of the felled vendor closest to her.

ZhiChao walked next to Yan as she made her way back to her dormitory. "You have been studying too hard. You look tired." He wished he were carrying her bag for her, but she seemed somehow determined not to let him.

"No matter." Yan hugged her shoulder bag into the side of her body. "We all study hard. None of us looks too fresh."

"Listen. I was thinking you may want to come home with me some weekend? Meet my family. My mother would love to feed you."

"*Your* family? Why?" Yan immediately saw Lei's face as it was during their time out on New Lake. She didn't want to be disloyal.

"You can taste proper, traditional Shanghai food. I realize that you likely are missing home-cooked meals. You have already been away from your home for almost two years. Right? My favorite dish is sweet tomato and eggs; our housekeeper used to make it for me as a child. It's tasty. Not like the canteen food."

"I am not sure. I have a lot of schoolwork to prepare. It's not easy for me."

"Or for me."

"Yes. That is true. It's just that—" Yan stopped, not sure of what she wanted.

"What?"

"Nothing."

The two walked in silence for some time. The early evening air felt warm and city life seemed perpetually bathed in light, either natural or artificial. Yan willed herself to mentally review the genetics lecture she had attended earlier in the day: the professor had taught them how to predict trait inheritance in children based on the genes of their parents. Yan noticed how long ZhiChao's legs were, his stride much greater than hers, and couldn't stop herself from wondering what would happen should her genes mix with his. What stride length would their children have? ZhiChao was walking slowly to keep at her pace; Yan immediately sped up so that he would not need to accommodate her.

"Evening." The security guard at the women's dormitory gate greeted Yan and ZhiChao and did not turn away as the two lingered for a moment.

"Tomorrow." Yan sensed the guard's eyes and ears tuned on them.

"Wait a little. Why hurry?" ZhiChao moved away from the gate and out of the light coming from the small guard booth.

"Too much to do. And I am tired, as you said." Yan noted she had started sharing excuses.

"You miss your family. I would also if I could not go home to see them. You know, you don't have to do everything on your own. Medical studies are not easy; the workload is heavy. It, and other things, could be made lighter by sharing the weight with a friend."

"Let's not talk about this."

"Okay. But I just want to say that I am your friend."

"Okay."

"Yan, I am a real friend."

Yan looked at ZhiChao, even as the light was leaving for the day, she could see his lips.

ZhiChao turned and looked at the guard, "Nice evening." He continued to look at the man, as if to will him away. The guard pulled out a cigarette and retreated into his booth, ostensibly to smoke in private.

ZhiChao reached out for Yan's hand, causing her bag to fall off her shoulder and down her arm. Hesitating for just a moment, Yan let her bag slide to the ground. ZhiChao reached out again, and Yan placed her hand in his.

Whispering, "Tomorrow," he then bowed his head and pressed his lips against the soft skin of her palm, making this the first day on which Yan had ever been kissed by anyone other than her mother.

———

On this first day of their courtship, neither Jiang nor LiLi was particularly pleased with their newly discovered matrimonial partner-to-be.

Upon arriving at the Farmer Master's courtyard, LiLi greeted AnRan by bowing her head and not lifting it again until AnRan invited her inside the house, at which point LiLi thanked "Wang TaiTai, Madam" several times.

Made uncomfortable by this exaggerated and seemingly practiced formality, AnRan tried to put the girl at ease. "Daughter, please call me Wang MaMa and call my husband, Wang BaBa. Please take care to relax your spirit. That will be better for all of us."

Dropping all pretense of submissiveness and quiet politeness suited the Cupcake Bride; LiLi quickly slipped back to her natural state, "Oh, Wang MaMa, I am so happy to be here safely. The New Market was so noisy due to some type of fight that was going on when I arrived. But this house is so peaceful and big. Why is it so big? Is it really my new home?" Unable to contain her excitement, she started down one of the hallways, letting her fingers run along the wall and leaving AnRan and Ayi to follow in quick step behind her.

"The next room is the study, where we will find Jiang," AnRan called after LiLi and, upon hearing this, the girl stopped.

Overcome with a sudden shyness, LiLi asked, "Wang MaMa, can you please go first and let him be ready to meet me?"

"Of course." AnRan slipped into the study, leaving LiLi with Ayi.

"How old are you, child?" Ayi looked at the child bride and could not believe it was possible that she had reached her first bleeding.

"Fourteen, but I will be fifteen by this year's end." LiLi's pouty lips and squeaky, high-pitched voice made Ayi wonder if the child was possibly mistaken.

AnRan appeared at the study door. "Come. Come and meet Jiang."

On seeing LiLi for the first time, Jiang, without making even the slightest change to his posture, his calligraphy brush held at the perfect angle above the surface of a clean sheet of paper, pronounced, "She's fat." He shared neither his accurate estimations of LiLi's weight and height, nor that he had found her face to be pleasantly shaped.

Not necessarily perturbed by Jiang's statement, but rather shocked at the frail-looking man on the other side of the table, LiLi simply responded, "You're old." She turned and exited the study, walking back to the spot at which Ayi was waiting in the hallway, and asked her when dinner would be ready.

———————————

On the first day of Long's incarceration, Lei lay at the foot of the wall that surrounded the prison, clutching her coat closed around her. Despite being exhausted, she did not sleep; she tried repeatedly to understand why it was that she had not been able to rescue her son as he had cried out for help. Her stomach grumbled with hunger, though she had no desire for food, and reminded her that she had wrapped the day's leftover flatbreads and placed them on the vending cart where they would remain uneaten. She closed her eyes and remembered Old Doctor telling her that he had no tonic strong enough to fix Long. Lei shook her head. No matter, her son could not stay behind this wall.

"TaiTai? Lei?" Bo staggered up to Lei and sank down on the ground next to her. "Bad cuts, that is all. Not a big problem."

"What? What are you saying?" Lei shook her head, not understanding her husband. She sat up next to him.

"No one has died. He was trying to be a good son. He was confused, that's all."

"I still don't understand."

"He was upset about Wang. I mean, he knew I was upset with Wang. This is what made him act out. Long is a good son; he just wanted to stand up for me. I don't know, maybe he was going to go and talk to the Farmer Master." Bo put his head in his hands and kneaded his skull while grasping at his hair.

"Bo! Six men are in the hospital. Long slashed them with a cleaver. Some of them have been sliced down to the bone. He thought he was chasing a dragon!"

"He was confused. He needs more sleep. I have overworked him."

"Husband, please listen to me. Old Doctor says this is some sort of mental deficiency. Our boy has the mind-splitting disease, and that …"

"Don't talk. Don't you dare talk! Close your mouth!" Bo began to scream, not just at Lei, but at anyone who could hear him. He pounded his fists against his thighs. "Don't talk. Don't say anything!"

Lei stood up and faced the wall. She stretched out her arms, put her palms on the wall and pushed against it with all her might. Head hanging down between her extended arms, she wept loudly, sounding animal-like. Her tears soaked the ground.

Bo, who had never heard this sound—the sound of his wife crying—was stunned into silence. He stood up, his legs shaking and threatening to forsake him. He put his hand on her shoulder. "Come, we will go home and explain everything to the authorities in the morning, when it is day and things are easier to see."

Lei ignored Bo. She placed her face up against the wall and, not wanting her son to be lonely, she began to sing to him.

Part Five

New Da Long & Shanghai
China, 2000

Chapter Twenty-Three

Seeds and Stitches

... The farmer plants seedlings
Plants them on the green trees
Plants them on the black mountains Plants
them on the white clouds Plants them on the
blue sky
  - *Planting Rice Seedlings* by Chan Ping

The nursery was full and ready to be drained of water. Each carefully germinated rice seed had been settled into its raised bed, fed and bathed with nutrient-rich water for three weeks, and had grown steadily from a tiny, green shoot into a hearty, twenty-centimeter-tall, fully leafed, branching seedling that was ready to be transplanted. Unearthing and separating the seedlings in preparation for their journey to the lower paddy took patience and a delicate touch, but it was no less back-breaking than the toil of the harvesting season, which would hopefully follow in several months.

The humid summer warmed Lei's back, and she allowed the heat to soothe her heart. She kept her head down and her hands working, thankful that day after day passed, for the most part, in her head. Digging her bare fingers into the soil and working around the base of each seedling, Lei loosened its root ball and then pulled it free, laying it carefully into the basket that hung off her lower back. On the mirrored surface of the seedling bed—a collection of warm water that crested just above Lei's ankles—lay the sky, clouds, trees and mountains at her feet. The voices of the other workers went unheard by Lei, who filled her head with private conversation.

"My son, the clouds are full of darkness today. The waters will rise."

"MaMa, will the seedlings drink all of it?"

"No, my son, they will take what they need, but we will help them not drown."

"You will let the water go down the hills to the lower paddy?"

"Yes, my son. You are a smart boy, and a good one, too."

"MaMa, how are the trees? Do they dance or stand still?"

"My son, today they do neither. Their arms just shake ever so slightly."

Lei passed every day this way, by herself. When the mid-day meal hour arrived, the other workers no longer asked Lei to walk with them down the terraces to the dry land below, where they gathered and gossiped. And though she was not with them, and though contempt of her could easily have flowed, the others left Lei alone to mend her heart. To lose a son was no easy thing, but to have him mad and caged for these past few years was worse yet.

Lei stood up and stretched her back. She reached into her pocket and pulled out a paper-wrapped, day-old flat bread which was chewy and oily with all its flake sogged through. From up here, in the high nursery, she could follow the downward wiggle of the terraces and see the Farmer Master's house. She spent no time on the possibility that he could be looking up at her. Over in the courtyard, she spotted a splotch of bright pink slipping in and out of the billowing white sheets that had been hung up to dry. She smiled at the now familiar sight of the Cupcake Bride dancing by herself. Beyond the house, further down the sloping terrain, she could see the Lake Ring Road and imagined the purring of the colored dots that moved along it. That some of the dots belonged to Pang and were plying the route transporting goods made her smile. She continued to talk while chewing:

"My son, your uncle is a good man and sends you his kind wishes."

"MaMa, does he talk about me? Do they all talk about me?"

"Oh, no. Not in any way that should make you scared." Lei shook her head vigorously. "They only speak of you with fondness and a sense of missing."

"What does Uncle Pang say?"

"He says he is happy to help BaBa. He takes him now, with the cart and all, to and from the New Market. He says he will do so until you come back to us."

"Will you still not go with them?"

"I am with them until Wang's Way. I work here. You know that."

"MaMa, I am sorry ... I ..."

"No need. I stand up from bed just a little earlier than before, but not much. I would have been lying there anyway, with my eyes open. Now I just put myself to use. I roll and fill all the flatbreads and curl them into pinwheels for BaBa."

"And then he rolls them flat and cooks them all alone, at the—"

"Yes, he does and sells them as well."

"Does he still throw his temper at you? Is he still not pleased about you being here?" "Shh ... No worries. I must get back to work."

Lei carefully re-wrapped her half-eaten flat bread and pushed it back into her pocket and rubbed the oil on her fingers into the backs of her hands. She pushed Bo's angry words out of her head; at the end of each workday, her pockets were heavier with the Farmer Master's pay than were Bo's from holding his meager flatbread earnings.

"MaMa?"

"Yes, my son." Lei, preparing for the work that would continue until the sun began to sag, massaged her hands, bringing blood into them.

"MaMa, when can I come home?"

"Soon, my son." Lei, unaware of her own self-deceit, bent back down and started again to release the tender seedlings.

The clouds broke open and rained red envelopes down onto the trees whose branches suddenly grew buds which bloomed into flowers with red envelope petals. Lei ran a hand back and forth through the water, trying to pick up the little packets. She thanked the ancestors for reminding her that all things were possible through the power of the glossy red paper pouches whose bellies she and Bo stuffed with their earnings. Shared in the right way, these little bribes opened the prison gates and allowed a mother to touch her frightened child for the first time in months, even if for just a few minutes, and to stroke the tangles out of his unwashed hair. They spirited toothpaste and soap into the dirtiest corners of a cell and allowed a son to have the dignity of clean breath and body. These same little red envelopes allowed a father to buy a candy bar for his son, even if the father would not be there to share it with him.

The red envelopes were how love made its way over the prison wall.

Her basket full of the young seedlings, Lei began to make her way down the slippery slopes of the terraced paddies. As she descended, she could now clearly see the Eagle's Eye and its frame filled by the Farmer

Master. She was grateful for this job and did not harbor any of Bo's ill will towards the man. She had bigger problems to deal with than Bo's ; fatter red envelopes would be needed to get Long out from behind the prison's walls.

Lei began to hum softly. Even as she walked her way down Wang's fields, she sat in a cell keeping her son company.

The general medicine ward of Shanghai's Number Three hospital was a single long room with two rows of thirty beds pushed up against opposite walls. A thin row of ventilation windows ran along the top of one side, set high up on the wall, almost abutting the ceiling. All the windows were flung wide open, though the wet air of the Shanghai summer was too lazy to move. Down the center of the room, in between the rows of beds, hung a fleet of fluorescent light tubes that dangled precariously by cheap electrical wire.

"Young Lady Doctor! Young Lady Doctor! My pain kills me." Grabbing his side through his grubby gown, a man staggered about his bed as he called to Yan, not recognizing she was one of the student doctors.

"Please, wait just a little time. The Doctor Professor will be with you shortly." Yan tried to quiet the man.

He persisted. "You, how pretty you are! I am happy to have you. Please, come. I have a red envelope for you. A thick one!"

Imprinted like ducklings on a wheeled metal cart messily stacked with clipboards, one for each patient on the ward, a gaggle of student doctors stood around the cart, chatting as the Doctor Professor worked his way through the last drags of his cigarette.

The Doctor Professor eyed Yan. "Fang Yan, you have your admirers, don't you? Maybe you should start off our morning rounds. Do you have the charts in order?"

"You, how pretty! Look at my leg. Please, I have a question. Look at how it does not work. Useless." A second patient stood up on his bed, unthinkingly letting his bed sheet drop and exposing his naked body as he pointed at Yan.

Yan's face warmed. "Sorry, sir."

"Not at all. A popular doctor is a wealthy doctor. Thankfully, your mind is worthy of such ... attention." The Doctor Professor pulled another cigarette from his pocket and one of Yan's classmates presented him with the ready flame of a BIC lighter. Moving rapidly from bed to bed and from broken body part to broken body part, the gaggle made its way through the ward, pushing the cart along and handing clipboard after clipboard to the Doctor Professor for his review and assessment. The students scribed every word the man uttered for later memorization. The patients also recorded his words in their own way: each patient engaged in a game of telephone, relaying every aspect of their own and everyone else's plights, as discussed by the Doctor Professor, to their neighbors in the adjacent beds.

Though her hand was cramping from furiously penning her notes, Yan did not dare stop. She was filled with a sense of awe at Doctor Professor's prodigious knowledge and his facility with its application. Flying from anatomy to physiology to biochemistry, the senior scholar shared his wisdom freely, in a way that made Yan's head take flight. She could dive into the common bile duct in one moment and follow the current of the blood as it raced through the four chambers of the heart in another; she danced confidently on the tangled neurons of the human brain or moved with water molecules pulled along the chemical gradient in the kidney's collecting ducts. That Yan's brain worked this way, allowing her to see the unseeable and touch the untouchable, fostered her reputation for being a medical prodigy. That her fellow students, and even a fair number of her professors, admired her was of little interest to Yan. At the end of each day her mind, while fed and full, always went into the night hungry for more.

Later that evening, lying in the bed of her dorm room with ZhiChao, Yan whispered to avoid waking her roommate, "There is so much more to learn. It seems unfair. Can we ever be satisfied?"

ZhiChao pulled Yan close to him. "I don't know. Your brain is impressively big. It needs to be filled."

Yan loved the way ZhiChao saw her, ever championing her thirst to know more. She kissed him and lay her head down on his chest, enjoying the softness of his shirt.

"Did you ask your parents?" ZhiChao stroked her hair.

"I did. My MaMa wrote to me. She's okay."

Yan fell precipitously silent. She did not tell ZhiChao that her parents had just visited Long on the two-year anniversary of his incarceration. Lei had taken the time to detail the excessive humidity of the day, the foods she had carefully prepared and packed to share, the brands of shampoo and toothpaste she had pressed into Long's rough hands, and how desperately thin he now had become. She did not have any word about what medications, if any, Long was receiving, even though Yan's last letter had stressed the importance of finding this out.

Yan felt her chest tighten. In her absence, life in New Da Long had pushed forward and erupted into a new form that she feared she would barely recognize. Long was in prison, Jiang was married, and Lei was once again working for Farmer Master Wang. The cityscape, just outside her window, often felt ceaseless and unrelenting, stretching into the forever of the horizon and almost blinding you to any other existence. But Yan knew that beyond the beyond lay her *laojia*.

Yan forced a heavy sigh to relieve the sense of pressure mounting within her and allowed herself to be distracted. Running her fingers along the stiff collar of ZhiChao's shirt, Yan could feel the stitching that secured its hem. The thread was so fine, it worked almost invisibly to hold the fabric in place. She immediately saw how this place, Shanghai, like the fabric, took shape and was morphed into something big and brilliant, held in place by the work of the unseen. Each migrant was an invisible stitch, sewn far from home. Was she just another stitch?

ZhiChao took a deep breath and ventured into Yan's silence, "When do you think we should leave?"

"I don't know." Her answer was truthful, and he knew that.

"At the end of the next school year, when we finish? That gives us enough time to prepare everything."

"I don't know." Yan closed her eyes.

"Yan, my father has used his connections. It was not easy, and the exchange of favors will play out for a long time to come, but we will both have our visas for America." ZhiChao's tongue broke down the word America into too many syllables.

"The Beautiful Country."

"Yes, the Beautiful Country."

Wanting to believe that the promise of the "Beautiful Country" was enough to make his point, to bring him a genius wife whose mind sought to be fed, to ferry a young couple across an ocean and into a strange new life, to make looking back impossible, ZhiChao let his words float in the air and waited for them to make a deep impression upon landing. The room was quiet except for the snores of Yan's roommate and a pair of dogs outside trying to out-bark one another. Feeling the rise and fall of Yan's chest against his body, ZhiChao waited patiently. When Yan's breathing slowed and her body became heavier against his, he realized his "Beautiful Country" had not fallen as it should have, and he shook Yan awake.

"You fell asleep!"

"Sorry, I'm so tired." Yan shifted in place.

"Yan, we need to make our plans. Your mother, what exactly did she say?"

Yan sat up, retrieved Lei's letter from her bag and handed it to ZhiChao who read it aloud, focusing on the last line, "Daughter, take the sky train and know your spirit will always be carried home. Love, MaMa." ZhiChao looked at Yan quizzically.

"She is telling me to join my greatest uncle, and that everything will be resolved on my death. That I will be brought home like the Celestials and their bones. My bones will be ..."

"What is she saying? I don't understand." ZhiChao was sitting up next to Yan.

"It is her way of blessing me to go."

"Really?" ZhiChao put his arms around Yan and hugged her close to him, "That's too good!"

Yan looked up at him, her eyes wide with disbelief. ZhiChao's quest for clarity and the ease with which he grabbed it was part of what she admired about him but, in this moment, she found it unnerving. For ZhiChao, life's math was so easy: Yan, the "beautiful and brilliant" woman he loved, plus family connections and wealth equaled "go to America" and take advantage of the opportunities it offered, wherever that might lead. The fact that Yan also happened to be a migrant with an incarcerated, mentally ill brother and parents who did not have a home of their own somehow got canceled out in his working of the equation. "You do see she didn't say anything relevant about my brother, other than he's lost weight. She barely mentioned my father, for that matter."

"She is a good MaMa. She sends you to seek answers."

"What can you possibly mean?" Yan forced herself to slow her breathing and to not pull out of his arms in frustration.

"Don't you want to understand why Long's illness started and how to stop it? You are the one, of all of us, who sees things most cannot. You dream of molecular biology and biochemistry, while the rest of us struggle to keep up. You see the brain chemicals diffusing across the synapses between neurons, gliding into their receptors, and lighting up electrical pathways in the brain. Tell me you haven't dreamt of seeing how those chemicals and pathways work in your brother's brain? In the Beautiful Country, all of these questions are being explored. The pathophysiology of myriad diseases and the mechanisms of action of the latest therapeutics—this is what the top minds are working on day and night."

Yan pulled away from ZhiChao so that she could see his face.

ZhiChao looked at Yan and could see that he had her full attention. "Yan, this is an amazing opportunity. One our own fathers never had.

Think of all the families right here who will benefit from what you learn. Wouldn't you want someone like you to go and bring back answers for someone like Long? Without answers, you know that he and those like him will be left to struggle."

Yan's jaw tightened painfully. She knew that her brother likely spent most of his waking hours trussed up in his cell, trying to keep up with a mind that moved from the real to the unreal without warning. These thoughts she kept out of her letters to Lei and Bo. "It will help them, yes? Leaving makes life better for him, for all of them. Right?" Her words were short and terse, her body stiff.

ZhiChao reached for Yan's hand, and she did not resist, "Your parents worked all those years in this city, and they work again for you to have something more, something better. You seek better and whatever you find, whatever you gain, you share."

"With them? When we come back?"

"Of course." His eyes were on hers, looking at her with true conviction.

"Okay." Yan managed a small smile of assent. She closed her eyes as she allowed her body to lean closer into him.

ZhiChao fell asleep, holding Yan securely. She waited for his arms to go limp and then freed herself. She went to the window and looked out into the night sky, wanting to count stars. The city's lights almost outshone the heavens, and Yan lovingly followed them all the way to the horizon, searching for the beyond.

Shanghai's appeal had revealed itself slowly to her. Her first year here, Yan had been filled with doubt about how to navigate such a place. The city was filled with soft-handed people who lived life above the earth, almost removed from it and from the people who worked the soil with their bodies. Then she had fallen in love with one such soft-handed man who laughed and loved so easily and looked at her, Yan, with such awe. ZhiChao had taken her to discover the nooks and crannies of the real Shanghai. Together they explored historic hutongs and ancient temples, city parks where people from all over came to relax and recover, bustling food markets and the bursting business district, a migrant shanty that lay under a bridge, the city's oldest orphanage that labored to take care of the youngest unwanted, and the expat villas, across the Huang Pu, filled with people from all over the world.

The city was like a centerless onion with endless layers of skin. It was in one of those layers that Yan felt most alive. Inside the city's most revered academic hospital, she immersed herself in a world of books, experimented in fully equipped laboratories, and was taught how to use the nation's most modern hospital machines. She spent month after month moving through different hospital departments, going from the operating theater to the oncology ward to the neonatal unit, and on and on. Shanghai was a multi-course meal in learning with one exquisite dish after another. The Beautiful Country, it was rumored, promised an even larger menu. Yan remembered what the beloved Doctor Professor had told her in her first year, when loneliness severely creased her forehead, "Don't grip so tightly onto the past that you have no strength to reach out to the future."

ZhiChao purred softly on her bed and Yan wondered about what the future held for them. She came back to bed and lay down next to him, tracing his lips with her fingers and letting her feet touch his. There was peace in his face; he was a good man. She put her hand up close to his mouth and nose and counted his breaths. She synchronized her breathing with his and felt electric.

Yan's mind drifted to Bo and his thoughts on love and marriage, shared with her on that night on the mountainside in the time when she had not yet known whether he had betrothed her to Jiang: "Yan, I did not love your mother in a passionate way. That type of love does not make a life. Ours was more a relationship of purpose."

She had not said anything to her father about what type of love she sought; she, herself, had not known. Bo had assumed her talk of leaving and seeing new things, included ideas of finding romantic "modern love." What if he was wrong? Wasn't all life about energy? Wasn't passion just another type of energy? Old Doctor always spoke in terms of energy flow, too much and too little of it determining health. What if this electricity inside of her, lying here next to ZhiChao and breathing each breath with him, was a power source fueling a relationship of purpose? What would that type of love build?

That night in her dreams, Yan saw the neat stitches of ZhiChao's collar pop loose and their invisible thread coil freely up and out the open window; let loose, the thread flew away in the wind.

———————

Ayi knew that indulging LiLi was not the solution, but she found herself helpless in the face of the girl's charms. The Cupcake Bride had brought a much-appreciated lightness to the heavy walls of the Farmer Master's home, but she had also seemingly rearranged time, perplexingly reversing its course. After finishing her studies at the New Da Long school with Ayi's assistance, LiLi had married Jiang with very little resistance. Ayi had suspected that LiLi had obediently followed the instructions of her mother and her sister, with whom the girl corresponded every few months. However, since her marriage several months earlier, LiLi had both grown rounder and had become younger with each filling in of the moon. Rather than maturing into her inevitable role of wife, she seemed to be regressing. Ayi and AnRan both felt compelled more than ever to mother the girl, and maybe this was okay, as she was only sixteen and marriage was an adjustment.

This explained the individually wrapped, dried sugar plums that Ayi now perpetually kept in her pocket ready for the offering to LiLi whenever the girl joined her in the kitchen or out in the courtyard. And even though it was unfortunate that LiLi preferred the company of Ayi to that of her own husband, Ayi did not have the heart to shun the girl and decided to try bribery instead.

"Little LiLi, you should not be out here. The sun is too hot for your skin; you will become dark like the workers in the fields. Why not go to the study to paint the landscape?" Ayi shielded her eyes, exaggerating the brightness of the sun. "I will bring in a bowl of creamy milk candies. The ones from Shanghai."

Though LiLi could taste the sticky sweetness in her mouth, knowing Jiang was in the first-floor study and that the Farmer Master sat in the second-floor office, she did not move, pressing her feet firmly into the ground. She missed going to school each day and wanted desperately to be free of the house. "Why can't I be here with you? The weather is so fair. I am covered. Help me tie my bonnet, the one Wang BaBa brought for me." LiLi pressed down the pink sun hat that was on her head and lifted her chin, exposing her neck so that Ayi could help tie the hat's straps. She eyed the woman carefully. "Ayi, you know I have a sister in Shanghai?"

"I did hear."

"MaMa told me that once a girl marries, she becomes part of her husband's family, and her own family comes second. She told me it was not likely I would see her or LuLu, my big sister, for quite some time."

"Well, your MaMa is to be followed. And your sister ... well, Shanghai is too far. It would be quite difficult."

"It's a fine city, I hear. Filled with interesting people."

"Yes." Ayi stepped back and admired LiLi, who now had a beautiful bow blooming from beneath her jawline. "So pretty you are."

LiLi broke into a smile, stood up, and began to sing and dance about the courtyard. Seeing the rabbit hutch, she ran over to it and reached through its chicken wire front to stroke the animals. After running her fingers along the rabbit noses, she turned to watch Ayi sweep the courtyard with a branch-bristle brush. "Ayi, you remind me of my MaMa."

"Really?"

"Yes. She's always sweeping the manger in our family home and chasing the chickens and goats out of her way. She works hard."

"I am sure. If she were here, she would want you inside ... with your husband, don't you think?"

"She would be happy I have a friend here." LiLi looked at the ground, not wanting Ayi to see her face.

"But I am an old woman."

"Yes, but my husband is an old man!" LiLi was desperate to tell someone—LuLu, MaMa, Ayi, anyone—how much Jiang scared her. His eyes never looked at hers and his sickly frame, that sometimes fluttered and then went loose like a rag, made her stomach turn over and over. She opened her mouth, but no noise came out. Instead, tears rained on the ground. Ayi rushed over to the girl and reached into her pocket with one hand while using the other to dab LiLi's face gently with her apron. "Hush, hush. These things take time." She unwrapped a sugary plum and popped it into LiLi's mouth, trying to soften the sounds of her crying.

Up through the atrium and straight through the door of Farmer Master's office came the familiar cries of the child bride. Standing at the window and looking up to the rice terraces, Wang ran his tongue back and forth over an ulceration on the inside of his right cheek. He was watching Fang Bo's wife, admiring the strength of her body and her evident distaste for the idle chatter of the other peasants. Looking at Lei's height, he recalled Yan's stature and, though he could not see Lei's face clearly from so far away, he knew that her expression was likely soothing in the same way as Yan's often had been. The girl who got away had a mother hooked to his land. This fact, having Lei working for him, was not enough to stop Wang from suddenly biting down on the ulcer and sending blood into his mouth.

Wang spat into a cup on his desk, slumped into his chair, and began to knead his forehead with his fingers. He pressed hard through his skin down onto his skull, hoping to distract himself from the sound of LiLi with an alternate source of discomfort. When this failed, he moved his hands over his ears as the stupid girl's crying grew louder and louder; in actuality, LiLi was no longer crying but was seated in the courtyard with a rabbit in her lap, happily sucking on a sugared plum candy. What Wang was hearing was a sound embedded deep in his head, coming from those masses of neurons responsible for memory. It was the sound that he had first heard while standing at the door of his son and daughter-in-law's bedroom with his ear pressed up against their door. It appeared that while LiLi had not resisted the idea of getting married, she had come to simply resist the reality of being married.

Wang's decision, several weeks earlier, to eavesdrop at the door of the newlyweds was in some ways the natural result of his unspoken plans for the girl.

From the moment LiLi had stepped down into the New Da Long Square, she had been watched ever so carefully from all directions by all manner of people. However, no one had watched her more closely, more keenly, or as persistently as the Farmer Master. He had watched her hands move with every word she spoke, fluttering this way or that. That she sucked hard on all sweet things she popped in her mouth, sang loudly off key, and danced in a clumsy succession of circles were all noted with intense interest by Wang, not because any of this was endearing or even irritating, but simply because this was her manner "before." All these observations served as a pre-marriage starting point. Any deviation from LiLi's pre-marriage baseline would be proof of their finally being an "after" marriage development.

As soon as LiLi's fingers looked pudgier, the fullness of her cheeks became fuller, and the puckering around the buttons on her vest became ever so slightly more pronounced as she sang and danced, Wang delighted in her commencing the "after" period.

That the Farmer Master suddenly walked with a softer tread, emerged from his office several times in the day to look out on the courtyard, and even took to standing outside in the sun, initially had AnRan confused. Soon enough, all became clear.

One morning, as she combed her hair in their bedroom, Wang suggested to AnRan, "TaiTai, daughter should be taken to see Old Doctor."

"Why? Is she ill?" AnRan, who had been pulling a heavy, wooden comb through a section of hair that was covering the front of her face, stopped and drew her hair aside.

"No. Not at all. Have you not noticed how she is changed?"

"Changed? Yes, I have. It has had Ayi and me both concerned."

"Concerned? What for? She is clearly, finally, with child."

AnRan contemplated her husband's words and wondered if, even hoped, he was right. The changes of pregnancy were known to be mercurial; this could explain LiLi's increasing penchant for sweets and her clinging to the womenfolk of the house.

AnRan's hope was very short-lived. Ayi, who stood just outside the doorway, now entered with clean linens and shook her head "no" at AnRan. Ayi laid the linens on the foot of the bed and left the room.

AnRan started to comb her hair again, bringing an even larger section of it forward over her face. From behind her shield, she spoke almost without sound, "The girl is not pregnant. She has recently bled."

Wang said nothing. His response, coming only from the wooden floors that creaked more loudly than ever with strain as he exited the bedroom, sent a chill down his wife's spine.

The next time LuLu met Wang, none of their customary pleasantries were exchanged.

"Why is she not pregnant? You said she was pure and whole!" Though Wang spoke quietly, his words vibrated against the stillness of LuLu's face. "What is wrong with her?"

"Relax. There is nothing wrong with her."

"It has been almost two years since she has been in my house and married to my son."

"Yes, I know. Do I need to remind you that I have not seen her in over two years! You promised me that I would see her as soon as the marriage was finalized, and I have not seen her!"

LuLu's words now flew fast at Wang. The couple stood on the sidewalk outside the barbershop, where the baldness of their words had no bearing on their surroundings. Streams of people sluiced past them.

"I have been waiting for her to be pregnant. To offer a reason for her to call on her sister for a visit."

"Like a reward? Or a payment for services rendered?" LuLu glared at Wang. She was his match. He let his shoulders drop and changed his stance, realizing that it might not be beyond her to claw at his face.

His voice softened. "I just thought that by now ..."

"Yes. I understand. How do you know your son is not broken?"

Wang searched LuLu's face, trying to see if she knew anything, but dismissed this as she continued, "I mean, he was inexperienced, no?"

"Yes."

"Is he different now? Does he walk or talk as a man, or is it possible he is still a boy?"

It was this conversation that prompted Wang, upon his return to New Da Long, to put his ear against the door of LiLi and Jiang's bedroom late in the night. Hearing the childish girl sobbing, once again, he refused to bite down on himself and instead he entered the room unannounced. It was only then that he discovered, door wide open, LiLi alone in the bed, wrapped up like a piece of candy in a silk nightgown that was buttoned up to her neck and cinched tightly around her waist. And it was there, on the floor in the corner of the room, that he saw Jiang huddled on a makeshift bed of folded blankets and sheets. And, in that moment, the Farmer Master, standing uninvited between the two of them, became privy to the only words the two had ever shared in their marital bed:

"I don't want him to touch me!"

"I will never touch her."

The Farmer Master, fighting the urge to take both fools in front of him by the neck, stormed out of the room. His mouth flooded with the taste of blood.

———————

Squatting in the yard, Bo and Fang MaMa found themselves alone, low to the ground, and facing each other as they had countless times before.

"I will not see her again." Bo watched as Fang MaMa handled a heavy cleaver, scrubbing it free of dirt. "Her mother has filled her head with silly stories and ideas, and this is what comes of it all."

"Cha! Yan ...Yan is to ... to ... to be married. She will have a city *hukou*."

"For a filthy city. A city that she will not even be in."

"Aiyah!" Wet exasperation flew out of Fang MaMa's mouth. She dropped the cleaver in the basin of water, the grip of her twisted hands too loose to hold onto it.

"I'll do it." Bo pulled the basin in front of him and reached into the soapy water for the cleaver. He used his nails to scrape the last bits of stubborn dough from its blade.

After the cleaver was clean, Bo placed it on a towel at Fang MaMa's feet, and she dabbed it dry.

"America! To the devil's land she goes, enticed by a devil man." Bo wiped his hands on his thighs. "I should have made her stay here, with me, with all of us."

"The way you make your wi ... wi ... wife ... stay?" Fang MaMa punctuated her words with single-hand air punches.

"She works for that bastard of her own mind. She knows he is responsible for Long."

"Bah! You don't know that. Nobody knows how ... how this happened." The old lady patted Bo on one knee. "Lei earns ... earns for your son. She went, so you did not have to ... beg ...beg the man for a job. She let you save face."

Looking at the ground between his feet, Bo said nothing. Lei had returned to working for the Farmer Master. A full three years earlier, she had simply stated, "Tomorrow I will work in the fields." Bo had pretended not to hear her, making believe that the New Market noise drowned out her voice as he continued to punch the dough against the sides of the metal bowl. Working the food cart was not a lucrative business, but it was theirs.

The next morning, when Pang had stopped his truck at the foot of the Old Wang Way, Lei had climbed out without a word and had simply made her way up to the Farmer Master's rice terraces. Bo sat stonelike, looking at nothing but the empty road that lay ahead.

Only at night, in their room, which was now empty but for the two of them, did he try to lash her with his words. But the words "pride," "dignity," "shame," fell in the space between the two of them and were not picked up. The tongue lashings didn't last for long, as Bo did not have the energy to sustain the effort, and he felt foolish doing so when Lei's substantial earnings helped fill the red envelopes faster. One night, under the cover of darkness as they lay in their bed, Bo did ask Lei if he shouldn't come up with her to work Wang's terraces.

Without hesitation, Lei answered, "No, Bo. You put the Farmer Master in his place when you turned down his bride bid for Yan. You must allow *him* to save face." Bo had been grateful that Lei could not see any part of him and had reached his feet over to warm hers.

"Pass me the pin." Reaching her hand towards Bo, Fang MaMa's arm trembled.

"MaMa, rest. I will do it." Bo placed the heavy wooden rolling pin into the basin and began to rub it down with water.

"Rest? Give it to me. You have worked all day." Fang MaMa splashed her hand in the water, but Bo pushed it away and she did not fight him.

"Your daughter is to be married, your wife works from dark to dark, and your ... son," Fang MaMa's tremble took on a faster frequency, and the pink lower rims of her eyes glistened, "he ... he ... Long lives."

Taking the towel from the ground, Bo dried Fang MaMa's hand. And then, as he had seen MeiLin do many a time, he squeezed each bony spot at the base of each of his mother's fingers between the pads of his own fingers. The old woman breathed easier and moaned in appreciation. From inside the house came the sounds of MeiLin preparing a meal. Bo looked around him. Far beyond his mother, he saw Wei and Tao soaping the bikes and Pang, who Bo now considered to be his brother, heaving Bo's flatbread grill out of the back of his cart and steadily placing it on the ground.

———

Lifting his face off his desk, the Farmer Master could see the moon through the Eagle's Eye. As he struggled to stand, the silver crescent began to swing back and forth, and the floor began to move as if afloat on the ocean. Falling forward against the desk, Wang's arms swung about and swept the open ledger onto the ground. Birds and flowers began to float up off the desk, and Wang tried to swat them out of his face. Certain that Earth MaMa was on the rise again, he listened out for the screams of his wife but was met with silence.

His eyes pulsed, and he tried to focus on a small object on the desk, certain it had some meaning; grasping for the object, he miscalculated and sent it hurtling off the desk and onto the floor where it shattered. Wang fell deep into darkness before recognizing it as an herbal sedative bottle from Old Man Doctor's clinic and before recalling that he had, attempting to still the pounding in his head, swallowed its entire contents several hours earlier.

Across the atrium, LiLi sat straight up in the bed, awoken by the sound of splintering glass. She immediately looked to the corner of the room and was relieved to see Jiang asleep on the floor, nowhere close to her. She lay back down with her eyes wide open, and was that way for some time, waiting for sleep to return. She occupied herself by compos-ing the text of a letter she wished to send her sister:

Dearest LuLu,
I know Shanghai is far, but not so far that I could not find my way to you.
I did not understand what it meant to have my husband be a sickly, old
man. Can your Mister Fu, your city husband, not find a way to set me free?

You two will start a family soon; maybe I could be your Ayi and help raise my niece or nephew so as not to be a burden to you both? Please LuLu, do not tell MaMa; she must not know. I believe Mister Wang tricked her. She would not be able to relax and ...

LiLi did not want to think of her mother worrying; she put the letter out of her mind and allowed her stomach to start talking to her. Its grumbling convinced her to climb out of bed and coaxed her quietly down the stairs and into the kitchen. She searched out Ayi's jar of milk candies and easily found it on the table as if it had been left there just in case she came looking. Opening several pieces, careful to scrunch the empty wrappers tightly in her hand, LiLi successively dropped one candy after another into her mouth and began to suck loudly on the sticky blob.

"Why are you here? What are you doing?" LiLi did not hear the Farmer Master enter the kitchen and almost choked with fright when his voice came out of the darkness.

"Wang BaBa! Oh, I was hungry." LiLi's voice trembled, and, in the darkness, she could not see just how close the Farmer Master was to her.

"What? What are you saying?"

She realized she could smell his breath. "I am sorry. Did I disturb you with my noise?"

Wang heard the girl's voice but could not fully understand what she was saying. Her words sounded so very far away, as if she were under water. "What? Speak properly!" His voice boomed through the kitchen. "What are you sorry about?"

Again, her voice came like water: "I said I did not mean to disturb you."

Wang looked at LiLi and saw LuLu. He was flooded with relief and reached out to grab her waist. "It's you!"

The girl squealed with fright and tried to pull away. "Wang BaBa! Please stop!"

"Don't call me that!" Wang's eyes were wide open, and the whites were streaked with red. His face was so close to her, that his mouth was all she could possibly see. Her shriek came blast-like into Wang's head, causing his teeth to clamp down so forcefully as to be painful. He reflexively put his hand over the source of the noise. He brought the noise down onto the floor and tried to crush it with his full weight.

LiLi's nostrils flared ferociously, and her chest heaved up and down rapidly. Her mouth moved under Wang's hand but made no sound.

Wang looked at the girl, and, in one flash, he saw LuLu, and, in the next, he saw LiLi. He shook his head violently from side to side, pushing down on her body, pressing down on her mouth. When he stopped, the girl, who had frozen, her eyes wide, confused him. In one moment, she was the woman who gave him everything she had, and, in the next, she was the girl who refused to give him the one thing he wanted.

A wicked combination of arousal and anger propelled Wang forward, and he thrust his way into LuLu and LiLi, forcefully demanding to be given and taking what he wanted.

Through the kitchen window, the night sky remained black.

Grey morning light crept into the lower part of the window and made its way to filling the kitchen. Ayi found LiLi curled up on the kitchen floor and saw the open jar of milk candies on the table.

"Silly girl! Come, stand up."

LiLi seemed determined not to open her eyes.

"Fine. I should leave you right there." Ayi looked down on LiLi and noticed that the girl was shivering. She bent down and grabbed the girl's hands with her own and pulled her up.

LiLi's eyes remained tightly shut, although she moved under her own power. The older woman wondered whether the girl might be sleep-walking and felt ashamed for scolding her. After helping the Cupcake Bride back into bed, Ayi went back to the kitchen to clean the girl's vomit, but first she knelt and picked up the several waxy candy wrappers that were scattered on the floor.

Chapter Twenty-Four

Sixes

The darkness of morning rendered the alley empty. Alternating the lifting of each side of her buttocks off the cold cement by clenching and releasing her muscles, the seamstress exercised while seated on the steps in front of her store. She methodically regulated her breathing, inhaling deeply with each muscle contraction and exhaling forcefully with each subsequent relaxation. Slowly rising, she began to beat blood into her upper body, slapping her right shoulder with her left hand and then slapping her left shoulder with her right hand, each slap stressed with an exhaled grunt. The old woman's effort fogged the air, for winter had come; her body reluctantly warmed beneath several layers of quilted garment.

Inside the shop, a pair of unornamented ceiling bulbs shone down over a large, wooden sewing table. The elements of the seamstress's craft lent topography to the table. In the center rose a soft mountain of brushed cotton fabric, its base obscured by several pools of satin and silk. At one end of the table, heavy and unyielding, a glossy, black sewing machine with a hand-cranked balance wheel waited to be used; spools of colored thread, some short and squat, others skinny and tall, clustered around the machine. As the seamstress entered the shop, a chilly gust of wind followed her and set the edges of several tissue paper pattern pieces at the other end of the table flapping, their centers weighed down by a large, smooth, river rock. Nearby sat a prickly, red, felt tomato stuffed with needles of various lengths, a pair of scissors with razor-sharp, straight-edged blades, and a set of pinking shears with jagged teeth.

Despite being indoors, the seamstress did not remove a single garment of clothing; the frugality of government authorities did not allow for the temperature inside the store to be meaningfully different from the temperature outside on the stoop. Unlike its compatriot cities to the north of the HuaiHe River, in which government authorities had powered up the centrally controlled heating of all buildings, Shanghai was allocated no heat; no warmth crept through its ducts.

Rubbing her hands together and puffing warm breaths between them, the seamstress eyed the materials of her craft. She set free the pattern pieces and laid them out carefully on the table, each one hand-scribed with myriad vectors of direction, symbols, and numbers of measure. Running her fingers along the edge of a small, bodice-shaped piece, the old woman's eyes turned watery, and her mind drifted to the rooms above. The plastic wall clock indicated that three minutes would bring the time to six. Her son would soon rise, and her daughter-in-law would bring her a thermos of steaming milk tea. She studied the pieces again and thought of her grandson, long gone from the house but not far, and remembered the many times these pieces had been used over the years to produce the garments she most loved to make. Each small piece, a patch of love and hope, stitched together to swaddle and protect a new life. Her pulse quickened with the pleasure of being alive to make another set. Through her shop window, she could see the barbershop; all its lights remained off. She had unreservedly served all the women of the store, including both of its Fu Tai Tais, the second of whom was counting on her.

Pulling loose a piece of snow-white cotton from the mountain, spreading it smooth and flat with her hands, and strategically arranging the tissue paper templates to minimize fabric waste, the seamstress now placed a half dozen pins between her lips. One by one, the pins secured pinches of paired fabric and tissue paper. Then, armed with her pinking shears, the old woman bit into the fabric, letting loose tiny sleeves, a bodice front and a bodice back, and two pant legs. Each bite of the toothy shears was marked with a foggy exhalation.

Yan stood silently at the patient's bedside, his wasted-thin wrist pinched between her thumb and index finger. She watched the second hand of the ward clock carefully as the six o'clock hour approached. A full sixty seconds passed and only thirty-six pulses drummed under Yan's finger. She focused for another minute, watching the rise and fall of the man's chest. The frenzied phase of his breathing had passed; six barely perceptible waves of breath washed up on the shore of the man's body as the second hand completed one more go around. It would not be long now.

Sixes everywhere.

The overnight shift had passed quickly, keeping Yan's brain and body busy, moving her from one patient's bed to the other. Now, with her lids weighing heavy and her mouth dry, Yan's head began to dream even as sleep evaded her. Sixes began to snake about. The Beautiful Land was six months off; in that time, she would have completed five years of medical studies, become a wife and moved to a land where, according to Zhi Chao, the sun would always be bright, the sky would always be blue, and golden sand perpetually met the sea. When would they return? Certainly not in another six months. But would it be six years, or six raised to the power of two for thirty-six years? Such long absences abroad were commonplace.

She gently placed the patient's wrist down on the bed; his sunken eyes were wide open but unseeing. He was covered with only a light sheet. Yan could easily make out all the bony landmarks of the man's body: the nubs at the base of his neck where his collar bones ended, the curved ridges of his ribs, the pair of bony protrusions demarcating his hips. All the markings vibrated as he shivered in the cold morning air. Yan unfolded a thin-weave, well-worn hospital blanket and laid it over him, fearing that even its insubstantial weight would press the last molecules of air from his body. Leaning against the wall next to the head of his bed, Yan would wait with the man and make sure his spirit found its way peacefully to the ancestors.

More sixes came for her.

Six years was the length of the sentence handed down by the Provincial Court back in the Old Home. This was how much additional time Long would now serve in prison; one year's retribution for each of the six New Market vendors who had been wounded on the day her brother had tried to slay a dragon. Yan had offered to return home to help her parents with Long. She could join them in their visits to the prison and work to help stuff those little red envelopes that they believe placed a little comfort into Long's life. They had simply said, "Go."

"Go." She compared that with ZhiChao's words, "To bring back something better." The young couple's positions had been secured in a famous hospital upon a hill in the Beautiful Country; Yan would be a junior researcher on one floor with a cell scientist, and ZhiChao a clinical fellow on another with a famous surgeon. Their heads would be filled and their curiosities fed, as their tongues and mouths became more proficient in making the words of a new language. Number-filled data tables, graphs with curves reaching infinity, and molecular models swirled all around her. Yan rubbed her eyes.

The patient's chest rattled and drew Yan closer to the bed.

She knew that what she would learn was beyond that which she could conjure.

She placed her hand on the patient's chest and felt it go still, his residual warmth seeped slowly away.

So much dwelled outside of her imagination, and yet she was certain that there were some things she would not learn: how to bring back an ever-bright sun to a cell bathed in blackness; how to bring back a blue sky to a place with a ceiling so low it grazed the top of Long's head; or how to bring back the certainty of sea meeting sand to the uncertain world of her only brother, a world filled with things unseen and the unheard by others.

Yan took the man's wrist into her fingers. No more sixes. She softly touched his lids and closed his eyes.

Like a poorly tuned organ, the sleeping Lao Fu emitted a cacophony of hissing wheezes and rumbling snores; he filled the back bedroom. The cold weather had made his and LuLu's bed, with its electric warming pad, the warmest place in the entire barbershop, and the old man had taken on a new routine that involved extensive afternoon napping. LuLu, lying on the couch with her wool coat buttoned all the way up to her neck, worked to focus on the box she was preparing. A bright pink, woolen scarf and matching hat, as well as a handmade pair of quilted, cream-colored, knee-high boots, had been carefully wrapped in tissue paper and placed in the box, leaving ample room for a final package to be added, as well, perhaps, as a few more items.

Looking about the room, singing silently to herself, LuLu's eyes wandered. The orchid plants on the sill were without blooms and looked to be no more than dry twigs stuck into pots of dirt. Filled with faces still unknown to her, several framed photos on the wall did not hold her attention. It was the curio cabinet that pulled her off the couch. Putting her face up to the cabinet's glass front, she came eye to eye with an elaborately coiled, orange-gold, glass snake with large glittery eyes. The snake's head was raised, and its fangs bared, but its eyes made it less frightful. She had seen it before but had not cared for it. Now she removed the snake carefully and held it in her hand, her palm a cradle for the precious figurine.

LuLu looked over to the bed and confirmed with her eyes what her ears had already told her: her husband remained lost deep beneath the blankets. She opened the leaves of tissue paper surrounding the scarf and hat and lay the snake down in the pink wool deep inside the box.

Invisible YuZhen's voice blocked out the wheezes and snores, "You lucky girl! It's providential.""Is it?" LuLu asked.

"Is it? Aiyah! The zodiac wheel turns soon. The year of the golden snake is coming, is it not?"

"Yes." LuLu ran her fingers along the coils of the snake's body. "But I don't like snakes."

"It's one of those signs of which Master Du speaks, don't you see it? The year of the golden snake brings you great blessings, LuLu. It's not about like, not like. Right, not right?"

"Right. I will see her in this year. I will see them both." LuLu thought of her last words with Wang; he had assured her LiLi was well. "Wang has promised me this."

A rush of warmth filled LuLu, and she unbuttoned the top of her coat. Quickly wrapping the figurine in its own sheet of tissue paper, she tucked it safely between the folds of the scarf. The golden snake was a sign. LuLu felt intimately connected to the first Fu TaiTai; she felt the woman had blessed LuLu and her mission in bedding Lao Fu. LuLu moved to the mirror and, for the first time since coming to live in this room, she tried to slip her feet into her predecessor's shoes, but her feet, encased in two sets of socks, were too big. Kicking off the shoes, LuLu reached beneath the silk robe hanging off the mirror and pulled out a corded, white fur muff. She held it for some time, losing her fingers in its plushness. She had not dared to wear it before, even as her fingers tingled with cold. Now she placed the muff's cords around her own neck and slipped her hands into its satin-lined center. Lao Fu stirred in the bed, snorting and pulling the covers over his head.

LuLu walked quickly down the street, holding her hands together inside the muff, and crossed over to the seamstress's store.

"Ahh. Fu TaiTai. Everything is ready." The seamstress welcomed LuLu by gesturing her attention towards several neatly folded piles of colorful clothing that sat on the sewing table.

"Ah! That is good. The courier will be here soon for my box." LuLu, taking her hands out of the muff, unfolded a tiny, cotton bodysuit and ran her finger along the curved line of tiny stitches securing the hem of its neck. "You are too good! A master. I cannot even feel them. Thank you."

"Ahh! Don't embarrass me! No need for such polite manners. I enjoyed making the little outfits." The seamstress eyed the muff as if yearning to touch it.

LuLu followed the woman's eyes. "I plan to send this ... as well, to my sister." LuLu held out the muff for the seamstress to examine. "I was only trying it for a short moment. It will help her stay warm."

"Yes. It is a fine piece." The old woman stroked the white fur gently and then studied the stitching attaching the neck cords to the muff. Pulling hard on the cords and satisfied that they were secure, she placed the muff, like a necklace, back around LuLu's neck and directed her hands back into the muff. "Well made."

Hearing the pride in the woman's voice, LuLu blushed and quickly removed her hands. "You made this?"

"I did." The old woman again placed LuLu's hands inside the tube of fabric. "Stay easy. It will keep your sister warm, Fu TaiTai."

———

"A rotten fruit hangs on the frozen terraces." AnRan searched the court-yard from the kitchen side of the window, her words frosting the glass. "The earth is so cold as to be solid; nevertheless, a pink bloom creeps along it, withering in the chill." She rubbed her condensed breath from the pane. "Rotten fruit is what they, all the villagers, are calling her and the little one. You know that. You've heard it said?"

"Aiyah! They do spew all manner of nonsense, but you know that!" Ayi tried to press down her own anxiety. "It's just the energies of the body in this condition. Unbalanced. And she is just a child."

"A child? She is six moons ripe, but ..."

"There!" Ayi wagged her finger, pointing through the window. "Look. She has come back." Blowing out a long exhalation, Ayi rushed to the kitchen door, opening it wide without concern for the bitter cold. "LiLi! Come inside. Hurry."

Running out into the courtyard, Ayi scrunched her shirt collar tightly around her neck. LiLi stood stone-still just within the gate, the wind whipping her clothes about her rigid form. "Child! LiLi! You cannot wear so little, you silly one. Hurry inside." Ayi put her arms around LiLi's shoulder and pulled the girl forward towards the house. Mud crusted the pink folds of LiLi's skirt and streaked the pink silk wings of her sleeves. The white fur of her vest was stained brown and clumped hard in some parts. Barely lifting her feet, LiLi dragged her satin bedroom slippers across the dirt and lost one of them before making it to the doorway. She did not look down or try to recover her shoe and came to stand in the kitchen with one foot completely bare. AnRan pulled a shawl from her own shoulders and hastened to wrap the girl up as Ayi began to rub heat into the girl's cheeks. Both women eyed each other quietly, saying nothing about the deep, sour smell rising off LiLi's body.

"To the ancestors! Have you been rolling in the dirt? Look. Look at your hair and your face." Ayi gently swept strands of matted hair out of LiLi's face and rubbed at the smudges of dirt on her face and neck. "Let me bring a hot cloth to wipe your face and hands."

"And her neck, and legs, and ..." AnRan looked briefly at LiLi's belly. Gone were the softness and the rolls of fat; now, only a small knot protruded outward from just below the girl's sagging breasts. AnRan turned away and sat back by the window, wringing her hands. She and Ayi did not need to speak out loud to wonder together about the child inside a child and how it had come to be. In the silence that lay between them, there were so many thoughts being shared.

On the day that LiLi's condition had been matter-of-factly pronounced by Old Doctor, AnRan and Ayi had been taken by surprise as the girl had been brought to the New Da Long clinic by the two women for the sole purpose of remedying LiLi's sudden lack of appetite. AnRan's eyes had locked in on those of her dearest and only friend. Ayi had silently shaken her head from side to side; Jiang still slept on the floor in the corner of the young couple's bedroom. With the passing months, the Cupcake Bride continued to drastically change—her hair was now stringy, unkempt, and unwashed. Her endless chatter and giggles had been replaced with firmly pressed lips, and her body, rather than joyously expanding, seemed thinned and exposed—even as Jiang was not in the smallest way different. LiLi had taken to wandering aimlessly for hours, and had been brought back to them one day by Pang, the uncle of Yan, who found her wandering in the New Da Long Square. The villagers who saw the Cupcake Bride that day, filthy and disheveled, spoke of it for days.

Neither AnRan nor Ayi directly put a single word of speculation or doubt out into the open, but that did not mean they did not exchange all manner of concern through suggestive gestures, shared looks, and oblique references. LiLi had always been free to wander into New Da Long, who she had come to befriend the two women could not possibly know.

"A hot cloth is not enough; it's no use. I must take you and the little one for a nice bath. We will get you all washed up and smelling pretty. You will like that," AnRan said.

LiLi did not speak. Ayi looked at AnRan who raised her eyebrows in doubt, prompting Ayi to answer emphatically for herself, "Yes!" Ayi ushered LiLi out of the kitchen, and the girl did not resist her gentle pushes. They moved past the kitchen table upon which sat a full, untouched jar of milk candies.

———————

Stuck suspended midway to a deep knee bend, Old Doctor cursed the cold that had locked his joints. Trying to oil his hinges with heat, he began to rub his knees vigorously. A curved hook sticking out of the tile floor; he slowly rose back to standing and shuffled his way across the room. Making it to the examining table that pushed up against one side of the New Da Long Clinic's solitary examining room, he stepped slowly up onto a small, wooden box, bent forward over the table, rolled over, and came to lie on his back on top of the table. His hand grazed the wall; the green-yellow tiles of the floor continued up the sides of the room, making it appear jaundiced. The bright white hue of the overhead light, along with its incessant buzzing, grated on Old Doctor, tempting him to retire right there and then. He looked about and wondered what his wife, who was likely resting on their bed in the peaceful darkness of their own home, would cook for their nightly meal. In all their married years, he had never thought to ask her this question. The smells rising from the coal stove of their house, which had served as his workplace for several decades, had usually been appreciated by the last few patients of the day and had always provided the answer. Now he was alone in the New Da Long Clinic, with its sterile smells, and he did not like it.

He opened his eyes to the sounds of a knock at the door. "Wait a small amount of time. I'm coming." After almost a full minute, at the door to the clinic, the Old Doctor found a trio of village women, all of them his patients.

"Why s-s-so long? It's cold!" Fang MaMa pushed her way past Old Doctor, turning and looking over her shoulder. "Come!"

"Sorry for disturbing you," MeiLin said as she followed her mother into the small space.

"Sorry," Lei added. With her entry into the room, the doctor's view of his space, including the examining table, his desk, a modest medicine and herb cabinet, and his bag of medical instruments, was completely obscured by faces. He wondered if this was a social call, as only space for talking was left.

"Too bright!" Fang MaMa swatted at the ceiling.

"I know." Old Doctor remained standing at the clinic door.

"You talk." Fang MaMa now waved one shaking arm up in front of MeiLin's face and used the hand of her other arm to wipe spit from her own chin. She slumped down onto the doctor's chair, the only one in the room. A silver metal stool was available for patients; neither MeiLin nor Lei chose to use it.

"We are here to talk about Long," MeiLin spoke softly to Old Doctor, "and about Lei." MeiLin glanced in Lei's direction, but Lei's eyes were focused on the tile floor.

"I understand. He remains in the prison." The doctor shifted his weight from one foot to the next. How many times had he tried to conjure hope out of nothing? "I understand he has not yet been granted a transfer to the Provincial Number Six Hospital." The doctor himself fought off a chill as he spoke these last words. The provincial mental health facility stood several hours drive from New Da Long, but even this was not far enough to keep Old Doctor from vomiting into the back of his throat. He covered his mouth with his hand and pretended to cough. Retching silently, he scolded himself, "Discipline the mind!" He focused on the idea of relative bleakness. While much of the misery Long experienced as a prisoner would remain unchanged even if transferred from the prison to the mental health facility—the physical restraints, beatings, poor nutrition and extremely poor hygiene would all persist and possibly become worse—it remained true that only in the latter institution did there exist a chance of clinical relief for the boy. If Long ever gained permission to transfer from the prison to the hospital, then medication could possibly flow, dampening the voices and visions in his head and soothing his tormented mind.

"They have tried, my brother and my sister, here, to help him get there." MeiLin again looked at Lei, who kept her eyes fixed on the floor. MeiLin did not mention that she and Pang had fed their own rolls of Kuai notes into the red envelope bellies, hoping that it was enough for Long to be in a better place. "But he has not been moved."

"Of course. But you know I can be of no help to you in this matter." Old Doctor did not dare to share his suspicion that the prison guards, too, were worthless; that securing a transfer required far more influence than any low-level sentinel could muster. This decision, to not share the whole truth, was a continuation of one he had made years prior, when Bo and Lei had first come to him and sought his advice on how to get their son, the would-be-dragonslayer, out of prison. The doctor had let the desperate parents believe that they might be able, with sufficient red-envelope-encouragement of the guards, to facilitate Long's transfer. Was this not what all parents needed to believe, that they could make life better for those whom they had brought into this world? To tell them the truth, then or now, would only have killed their hope.

MeiLin continued, taking Lei's hand in hers. "We are not here for that. We understand that you cannot help Long. But Lei, we are here for you to help her. To have you tell her to stop."

Lei gently pulled her hand away from MeiLin.

Fang MaMa pulled herself up. Her lips trembled, "Show him!" Saliva specks flew from her mouth.

Lei slowly pulled the sleeves of her shirt up above her elbows and turned her arms to reveal the soft underside of her arms. Bruised a deep purple color and scabbed with dozens of puncture wounds, Lei's arms caused the doctor to lean back against the closed clinic door. Fang MaMa sucked on her teeth and looked up to the ceiling, shaking her head in disgust.

MeiLin took Lei's hand again, and Old Doctor could see tears in both women's eyes. He took Lei's arms into his hands and rotated them, letting the light fall at different angles upon the broken surfaces, "How long? How often?" His body suddenly felt too tired and heavy, as if he himself was exhausted from having battered Lei's arms.

"Aiyah! Too long and too often. She must stop! Tell her!" Fang MaMa closed her mouth with a snap and pressed her upper molars downward with force. Her small chest now moved up and down noticeably.

"Please, Lei. Tell the doctor what you are thinking." MeiLin's voice tried to rise angrily but quickly softened with tears. "Tell him about the organ dealer."

Old Doctor dropped Lei's arms and motioned to MeiLin to have Lei sit in the empty stool. He stood with his head hung. "There is no point in cutting yourself up, in selling your blood. Your heart is already outside of you, locked up, and the money will not get him moved."

Raising her eyes, it was now Lei's turn to look at the doctor who had fixed his gaze on the tile floor. "I can get more money. The organ dealers have offered me a large sum for a kidney. I will do it for him. You can help me to do it safely. Please."

"No. No." Old Doctor shook his head with a force that moved his shoulders. "It will do no good."

Lei would not listen. "The guards have promised me that with enough money, they can make sure to spread it around in just the right way, to just the right people, and get Long transferred to the hospital."

The old man pulled himself up as tall as he could and looked Lei in the eyes. "Those vultures, the guards, have promised you something that is not in their authority or capacity to do. They will take more of your money, but it will never be enough. They cannot deliver on a transfer for Long. Only a judge at the Provincial Court can make that happen. There is neither a guard connected enough nor do you have organs enough to sell for the kind of money needed to sweeten such a man. I'm so sorry for ever letting you think otherwise."

Lei held out her arms and turned them back and forth. Every bloody scar that marked her skin represented the invasion site of a needled tube that had carried away a part of her into the plasma sellers' dirty little collection bags. She had turned her red blood into dozens upon dozens of useless red envelopes. Filling the room with her despair and refusing to be consoled, Lei began lowing and thrashing her arms against her body.

The skin beneath his eyes was heavy, and Old Doctor breathed hard as he took in the once again empty room. Lei's visit had left him exhausted. Thankfully, everything was as he had found it this morning. The examining table was up against the wall, the desk and chair were paired in one corner, the medicine cabinet was locked, and the patient stool was wiped clean. He pulled on his coat and cap and was about to silence the brazen overhead light when a loud thumping on the clinic door almost toppled him with fright.

The door flung open before the doctor could get his hand on its handle, and the Farmer Master was in the frame. "She is killing my grandchild!" The force of Wang's words pushed against Old Doctor, who stumble-stepped backwards onto the spot directly below the harsh light.

"Who? Who is?"

"The child bride. She has become a filthy fool, wandering the fields and refusing to talk and to eat." Wang spoke as if throwing punches.

Old Doctor studied the Farmer Master. The skin of his bloated face was rough with stubble and his unwashed hair, heavy with oil, was furrowed from the teeth of a comb. Red vessels filled the whites of his eyes, and his clothes were rumpled, presumably from having been slept in.

Letting his coat drop back off his shoulder, the old man directed Wang to the empty stool. "Little Wang," Old Doctor caught himself. "Excuse me, Farmer Master, come in and take relaxation. Sit and tell me what is happening."

The gentleness of the doctor's tone jarred Wang, who sat down quickly as if he had received something he did not deserve. Seated, he spoke more softly and slowly. "I ... I don't know what is happening. Will my grandchild be okay?"

"Mother and child go together."

"Of course." Wang now put his head down and began to run his thick fingers through his hair. "She needs to be stronger, but she is not like ..." he caught himself. "She is weak in the mind and therefore has become weak in the body."

"Her body builds a child, does it not?" Old Doctor looked at Wang with one eyebrow raised and a half smile. "Does she sleep?"

"Little. The women say she wanders the fields early and late."

"Is she eating full foods?"

"Ayi says little has passed her lips in days." Wang ran his fingers through his hair again.

"And you have come alone; you did not bring her to me."

Wang eyed the doctor, trying to size up his words, and felt heat rise up his neck. "No."

The doctor went on, "What has happened? She did not arrive here in this condition, right?"

There was not a trace of accusation in the doctor's croaky voice, just concern, and Wang immediately felt despair once again. "Right. She was … fine, and then … she was not." Wang fell silent, unsure that he would not confess to his part in the conflict that played out in LiLi's body; the forces for her expansion clearly were losing to the forces for her disintegration. Was he not the embodiment of those forces? Had he not made her as she was now, in every way? He was scared to look at the man.

Old Doctor thought of Lei, who had taken a similar posture on the stool not so long before; after she had no more water for tears and no more energy for moaning and thrashing, she had slumped down on the stool, held in place by MeiLin. With the passing of time, how many patients would come to sit on that stool with their heads hung and their eyes counting floor tiles? How many would come to him for a remedy? Hope. Where to find it? The Farmer Master was no different than the others who sought him out. He had come looking for a way out of his pain and powerlessness. A way to get the child bride to a better place.

Wang, fearing being exposed for his role in LiLi's current state, regretted coming to see the old healer.

Old Doctor kept probing. "How about her mother? A girl's mother is often helpful in preparing her for this transition. A young girl can be like a plant; transplanted too hastily it may have trouble in new soil."

"The mother is not well," Wang said. The truth was, he knew scant little about the woman's health.

"I understand. And the sister?" Old Doctor paused, waiting to hear the Farmer Master's answer. Wang seemed to be confused by the question, his brow furrowed. "The girl has a sister. Right, not right?"

"Right ... of course ... she ..." Wang's stomach turned. "She ..."

LuLu's face had been etched with pain when he had declined her offer to come to New Da Long and stay with her little sister during this time. She had voiced concern about the young girl being pregnant and so far from her own womenfolk. Wang had described LiLi as being the type of pregnant woman who became more radiant with each passing day. He had laughed off her concern. "Relax. There is no need to worry."

Remembering his deceit of LuLu, Wang's bowels begin to gurgle and sweat leaked from his skin despite the coldness of the clinic. He clenched the deep muscles of his rectum to avoid soiling himself. He felt the doctor place his hand on his arm and looked up to find the old man looking at him with the tenderness of a parent. Thinking of his own father, Wang's own body humiliated him. He stood up from the stool, kicking it back behind him with his feet. Widening his stance and fixing his eyes on those of Old Doctor, he delivered his words clearly, with a forced air of dismissal, "She cannot take leave of her life in Shanghai. LuLu, the sister, wishes for the baby to arrive safely and for her to come and join in the newborn's one-hundred-day celebration. She is traditional; it would be unlucky to come before the baby has arrived."

The Farmer Master wanted to believe his own words. He wanted to not have betrayed LuLu. He wanted LuLu to come to New Da Long one day soon and find LiLi as she had been before. But more than anything, what he wanted to be true—that needed to be true, that he would make true—was the safe arrival of the baby, his legacy bearer.

The rice seedlings in his fields, transplanted from the high fields of the nursery to the lower crop fields, were made to grow; each one was carefully cultivated, watered, fertilized, sprayed with government-concocted insecticide. They were coaxed to grow. They did not survive without being made to survive.

Wang's mind jumped over LiLi to the unborn Wang. His focus had been misplaced, for the mother was nothing more than a conduit. "A plant must eat. I must nourish my grandchild."

"Yes, but the mother's frame of mind—"

Ignoring him, Wang sprang swiftly to open the door and was well beyond its frame when he called out, "She will eat."

The doctor shuffled over to the stool and pulled it forward. He put on his coat, adjusted his cap, and turned off the light, leaving the small room in darkness and silence.

Chapter Twenty-Five

Stars and Snakes

B lazing high above its planetary sisters, cresting the earth's lunar companion, Jupiter traveled its path around the sun and drew Jiang off the bedroom floor, pulling him down along the upper hallway that lined the atrium to the window in his father's office. He gazed up through the Eagle's Eye and was transfixed. The twinkling ball of gas, still visible in the near dark, morning sky, though separated from him by hundreds of millions of kilometers, delighted Jiang. He recognized the astronomical power of the zodiac and how it had worked its magic on the girl everyone considered to be his wife.

That a LiLi resembling the LiLi of "when she first arrived" had reappeared—passing her time in the study playing with the rabbits and her bird, helping herself once again to all the rich treats Ayi prepared—was an accomplishment attributed by everyone, except Jiang, to the cunning of the Farmer Master.

After abruptly departing the New Da Long Clinic two months earlier and leaving Old Doctor to wonder if he had truly been of any help to anyone in all his years as the village healer, the Farmer Master had left New Da Long. Making his way to the provincial capital and boarding the first train he could find to Shanghai, he had journeyed for almost two days before finding himself at that city's finest markets. There, he had harangued every vendor for their most exotic, most tantalizing, and most expensive treats. The only limit on his purchases was a foggy notion he had about what a child would want. Wang had reminded himself of one simple truth: though LiLi was woman enough to bring forth a baby, she was still no more than a simple, peasant child. Whatever fugue state her feeble mind had found itself in would be thrown off by appealing to her childish senses. He would coax her into being what he wanted her to be. Just like his seedlings, LiLi needed the right fertilizer.

In a rush of purchasing, Wang had taken only one pause. Amid bargaining with a particularly wily fur vendor from somewhere in the north, it had struck him that in addition to luring LiLi back to health, he may actually succeed in having the child forgive him. Aside from the one moment in which he had been on the verge of confessing his behavior to Old Doctor, Wang had not felt any need to be cleansed of his doings. But now, as he let the money he had so carefully recorded in his ledger flow out of his pockets, he was particularly pleased with the genius of his plan. He did not need her forgiveness, but she likely needed to forgive him. He heartily clapped the vendor on his back and paid the man's asking price for a glossy and plush, black fur capelet.

Of course, it was neither the Farmer Master nor Jupiter that brought light spirited LiLi back.

It was LuLu.

At the same time that the Farmer Master was gone from New Da Long, LuLu, by way of a heavy Lunar New Year's gift box, had arrived. Up until a couple of hours after the box's arrival in the Farmer Master's courtyard, disheveled, "not of this world" LiLi had still been floating and lolling about the frozen rice fields, much like a pink blossom torn from a tree and carried along aimlessly by spurts of wind.

Shivering and losing sensation in her feet, Ayi had found LiLi and dragged her home, Telling the girl of the gift that awaited her, she had begged, to no avail, for LiLi to walk faster. As was her new custom, LiLi dragged her feet along the ground, muddying the tops of her cloth shoes. The lower edge of her dress, only cleaned a couple of days prior, was rimmed brown and had taken up water. Ayi talked on, speaking for both of them, not wanting the chance to really look at the girl. The continuous sound coming out of Ayi's mouth floated up to LiLi's eardrums and went no further, no higher processing for meaning was happening, until out of Ayi's mouth came a word that broke into LiLi's hibernating mind and knocked her back into the world of comprehension: "LuLu."

LiLi suddenly began to lift her feet, easily keeping pace with Ayi, almost moving ahead of the startled woman. LiLi focused on the house and said nothing to the now silent Ayi. Once at the house, LiLi began to move more quickly in the direction of the study, though her haste was mitigated by the weakness of her underfed, very pregnant body. Ayi and AnRan, confused by the spectacle of the bedraggled, previously languid girl suddenly struggling to come back to life, followed closely behind her. Ayi held her arms out, as if ready to catch LiLi should she fall.

LuLu's love sat waiting for LiLi on the study table.

LiLi embraced the box and squeezed it tightly with her stick-like arms.

Jiang, who had been painting a scene of the frozen landscape, looked at his wife and stated simply, "She needs to bathe."

"LuLu. LuLu. LuLu," LiLi repeatedly read her sister's name, tracing the lines of the signature she found at the bottom of a piece of sketch paper that lay on top of the box's contents. Unfolding a fuzzy, pink scarf carefully, LiLi could hear MaMa's voice, "Careful! Open everything with care. Your big sister always tucks little extras safely in the folds."

Finding the snake, crafted of beautiful orange-gold glass and embellished with glittery eyes, LiLi immediately studied LuLu's sketch and began to cry, her chest heaving rapidly up and down like it would pull her off her feet. AnRan and Ayi stood perfectly still, stretching their hands out even further in LiLi's direction but not daring to touch her. Both women, without speaking, shared the same fear that touching the girl could shift her inner energy balance and send her back to some place not in this world. Adding to their shared sense of paralysis, LiLi's crying took on a strange tone, her voice rising into a laugh. The tears streaming down her face seemed to be fueled by joy and not despair.

Not noticed by LiLi, Jiang approached her and unceremoniously took the golden snake out of her hand, before turning his back on her and picking up LuLu's sketch from the table. He studied the sketch carefully and then turned the snake over and over in his hand. "Her sister has sent this to bless the baby, for he will be born in the year of the snake. Specifically, he will be born in the year of the golden snake." Jiang placed LuLu's sketch down on the table and put the glass snake on top of it; he then sat down and resumed painting, all the while sensing the vibrations of LiLi's joy. LiLi remained cry-laughing.

"Did he say 'he'?" AnRan asked as she and Ayi moved to the table. AnRan held up the sketch and admired the fine lead lines and smudges that came together into a portrait of LiLi sitting on a park bench. Next to her sat a young woman with the same eyes as LiLi, but she was thinner, and her skin had been shaded by the artist with more force. AnRan knew this must be LuLu, the sister. Together, the young sisters held a tiny, swaddled baby; the threesome were shaded by the bloom-filled branches of a cherry blossom tree. Next to the family portrait, an orange snake with large dark eyes had been drawn, as if it sat guard over the tiny clan. Down the side of the sketch was a calligraphed message: "May treasures fill our home."

Later that night, when she had no more tears left, LiLi finally gave way to her body's exhaustion and fell into her bed. The sound of LiLi's soft purring snores came as music to Ayi's ears, and she quickly covered the girl with a blanket, leaving her face tear-stained and her body directly swaddled in muddied clothes.

LiLi's brain, filled with images of dearest LuLu, the newborn, and herself all together, began to replenish itself by feeding off a dream that the girl now had. LuLu had come for her today. LuLu had called LiLi and the soon-to-be-born golden snake boy, who would grow to watch over them, to join her!

In the highest heavens, Jupiter's light once again burst forth; while LiLi was busy dreaming, the Farmer Master, having just arrived home, stared up at the star while standing just outside the courtyard. He carried his numerous city purchases into the house and arranged them enticingly on the kitchen table, proclaiming to himself, "She will eat!"

The next morning, the Cupcake Bride re-emerged. Sitting up in her bed, she touched her face, held out her arms, and was surprised to find herself wearing a dress. She looked at the soiled sleeves of the dress and quickly pulled back her blankets and gasped when she saw chunks of mud scattered about her sheets. She touched the top of her head and ran her fingers through her unwashed hair, catching them in knots and tangles. Like a butterfly desperately struggling to shed its husk-like chrysalis, LiLi began to pull at her clothes and called out loudly, but sweetly, "Ayi. Ayi! Come help me. I need to be washed, dressed, and fed!"

———————

Every soul living beneath the Farmer Master's roof was happy.

The Farmer Master could hear the Cupcake Bride devouring Swiss chocolates, Japanese jellies, Australian cheeses, and the other assorted foods he had brought from Shanghai; when she was not eating, she remained in the study and amused herself with the many diversions he had procured. Her giggles and laughter confirmed his truth: every person could be bought. That LiLi did not come near him or utter a single word of gratitude for any of the gifts with which he believed he was pacifying her temperamental way did not upset Wang. This behavior of hers had no practical consequence for the Farmer Master, who himself preferred to not be seen by her or anyone and spent these days up in his office, victorious, carefully penning numbers into his ledger.

LiLi grew stronger, larger, and more radiant with each passing day. As her belly ballooned and the golden snake boy moved inside of her, she delighted in having a dedicated-to-her-alone playmate. Loving sweets, she ate generously, sharing with her unborn child and waiting to feel it wriggle with happiness. LiLi watched the tight surface of her belly for the bulge of a moving arm or leg, giggling each and every time; not once did she ask for the rabbits to be brought to her from their courtyard hutch.

AnRan had a chair brought to the study and made this her new perch, sewing and watching carefully over her children, Jiang, LiLi, and their child-to-be. Streams of orange sunlight, colored in part by the dozens of painted snakes that graced the windows, warmed the study. LiLi kept LuLu's talisman at the center of the study table; she looked at it often, as if needing to see it to stay on course. That Jiang, maybe seeing LiLi's frequent seeking of the talisman, chose to paint multiple renditions of the character such as to surround his wife with its image pleased her, and made the room into a sanctuary of sorts for LiLi's dreaming and planning.

Ayi now served all meals, except for those of the Farmer Master, in the study. She carefully paired foods to harmoniously balance LiLi's yin and yang. Sweet potatoes to detoxify the spleen, eggs to calm the mind, and spinach to strengthen the baby's organs featured prominently in the menu. And, although Ayi found herself suspiciously eyeing some of the foreign foods brought for LiLi by the Farmer Master, she did not hold back on serving them as well, though in small portions that she assured herself would not throw the girl out of balance.

AnRan sewed for the baby, Ayi cooked for mother and child, Jiang painted for LiLi, and LiLi played to amuse herself. The two women ignored the surrounding snakes and did not question their presence. Whatever had brought LiLi back to them was not to be questioned, in the same way that whatever had created the "not of this world" LiLi, the LiLi who seemed to have abandoned herself and her child, was not queried. AnRan and Ayi let LiLi's recent past go, attributing everything to the capriciousness of youth combining with the ferocious energies of reproduction. While both women, at different times, thought that each one of the parents-to-be was indeed peculiar in relation to one another, they were ever so grateful that the pair were on course to be fruitful.

LiLi, one moon cycle from birth, stepped out of the study, her swollen feet wide apart and outward pointing. She began down one of the atrium corridors on the first floor in search of Ayi. AnRan had fallen asleep mid-stitch, and Jiang was tending to the rabbits, leaving LiLi with no one to complain to about her discomfort or to help her to the toilet. She found Ayi sweeping the kitchen floor.

"Ayi, I want to pass water. Please help me?"

"Yes, come." Ayi helped LiLi up the stairs.

The girl's breathing grew louder as she came up the stairs, and from the sounds of their steps, the Farmer Master knew she was accompanied by Ayi alone. He had hardly seen the girl, but his ears let him know she had become heavier. After he was sure LiLi and Ayi were deep beyond the bedroom, inside the bathroom and unable to see into the hallway, Wang quickly made his way to that familiar spot just outside LiLi's bedroom door and listened.

Ayi helped LiLi to the bathroom adjoining her bedroom, leaving the bedroom door open, and listened as the girl urinated.

"You're finished?" "I am, but I'm not."

"Just sit a little then," Ayi voiced patiently.

"Talk to me, Ayi." "Very good. I feel it is time we start preparing you for after the little prince is here."

The Farmer Master nodded his head in agreement.

LiLi responded, "Yes. But I will spend my first month in sitting, no?" "Certainly. You will stay indoors and not bathe for the first full month. I will help you express your milk and feed the baby."

The Farmer Master wrinkled his nose.

Ayi continued, "I will stay with you both in the night and help to keep you both clean and rested."

"Yes."

"And then after, I will teach you the ways to hold and bathe the baby and how to prepare yourself to give him your breast at night. Of course, I will still be with you."

"You will? Can you help me up?" Wang could hear LiLi heaving herself forward off the toilet bowl.

"Of course! You need to wash your hands."

The sound of running water obscured LiLi's and Ayi's voices. The Farmer Master scrunched his eyes, as if this would help him hear more clearly.

"Ayi, you will come to Shanghai with me?"

"Shanghai?" Ayi chuckled. "You will not be going anywhere for some time."

"I will. I must." LiLi's voice was emphatic.

"My sweet child, I'm sorry. I don't understand."

"My sister, LuLu has called me to Shanghai to live with her and her Mister Fu."

The thumping in his chest came so hard and fast that the Farmer Master stepped away from the door, convinced it would be heard by LiLi and Ayi. He dug his nails into his palms. He made himself heavy and fought his own body from charging into the bedroom. *Listen. Listen. Listen!* Wang screamed to himself.

"LiLi, your sister has asked you to Shanghai?"

"Yes." The girl's voice took on a higher pitch, "Ayi, you saw it. She sent me the sketch with us all in the park, the one near her city home. It is the one she told me about before I came here. She told me how beautiful it is and how we could sit under the cherry blossom trees. She wanted us to be together. Well, back then, it was to be just the two of us and her Mister Fu. But now, she has sent the golden snake to let me know she wants the baby as well."

Wang stood speechless, trying to untwist the girl's logic. It seemed Ayi was doing the same, for she said nothing.

"Ayi, please hand me a towel."

"Yes. Of course. LiLi?"

"Hmm?"

"Have you mentioned this to Wang BaBa?"

"No. But he cannot know, Ayi. LuLu will come and when I tell her everything, she will help me. She will take me and the baby home to Shanghai."

"I understand. Or maybe I will in time." Ayi's voice was hesitant, almost questioning, but, to Wang's relief, she did not ask what the "everything" was that LiLi would tell LuLu. "All that matters now is that we keep you healthy, relaxed and well nourished. Come now, shall I prepare you a treat?"

"Yes. I am hungry, again." LiLi answered as she and Ayi began to move towards the bedroom door. Wang snuck away quickly, hearing Ayi chuckle as she affectionately teased, "Well, in that way you are most unchanging. Let's go and see what we find."

The golden snake boy wiggled and jabbed LiLi's insides with his tail, and she took this as a sign of his displeasure. Looking out beyond Jiang's painted, tangerine-hued snakes, she was beckoned by an orange sky streaked with wisps of bright pink and yellow. Feeling as restless as the baby, LiLi sought to be outside and told AnRan, who had confined the very pregnant child to the house, that she was going to the kitchen. AnRan nodded her approval, barely looking up from the massive needlepoint magnolia lying in her lap for fear of losing her stitch count.

In the kitchen, Ayi was cradling a large bowl of boiled taro which she was mashing for the evening meal. "You want to eat already?" She kept working the contents of the bowl with a heavy wooden spoon. "I have minced the pork already; it will not be so long."

"No, I just want to take a little walk in the courtyard."

"Alone? Wait now, and I will come with you." Ayi, surprised to not have enticed LiLi with one of her favorite foods, placed the bowl on the table. "It will be dark soon. Let me get my coat."

"No need. You can see me through the window." Sitting down on the window bench, LiLi reached beneath it and pulled out the cream boots gifted to her by LuLu. She leaned forward and spread her knees to allow her belly space. She let out little huffs as she tried to shimmy her foot into a boot.

"Child, give it to me." Ayi knelt on the floor at LiLi's feet. Taking one foot at a time into her hands, Ayi rubbed them gently, making LiLi giggle, before placing them into the boots. Ayi then grabbed the black fur capelet from the window bench and secured it around LiLi's shoulders. "You don't need a lot of time out there. Understand?"

"Understand." Breathing heavily, LiLi pushed her way out through the kitchen door.

Cloaked in a façade of concern, the Farmer Master had taken to passing through areas of the house which he had previously never frequented with the express aim of catching a glimpse of LiLi. He had not yet devised a scheme by which to squash the girl's plan to "tell everything" to LuLu. He was not worried. He was so close to having the fruit of his labor, that he simply focused on not letting the girl out of his sight for too long. He walked into the kitchen just as the door out to the courtyard was closing.

Outside, the air of late winter pricked at LiLi's cheeks, turning them into pink roses. She closed her eyes and held her face up to the early evening sun; she began to spin slowly, the whole time with her feet widely based. Her stomach did not keep up with her spinning, and LiLi came to an abrupt stop and felt her head continuing to move. Blurry-eyed, but not enough to be mistaken, she suddenly saw the Farmer Master through the kitchen window, standing as he had on that night when he found her sucking on milk candies.

A sickening flood of sweet saliva filled LiLi's mouth. She wanted to spit at the ground, but the sensation of being suffocated made her put her hands up to her neck. Her heart racing, she fought to pull air into her lungs. Her neck muscles contracted in an attempt to help heave her diaphragm up and down.

Through the window, Wang pointed at LiLi. A wave of panic roared inside the girl, lifting her off the ground and commanding her to move. *Move! Move!*

LiLi could not stop moving. Through the gate, along the outer wall, and away from the house she ran. The rice terraces were before her, earthen steps climbing up the side of the mountain, and finding the sloped path that led upwards, she scrambled up to the first terrace. She knew not to let fall silent the crunching sound of her feet on the soil. Partially frozen puddles of rainwater gave way under her weight, and LiLi's feet were intermittently submerged. Cold water seeped through the quilting of her boots. "Move! Move! Move! LiLi, don't stop moving your feet," LiLi heard her sister's voice, inside her head, spurring her on.

"I don't want to, LuLu, but I have no breath." LiLi cried out into the coldness. Her chest rose and sank violently, and she was forced to slow down. She kept trying to lift her feet forward, but air hunger forced her to stop. She turned her head back in the direction of the house and saw the Farmer Master making his way towards her, along the lower terrace.

"Stop. Stop! This is dangerous!" Wang screamed out.

Lowering herself down to the ground and crawling on her hands and knees, LiLi started up the second slope that connected the lower terrace to the one above it. She just managed the low grade and made it to the top of the middle terrace. She staggered to her feet, grabbed her belly on either side with both of her hands, and bent over. She raised her head and could now see Wang's face as he approached the bottom of the slope she had just scaled.

"Stay away from me!" LiLi tried to scream, but only soft, soundless words came out of her. Her eyes were wide and her teeth bared as she let out a low guttural growl. Wang immediately stopped moving and raised his hands, palms forward, to the level of his shoulders. He seemed to recognize that a frightened animal was an unpredictable one.

"Stop. Please, child. This is too dangerous."

LiLi instinctively moved back and away from Wang, despite him being motionless.

"LiLi. Listen to me. I just want to help you home."

"This ... is not ... my home. My home is with LuLu." LiLi turned and headed in the direction of the next embankment, at the top of which lay the upper terrace. On reaching the next steeply inclined, upward pathway, LiLi stopped and let out a horrible groan over which she had no control, a sound that found a means to be heard. Wang, who was already up on the middle terrace, stopped in his tracks. The top parts of the girl's cream-colored boots, which rested against the inside of each knee, turned bright red. LiLi pitched forward into the mud, her arms outstretched, and rolled onto her side. Struggling to lift her feet, trying to pump her knees, she was pedaling slowly into the air.

Wang slowly approached LiLi. "We must get you to Old Doctor. Right now!"

"No! No! No!" Screaming in pain and fear, feeling chords of muscle bulging hideously along her neck, LiLi pulled her lips back, revealing tightly clenched teeth. She turned onto her knees and began grabbing at the dirt in front of her, trying to pull herself up the slope.

"You will lose my baby! *Stop!*" Wang reached forward and tried to grab LiLi's legs, but she kicked backwards at him, catching him in the face, and he fell back and away. Wang now scrambled forward onto his knees and dove towards LiLi, landing on her legs. Feeling his weight on her, once again, LiLi tried to scream but was stopped by a sensation that flooded her lower body and her inner thighs. A warm stream of blood and water soaked through her dress, flowed into her boots, and wet the top of Wang's shirt. LiLi writhed ferociously. Wang heaved himself up and onto LiLi's back and tried to grab her hands, which were clawing at the mud.

Wang could feel LiLi's body heaving under his. "Stop!"

Crying, LiLi lifted her head. "LuLu! LuLu!"

"LiLi! LiLi!" Ayi's voice could be heard coming from somewhere far off.

Wang rolled off the girl. LiLi's cries did not stop. "Shh! I am taking you to the clinic." He reached over and placed his hands on the back of her shoulders, trying to help pull her up and around to face him. As her body turned, LiLi reached around and swung her fist into the side of Wang's face, causing him to stumble back. As if a surge of momentum charged her body, she began to crawl up the slope. Wang, grabbing the side of his head with one hand, stood up and wiped blood from his face. He started up the slope behind LiLi, moving faster than her. LiLi, pulling herself up onto the upper terrace, turned and saw Wang and tried to lift one knee up onto the plain of the upper terrace, but her knee missed. LiLi's feet failed to find purchase on the slippery slope. Losing her balance, LiLi slid down the embankment, into Wang. The two bodies pitched backward, fell about a meter and a half, and landed forcefully onto the middle plain on their backs.

Wang waited for LiLi's cries. All he heard were the full-throated shrieks of Ayi. He waited for the girl to move. But everything had stopped. LiLi did not move. Wang's body stiffened, and he suddenly felt the cold.

An unbearable weight of silence filled the frozen fields.

Chapter Twenty-Six

Old Home

The longest day of the year arrived bathed in sunlight, and, though not a cloud sailed the blue skies, the windless air was heavy with water. Every vista within the heartland dripped with life. Heat, moisture, and calm had come together to create the perfect conditions for rebirth: the rebirth of flowers, grasses, trees and creatures long liberated from the frosts of winter. Even the mesmerizing algae that crowded the surface of the lake had exploded overnight; the galaxy appeared to be displayed skyward, projected up from the surface of the earth, for the ancestors to admire. Strands and swirls of luminescent greens and crystal-like teals came together in tight pinwheels with impossible-to-find centers and, at their outer limits, loose, free-dancing tendrils reached for the far ends of the cosmos. Framing this earthbound, celestial map were myriad deep-bending, unbreakable, boughs of weeping willows, each one lime-yellow and brilliant. Rising away from and circling around this cosmos were green folds of mountain, arrayed like a stone curtain drawn protectively about this precious jewel.

Holding up her thumb and index finger in an unclosed loop just in front of one open eye, and squinting her other eye closed, Yan pretended to hold the whole of the cosmos, upon which she spied, between her fingers. She ignored the sweat that beaded her brow and wet the plain between her shoulder blades, and she was unbothered by the insects that buzzed around her ears and up her nostrils. Wanting to fill herself with the Old Home, she closed her eyes and drew in a deep breath between her lips, careful to keep her teeth closed.

A motor purred behind her, and she stayed as she was.

"Good?" Pang called out to Yan from inside the cabin of a small, flatbed truck that was piled high with cut and trussed bamboo culms. "We have time if you want to wait a little."

"No need. Better to get down the mountain before the traffic comes." Yan climbed in next to her uncle and found a paper-wrapped scallion pancake on her seat. She set it on her lap, its warmth letting her know it had just come off the pan.

"Auntie MeiLin sent that for you, for the journey." Pang raised one buttock cheek off the seat and felt in his back pocket for his wallet, which he secured against the wheel with one hand. He pulled out two one-hun-dred-Kuai notes and pushed them in Yan's direction. "For later."

"It's okay." Yan playfully pushed the money back in her uncle's direc-tion. A wide grin broke out across Pang's face as he pretended not to see her. "Uncle, please."

"Is that what the city has taught you? To disrespect your elders? You might be twenty-two, but I can still tell you what to do." Pang started laughing. "Keep it, Little Face."

The wheels of the truck bounced down the dirt road and sent bamboo clacking loudly against the bed. The world outside the window was a jumping blur of different shades of green and yellow, and Yan let the sunshine heat her face as the truck circled the mountain. On Lake Ring

Road, Yan pressed her face up against the glass and took in all the restitution houses. Little had changed; the houses still looked thrown together, and the yards were little more than dirt clearings with random items—a broken chair, a muddy ball, a rusted-out moped—tossed about.

Opening her eyes wide, taking in as much as possible, Yan was still surprised by the sight of her parents' patch of land. Distinctive for having been fastidiously stripped bare of all vegetation and having a neat, flattened, dirt surface that covered the entire lot, the place emitted a sense of purpose beyond mere survival. A meter-high, stone wall demarcated the rectangle's perimeter and enclosed multiple rows of delivery vehicles—both large and small, some with flatbeds, others with pickup beds. Along the lot's deep edge, running parallel to the road, stood a new, low-lying, wooden mechanics shed. Completely open in the front when its barn-style doors were swung all the way back, as they were now, it had been constructed with ports for several vehicles. The roof of the shed was covered with discarded tires, metal bike fenders, mismatched mud flaps, several yellow, plastic petrol cans, and lengths of rubber tubing. The shed walls and practically everything inside the walls, save the vehicles wanting repair, were black with grease. The work benches, the tools that hung off the walls and the rags that were strewn about were all thick with muck and grime. Pang stutter-pressed on the brakes and leaned on his horn. A grease-covered Brother Shu emerged from the shed. Yan rolled down the truck window and hoisted herself halfway out, frantically waving back and yelled, "Until we meet again!" The roar of the wheels and the thumping of the bamboo drowned out her voice. Shu ran towards the front of the lot waving at Yan as she disappeared down the road.

"It is good of your parents to let us use their land for the business. Such a convenient location. Much better than up the mountain." Pang kept his eyes on the road.

"It is good of you to use the land for the business. You are too good." Yan wanted to openly thank her uncle for the rent payments he was making to Bo and Lei for the use of their lot. He was the type of man who had paid for the land to be both cleared and leveled, and who had nonchalantly chalked the expense up to the cost of doing business.

Yan resisted reaching over and hugging Pang. She would write him a letter of thanks, once she was gone and he would not need to react or say anything in front of her. She would make sure he knew that she knew how generous he had been all these years. He had never once asked Bo and Lei to pay rent or for their share of the expenses when they had lived in his house on the mountainside. Yan thought of her father's face and checked herself. She continued to look straight ahead and said matter-of-factly, "I mean, of course, it makes sense to have a business in such a convenient location."

The truck took the last curve in the road before the mouth of Wang's Way opened on the right. Yan looked up the comparatively narrow, paved strip and admired the decorative flower arch that still curved in welcome across the road, within a yard or two of the junction. The wetness in the air had kept the flowers fresh, even a full week past the new baby's one-hundred-day celebration, their red and yellow petals still vivid and pert. Remnants of balloons and gold tinsel hung limply between the flowers.

Pang pulled the truck over to the side of the road and turned on his blinkers. "I will wait. You go and say goodbye."

"You don't want to come to see AiGuo, Jiang's son?"

"I will see him enough. My business brings me here." Pang looked out at the New Lake. "It's too beautiful. I will take one round. Go on now."

Yan climbed up the road to the Farmer Master's house. Along the way, she pulled free a few stray pieces of gold tinsel that were caught in the grass and wound them around the base of her fourth finger. She studied the tinsel ring, letting it catch the sunlight, and then unraveled and shoved the tinsel in her pocket.

Inside the gate, standing in the courtyard that had once served as her favorite school, Yan looked at the snake-adorned paper lanterns and the banner of congratulations that hung over the kitchen window and knew they were not enough to disguise the deep sadness emanating from the house.

"Yan?" Ayi emerged from the door; her eyes looked small, almost lost in a surround of puffy, pink skin and she moved slowly.

"I came to see you all before I leave." Yan reached forward to take the woman's hands.

"AiGuo, you mean. Certainly, the baby pulls you here." Ayi looked at Yan with a raised eyebrow but appeared too tired to tease around as she usually would. She let Yan cradle her hands.

"AiGuo. You. Both work for me, though I do hear that he is quite special." Yan tried to laugh; she wanted Ayi to laugh back, but she did not. Though Yan had never met LiLi, just seeing Ayi's grief was enough to fill her with a tangible sense of loss. Ayi pulled her hands free and wiggle-walked her fingers, hastening Yan through the kitchen door. "They are in the study. Jiang doesn't leave the child's side. Go enjoy the baby; he is beautiful. I have work to do." She turned away from Yan, moving into the courtyard, and began to sob.

When pulled all the way down with its lower edge resting on the sill, the window shade kept out the sun, the moon and the stars, and the barbershop's room was left with only a few lamps to provide light. All clocks had been removed and the decades-old Shanghai pin-up girls calendar that had hung next to the orchids had been taken down, leaving behind only a light rectangular patch of wall. The orchids themselves no longer graced the sill. They had come to land on top of the menagerie of glass animals tossed into the bottom of a large, metal rubbish barrel. They were not alone, soon being joined by, amongst other things, scarves, magazines, pillows, shoes, blankets, and sheets. Under LuLu's command, the girls of the barbershop had made quick work of clearing her and Lao Fu's bedroom of practically everything that had made it different from the rest of the back rooms, save Lao Fu himself.

From the moment LuLu had returned from New Da Long, Lao Fu and all the girls of the shop sensed they were in danger. Not saying a word, LuLu had dragged the metal garbage barrel from the street into the center of the bedroom before summoning the girls and giving them a simple instruction, "Everything goes, except for the furniture."

When one of the younger girls, running her hand along a scarf that hung off the standing mirror, had asked if she could keep any of the items, LuLu had looked at her for but a fraction of a moment before slapping her across the face. For the rest of that afternoon, the old pimp had sat on the sofa in stunned silence as LuLu calmly directed the ravaging of the room.

Lao Fu had watched as each item was tossed into the barrel and felt himself tossed onto a sea of memories. From that spot on the sofa, Lao Fu visited places to which he had not ventured in far too long. The first Fu Tai Tai's deck of playing cards reminded him that they used to play rummy late into the night, and that, when he grew tired, she had always taken advantage of her role as the dealer. He smiled, recalling she was a terrific cheat. When the trash collectors, commissioned by LuLu, arrived and easily heaved the old mattress out of the room, Lao Fu laughed to himself. He recalled how he and the first Fu Tai had struggled to get the mattress home from the store, too tight-fisted to pay for it to be delivered.

She had such delicate arms and legs, his first wife, thin like a bird and small. She had dropped the mattress every few meters. Thinking of her body made him warm and sad. The glass animals had each come to the back of the barbershop with a story: a how, a who, a where, or a when. Since her death, he had not looked in on those creatures sitting behind the glass of the curio cabinet, and guilt came over him. Steeped in pain, Lao Fu saw the beauty of each of the figurines, his eyes following each of them on their final journey from cabinet to barrel. He saw them through the first Fu Tai Tai's eyes. He had no anger in him as he watched LuLu strip bare the room of his long-dead wife; in all these years, he had not kept her alive, so how could he expect to do so now? He wanted to close his eyes, to turn away from the room and sleep, but he would not do that to his late wife.

Now, LuLu lay on the bed, its new mattress and pillows dressed in stark white bedding. A cheap, clip-on lamp, that looked out of place affixed to the wooden headboard of the antique bed, shone down on her head. Lao Fu was asleep on the sofa, the only part of the new room he dared or desired to claim.

Turning on her side, LuLu stared at the faces captured in the three picture frames on her bedside table: YuZhen, LiLi, and AiGuo. The portraits of YuZhen and LiLi were old pencil sketches, the ones LuLu had drawn so many years ago: YuZhen when she was still beautiful, and LiLi when she was just about to turn three. LuLu had recovered them from her old, purple backpack along with the old panda whose seams were tearing apart with wear. She had also found the yellow paper bird she had received at Master Du's temple. The panda she had left for Ai Guo, letting his grandmother, AnRan, know that it had belonged to the baby's mother. The bird she had tried to burn, wanting to destroy its lacy wings with the flame of her cigarette lighter, but YuZhen had once placed the bird directly into her hands and this was enough to save it.

The portrait of AiGuo was in vivid color, a photograph taken in New Da Long at the boy's one-hundred-day ceremony. He had a shock of black hair, and his pudgy body filled out his red and gold silk pajamas. The picture captured the rosiness of his full cheeks and the creaminess of his skin; his resemblance to his mother was unmistakable. He lay on his back in his crib. Seeing LiLi's face in the boy's, LuLu could not stop herself from seeing LiLi lying on her back with the same fullness and color of youth, but frozen cold against the black dirt of a rice terrace. LuLu hugged her body tightly. She commanded herself to imagine LiLi on a happier day and conjured an image of the girl as the dancing Cup-cake Bride in New Da Long Square. LuLu began to cry, for visions of the square took her back to her own first day in New Da Long.

That Wang had not come himself to collect LuLu upon her arrival in New Da Long Square caused her to bristle. She had planned to show him some gratitude for finally making good on his promise to reunite her with her sister. She had even looked forward to sharing a tender moment while riding alone with him to his house; she thought she would enjoy hearing him brag about his new grandson, her nephew. Instead, Wang sent one of his workers to pick her up. LuLu wondered if the man was mute, for he did not utter a single word on the entire drive to the Farmer Master's home. On their arrival, the worker unloaded all of LuLu's suitcases and the numerous gift boxes that she had tied together into bundles with handles fashioned from string. Strangely, he did not take her things into the house, but rather left them just inside the courtyard gate, as if he knew they should not make it any further.

Wang alone came out of the house and politely welcomed her, "Fu TaiTai," to his home and told her he was honored that she had made the long journey from Shanghai to meet his grandson. She thanked him with a grand show of politeness, wondering if his wife's eyes watched her. Wang stood silently for what felt like a prolonged moment, before bowing his head and looking down at the ground. He began to tremble as he whispered her name, "LuLu, LuLu, LuLu." She wanted to reach out and touch him, but she instinctively knew she shouldn't. She stood stone still.

Before Wang had said another word, LuLu became acutely aware of a breeze moving through the courtyard and of the fact that the only sounds she heard came from a collection of colorfully painted paper lanterns jostling about their wire stems and a congratulations banner flapping up against the house. There were no animals scratching about. No workers' voices floated over from the fields. No sounds of cooking or cleaning escaped from under the front door or through an open window. She looked about the courtyard more carefully. The floor had been spotlessly swept, all the farm tools were hung up on hooks, and the weighing scale had been wiped clean. No laboring had taken place here for some time. She searched the face of the house; every window was closed and dark. The lanterns and the banner looked almost grotesque. LuLu's body went cold. This was a place in mourning.

LuLu's chest moved up and down too quickly, her breaths were cut short, and her fingers began to tingle. Where were the joyous screams of her name and the pattering of feet running towards her? Blood rushed through her ears and, with all the air she had in her body, LuLu screamed for her sister.

"LiLi! LiLi! Where are you? Wang! Please, in the name of all that is in heaven, bring me my sister!"

Wang did not raise his head. "She's gone. She's gone."

LuLu's memories of what happened after she learned of her sister's

death, those few days she spent in New Da Long, were like jagged shards of a mirror offering her an incomplete reflection and quick to cut. Someone, likely the Ayi, had shown her the highest rice terrace where LiLi had tumbled. AnRan, the mouse-like wife, had cried as she put AiGuo in LuLu's arms for the first time. Or was it the baby who had cried? AiGuo had gripped her fingers so gently with his perfect little fingers, but she could only remember feeling pain. And then there was Jiang. No matter how hard LuLu tried, his face and voice escaped her. The young man had stayed in the study, calligraphing poetry for hours. He seemed unable to bring himself to talk to LuLu. No matter. She did not care to judge his grief.

Presently, LuLu sat up in her bed and wiped her face roughly with her new sheets. She could feel anger and bitterness clawing up the back of her throat and she fought to swallow it. What angered LuLu was the part of those horrible days that centered on Wang. Much like his son, he had taken every chance to avoid her, secreting up to his office. Further upsetting her was the way he would watch her from the Eagle's Eye; she had caught him looking at her every time she had, in her quest to understand what had happened, taken to walking the terraces. On her last night in New Da Long, she had waited for him in the darkness of his office and forced him to join her in the fields. He had hardly opened his mouth, and LuLu had wanted to throw her fists at his face.

"Why? Why did this happen? How did you let her alone? Why would she be climbing here?" She had demanded answers and had received none. Wang kept insisting that he had done everything to help LiLi. "Everything? You did everything but keep her safe."

Wang had not argued with her.

"She should have been buried with her ancestors! You owed her that!" She had sobbed wildly, thinking of LiLi lying against the cardboard of her cremation casket and her body being burned to ash. "She will be all alone now."

Here Wang nodded in agreement, as if genuinely sorry. "The Party doesn't allow burials, you know that. I am the township leader; I did my best."

LuLu did not wave to Wang as he stood watching her bus pull out of New Da Long Square. She watched him grow smaller and smaller and thought how pathetic he had become. In better days, she could have worried for him, but now he was just another man who had not kept his promise.

LuLu picked up AiGuo's framed picture and held it to her chest. From the corner of the room came the scratching sound of LiLi's bird tottering around on the floor of its cage. AnRan had insisted that LuLu keep the bird close to her in Shanghai. She whistled into the air and the bird chirped back. She was glad to have it safely here with her: a life held in place, looking out on the world, but far from the danger of being in it.

———————

Ayi wiped tears from her cheeks. She stood quickly and looked about the kitchen to see what she should do next. "Busy hands. Busy hands," she chanted the words like a mantra. She had let Yan sit her down, but she should have put herself to work. She turned her attention to AiGuo's dirty clothing and went to fill the wash pot with water. Using two hands, she set the water-filled pot on the stove, opened the valve to the propane tank and lit the fire. She sorted AiGuo's little cotton pajamas and rompers, looking for stains that needed extra scrubbing.

Ayi waited for the water to boil. Staring at the water's surface, smooth within the confines of the pot, she found herself begging, "Please boil. Please boil. Hurry. Please boil." She had pleaded, almost prayed, the same lines on the night that she had done everything she could to save LiLi. Playing like a movie on the surface of the water, Ayi could not stop herself from seeing everything once again:

As LiLi fell backwards, off the top of the slope leading to the highest terrace, Ayi came up the way from the house and saw only a flicker of pink falling to the earth. The Farmer Master was there, but Ayi could not make out what he was doing. He had fallen with the child. She could not tell whether he had been trying to bring LiLi down or help her up. Why was the child there?

Running towards the three lives down on the ground, Ayi started calling to the ancestors for help. Coming up on the girl, Ayi found LiLi lying stone-still against the earth, with her eyes closed and her lips parted slightly. The Farmer Master reached under the child and picked LiLi up into his arms and started to move.

"Is she breathing? What happened? Master, is she breathing?" Ayi was on the move following Wang, who was moving with unimaginable speed. Somehow, Ayi managed to keep up, to be right behind him and LiLi.

In a blur, Ayi was climbing into the back of Wang's truck and receiving LiLi from his arms.

"Keep her warm!" Wang shouted as he jumped in the truck's cab and started driving.

It was already past dusk, and Old Doctor and his wife were at home as Wang drove ferociously along the Lake Ring Road. The couple sat across from one another at the wooden table in the center of their home.

Steam rose from their bowls of soup, obscuring their views of one another's faces. Slurping heartily without pausing to speak, Old Doctor did not need to smile approvingly at his wife to let her know how much he was enjoying her cooking. The old woman rose from her chair, shuffled over to the stove which also served as the home's sole source of heat, and used a metal rod to jab at the ashy coals, hoping to release a little more warmth into the home.

"Add some more." Old Doctor spoke slowly, directing his wife between slurps.

"I know." The old woman reached into the coal bin; her frugality allowing her to add only two small lumps to the stove fire. She slowly shuffled back to the table and had just settled back on her chair to finish her meal, when the sound of someone kicking at the door made her put her bowl back down on the table.

"Aiyah! Who is it?" Irritated, the old woman stayed seated and tried to raise her voice, but only a low huskiness came from her throat. Speaking to her husband, "We will have to open the door and let in cold."

"Yes." Old Doctor did not move. He kept slurping, knowing his soup could soon be rendered cold and used his eyes to gesture his wife to the door.

More kicks came hard against the door, and a man's voice called out, "Open the door!"

The old woman did not move any faster. When she finally opened the door, the Farmer Master barged in with the limp-bodied Cupcake Bride in his arms and Ayi at his back.

Old Doctor stood up, took both soup bowls into his hand, and placed them on the floor under the table. He then directed Wang, slapping his hand on the table's surface, "Here. Put her here." Turning to his wife and Ayi, he firmly ordered, "Boil water."

LiLi lay motionless; her skin was pale as steam. The lower half of her dress and the quilting of her boots were soaked a horrifying scarlet. Old Doctor took LiLi's wrist in his hand and closed his eyes and waited for any movement beneath the pad of his index finger. Nothing. He put his index finger and forefinger up against LiLi's neck, tucked in under her jaw, and again waited for any movement to guide his next steps. He put his head to her chest and listened for the beat of her heart, watching for any rise or fall that would let him know her lungs were still working. While she was the color of steam, she was not yet the temperature of ice, and so he lingered waiting for any sign that she could be saved.

"My grandchild! Can you save it?" The Farmer Master was at the table, his head lowered so that his eyes were level with Old Doctor's, just above LiLi's chest.

"Little Wang! Get back! Now!"

The Farmer Master shrank back from the table, ashamed as if chastened by his own father.

"More coal. We need more coal to bring this to a boil." Ayi looked pleadingly at the Old Doctor's wife with fear in her eyes, and then back to the surface of the water that sat in a large pot on the coal stove. "Please boil. Please boil."

"Do not watch it." The old woman put her hand on Ayi's arm, trying to calm her.

Ayi turned back to the table and moved next to LiLi's face. She stroked the hair from her face and whispered, "LiLi. Child, please open your eyes. Please talk to us."

"Too much blood has escaped her. She is stepping into death." Old Doctor raised his head off LiLi's chest.

"But my grandchild is alive!" Wang screamed out.

"Yes, but the mother will need all her energy to survive. If she survives."

"Save the child!" Both Wang and Ayi cried out at the same time. They turned to look at each other, horrified by the realization that they were not speaking of saving the same soul.

———————————

The existence of AiGuo, the infant child of the child bride, plagued the Farmer Master. The thinnest of the baby's cries and the least pungent of his odors seemed to drift out from the study, rise up through the atrium, and enter the man's office. The newborn's soft whimpers, irritable cries, and full-bodied bellows all sent unpleasant tingles down the line that ran from Wang's sternum to his groin. And, suddenly tormented with an even keener nose than before, one of supernatural acuity, Wang gagged each time the tinniest Wang burped or produced a foul nappy, rendering the man miserable and driving him to clamp his hand tightly over his nose and mouth.

Desperate to stop all sounds and scents from reaching him, the Farmer Master commissioned the fabrication of an airtight door for his office which would effectively seal him off from the rest of the house. But it was not only the door that required renovation. Wang had also demanded that the Eagle's Eye be bricked up. He told AnRan that his eyes had become too sensitive to the sunlight that streamed through its opening; the wife did not question her husband for that had never been their way. Furthermore, Jiang had taken to organizing the workers in the field and designing an elaborate new configuration of crop planting; Wang's oversight was obsolete. Only Wang knew the real reason for the aperture to be permanently closed: it was through the Eagle's Eye that *she* had first come to visit him.

Presently, Wang hastened out of the office and looked down into the atrium. He stood silently for almost an hour, hearing nothing more than Yan's laughter and AnRan's cooing. Nothing happened. He went back into his office, closed the door, sat down at his desk, and waited. Nothing happened.

The ledgers on his desk had been untouched for weeks, and Wang heard the voice of his father deriding him for failing to account for all manner of happenings: "Fool! Fool! Fool!"

Wang began filling the columns in the books with relevant calculations. Hours passed. "Numbers are real; they represent tangible results," Wang chanted repeatedly. Looking over at the bricked-up Eagle's Eye, he shook his head and proclaimed himself an "Idiot!"

The Farmer Master had just resolved to have the window reopened when his thoughts were interrupted by the resumption of AiGuo's cries. Wang reminded himself that all babies cry. The infant's call grew louder and more frantic by the second and penetrated the door with ease. Wang covered his ears, but the noise reverberated in his head. Blood thumped through his temples. He sank off his chair, onto the floor, and under his desk. He tried to control his breathing, but his efforts gave way to a searing pain; his abdomen began to burn intensely. Panicked, he lifted his shirt and ran his hand over his skin, relieved to find it was still smooth and intact.

He whipped his head back and forth, looking around, and knew with certainty that *she* had once again returned. She had first shown up on the night Wang had begged Old Doctor to save AiGuo.

"Was that wrong?" Wang pleaded out loud. "Would you not have wanted the child to be saved?"

"I was a child, was I not?" Pale and sickly, LiLi appeared in front of the Farmer Master, who contorted his body ever more tightly, squeezing to make himself as small as possible.

"Please, forgive me. I promise you, AiGuo will have everything," Wang sobbed. "I will raise him well, to be a patriot. His name means love of country! Everyone will praise him and know you were his mother. I will make sure of it. You will live on, through Ai Guo!"

"You too will live on, through Ai Guo. That is what I cannot forgive. Look at me! Look at what you did to me!"

Wang pressed his hands harder over his ears, trying to dampen AiGuo's cries, and foolishly closed his eyes tightly, refusing to look at LiLi. It was all futile. LiLi did not need Wang's eyes to be open to be seen by him. Her body, sliced open from her sternum to her groin, splayed and empty, lurched forward and enveloped the writhing Wang into its eternal darkness.

Struggling for air and clawing at his neck, Wang felt an intense chill descend upon him. He opened his eyes and saw nothing. He was alone. The room was both unnaturally silent and dark, with only the smell of his own waste filling the void.

AiGuo wailed in Yan's arms with such force, his legs kicking into the air, that Yan looked pleadingly to Jiang for help. Jiang calmly took the bawling bundle and confidently positioned AiGuo against his chest with his head peering out over Jiang's shoulder. Rhythmically tapping Aiguo's back as he stepped to and fro in front of the study windows,

Jiang gently coaxed a guttural burp out of the child, after which AiGuo's lids, heavy with fatigue, drifted downward.

"He is beautiful, Jiang!"

"Yes. At one hundred and four days old, his head has a circumference of thirty-nine and a half-centimeters, he is sixty-three-centimeters long, his weight is six and one-fifth kilograms, and he is feeding every two and a half hours. His cries are wavelike and lower-pitched when he is hungry, but more disorganized when he wants to be changed, and his highest pitch is reserved for when he needs to be burped. Of most importance, he smiles when I tell him the names of all the flowers and trees surrounding New Lake and laughs when I recite the famous poems of our ancestors. He's discerning the different melodies in my voice."

"You have it all figured out."

"Yes. We all have our patterns."

Jiang knew with certainty he was not AiGuo's father just as he was certain that the child shared his ancestry. He did not tell Yan about all the mathematical ways in which AiGuo's facial features—the angle of his inner eyes, the ratio of his forehead height to his total face length, the relative height of his philtrum—matched that of the Farmer Master. On the night on which AiGou had been born, Jiang had looked up at the stars and, instead of seeing constellations, had seen his ancestral family tree. Stretching back in time, reaching to the corners of galaxy, the tree was a fluid, shimmering network comprised of thousands upon thousands of connecting lineage lines. The lines were highly variable: long, short, some blazed boldly, while others flickered faintly fragile. No matter: Jiang knew instantly that the difference in the distance between father and son versus that between brothers was of little consequence and that AiGuo would need him.

Aiguo purred softly against Jiang's neck, prompting him to smile and pull wooly earplugs from his ears. "I have found that these prove to be both necessary and very helpful."

Yan's laughing response was promptly shushed by AnRan, who was delighting in watching the two friends and her grandson from her chair in the corner.

––––––––

Pang pulled the truck up in front of the New Market. "You still have half an hour before your bus arrives. I can wait with you."

"No need, Uncle. I have a few more people to see before the bus comes." Yan climbed out of the cabin and looked back through its open window. She looked at the ground and wiped tears from the corners of her eyes before looking back up. "Until we see again."

"Until we see again." Pang let the truck drift away for several seconds, waving to Yan in his rearview mirror, before applying pressure to the gas pedal.

Yan walked into the New Market and stood just inside the plastic strip curtain. Sounds and sights, both past and present, flooded over her, and she struggled to stay composed. The full bloom of summer fruits drew her eyes; the sight of glossy red apples and powdery, orange-yellow peaches coaxed her stomach. Hong and Min, standing at their posts behind adjacent fruit stalls, were watching their customers carefully when Yan called out to them, "Hey, you two! Are your bellies full?"

Spotting Yan at the same time, the sisters cried out in unison, "Full!" They waved while sharing their crooked-teeth-filled grins. "Safe travels, Yan!"

Not wanting to go in any further, Yan backed out of the market, making the plastic curtain strips yield to her will. She slowly scanned the square and was delighted to find it full of villagers who were occupied with gossiping, eating, laughing, singing, exercising, people-watching, and simply living. In front of the Great Quake Legacy Memorial, Yan pressed two fingers to her lips and placed them atop the stone, before finding her way over to the New School.

As Yan walked through the school's unfamiliar hallways, she heard several young students call out from inside their classrooms, "It's Yan! The girl on the posters!" Yan smiled without exposing her teeth, not wanting to encourage any disruptions to the ongoing lessons. She found Teacher Zhou in a back room, filled with windows that looked out the back of the building onto an alleyway filled with garbage cans. The view had been judiciously obscured by several pieces of butcher paper, each one graced with a different student's water-color rendering of the New Lake.

"Yan!" Teacher Zhou stood up from behind his desk and reflexively smoothed his robes. "You must be on your way to your next adventure."

"Yes. My bus is not far off, but I have time. I wanted to be certain to say goodbye."

"Ahh, Beautiful Country talk? I do think our way is much better. 'Until we meet again.' It's so much more hopeful. No?"

"Until we meet again is much better. You are right, as usual!" Yan bowed deferentially to her teacher, as she had so many times in their earlier years together.

"I'm glad you are here. I have something for you." Reaching under his desk, the teacher brought out a red, cloth-covered scroll box which he placed in Yan's hands. "Go ahead and open it."

A faint, sweet smell of tree bark curled through the air as Yan opened the box. She ran her fingers over the tightly wound scroll within, marveling at the softness of its fabric-like paper. Falling like perfectly formed, inky snowflakes, ornate running-style characters cascaded their message in a perfect vertical row down the scroll's face: "Home is where we hear the echoes of our past and the ancestors sing." Yan traced the characters without touching them; the delicate strokes, having been masterfully crafted using different brush angles and degrees of pressure, danced across the paper.

"It's so beautiful." Yan looked across the desk to Teacher Zhou. "This is *your* work! Am I right?"

Allowing himself only the slightest smile, the teacher picked up Yan's backpack from the floor and slipped it over his shoulder. "Come let me walk out with you and ensure that you do not miss your bus."

On his way back to the New School, the teacher thought about Yan and knew it would be a long time before he had another student like her, or even another one like Jiang. The two of them, with their own unspoken understanding, had made him a better, more humble man. Jiang had always become restless whenever Yan had missed one of their joint classes. That restlessness had let the teacher know that the boy had a true affection for Yan and not merely a tolerance for her. It had been

Yan seated next to Jiang, not the teacher and his lessons, who had made it possible for the boy to conquer the hours-long *gaokao*.

He could still feel the weight of Yan's backpack on his shoulder and imagined it being filled with opportunity. He was suddenly thankful to have made it to this point in history and decided to pick up his pace.

Once at his desk, Teacher Zhou carefully lifted a letter out of the top drawer. He placed it on the wooden surface in front of him and stared at it for some time. First, rubbing his hands together so that excessive oil would not mar the missive's delicate, pale blue stationery, he then touched it to his lips. He imagined the sender's long fingers cradling her pen, her face tilted in the sunlight as she carefully chose her words, and possibly even a few tears welling in her eyes as she had written to him.

She had answered him, and he was filled with hope.

He had known her so long ago, before blood, fear, and the grinding momentum of progress had expelled him so far westward. Crawling back east on his hands and knees, to find her amidst the tumult, scarring the idealism of his youth, had not seemed impossible back then. He had been determined to unite with her in blazing the right course for the country. But, The Party had kept him put, proved him wrong and, some would even say, set him straight. Had he not been put to good use? Maybe he had even been put to his best use?

Zhou had neither written to her about his position and the generous housing allowance that came with it nor that his application to become a Party member was pending. The latter was not a matter of concern, for how could the Farmer Master, who was in charge of such matters, deny the teacher without himself losing face? No need to rush; he had waited this long. Zhou would wait patiently to understand what time had done to her sensibilities.

A bell rang out, and students flooded the hallways of the New Da Long School, chatting and giggling as they rushed to their next class. The teacher moved into the hallway and smiled over his children. Was this not how power was to be used? To guide the future along the correct course, especially if the path was not an obvious one? Several students, caught in a volley of banter, dawdled outside the door of the math room. Teacher Zhou looked at them sternly, "Move along. Remember, do not be late to your future!"

―――――――――

The afternoon sun was beginning to come down over the provincial capital, and the hottest part of the day had passed. Women and men sat out on the city's sidewalks fanning themselves and chatting loudly. They compared the prices of vegetables and gossiped about wayward husbands and, far worse, wayward children. This place was not so different than the Shanghai that Yan had left behind, but the people seemed more relaxed; she heard more laughter as she made her way from the bus station.

The smell of frying sesame paste balls caught her nose and led Yan to a busy street vendor's cart. She bought half a dozen of the treats and stashed them in the top of her bag. She moved quickly now, wanting to reach her destination in time to enjoy the end of the day. Overhead, the roaring sound of a large airplane drew Yan's eyes upward. Admiring the thick, white contrail that streaked the sky, she wondered where ZhiChao was right in this moment.

"You always tell me to seek better and whatever I find, whatever I gain, I will share." Yan had reminded ZhiChao of his words as they lay next to each other in her bed just a month earlier during their last conversation. "You remember?"

"Yes." He had answered without thinking too much, without fully taking in her meaning.

"You said I will help my family by bringing back something better."

He had reached for her hand. "Yan, what are you saying?"

"I am not saying, I am asking." Yan had turned on her side and looked at ZhiChao as she had done hundreds of times, and she had known in that moment that she would likely not look at him in this way again for the rest of her life. "I came here five years ago to study and learn to be a junior doctor. I thought that was my something better and that going to the Beautiful Country, with you, was my way of building that something better into more."

"But it is."

"No." She touched his face with the palm of her hand, wishing to relax the lines out of his brow. "You are my something better. I am going to bring a little part of you back with me."

ZhiChao had sat up abruptly. "What are you saying? I don't understand."

Yan now moved quickly through the Provincial Number Six Hospital, making her way through its warren-like maze of corridors. Patients roamed the halls, some partially undressed; doctors and nurses bustled about, a few barking orders, others trying not to see all that was around them. Yan kept focused, ignoring the unpleasant odors that wafted about, found her way to the rear of the building, and slipped out through the back double doors. A slight breeze moved through the leaves of the garden in a whispered welcome. She spotted them sitting on Long's favorite bench, the one next to the patient therapy plot that was currently crowded with dozens of blooming sunflower plants. The heads of the blooms were oriented towards the bench as if they were eavesdropping on whatever conversation was taking place there.

"I am here." Yan put her hand on Long's shoulder, very gently.

"Sister, softly. MaMa is sleeping." Long put a finger to his lips. Lei was lying on her back, stretched out on the bench with her head in Long's lap.

"Yan, you've come?" Lei asked, opening her eyes.

"Yes, MaMa. You rest. We have a little more time."

Bo sat on the ground with his back up against the bench and with his legs stretched out in front of him. He motioned for Yan's bag. "It looks heavy. Give it here."

Yan sat down next to her father and opened her bag. She handed him the bag of sesame paste balls, which he immediately offered to Long so that he could pick first. The family was clustered together.

Yan silently thanked ZhiChao and wished him well, again, as she had every single day since their last night together, and as she would for the rest of her days. He had not spoken to her after that final conversation, but he had done everything exactly as she had asked. He had helped her convert the currency of relationships, the power of *guanxi,* into that something "better." It was ZhiChao's father's connections that finally procured Long a transfer out of prison and into the provincial mental hospital, where he finally received the medical attention he needed. And it was the Doctor Professor who helped secure Yan a position at this same hospital for her medical apprenticeship, allowing her to protect Long and help oversee his care.

Yan asked the ancestors to watch over both men's families.

Yan turned around and saw that Lei was sleeping. She stood up and took the opportunity to examine Lei's arms, something her mother would have avoided if she were awake. Yan ran her fingers over the previously battered skin and was satisfied that it was healing.

She sat back down and, on hearing the sound of Long sucking sesame paste off the roof of his mouth, she reached her hand up and behind her, prompting him to place a fried ball into her hand. She held the ball between her index finger and her thumb and thought about how, just this morning, she had held the cosmos between these same fingers. In this moment, she knew it to be true: one did not have to go anywhere to feel everything; to get the best of yourself; to experience all the terrible and wonderful things the world had to offer.

Bo's head weighed on Yan's shoulder as he nodded off, and she relaxed into her spot. The sun would soon be gone, and she knew it would be time to go to the apartment with her parents; she prepared Long, "Little brother, we will be going for a little while, but we will meet tomorrow."

"Meet tomorrow," Long repeated back. "Before you go, Yan, will you sing to me?"

Yan put the sesame ball down in her lap. She raised her face up to the sky, trying to catch the last of the day's rays, and ever so softly she sang the songs Lei had once taught her.

Acknowledgments

My deepest thanks

To Ayi, Xiao Fen, and A-Lan for sharing so generously.

To Paige, Ann, Su, Kathy, and Shaun for reading this book when it was in its infancy.

To Alex Brown and Tina Beier for editing and bringing my book to life.

To Mar Fenech for her ever-careful read and precious author-to-author support.

To Julia Borcherts for helping to get my book out into the world.

To Kooi Lin Chaddah and Laurel Ince for being my moms.

To Yani and Ayo for loving me all the way through this process.

And to Avery for everything.

About the Author

Born in London to an East Indian father and a Malaysian Chinese mother, Radha grew up in Kenya, the UK, and the US. She majored in Biology at the University of Chicago, earned medical and law degrees at the University of Illinois, and a Master of Public Health at Harvard University. She completed Internal Medicine residency training, and later practiced at Massachusetts General Hospital/Harvard Medical School in Boston. Along the way, Radha developed a deep commitment to patient advocacy, to "meeting the patients where they are", and to combating stigma around mental health. During these busy years, Radha married her wonderful husband and best friend, Avery, and had two terrific daughters, Yani and Ayo.

Life did not slow down! Radha and her family moved, over the course of 20 years, from Boston to NYC to Taipei to Shanghai to Beijing to Princeton, and finally to Philadelphia. GO BIRDS! Each of these places was filled with amazing people, wonderful culture, and incredible personal and work experiences. Radha worked as a primary care physician in Boston, NYC and Beijing; worked with the China CDC to co-write the book, *HIV/AIDS: Beyond the Numbers*; and provided mental healthcare to patients in several states as a telemedicine doctor upon settling in Philadelphia. Especially treasured by Radha are the first-hand stories she has been privileged to hear from patients, colleagues, friends, and family alike. These stories, and the storytellers that birthed them, fuel Radha's passion to write.

Radha enjoys learning new Mandarin characters, tackling novice knitting projects, painting with watercolors and acrylics, catching a live, stand-up comedy show with Avery, trying out new recipes with Yani and Ayo, and, of course, jotting down story notes for her next writing project.